AFTERLIGHT

FIRST LIGHT - HALF LIGHT - NEW LIGHT

ALICE VL

AFTERLIGHT

Alice VL

AFTERLIGHT

"When you realize that other dimensions exist, you'll never think of life, death, yourself, or the Universe in the same way again."

The Afterlife of Billy Fingers

By Annie Kagan

Alice VL

AFTERLIGHT

Alice VL

6

AFTERLIGHT

Alice VL

CONTENTS

Alice VL

DEDICATION

For W.

Beyond time,

through universes,

amidst dimensions.

Alice VL

AFTERLIGHT

Alice VL

AFTERLIGHT I – FIRST LIGHT

1

Misty-Bleu wrapped her unbuttoned, pale blue sweater tightly around her as she scurried down the path of the Coral Hill Oncology Hospital and Treatment Centre, on an unusually icy, summer's evening. As she folded her arms snugly around her waist, she was suddenly unconvinced that the abrupt cold that had crept up on her, was simply due to the frostiness in the air, or if in fact, her bravery was beginning to forsake her. She instinctively placed one foot in front of the other, determined to see William again.

As she nervously made her way down the dark path of a park, she looked up at the sky above her, and realized that it was only the light of the moon that was sympathetically casting a light down on the path ahead of her, almost as though it was giving her its approval, and swearing to remain like a silvery gown around her. When she glanced around her, she noticed how haunting it felt to her as she passed by the empty park benches, one at a time. She was at once saddened by the harsh reality that those benches were reserved for terminal patients and their families. A place where they could visit and discuss funeral plans and eventually, life as they would have it after they leave someday. Benches where they were forced to make decisions about their last days, and how they would spend it.

They were empty seats where the dying would sit and reflect on their lives, and where they would be compelled to accept their mortality. Misty-Bleu frowned when she suddenly realized how much anger, frustration, and devastation that very same park hides from the healthy. She could barely imagine the pain and heartache that had taken place in that very park, and how much heartache and devastation would still be to come.

She silently prayed to never own a sad story on one of those park benches, and she pleaded from deep within that their story; that William's story would not be confined to a bench in that park. Misty-Bleu felt an enormous, restricting lump make its way into her throat as contradicting thoughts rushed through her mind. She felt her hands grow colder through the unwelcome shudders of angst and fear that had made its way into her entire body, "He's going to be okay, he has to. God, please hear me ..." Her soft, panicky voice trailed off as she silently and selfishly pleaded for William to survive. "Let him be the one number that gets better. I beg you, Dear God. For me, for him. Please save him Lord!"

Alice VL

AFTERLIGHT

She slowed down when she let out a faint whimper, at once terrified of the reality that was waiting for her when she was to see him again after all the years. It was late. It was much later than she had planned on being there, but had she given in to her initial, overthrowing hesitation, she knew that her nerve would fail her in the end, and she would not be there at all. It was only moments before that she had announced herself at the nurse's station of the Oncology Department.

Misty-Bleu was relieved and thankful that William had wandered off into the lush park of the hospital grounds when the rest of the patients were settled in for the night, and asleep. She was deeply thankful that her reunion with William would not be in a hospital bed, and she was grateful that there would be nothing to persuade her of how sick he was. She smiled when she thought back to the last time she saw him. She remembered him as strong, healthy, and proud. Misty-Bleu could barely imagine a reality where William would appear as frail and weak.

It was overwhelmingly intimidating as Misty-Bleu anticipated seeing William Carmichael again under any normal circumstances, but to find him in a hospital ward, surrounded by all things clinical scared her almost to death. The mere idea that he would be fenced in by devices that would tell her that he was ill, gravely ill and that he might not survive, was a thought she

Alice VL

could barely wrap her head around. It was a thought she could in no way at all picture, and it frightened her immensely to consider a certainty that his life had become so extremely vulnerable. All she knew, was the boy she had once left behind. The boy that was on the verge of becoming a man. The strong, healthy, and beautiful man.

At the age of 18, he had reached almost 6 feet and wholly towered over her. She could clearly remember his dark hair and equally dark eyes that were framed by his endless supply of eyelashes. Misty-Bleu often evoked the stories his eyes would tell her and when she closed hers, she could still distinctly see his eyes looking back at her. Misty-Bleu was nothing at all like William. She was almost an entire person shorter than him, but her hair virtually trailed down her back and rested just beneath her bottom. Misty-Bleu smiled as she clutched at her hair, tossing it behind her.

She could clearly recall how William would admire the beautiful curls that would flow down her back, while he would claim to be hypnotized by her frosty blue eyes. She smiled again when she remembered how dissimilar they were on the outside, yet they could not be more alike. William was her very first love. He was the boy she had fallen in love with shortly after she began her Grade 10 year in Pascal High School where they both grew up in Shadow Falls. He was about to begin Grade 11 in that same year, making him a year older than her. They had initially met when Misty-Bleu's parents moved her into the neighborhood in Shadow Falls that William was born in, when they were both still in primary school.

Although they were nothing more than friends at first, William became secretly aware of his growing and intensely protective feelings for her when she was promoted to grade eight and he to grade nine. Much to Misty-Bleu's delight, he spent an increasing amount of time with her after school and would make a distinct effort to see her at breaks during school hours. She had, for as long as she could remember, been penetratingly aware of her love and admiration for him long before high school began but having been raised in an exceptionally strict and disciplined home, she thought it too forward to show William any other indication or attraction, but friendship. Misty-Bleu's father had instilled old-fashioned values and principals in her and would surely oppose any relationship that Misty-Bleu would ultimately, be the hunter of.

Misty-Bleu learned very early on that John Buchanan was a no-nonsense disciplinarian, and she knew only too well of his wrath should she ever disobey him. She had learned by then that she would never find shelter in the arms of her mother, Susan.

Alice VL

AFTERLIGHT

She had reluctantly resigned herself to a life under their rules and on their terms. Misty-Bleu feared her parents more than death, and she would place tremendous pressure on herself to obey them as though her life depended on it. But, Misty-Bleu was proud, and desperate to fit in at school.

She was frenetic to blend in amongst the crowd at school, and the thought of her standing out for any reason, was something she had avoided at all cost. Even though she was eager to keep up the facades of a loving home and equally devoted parents with William and her friends at school, when the doors to her home closed each day, Misty-Bleu would find herself caught up in a kind of hell she could and would never dare tell anyone about. She was afraid that no-one would believe her. She was terrified that her hometown would condemn her and banish her to an eternity of hell.

Her closest and very first friend, Blakesley, would often notice bruises on Misty-Bleu's body, but whenever she asked her about them, Misty-Bleu would laugh it off and blame her awkwardness on her unfortunate injuries. For Misty-Bleu, stepping into the home that was meant to keep her safe and shielded was almost as though she was voluntarily marching onto the devil's playground. She hated her parents and when she funneled into the house, she was forced to share with them, she became silent. She had learned by then that she could not suppress the shudder that would be evident in her voice each time she would speak.

She had learned to never utter a word to them, unless she was spoken to. Her answers would be short, and it would be all that they needed to hear, through her painful stutters. She never dared tell them about Blakesley, and she never dared mention William's name in front of them. She knew only too well that she was never to ask permission to see her friends socially, and she was in no way at all to form social relationships at school or afterwards.

As far as John and Susan were concerned, Misty-Bleu would leave home merely to attend school and return shortly and promptly after the last school bell rang each day. They declined her requests to take part in any after school activities and would only allow her to participate in school events if they were compulsory, and after a call to the headmaster. Misty-Bleu knew better than to ask for anything. She no longer lived with the hope that someday, they would change and be better. She no longer thought that if she had proved to be loyal and loving to them, that they would allow her freedom to enjoy with her friends.

She was no longer convinced that being the good girl, the

daughter they expected her to be, would finally buy her liberty or joy. She no longer longed for a normal or caring childhood, and she no longer craved shelter from her parents. She spent her days hidden behind the locked doors of her bedroom where she kept a secret journal she had started writing in, in grade five. She found a valuable escape through stories that had begun to cause untaught but welcomed chaos in her mind. As she began to make sense of the people living in her head, she began to write about them and then, she began to write about her love for William.

As though the stories had begun writing themselves, she was surprised to find William domineering each and every one of her tales. She couldn't wait to open her journals, and re-read stories she had written, simply so she could relive a wonderful fraction or a beautiful moment she had created. It brought her immense peace and absolute joy to close her eyes, and run into a world that would ultimately, become her safe place. She unwittingly created an alternate reality where she could breathe freely and easily in, a new life where she could love him anytime she wanted. As she closed her eyes to find William there, she would grab his hands and gently kiss him on his lips almost as though she wanted the whole world to see.

It was a beautiful creation; one she would escape to every chance she had. A place she would linger in for as long as she could. She would lie in bed at night and fall asleep while stuck in a world that embraced and recognized her. The unmistakable evidence would be in her eyes as she drifted off and rushed into her world of magic.

Blakesley could almost see her leave, and often wondered where it was that Misty-Bleu would escape to when she became silent and distant. She would look closely at Misty-Bleu, and unknowingly watch her as she ran into a universe that would allow her to love him and live freely with William.

It was a flawless world. It was a life she could tailor-make and change as she needed it to grow and progress. It was a world she felt safe in, guarded, and fiercely protected. One she never wanted to come back from, but one she often thought of dying for. Misty-Bleu would take flight into her cosmos whenever John or Susan's behavior threatened and scared her. She would shamelessly dawdle there with William until she could safely return to the life she was trapped and imprisoned in. Her journal would tell of her dream of someday, escaping and running away from her parents.

It told of a young woman in pursuit of becoming someone wonderful. Someone William would be honored by and someone, she would be immensely proud of. It told stories of great distances between her and her parents, and it kept secrets of her yearning to belong somewhere else, even if only to herself. Her journal gave away secrets of the Christmas tree farm she dreamed of owning, and it told of the books she would someday write, to give a home to all the stories in her head. It promised her of a reality of the horses she would own and ride off on when she had grown up, and when she had become magnificent.

John Buchanan was an unreasonably, enormously strict disciplinarian with enormous wealth and who held immense power over the citizens of Shadow Falls. It was often whispered amongst residents that he controlled people in high places, and that he kept the right people in the right places, and in his pockets. John was a man loved and adored by many. Both he and Sarah diligently participated in their community and would host numerous charity events. The local pastor, Pastor Byron would regularly stop by and seek advice or financial assistance from the Buchanans. John had deep pockets and enormous wealth. He would gladly spread around his good fortune in an attempt to retain power over the community of Shadow Falls.

Mayor Edwards was often seen cozying up to John in local pubs, and it came as no surprise when John would succeed in restricting certain youthful events in his town. He furiously guarded social activities amongst the youth, and he would regularly limit school gatherings to exclude his daughter. John Buchanan was not a man who was easily crossed, and he was certainly not a man that would be questioned. The wealthiest of families in Shadow Falls admired him, while the poorest of the poor feared his power and domination.

He blatantly and meticulously limited and structured who Misty-Bleu was permitted to befriend and converse with, and he unashamedly turned a blind eye to the fact that Susan could barely stand the sight of their daughter. Whenever Misty-Bleu would become desperate and confront Susan about her father's severe anger and savage beatings, Susan would fly into a fit of rage and beat her almost as brutally. Misty-Bleu took the brunt of their thrashings and would almost instantly be flung into the world she dreamed of with William, and in her beautiful world, her parents would never find her. It was almost as though only her body would remain behind for beatings when she left to love him in her mind. She committed herself to hard work at school, and she learned to obey her parents, simply to survive their cruelty and to finally, grow up.

William instinctively knew that Misty-Bleu was hiding secrets from behind the closed doors of her home. He intuitively knew never to mention her parents or question the marks that would randomly show up on her body. Each time he stared into her pale blue eyes, he was told of a thousand stories that would confirm how desperate she was to hide a world of extreme agony and anguish. Yet, what William could never have known, was how she would reach out for him and escape to him in her mind and turn to her safe place once more. She would make herself as small as she could and hide behind all her hair before she closed her eyes, desperate to become someone else. She would disappear and go hide there to escape her father's unprovoked rage and subsequent cruelty. William would be right there, waiting to take her hand and lead her far away from her parents.

He would hold her safely against him so that she no longer felt the pain inflicted upon her by her father or her mother. When the beatings would finally be over, William would let go of her hand and lead her back to return to the heartless world her parents had brought her into. What William couldn't know was how actively he lived in her world, and how he had given her the shelter she so desperately needed. What William could not know was how he saved her from them, over and over again.

Misty-Bleu would lay awake at night after the beatings and dream of her life with William someday. She would make plans and she would memorize all the things she would say to him when the time was right, when they had grown up and become adults. She desperately prayed and begged God each night that William never discovers the truth of all that would take place behind those large double doors and even larger gates. She asked God that when those gates were closed, that William would know instinctively, never to come looking for her.

It was at the beginning of the first semester, shortly after she was promoted to grade ten that William first revealed his true feelings to Misty-Bleu. She could vividly remember the night that changed it all for her. It was the very first time she felt true joy and elation. The night she would remember as her one night of pure ecstasy. It was a compulsory valentine's ball that they both attended at their high school. John agreed that she attend on condition that she was accompanied by Gary Long, a boy in grade eleven. Gary Long was the only child of Grace and Jack Long, and heir to their immense fortune. Jack was a close friend and business partner of John in his oil purification company, one they had begun almost twenty years before.

Gary won over John's approval when John learned that he had been accepted to Harvard and was at once enamored by the young man with impeccable manners and vast knowledge. Misty-Bleu was embarrassed by the fact that John and Susan had arranged for Gary to accompany her, but she was thankful that she could be free to join her friends for one night out. She giggled into her sleeve when she realized that John and Susan had by no means at all, known the true traits of Gary, and that they were oblivious to his actual nature. Gary was a brilliant disguise but would often get caught at school drinking alcohol or smoking on the sly behind the old school hall. Only the year earlier, did Grace and Jack Long pay off a fifteen-year-old schoolgirl who had fallen pregnant after a one-night stand with Gary. Quietly and without much of a scene, she disappeared almost overnight from Shadow Falls. It was later whispered and gossiped that she had been whisked away to the city for a secret abortion.

William on the other hand, arrived at the ball alone and without a date at his side. They had scarcely been at the ball for an hour when Gary began to slur and fall over his feet. It was clear to Misty-Bleu and William that he had had far too much to drink and was in no position to drive Misty-Bleu home. William insisted that she rode with him and refused to allow Gary behind the wheel of his car, and Misty-Bleu his passenger. "Gary, if you don't mind, I'm going to get another ride home?" "What? No, what are you talking about? You know your father insists that I bring you home?" Gary almost fell over as he pressed himself firmly against Misty-Bleu. William was at once unnerved by Gary's demeanor when he took her chin into his hands. "Don't worry about it bro, I am leaving, I'll drop her off at home." William hurriedly grabbed onto Gary's arms, afraid that he might fall over. "I know all about you, you and Misty. I have no problem telling John ..." Gary was slurring as he glanced threateningly over at Misty-Bleu, grinning from ear to ear. She had begun to quiver slightly before William tightened his grip around Gary's arm. "You don't want to do that, Long. Your family does not want to get into a war with my family."

William Carmichael came from four generations of international fishing trawler owners. The Carmichael Fishing Group of Companies operated a large fleet of fishing vessels, together with an industry compliant seafood processing facility and a growing number of fish farms across the country. The company supplied seafood wholesalers and retailers with quality fresh and frozen seafood products, ranging from hake to abalone and pink prawns. Carmichael Fishing was founded in 1877 and had been built on long-standing relationships with corporate clients, suppliers, and employees. David Carmichael ran the entire company and was eager for William to take over the reins someday. At the time, the company employed in excess of 15000 staff across its fishing, processing, and fish farming operations. The company also held substantial interests in aquaculture, making them one of the largest fishing companies in the world.

Although Misty-Bleu was enormously embarrassed by

the scene Gary had caused, she was thankful that William had insisted on taking her home. She could remember the entire drive that evening, and she could clearly recall their conversation as William pulled up to the corner, a few meters away from her parent's home. "Misty-Bleu, please don't be mad at me?" He was instantly anxious of the fact that Misty-Bleu might have been humiliated by the unexpected commotion between William and Gary. "I don't want to get you into trouble with your father, but I couldn't let you drive with him either?"

She lowered her head and smiled, before she turned to face him. Misty-Bleu was intensely aware of the hammering of her heart, convinced that William could hear the incessant pounding and fluttering of her heart. She gazed into his dark eyes and could not ignore the fear and sadness that was staring back at her. "I'm not mad at you, William. I'm always in trouble with my parents anyway, plus my dad wouldn't believe me if I told him about Gary's drinking and bad behavior." She smiled again as she searched his eyes for a hint to tell her that his heart is pounding as fiercely as hers was. "But it doesn't matter. I can handle them." She smiled sadly at William when she realized that her father's wrath would come down like a ton of bricks on her, but she no longer cared that he knew about William. For the first time in Misty-Bleu's life, she did not care about John Buchanan's anger.

Alice VL

Someone else, someone who mattered to her had cared enough to bring her home safely and unhurt.

"I don't know much about what goes on at your house, Misty-Bleu, but you can tell me anything. I see how scared you are sometimes, and it scares me too. You never say anything, and you never talk about your parents. Just know that I am here if you need me. I know your father is strict, and word around town is that his word is law, but I know things aren't the way they should be with you and your parents." He looked up as he let out a faint sigh, "You don't have to tell me anything you don't want to, but, sometimes, it helps to talk. It helps to have someone help carry your burden, you know?"

Misty-Bleu smiled when she heard him tell her that she could turn to him if she needed him. By the look in his eyes, she knew that she could tell him anything she wanted to. But, she could in no way at all, find the proof in his eyes to assure her that he would never turn his back on her if he knew the truth about her.

How desperately she wanted to tell him about the world she had dreamed up and created for them. She wanted to excitedly blurt out that he had saved her so many times before, and that no matter how much rage and fury John Buchanan would bestow upon her, he would be waiting to take her hand and sneak into her enchanted universe with her. She chuckled at the way it sounded in her head, and when she turned away from him, she knew that she could not tell him how he already knows her, even if it was only in their own magical world; a world he was unknowingly an enormous part of.

William stared at her and realized how profusely he adored what he thought to be the most beautiful smile in the entire world. He loved the way her dimples made no apology for forming around her mouth, almost as though they were capturing and framing a smile straight out of her soul. It was something William did not see often but savored in the vision each time he would see the joy travel from her mouth and into her eyes. His heart had begun to thump enormously as he gazed into her arctic blue eyes, almost afraid that it might thump straight from his chest. He took in a deep breath and knew that he could not leave without telling her how he adored her. "I care about you, Misty-Bleu, more than you know, more than I'm willing to admit to, actually. More than your father would approve of, maybe more than I'm allowed to. But, I do. My heart is beating so fast right now, and I just, I am in love with you, Misty-Bleu, I have always been. I can't think of one day that I didn't wake up excited to see you?"

Alice VL

Misty-Bleu was taken aback by his unanticipated confession and sudden sensitivity. She had no idea of how to respond to his declaration of love, and instead, she lowered her head again and glowered in response before she nervously bolted from his car. She ran up through the gates of their mansion, but before she opened the front door of her home, she smiled broadly before she turned to wave him goodbye. At that very moment, and as she looked back at William, Misty-Bleu knew that she was wholly besotted and entirely obsessed with him.

Her heart was racing at the speed of a freight train. She wanted to shout out how deeply she adored him too. She thought about their secret world and how she could once again alter it and change the way they were living there. In a way, she had found validation from William, and for the first time, she knew that she could love him more passionately, more enthusiastically and freely. It was almost as though he had given her permission to live in her magical world on her own terms and plan out a perfect future for them.

By an unforeseen stroke of luck, John Buchanan remained blissfully unaware of the fact that William had driven Misty-Bleu home. He had fallen asleep in front of the blaring television on the living room couch as he sat up waiting for her to return home by curfew. When Misty-Bleu quietly walked in, and noticed that her father was asleep, she gently covered him with a throw and tip-toed into her bedroom. She lay down on her bed, deeply relieved that he would never know that it was William who had brought her home that night.

She was thankful that there would be no arguments and no beatings, making it almost a perfect evening. She closed her eyes and relived each word William had said to her only moments before. She smiled again when she felt the familiar thumping of her heart, and when she felt the fluttering in her stomach, she turned on her side and rushed back into her very own world where they could pick up where they left off a little while ago.

William sat in his car and stared blankly at the house she had disappeared into only moments before. He remained silent as he nervously listened for raised voices and watched closely for the light in her bedroom to come on. He was terrified that John Buchanan would hurt Misty-Bleu, but he had no inkling of how to save her from her parents. He placed both his hands on his steering wheel and lowered his head. "Someday Misty, someday I am coming for you. Just be okay until then, just wait." He whispered sadly before he started his car and headed home.

Following the events of the night of the valentine's ball,

both William and Misty-Bleu found themselves unexpectedly, yet entirely uncomfortable and out of sorts around one another. They were at once acutely aware of the unmistakable attraction and tensions brewing between one another. Misty-Bleu's heart would ferociously begin to hammer each time she heard William's voice, while he felt as though he was drowning in her frosty blue, bewitching eyes. He was desperate to save her, and he was desperate to hear the words she was not saying. He was relieved to notice that she had begun to smile more often, and he was thankful that she seemed more at peace.

Unbeknownst to Misty-Bleu, William intentionally failed grade twelve which was to be his final year of high school, for the sole reason of spending her final year at school with her. They both dreamed of attending a college in Coral Hill together, while William was keen to complete a degree in financial management, and Misty-Bleu was excited to study the English language and fulfill her dreams of becoming a writer and novelist. "I want to write. I want to tell the world about the stories in my head!" She shouted out excitely as they sat under a tree during lunch break at school just as the year was about to end. "Oh? You have stories in your head? Are any of them about me?" He laughed out loud when he detected the almost unheard-of exhilaration in her voice and equal excitement in her eyes. "They're always about you …" She whispered as she felt the blood rush to her head. "Then tell your stories, Misty, write about them and let the world know what goes on in that beautiful mind of yours." "I want to live on a Christmas tree farm someday and own two horses. At least! I want to sit amongst those trees and under the stars and write about the things that once saved me." He moved closer and playfully tickled her. "Then I would have to work damn hard for you, Misty-Bleu, so that I can save you!" She burst out laughing when he relentlessly continued to tickle her. "No, I'll write good books, you'll see! I'll buy us the farm!" "And a dozen kids. We must fill that farmhouse with kids! A whole bunch of us running around!"

Misty-Bleu was at once caught off-guard by the mere mention of having children someday. She was instantly saddened by the very notion of bringing their children into a world that seemed nothing but crooked and cruel to her, It was a world that showed her no mercy and no compassion. She nervously turned away from him before she anxiously began to fidget. "What's the matter, Misty? Did I just say something I shouldn't have?" Misty-Bleu hesitantly turned back to face him, unsure of what to say next. "I, I don't know, William. I mean, I never thought, I'm just not sure if children are in the stars for me. I mean, don't you think this world is far too cruel to bring kids into? Don't you think that life is just too hard?"

"No Misty, what are you talking about? Life is beautiful."
He sat up straight and took her hands into his, "I mean, love is
wonderful and beautiful, and then it's not. But then, Misty, then
it is again. Don't you want children someday? Don't you want a
family of your own?" She glowered as she gazed into his dark,
interrogative eyes. "No. I'm scared to. I don't, I don't want … my
parents, you know?" "Misty-Bleu, you are not your mother, and
our children will never have your life, I swear." She lowered her
head before she burst into tears. William placed his arms around
her and gently pulled her closer to him. "I love you, Misty.
Someday you will be wonderful, and our life will be magnificent.
We'll leave all this behind. I swear it …" "They'll never let me go,
you know?" She whispered softly through the tears that were
shimmering in her eyes as he held her firmly against him.

William was frantic to keep Misty-Bleu close to him and
refused to entertain the idea that she would be left behind for an
entire year without him. He was overcome by a desperate and
inexplicable need to keep a vigilant eye on her. William could in
no way at all, explain a nudge from deep within him that Misty-
Bleu might be in greater danger than he initially considered. He
was terrified of leaving for Coral Hill without out her, afraid to
leave her at the mercy of her parents.

Alice VL

Misty-Bleu was secretly relieved when she heard that William had failed his final year at school, but she could not shake the pity she felt for him for the wasted year. A year she knew he would have to start all over again. She had no inclination at all that William had intentionally flunked his final year simply to be around for her final stretch.

"William? You failed grade twelve? How did that happen?" Blakesley ran into William outside the school hall shortly after they received their final results. She was stunned that William had failed his entire last year when he had previously sailed through each of his years. "I mean, you are an A student. You've always been right at the top of your class? Every semester and every year, you've been an A student for all of your life? What happened? What went wrong?" William lowered his head in unanticipated shame, and gently shook it, "You can't tell Misty-Bleu, Blakesley, promise me?" "Misty-Bleu? Oh my gosh! You failed to stay behind with her?" Blakesley at once realized that William had every intention of remaining behind in Shadow Falls with Misty-Bleu. "You can't tell her, Blakesley! You must swear it!" Blakesley grimaced and was at once concerned when she noticed the anxiety and desolation in his eyes. "You and I both know that something's not right at her house, Blake. You know it! We never say it, but you and I both know. Have you ever

Alice VL

been to her house? Has anyone ever been there? I can't leave her here alone, with them. I know something's not right. I know, I can feel it, and I just can't leave her here." "No, you're right. She always has an excuse when I want to come over. I don't think she's allowed to have friends. She never speaks to any of us at Church. I see how stressed she is when I greet her in front of her parents."

Blakesley frowned as she considered the reality that she had never been invited to Misty-Bleu's house or that she kept her distance from her friends whenever she was around her parents. "Right, and she never goes anywhere, except to school or compulsory school events, and Church, with them." "Yeah?" "So, Blake, she's not safe here. You've seen the marks on her, we all have. Nobody talks about it. Nobody says anything, but we all see it. She always blames the fact that she's clumsy or awkward, but I know, I know they hurt her." "But, what can we do about it? Nobody will believe that John and Susan Buchanan are hurting their daughter? There's nothing you can do, William, is there?" "I know, I know that the Buchanan's are powerful. I know they have clout, and that is exactly why I must stay here until she can leave with me. I have to watch out for her. They keep her a prisoner in that house, I know they do." Blakesley bowed her head and nodded while reluctantly agreeing with him.

Alice VL

William's heart began to tremble when he heard Misty-Bleu's unanticipated voice behind him, "William? I just saw the results and, you, are you doing grade twelve again?" William nodded when he noticed the sadness in her eyes. He turned away, unable to look her in the eye, afraid that she might discover his secret. "You can't do the entire year all over again! They must have made a mistake!" "Nope, no mistake. I failed. Fair and square! I just didn't think, and studying was just not that big a deal this year. I don't mind doing it again." "William? You need to go see the headmaster. Your parents are going to kill you!" William smiled when he detected the sudden panic in Misty-Bleu's voice. "My parents know, Misty-Bleu, and there is nothing that the headmaster can do. I guess you're going to have me around for another year, this time as equals." He lied, desperate to keep his secret from her. "I'm so sorry, William. I know how eager you were to get to Coral Hill."

Misty-Bleu was overwhelmed by sadness, but as she searched his eyes, she failed to detect the disappointment on his face. For a moment, she was unnerved by his acceptance, almost as though he had expected it. "Another year won't hurt; besides, it just means that you can't cheat on me. It just means that I can be around you for six whole hours a day!" He winked playfully before he seized her firmly into his arms. "I love you, Misty-Bleu

Alice VL

Buchanan …" "I love you, William Carmichael. I don't want to cheat on you, ever."

When William returned home that same day, his parents, Julia and David Carmichael were anxiously awaiting an explanation from him for what had gone so wide off the mark during his final year in high school. They could barely fathom what it was that had gone so wrong that would result in him having to repeat his entire senior year all over again. As he reluctantly made his way up the steps to the front door of his home, he knew that he was in for bigger chaos than he cared to admit.

David Carmichael made way for his son to enter as William walked through the front door. Julia Carmichael cautiously showed him to the dining room, and by the look on her face, William was sure that she had aged ten years since that morning. He let out a fretful sigh before he took an empty seat, and determinedly, folded his hands on the table. "So, your mother and I want to talk about your final year's results. Anything you want to tell us?" David was desperate to remain calm as he searched his son's eyes for answers. "Nope dad, it is what it is." "Son, come on. This isn't you? What happened? Is it drugs? Are you in trouble?" "No dad! Of course, it's not drugs! I don't know? I guess this year was just tougher than I thought it would be.

AFTERLIGHT

Perhaps I slacked a little this year?"

"William, nothing is tougher than you thought it would be. Something else is going on here and I am going to make an appointment with Mr. Sloane, your Headmaster and find out what's going on here. There must be a mistake. I am going to insist on a remark. But, you could always rewrite in January. Perhaps we should work towards that, if all else fails ..." Julia was desperate to make sense of her son's dismal results during his very last year of high school. "Stop mom, just stop! I failed. I wanted to fail! I am glad I failed! If you make me rewrite in January, I'll just fail again!" William slammed his fists on the table, desperate for his parents to accept the fact that he had failed his very last year. "It's Misty-Bleu, isn't it?" Julia was at once angered by his irresponsible behavior. "Please mom, dad, I want to stay for her. I love her. I can't leave her here, with them." "You can't give up your future, your life, for her? You are not thinking clearly William, and you are behaving enormously irresponsibly." "I'm not, dad. I'm just postponing it a little. Please. I swear, I'll work hard and study hard at university the minute I graduate from high school, just please, let me have this year. Think of it as my gap year if you must, just please, leave things as they are. Let me repeat my final year, please?"

"William, do you know something about Misty-Bleu we

don't? Is there anything we can do to help her? There must be something we can do?" Julia was concerned at once when she discovered the unnatural desperation in William's voice. "No mom, I don't. I just know what I see. I see the marks on her. I see the fear in her eyes. I know things are rough for her, but she doesn't say anything. She never says anything. She doesn't talk about it to anyone." "Do you want us to step in and speak to someone? Perhaps we can talk to the Priest?" "Yeah, that would be great. Only, John Buchanan just about owns this entire town and the priests. It'll just make things worse for her, mom. She's been okay so far, we just need one more year. Just one."

William was frustrated when he realized that Misty-Bleu's father was one of the most powerful men in Shadow Falls. David squeezed William's shoulder before Julia got up, and desolately made her way into the kitchen. "Alright son. Just this one year." He whispered almost inaudibly, before he followed Julia into the kitchen.

When he reached Julia, he anxiously ran his fingers through his hair. She looked up at him and could not ignore the expected worry in his eyes. "We must do something, Jules? I can't let William throw his year away like that?" "I know, but I just don't know if there is anything we can do?" "What if we speak to the headmaster? He should know who to get in touch with?" "I'm just, I'm scared of the backlash. Misty-Bleu is such a wonderful girl. I don't want to put her through unnecessary stress?" "We have to think of William now. He's young, he's not thinking straight, and has no clue what he's getting himself into. We must do something, before it's too late." David took Julia's hands into his, and anxiously squeezed them. "William will never forgive us if anything happens to Misty-Bleu, David. I don't know, I don't know if I can do this?" Julia brought his hands to her chest as unexpected fear began to overwhelm her. "What if, what if William retaliates? What if they do something to Misty-Bleu? I don't know if I'm willing to betray our son like that. We should support him, Dave, we should respect his decision." "I can't Julia. I just cannot see him discard an entire year, and for what? They are kids who think they are in love! They don't know anything! In a year or two, William won't even remember who she is. He'll regret this, Jules, he will." David placed his arms around her and held her closer. "Alright then, Dave. Just know that I don't agree with any of this. I don't have a good feeling about any of this." "I will take full responsibility for this. William will thank me for this someday." He whispered gently before he kissed her on her forehead.

Just days after David and Julia Carmichael met with Mr. Sloane, John Buchanan suddenly and irrationally moved his family to a town at the opposite side of the country. Misty-Bleu had come home from school shortly before the semester was due to end when John and Susan were anxiously awaiting her in their dining room. Misty-Bleu was instinctively paralyzed with fear when she found them sitting quietly, the curtains drawn, drowning out all the light from the outside. It was dark and somber, and she could barely ignore the anger and rage that were emanating from their eyes. She was sure that she was about to receive a beating and, in a moment, all she had ever done to disobey them had begun to play over and over in her mind, almost like an old, silent movie.

"Mom, dad?" She cautiously and nervously approached her parents after she slowly placed her sling bag on the floor. "Sit, Misty-Bleu." John pointed to an empty chair before she hesitantly sat down, unable to take her eyes off him. Misty-Bleu's entire body began to quiver uncontrollably She was convinced that her heart was about to hammer right out of her chest. She hurriedly glanced around her and noticed that everything they had ever owned had been packed into moving boxes. Paintings and photographs that once adorned the walls of their five-bedroomed mansion were taken down, leaving the walls naked and cold. "What's going on?"

Misty-Bleu felt panic make its way into the very core of

her as she folded her hands on her lap, desperate for them to stop shaking. "Don't bother changing, all your things are packed up. I have packed you an overnight bag. We are about to leave Shadow Falls. Our plane leaves in a couple of hours." Susan mentioned matter-of-factly before Misty-Bleu's eyes trailed over to her father. "Leave? Leave where?" "You'll see when we get there." Dave got up from his seat and aggressively pulled Misty-Bleu up with him. "What have you told that Blakesley girl? Who have you been talking to? Did you think I'd never find out?"

He tightened his grip around her arm, as he yelled angrily at her, ready to punish her for betraying her parents. "Nothing. I haven't told her anything! I haven't said anything, I swear! I didn't tell anyone anything!" Misty-Bleu was painfully aware of a confining lump that had made its way into her throat as she hoarsely pleaded with her father to believe her. "Somebody said something, Misty-Bleu! Mr. Sloane and Father Jones were here this morning. They were decent enough to come and warn us." "It wasn't me, daddy! Blakesley doesn't know anything! I have never told anyone anything! I won't, I will never!" Misty-Bleu was desperate to make her father understand that she would never betray him in such a way. "Well, we're leaving Shadow Falls today. This is what happens when you speak out! Let this be a reminder of how quickly things can change!"

Alice VL

Susan came closer and grabbed Misty-Bleu's hand before she twisted her arm. "It's that boy, William, that Carmichael boy? I've heard the stories about you and him. The whole town is talking about your canoodling with that Carmichael boy!" "What? No! I swear mom, I never said anything!" Misty-Bleu stood still, cringing, as she desperately tried to absorb and understand all that was happening at that very moment. She had never told a single soul about any of the beatings she had suffered at the hands of her parents. She was meticulous in hiding the bruises that bore witness to her abuse. "We can't leave! I don't want to!"

Misty-Bleu shouted out as she desperately tried to free herself from Susan's grip. When she turned to face John, the last thing she could remember, was his enormous, angry fist coming at her.

Alice VL

AFTERLIGHT

2

William awoke to a loud and urgent knock on his bedroom door the following morning. He quickly glanced at his wristwatch and was at once bewildered by the perseverance when he noticed it was barely 6 am. "Yeah? Who is it?" "William! It's me, Blake!" "Blakesley? Come in?" William sat up straight when Blakesley anxiously made her way into his bedroom. "It's Misty-Bleu! She's gone!" Blakesley became ashen as she stammered over her words, desperate to inform William that Misty-Bleu had left, and seemingly disappeared without a trace. "Their house, it's empty. They're just gone. Like, gone! I mean, everything was normal yesterday, and today, there's nothing?"

William shot to his feet and placed both his shuddering hands on her shoulders, aware that his heart was about to thump right out of his chest. "What do you mean, gone? Gone where? Blakesley, you're not making any sense!" "I don't know? I mean, they moved. Their house is empty. It's like, it's like she was never here?" "Overnight? They moved overnight? I saw Misty-Bleu yesterday? They couldn't have moved overnight. Could they?" He agitatedly tightened his grip on her shoulders, unsure if he had even understood exactly what Blakesley had said only seconds earlier. "Yeah, they moved, William! They've moved out of Shadow Falls! I asked my mom if she knew anything, and she called Gary's mom, and she said that John had decided to branch out and, he'd send word the moment they're settled?"

"They know, Blake! Someone must have said something. Someone must have said something about the bruises and marks on her!" William hurriedly pulled on a pair of jeans and threw on a sweater before he abruptly bolted down the passage. He grabbed his father's car keys, and frantically dashed out to his car. William raced through the streets of Shadow Falls as though he could not reach Misty-Bleu's house fast enough. When he finally pulled into her driveway, he stood as though frozen in time when he discovered the house empty and abandoned. He ran up to the front door and banged on the door with all his might. He felt his heart race at a frightening speed and could barely breathe when he realized that they had taken Misty-Bleu away from him. When there was no answer, he frenetically ran around to the back, and peeked through the windows, only to discover that there were no traces of her, or where she had gone to.

There was nothing to tell him that Misty-Bleu still lived there, and that she'd be home soon. William sat down on a step at the back door, and defeatedly, he clutched his head in his hands. He was entirely overwhelmed and wholly confused, while panic began to invade the very core of him. It felt as though the world had crash landed on his shoulders. He was sure that his heart had shattered into a million pieces. He stared straight ahead of him, and aggressively swallowed back on a hampering lump in his throat. She was gone. Misty-Bleu had vanished into thin air, and there was nothing he could do to find her and bring her home. For the first time in his life, William did not have a plan.

He did not know where to start or what to do. At that very moment, William understood how defeated and powerless he was, and that John Buchanan had finally broken his daughter, and in the process, he destroyed William's heart. As though in a stunned haze, William slowly and desolately made his way back to David's car. As he strolled through the enormous, unlocked gates that was once home to the Buchanan's, he noticed a neatly folded sheet of paper. He picked it up, and immediately recognized his name, hurriedly scribbled down in Misty-Bleu's handwriting. As he unfolded the tiny block of paper, he was at once convinced that someone had taken a hold of his heart, and gripped it into both of their hands, as they squeezed the life out of it. He gasped for breath when he read her swiftly written note,

'William, I am sorry! They think I told someone! I don't know where we're going? Please don't tell on me! Please don't

Alice VL

tell on my parents! Please don't look for me! I'll find you! William! I didn't choose this! I love you! Don't forget me! M xx'

William gasped for air once again when he detected the fear and desperation in her note. He gently rubbed over her words when he noticed the smudges of her tears. He hurriedly wiped his own tears that had begun to roll carelessly onto his cheeks. He looked up and swallowed back on that almost familiar and confining lump in his throat. "Misty-Bleu …" He was entirely overwhelmed and crushed by her unexpected departure. He knew that she was not safe, and for the second time in his life, he was utterly powerless to save her.

When William arrived back home, he caught a glimpse of David standing on the front porch, sipping his coffee as he peered over his cup at William. William walked up to him, and collapsed in his father's arms, just as he did when he was only a little boy. "Son?" David was at once disturbed by his son's sudden and unexpected devastation. "She's gone, dad. He took her." "Misty-Bleu? Who took her?" "The Buchanan's are gone. They think she said something about them, hurting her …" William began sobbing as David gently stroked his crushed son's hair. "Everything was for nothing! It was all for nothing! Staying behind another year was for nothing! It was all for nothing!" "No, William, it wasn't …"

Alice VL

William retreated slightly and turned to face Julia when he heard her voice behind him. He was devastated when he saw the expression on her face and horrified by the notion that she may have intervened and spoke out against the Buchanan's. "It was you? You did this? Mother! What did you do?" "I couldn't let you waste a year of your life. Mr. Sloane has promoted you. You have officially graduated on past results." "What did you do?" William had become hysterical when he realized that she had placed Misty-Bleu in a life-threatening situation with her parents. "I just, I thought I could help both of you?" "Mother! You have no idea what you've done! If anything happens to Misty-Bleu, I will never, ever speak to you again! Do you hear me? I will never forgive you!"

William brushed past her and angrily made his way back into his bedroom. David followed closely behind him, afraid of what William might do next. "Did you know?" William stood glaring at his father who came to a standstill in his doorway, overwhelmed by the anger that had entirely begun to consume him. "William, after a while you'll forget her. You're both still kids. We couldn't leave you to make the biggest mistake of your life." "Dad, you don't know what you're talking about! I love her. I love, love her, and I will never forgive either of you if anything happens to her, never!"

Alice VL

AFTERLIGHT

When Misty-Bleu left Shadow Falls almost ten years earlier, she could never have predicted that it would take her almost as many years to pluck up the courage to find William again. She could never have anticipated all that would stand in her way from returning to him. She was a mere seventeen years old when her parents forcefully moved her away to what felt like the other end of the world for her. Susan kept a watchful and anxious eye on Misty-Bleu and discouraged any form of communication between her and the outside world. It was impossible for Misty-Bleu to make contact with anyone outside of her home. There was no way she could contact Blakesley or William. John Buchanan had employed a world class educator to home-school Misty-Bleu in a desperate attempt to shield her from the outside world, and all the negative influences he believed would taint her. It was nothing more than a desperate attempt to shield himself and Susan from the persecution of the rest of the world.

Misty-Bleu swore to herself that the moment she was old enough, she would promptly and without hesitation, return to the only home she had ever known, and to the only life she had ever wanted. She would waste no time in going back to the little town where she had first met William, where she felt understood and where nothing in her life could alter the way William made

Alice VL

her look forward to each new day as a promise of a better tomorrow. In the meantime, she found comfort in her mind and in her stories. She had kept them safely hidden in her heart and from her parents. As often as she could, she would close her eyes, and run back into his waiting arms where he once again, saved her from the cruelty of the only life she had ever known. "Wait for me, William, please wait ..."

Misty-Bleu would whisper almost inaudibly as she drifted off to sleep each night. She was desperately afraid that he might forget her. She was terrified that he would move on with his life without her. He was the boy in her dreams, the boy she could never forget and whose name brought her soul back to life.

After much planning and careful scheming, Misty-Bleu was finally able to escape and break free from John and Susan Buchanan. From the innermost core of her, she knew that returning to William would hardly be as simple as she once thought it would be, when she was so sure he would wait for her and welcome her with open arms. The time had passed when she was once so sure that love was all that mattered, and life was as simple as picking up where they once left off. They had no form of contact since she had left him her scribbled note. She had no idea of how to simply show up and walk back into his life, as though she had never left. Misty-Bleu did not dare try and contact him again. She could not endure a possibility where William might reject her. She could not stand the notion that he would have discarded her by then now that they had finally grown up.

She knew that William knew far more about her childhood, more than she would have liked him to know, and so much more than he would ever admit to knowing. Misty-Bleu wanted to be worthy of him. She was desperate to become wonderful for him, and she was determined to first, create an authentic life for herself that she could be proud of. A life William would have no choice but be honored by. A life where she would never be compelled to explain away her past, one that no-one else would ever know about. A past she was desperately ashamed of. One that lugged secrets she was fiercely guarding from him and from the rest of the world. Secrets she was defending, almost as though she was loyally cherishing them, but at the same time, a past she had no influence over and was immensely abashed by.

Misty-Bleu knew it was a past that he may never truly know all there was to know of, and the longer she delayed in finding him, the greater her excuses to return to him became. The longer she waited, the older she became, and the more unworthy she felt of a life she had once dreamed of, and was sure she deserved with William. Misty-Bleu knew that William was wholly untainted by the darker turns of life, and the cruel twists of fate it had bestowed upon her. It was a life he had not led, or had much experience in. William knew of love and care; he knew of family and devotion. She was desperate to shield him from the life she had lived, and the darkness that had surrounded her. She could in no way at all, ever expose him to any of the damage or suffering she had once endured at the hands of her parents. Misty-Bleu had survived a life she never thought she would, and that was enough for her. She had clawed her way out when she should have curled up and surrendered to what she once thought was her fate. She had fought with all her might to rise above the cruelty and brutality of her parents in a way the world would never guess she had once suffered. With each tormenting defeat, she fought harder and became stronger until she became unstoppable. She was determined to become someone the world would take notice of.

It was only a couple of days before her visit to the hospital, that she had plucked up the courage to make contact with and reach out to Blakesley again after all the years. She was overjoyed to hear her familiar, unchanged voice, but devastated to learn that that William was ill, and that he was dying. Blakesley begged her to keep a safe distance from William. She was desperate that Misty-Bleu avoid all contact with him, following William's years of anger and resentment after she had left so abruptly. But, it was hardly as simple as staying away for Misty-Bleu. She was overwhelmingly nudged and desperate to see him again, even if was only to tell him that because of him, she had survived. She wanted to outlast the life she was so carelessly flung into for him, and she wanted to survive simply because he loved her once. He was her safe place. He was her escape.

She found a home in his heart, and she found a world she could run away to. She wanted him to fight for her, and she was desperate that he holds on to his life, so that they could finish all that was unfinished between them. Misty-Bleu could not contemplate the possibility that William might die. She could not at all consider the likelihood that he was ill and about to leave her all over again, this time never to return to her. She was frantic to reach out to him and beg him to stay alive for her. There was no way at all for Misty-Bleu to ignore the fact that William was sick. She could not pretend she did not know, and she could no longer make excuses to find him again. She was devastated and entirely crushed by the prospect that his life might be over before it had even begun. Misty-Bleu knew that if William were to leave this world, she would certainly follow closely. There would be nothing left for her, and nothing more to live for. She had survived for him, and now it was time for William to survive for her.

Misty-Bleu took a job as a lounge singer and waitress at a local pub as soon as she reached Coral Hill. She was happy to move into a rent-free, one-roomed apartment upstairs. She would spend her days writing, and her nights serving and singing. Misty-Bleu had met Bryan Shaw, who was a regular performer and entertainer at the pub, and she would often share the stage with him and his band. After successfully publishing her first novel almost a year later, one she had written after recklessly tossed into an afterwards of complete and utter despair, Misty-Bleu found herself standing and caught up in a crossroads where careful choices had to be made. She could choose to take one road and return to William, the safe place she had created for herself, or she could follow another, and create her very own safe place while becoming wonderful for him before she was to find her way back to him. She ultimately settled for a quaint farm she had purchased all on her own, and where she had dreamed of creating and growing her very own Christmas tree farm. She had bought two beautiful riding horses which she proudly named Captain Nimo and the beautiful and elegant, Wilhelmina.

Misty-Bleu had created a life for herself in her beautiful country farmhouse. A life she was immensely proud of and found ultimate peace and safety in. At 6am each morning, she would make her way out to the stables in her old red barn just as the sun was about to rise and walk Captain Nimo and Wilhelmina out to the riding fields. Misty-Bleu adored her horses and found solace and peace whenever she was around them. She would spend hours at their side, and even more brushing and engaging in conversation with them.

At times, she would climb onto the rails of a charming enclosure she had built and sit quietly as she stared at them galloping and trotting the day away. After brushing them down each day as the sun was about to set, Misty-Bleu would lead them back to the stables, and close off the barn for the night.

Some mornings, she would swiftly make her way back into her farmhouse after she had led them out into the fields and begin her day writing one of the many stories that were fighting for a place in her books. She had finally found the peace she had been searching for her entire life. She had created a world for herself, and she had finally established a fitting identity for herself. She had found all that she was looking for, but she was never quite ready to bring William home to her. She continuously pushed herself to be better and become better, so that she was worthy of the only man she had ever loved. She was no longer the shy, fearful and quiet girl that had once disappeared from his life. Her voice became louder, and the shudders and stutters had vanished. She stood tall and proudly, and she attracted friendships through her beautiful, and caring nature.

She was finally someone. Someone who had carved out a living and a life for herself. Her name was important. Her books were loved. Her Christmas trees were the highlight of her year when families rushed to the farm, hoping to find the biggest and most beautiful tree. Misty-Bleu never sold one tree, but happily gave them away to anyone who needed joy and cheer in their homes. She would gladly allow them to cut down the perfect tree, on condition that they return the trees after Christmas to be replanted. Misty-Bleu loved the smell of her Christmas trees, and secretly dreamed that someday, she would own a million trees that would light up the skies on her farm. For Misty-Bleu, Christmas trees were magical.

Misty-Bleu always reminded herself of the legend that once, on a cold Christmas Eve night, a forester and his family were in their cottage gathered round the fire to keep warm. Suddenly there was a knock on the door. When the forester opened the door, he found a poor little boy standing on the doorstep, lost and alone. The forester welcomed him into his house, and the family fed and washed him, and put him to bed in the youngest son's own bed. The next morning, Christmas morning, the family were woken up by a choir of angels, and the poor little boy had turned into Jesus, the Christ Child. The Christ Child went into the front garden of the cottage and broke a branch off a Fir tree. He gave it to the family as a gift to thank them for looking after him. So, ever since then, people have remembered that night by bringing a Christmas tree into their homes.

Misty-Bleu had grown extraordinarily fond of two young men she had met at a book signing in Bronlyn after she had published her very first novel. She would make a concerted and regular effort to spend time on the phone with them and was saddened that they saw one another only during holidays. She adored Shaun and Kevin and was happy to speak to them as often as she could. She had met them at an after party that was organized by her publisher shortly after the book signing, in a town she had never been to before. After drinking a few glasses of champagne too many, Misty-Bleu hopped up onto the stage of a band that was hired for the evening, one she had often performed with in Coral Hill, and playfully grabbed the mic from the lead singer, Bryan Shaw. She unashamedly belted out her very own version of 'Put me on a dragon and take me home for the night,' much to the audience's delight. After her rendition of the popular song, the band insisted that Misty-Bleu perform alongside them for the remainder of the party.

Misty-Bleu never dreamed of becoming a famous singer, but she was proud to hold her own against one of the greatest performers she had ever met. She loved singing, and she loved the fact that she could let her hair down and become one of them even for only a couple of hours. Bryan Shaw regularly invited her out to perform gigs with them and would persistently persuade her to perform on a selected number of tracks on each new album he was about to release, and when he was in Coral Hill. She was happy to oblige as a favour to him, but insisted he leave her name off the tracks and never at all, acknowledge her as the singer accompanying him on any of his songs. Shaun and Kevin, who were affectionately known as Shakes, fell in love with her voice and her spirit that very evening, and even though they lived in two entirely different countries, they had clicked on a level Misty-Bleu thought would never be possible.

She often found herself in awe of the love the two shared for one another, and secretly reveled in the fact that these two same sex couples chose her as their devoted, and best girlfriend. "Oh my gosh, girl!" Shaun yelled out excitedly as Misty-Bleu made her way back to the table she had shared with the couple at the after party. Misty-Bleu smiled bashfully when Shaun embraced her. "You should do this, you should sing!" "No, no.

AFTERLIGHT

This isn't the life for me. I much prefer my books." Misty-Bleu giggled shyly as she peered back at Bryan Shaw and his crew. Shaun was a successful Realtor who had been in the industry since he relocated to Bronlyn more than ten years ago, and at the tender age of twenty-three. He met Kevin at an art exhibition shortly afterwards, and the two became inseparable. Kevin had emigrated to Bronlyn from Africa only months before, but was instantly recognized for his art. They were legally married only months before her book signing. Misty-Bleu tremendously admired the two men who were keen to start a family. "So, Misty-Bleu, when do you go back to Coral Hill?" "First thing in the morning, I am so over the night-life and city noises!" "You don't like it?" Kevin frowned as he gazed questioningly into her eyes. "Not even a bit. I wouldn't even be here if it wasn't for the book signing." "Coral Hill, is it not a city too?" "No, well, yes. I live outside of the city on a farm." "Oh? A farm?" Shaun moved closer, eager to learn more about Misty-Bleu. "Yes, a beautiful farm with hundreds of Christmas trees and two horses. I love it there; you guys should come visit?" "Actually, we're in the process of looking for a surrogate. We are so keen to start a family, you perhaps interested?" "Oh no, no, no. That isn't for me!"

Kevin winked at Shaun, while fascinated by Misty-Bleu.

Alice VL

"So, tell us about the hunk in your life, or goddess?" She burst out laughing and grabbed Shaun by his hand, "There is no hunk or goddess!" "Really? You have no-one? You live alone on that farm?" "Yes, and no, it's not like I have no-one. I have my horses and my stories. I'm quite happy with my life just as it is." "But Misty-Bleu?" Kevin moved closer and placed his hand on top of her and Shaun's, "Don't you want somebody? I mean, don't you want to share all this with someone? You are gorgeous, successful and a great writer and singer. You have so much to offer." "Nope, I am quite content. Really guys, I am happy as is. I've dated on and off, but it's just not for me." She smiled when she gazed at the two men staring curiously back at her. "Someone must have broken her heart …" Shaun turned to Kevin before they sat back in their seats. "There was someone once, and if you read my book, you'll get it." She smiled sadly before she lowered her head. "So, handsomes, I am going to say goodnight. I have an early flight out tomorrow. I hope I will see you again. Please keep in touch?"

She hurriedly handed Kevin her author's card before she swiftly kissed him on his cheek. "Here's my number and details. Please, please keep in touch. And you Shaun, you need to find that surrogate soon!" "You sure you won't be her for us?" Misty-Bleu smiled before she kissed Shaun on the cheek too. "Who knows? Maybe someday?" She waived them goodbye, before she left to return to her hotel room, happy to have met the couple.

Alice VL

3

As she continued down the path of the hospital, Misty-Bleu glanced around her, and realized with great anguish that she had forgotten when it was that she had last noticed how bright and low the moon felt, while at the same time, surrounded by a million brightly lit stars. The light of the moon shone so brightly, it almost blinded her. As she gazed mesmerizingly at the moon, she felt as though she could reach up, and almost touch it. She smiled at the stars shining brightly above her and imagined it to be a silvery gown covering her while leading the way to William.

She stopped and gasped for air when she saw William alone on an isolated park bench, just meters away from her, and under the same light of the moon she was walking under. Misty-Bleu was at once debilitated by the thumping of her racing heart. She desperately tried to evoke when exactly it was that she had last seen him. She could suddenly not quite remember when it was that she last felt his arms around her. She could barely recall when it was that she last gazed into his beautiful, brown eyes. She knew she was only seventeen years old, yet it felt more like a lifetime ago, almost as though they had existed in a whole different universe. Ten years had passed since that very moment, yet, as Misty-Bleu stood staring at him, he felt as familiar to her, as he did when she so abruptly, and without explanation, left him behind all those years ago. Misty-Bleu was desperately afraid that he might not recognize her. She was terrified that he might rebuke her for their broken hearts. She was overcome with horror at the notion that he may possibly have discarded every memory of her, and that he would not even remember her name.

She quietly slipped in beside him, before she hesitantly sat down, without as much as looking in his direction. Her hands had begun to quiver. It felt to her as though her heart was about to hammer right out of her chest.

He sat in silence as he stared out in front of him and took no notice of the stranger that had taken a seat right beside him. He was at once exasperated by the fact that she would so carelessly invade his privacy, when there were countless other benches, he was convinced, she would be more comfortable on. William was irritated that she slid in next to him and was about to get up when he heard her speak. "Do you mind if I sit here?" Misty-Bleu's voice shuddered slightly when she whispered softly before she finally turned to face him. When she caught a glimpse of his familiar face on that extraordinarily dark night, she smiled sadly, and realized that she had unexpectedly become

Alice VL

apprehensive about seeing him again for the first time. There was nothing about him that seemed different to her, except perhaps that he had grown into the man she always knew he would someday. His dark hair seemed darker, and his skin seemed paler, but to her, he was still the most beautiful man she had ever laid her eyes on. As she sat staring at him, Misty-Bleu realized that she would never have thought him to be ill, and at once, she felt her entire world crashing down on her. He seemed sadder than she remembered but, there was nothing to tell her that he was gravely ill. She wondered what he was thinking of, and she cringed when she saw the pained expression on his face.

William was surprisingly unnerved by the sound of her voice. The stranger beside him sounded familiar. Her voice was soft and shaky, but it was a voice he had heard before. He swiftly glanced over at her and grimaced questioningly. He tried to remain subtle, not wanting her to notice him staring at her, but desperate to identify where it was that he knew her from, and where he had heard her voice before.

"So, do you mind if I sit here?" Misty-Bleu hoarsely asked again, desperate to get his attention, and frantic for him to look at her, and recognize her. She was frenetic for him to feel her. She desperately wanted his soul to recognize hers, even in the midst of one of the darkest nights of the year.

Alice VL

AFTERLIGHT

William frowned when he tried to identify her with only the light of the moon to expose her facial features, and when she gazed into his recognizable eyes, she was instantly discouraged and saddened to detect the utter confusion that was evident on his face. His eyes glared questioningly at her while she prayed for him to recognize her. As he sat staring at her, William knew that he had seen her face before, but at that very moment, he could not quite place her. He stared at her, unsure of what she looked like with only the light of the stars shining down on her. It was dark, darker than any other night before. He could not see the color of her eyes, or the color of her hair. He felt an unanticipated shudder run down his spine when he heard her voice once more and knew into the very core of him, it was a voice he once must have known intimately.

He unashamedly admired her long hair as it flowed down her back, but it was when he gazed into her eyes that he felt into his soul, he had seen them before. He stared cautiously at her in an effort to identify her, afraid that the darkness of the night might be playing tricks on his mind. Misty-Bleu smiled tenderly and was promptly reminded of how awfully she had missed the boy she had fallen in love with so many years ago. "Sure, I guess you can sit anywhere you want." He whispered huskily before he turned away from her and nervously lowered his head.

Alice VL

AFTERLIGHT

"I don't mean to intrude, and I know what you must be thinking. I bet you are wondering why I chose this park bench to sit on, when there are a hundred empty ones around us? But, you know, when I was a little girl, I had a friend, someone I loved so much …" She sniggered nervously as she began telling William who she was. William glanced tensely at Misty-Bleu, confused as to why she was engaging in conversation with him. "He used to look out for me all the time, and he made me feel so safe and protected, like nothing in the world could ever hurt me. Whenever I became ill and landed up in hospital, he would sit beside me, and hold my hand. He would insist that I get better soon. He would sneak in after my dad left, and sneak out before my dad came back in. That always made me feel better. What he never knew was that he gave me a home, he gave my heart a safe place. He let me create a world that I could escape to, and as sure as you and I are sitting here now, he would be there to meet me, every single time. He gave me a way out. He became home to me. He saved me …"

She smiled sadly as his jumbled eyes met hers once again. Misty-Bleu got up almost as though in a wandering haze and knelt before him. She grabbed his hands, and bowed her head when that familiar, curbing lump made its way back into her throat. "I know that he … I've heard that he's sick now. They say,

Alice VL

he's really, really sick. I just wanted to see him and be with him again. I've been putting it off for so long. So much longer than I should have, you know? There were so many things I was running from, and there were so many things I wanted to get right, before … before I walked back into his life. I left it for so long and it, it was just never the right time. I was so ashamed of myself; of the life I had once lived. I didn't want to taint him with all that had happened to me. I wanted to become wonderful first. I wanted to deserve him first. And now, now his time is up. We have no more time. I wasted it all, but I never … I never forgot him, and I never, ever stopped loving him …" She lifted her head and smiled sorrowfully through the tears that were bucketing from her eyes. "William, it's me, Misty-Bleu …" She lowered her head as she desperately swabbed at the tears that were rolling unreservedly down her cheeks. She anxiously peered up at him and was at once aware of the recognition that had begun to flicker in his eyes.

When she saw the tears shimmer in his own eyes, she was at once relieved that he had finally recognized her. In one motion, William shot to his feet before he pulled her up with him. He seized her in his arms, before he tightly embraced her, and held her for what felt like forever. "Misty-Bleu? Oh God, Misty-Bleu? You're here? Is it really you?" William held her firmly against him, overwhelmed by the fact that she was standing in front of him. She held on tightly, and for the first time in so many years, she remembered in one moment, how it felt to feel safe again.

Her entire body had begun to shudder as he squeezed her firmly against him. He slowly retreated from her, and stood staring into her eyes, unsure of what to say next, but overjoyed by the fact that Misty-Bleu had found him. "How did you know? How did you find me?" Misty-Bleu could detect the indisputable confusion in his voice. "I mean, how did you know about any of this?" Misty-Bleu took his hand into hers and smiled sadly at him. "I wanted to see you again. I've never gone back to Shadow Falls since I left, and I'm making some changes in my life. I reached out to Blakesley. I wanted to find you. I missed you so, William. I know … I know I shouldn't have come but, I missed you. I had to see you again. Our story was just so unfinished. Everything was wrong with the way we left things; you know?" Misty-Bleu whispered gruffly as her tears continued to batter down her cheeks. "Misty-Bleu, it is so good to see you again. I never thought … I just never thought I'd see you again?" William was at once saddened to witness the extreme sorrow that had begun to overwhelm her. "How have you been, Misty-Bleu? What happened?" William held her hands firmly in his when he really wanted to hold her in his arms. She smiled through her crushing tears, desperate to swallow back on that all-too familiar and imprisoning lump in her throat, "I'm fine, William, I'm good … now …" "It's been so long, Misty-Bleu, what happened to you?" He squeezed her hand tighter, desperate to know that Misty-Bleu was in fact, alright. "Life William, life. Just things …"

She swallowed and took in a deep breath, "How about you? How have you been?" He gazed despondently out in front of him after he sat back down on the bench. He pulled her down beside him without letting go of her hand. Misty-Bleu stared guardedly at him, devastated by the fact that William was ill. "So, what's up William? What's the matter? Why are you here?" William remained silent, unsure of what to say or how to break the news to her. When he finally spoke, she was sure that her entire world was about to collapse around her. "I'm dying Misty-Bleu. I mean, the tests haven't come back yet, but my doctors tell me it's only a confirmation of what they already know. I have months at the most. There's nothing they can really do …" He let go of her hands and bowed his head, overcome by intense devastation and sadness. "They did the tests today. I should know soon, but they want to begin chemo and radiation tomorrow as a precaution." Misty-Bleu felt as though someone had stabbed her through heart with a blunt knife as she struggled to catch her breath. She took his hand back into hers and turned to face him. "Nothing is definite, William. Nothing is written in stone yet." She was devastated to realize that William Carmichael was falling apart, and there was nothing she could do to save him. "I mean, they don't know. What is the diagnosis and, what is the next step?"

"Ewing Sarcoma. It is inoperable and incurable. They suspect it has metastasized into my thigh bone and the prognosis isn't good. It never is. There is just no survival rate." Misty-Bleu was desperate to fight back the tears when she understood the finality of what he was saying. "I will have rounds and rounds of chemotherapy and radiation only to extend what will inevitably happen in the end. I will wither away slowly and die …" William's voice drifted off until he became silent. "Nothing is definite William. You have to have faith. Just promise me. William, promise me that you won't start any treatment until after Friday, until after you have your results. William, I am begging you, please. Chemo and radiation on its own can kill you. Please be sure first, promise me?" He stared at her in disbelief but saddened to witness the pleading and devastation in her eyes. "We'll see, I don't have much of anything right now, and faith is definitely not one of them."

"William, I didn't come here to hear you quit. You can't

quit. I never did, and you can't either! You taught me to fight! You taught me to be strong! You, William, you gave me hope. You gave me a reason to fight! Don't let it be for nothing. I am begging you, William, I can't lose you …" "Misty-Bleu? What happened to you?" "William, it doesn't matter, and not now. I can't talk about any of this now. I am here now, for you. This is about you. I want you to have life, for me, for us. It can't end like this! It just can't. Please don't let it." "Just tell me this, did he hurt you, Misty-Bleu? I never really knew, and you never told anyone anything?" "I am fine, William. I did good. I am good, and I found my wonderful. I found you again. They don't matter anymore. I have a beautiful life. I have peace and I have you, nothing matters anymore." She paused to take in a deep breath before she turned back to him, "William, let's not do this now. Let's just be like we were before. When we were little. When we were younger. Let's go back there for a while, I am begging you. Let's live where this isn't happening, let's just go back for a while …" She buried her head in his chest and began sobbing violently. He placed his arms around her and held her securely against him.

"Do you want to walk me back to my fancy hospital room? I want to hear all about you and what you've been up to since you left. I want to go back to before, with you." He stood up and held out his hand to help her up. "Won't they kick me

Alice VL

out?" "They wouldn't dare ..." He winked playfully, before he placed his arm around her waist. When she rested her head against him, they strolled back into the hospital.

When they reached William's room, Misty-Bleu was startled to find a man seated in a visitor's chair next to his bed. "Oh, Josh is here. I forgot he was coming ..." Misty-Bleu clutched his hand, and nervously turned him around to face her. "Maybe I should come back tomorrow?" "Please don't go, Misty-Bleu. I don't want you to go. Josh won't stay too long." When Joshua Stark saw William enter, he hurriedly rose to his feet. "Hey buddy ... I didn't know you had company?" Joshua took William's hand, and firmly shook it. "Have you been waiting for me?" "No, well yeah. I saw you out in the garden, and I ... I didn't want to intrude." Joshua fixed a gaze on Misty-Bleu, anxious for William to introduce her. "This is Misty-Bleu. Misty-Bleu Buchanan, an old friend of mine." He smiled before he turned to face Misty-Bleu, "This is Joshua Stark. My doctor, my psychiatrist and world-famous singer." Misty-Bleu shook his extended hand and smiled gracefully. "You look so familiar, Misty-Bleu, have we met?"

Joshua was at once stunned by her beauty and could not help but notice her red and swollen eyes. "No, I don't think so? But, I know who you are. I've heard you sing, and you might have performed with Bryan Shaw in the past?" "Yeah, I have. Aren't you the author, Misty-Bleu Buchanan?" Misty-Bleu nodded and turned away bashfully. "We actually met a while ago. At a book signing. You took over the stage at the after party. Wow! I remember your voice so well! Great voice! If I'm not mistaken, you were actually sharing the stage with Bryan and his crew?" He was genuinely pleased to meet Misty-Bleu. William smiled as he stood staring at Misty-Bleu, stunned to realize that she had met Joshua once before. "Yeah, no, that wasn't me. That was the champagne ..." Misty-Bleu was mortified that Joshua had recognized her but giggled nervously at the mere thought. "Seriously, you should enter The Academy with that voice. I heard from the band mates that night that you actually performed with them a few times for fun? What a small, small world ..." She smiled shyly before squeezing William's hand tighter. "So, listen bro, I just wanted to check up on you. Are you ready to start your chemo tomorrow?"

"Actually Josh, I was thinking of waiting for the results. I'd hate to start something without a confirmed diagnosis. I've read somewhere that chemo just makes you sicker and could actually kill you in the end? I'd rather we be sure ..." "Okay, well, if that's what you want? You're right, it is a whole lot of poison to be pumping into a healthy body, but you would have to stay until your results come back." Misty-Bleu smiled sadly when she noticed the immediate confusion and concern on Joshua's face. "Misty-Bleu, lovely to meet you. I hope you join us on stage sometime?" "It was nice meeting you too, but no, I have no business sharing a stage with a Grammy winner." Joshua burst out laughing before he squeezed her shoulder, "Take care of him for me, and call me if he gives you a hard time. Bye guys!" Joshua waved before he turned to leave.

William hurriedly made his way over to his bed, but before Misty-Bleu was able to take the seat next to him, he took her by the arm, "Come sit here with me ..." Misty-Bleu climbed onto the bed and sat directly across from William. "So, you sing too?" Misty-Bleu giggled self-consciously, "No, no. I was pretty drunk that night. It was the after party of my book signing. I met a gay couple, and we sort of hit it off straight away. There was way too much champagne at our table, and well ..." "I never knew you could sing too? Anyway Misty, are we going to talk about what happened?" "William, please. Please can we not? I just want to be here, with you. In the moment ..." "Okay, but you're going to have to give me something, what have you been up to? Other than singing your heart out while under the influence?"

Misty-Bleu giggled again when she detected the sarcasm in William's voice. "I write. I've published a few books. I have a Christmas tree farm and two horses. Not too far from here ..."

Alice VL

AFTERLIGHT

"A Christmas tree farm? Really? You got your Christmas tree farm?" "Yeah, and it's great. The trees are beautiful and the farm smells of pine and fir. I only work for two months out of the year which leaves me ten months to write. And you? What have you been up to, William? Where has life taken you?" "I am an investment broker. I have my own firm, and I'm doing all I ever wanted to do. I have a little place up in Cotton Road, and I travel as often as I can." He smiled when he recalled all the dreams they had once dreamed of together. "How long have you been in Coral Hill?" William was surprised to hear that Misty-Bleu had settled close by. "About six years ..." "Wow Misty-Bleu, six years? Really? And you're only now showing your face?" "William, there's so much you don't know, and I just don't want to go there right now. I know I should have come sooner. I know now more than ever that I should have reached out to you. But William, there were so many things I wanted to get right first. I wanted you, and everyone else to know my name and say it proudly. I wanted to create something wonderful first, you know?"

William shook his head before he took her hands into his. "You are wonderful, you always have been. Your wonderful has always been you. We had dreams to create our wonderful together, remember? You had nothing to prove, Misty-Bleu, and no-one to prove anything to. And now for the most important question, are you seeing anyone?" Misty-Bleu lowered her head, "No, I have two best friends, though. Shaun and Kevin, the guys I mentioned earlier. Yeah, they are wonderful guys, my guys ..." She teased playfully before she squeezed his hands, "You? Anyone special lurking around?" "Well, you know? On and off. One here and two over there. You know how it is?" "Oh my, Mr Carmichael, on and off? And no, I don't know how it is?" She giggled before she playfully punched him on his shoulder. "We're not going to talk about that either then!"

He began tickling her and for the first time in what felt like forever, Misty-Bleu felt as though she had finally come home. Her heart was finally thumping like it should be beating, for William. "Could you be any more beautiful, Misty?" William gently stroked her cheek as he brushed her hair back with his other hand. She smiled shyly, before she lowered her head. "You are even more beautiful than I remember ..." She looked up into his eyes and was saddened by the indignant expression that was looking back at her.

William stared into her eyes, wanting to take in everything about her again. He could barely recall her eyes as arctic as they were at that very moment. There were traces of pain and sadness, and as William counted the darker shades of blue, he found evidence of stories that were hiding behind them.

Alice VL

His heart fluttered when she looked back at him, and for an instant, he considered kissing her lips once more. "You are exactly as I remember you, only, I never thought you could be any more handsome than you were way back then!" She giggled softly before she lowered her head. "How are your parents, William?" "They're worried about me, that's for sure. They are here every day, almost all-day long." "I mean, William, you are sick ..." He took her hands into his and squeezed them gently. "You're here, and there's nothing else I want to think about tonight."

They sat together on his hospital bed, as they reminisced about the past and spoke about all that had gone by for them. They discussed moments that had turned spectacular in their lives, and they reminded one another of the dreams they once had.

William was careful to avoid questioning her about her parents, while Misty-Bleu was cautious not to let too much of her past slip out. They laughed about their old times and all they once went through. They spoke about how they once, meant the world to one another.

William hugged her often while Misty-Bleu buried herself in his chest as often as she could. She felt like she had finally come home, even though she could not quite discard the nagging feeling that it wouldn't last.

Alice VL

AFTERLIGHT

4

Misty-Bleu unintentionally fell asleep beside William on his hospital bed. When she awoke, William was asleep behind her with his arms firmly gripped around her. Gazing out in front of her through the enormous glass window with a view down the passage, Misty-Bleu was horrified to discover his parents standing there in silence, watching her and William sleep.

She shot out of his bed and was suddenly deeply mortified that she had fallen asleep in his arms. He groggily opened his eyes when he became aware of the commotion Misty-Bleu had caused and sat up straight while rubbing his sleepy eyes. "Your parents are here …" She hurriedly made her way to the closed door of his hospital room and opened it in a panic. "Mr. and Mrs. Carmichael." Misty-Bleu politely greeted them as they entered William's room. "Hello?" She instinctively placed her arms around William's mother, and excitedly embraced her. "It's Misty-Bleu, mom." William hurriedly reminded his mother before Julia Carmichael frowned, but hugged Misty-Bleu tighter. Dave Carmichael placed his arms around both of the women, and when Misty-Bleu smiled, she knew that they were truly happy to see her again. "Misty-Bleu! Goodness, how you have grown. I am so happy to see you again. You have no idea how good it is to see you again." Julia was relieved to see Misty-Bleu again after all the years. She secretly berated herself for the chaos and destruction she had caused all those years ago when William failed his final year of high school. She would lay awake at night and pray for Misty-Bleu. She punished herself immensely for her disappearance almost overnight. Through the years, she often tried to find her again, and grew anxious whenever her leads turned out to be a dead-end each time. Julia hugged her again, deeply thankful that she seemed safe and normal, not that she quite knew what she expected. Perhaps, she thought that if Misty-Bleu had been hurt, the scars would appear throughout her body. "It's so good to see you again, Mrs. Carmichael ..." Misty-Bleu swallowed back on the tears that were once again, threatening to escape through her eyes. She swiftly made her way over to William, who was smiling at his parents. "So, I am going to leave you and give you some privacy ..." Misty-Bleu began to excuse herself before William abruptly interrupted her. "Please don't go, Misty-Bleu."

William anxiously grabbed at her hand, while pleading with her to stay. "The doctor will be here soon, William, plus, I desperately need a shower. I promise I'll come back." "Here, put your number into my phone." William handed her his mobile phone before Misty-Bleu hurriedly saved her number for him. "I have to let the horses out. I'll have a quick shower, and then I'll come straight back here, I promise." Misty-Bleu was desperate not to intrude or interfere with William's parents being there. She grabbed her bag, and hurriedly walked out of his room, without turning back.

She had barely made her way to the elevator when her phone bleeped unexpectedly. She swiftly grabbed her phone and smiled when she realized that William had sent her a text. 'Please come back.' She grinned when she turned to see if she could still see him. She caught a distant glimpse of William staring at the screen on his phone before she hurriedly responded to his text. "I promise. Just try and stop me!"

Misty-Bleu walked into the elevator and was relieved that she was entirely alone. She peered to her right and caught a glimpse of her own reflection in the mirror. As she stood glaring at the dark circles under her eyes, the power suddenly went out and everything around her turned dark. She stood motionlessly and tense, as she anxiously waited for the power to be restored. She could hardly see her hand in front of her, but before she could reach for the emergency button, there was a bright flash that instantly blinded her. She lost her balance at once and grabbed onto the railing behind her. She closed her eyes as tightly as she could but was still overwhelmed by a light she had no idea where it was coming from. "Forgive me, Misty-Bleu, stay with me ..." She was at once aware of William's familiar voice behind her, but as she reached out to him in the darkness, she could not feel him anywhere. "William?"

There was a haunting silence that began to deafen her at once, but only a moment later, the power was restored, and the elevator doors opened again. Misty-Bleu realized that she was still on the same floor as William, and just as the doors were about to close again, Misty-Bleu slid back out, and ran down the passage, back to William. She was desperate to return to him. Misty-Bleu was nudged by an untaught sensation that compelled her to go back to him. "I, I don't want to leave you? I, I don't know what just happened, when the power went out?" "What do you mean, Misty? The power didn't go out?" "Are you sure? I mean, the elevator's power was out for a minute at the most. Were you not just there? I could have sworn I heard your voice ..."

She stood in the doorway, overwhelmed by sudden mortification, and overcome by confusion. She was at once enormously afraid of his test results, and terrified that if she walked out of the hospital, she might never see him again. She felt a wave of sadness overwhelm her. At that very moment,

Misty-Bleu felt like she was drowning, and could hardly breathe. "I've been here the entire time. But I'm glad you came back. Please stay Misty-Bleu. Are you alright? It looks like you've seen a ghost?" William grabbed her ice-cold hand as she approached him, aware of the fact that she had turned ashen. She was at once confused as to why she so robotically made her way back to William, but discarded all her fears and confusion when Dr. Zahn and Joshua Stark unexpectedly walked into William's room.

Julia Carmichael grabbed Misty-Bleu's hand as they anxiously awaited the results of William's tests, while David made his way over to his son. Dr. Zahn took his place next to William, while Joshua made his way over to the foot end of his bed. "Mr. and Mrs. Carmichael, William ..." His voice trailed off as he opened William's medical folder. Dr. Zahn began explaining the results as he flipped through the sheets that were neatly clipped onto his clipboard. "We have never been wrong before. The x-rays have never been wrong, ever, but following thorough testing of the biopsy, it is definitely not malignant. It seems to be a clustered pocket of adipose cells that we can easily remove through local anaesthetic. The reason it's causing such severe swelling and pain is due to the strenuous effect it has on your thigh bone which causes continuous inflammation, and then results in pain and discomfort as well as swelling. I would like to schedule the removal of these cells for first thing in the morning and then, well, you can go home and get on with your life. We were wrong, and for once, I am glad we were."

Dr. Zahn smiled, entirely confused by William's test results, while Joshua shook William's hand in relief. His parents embraced one another, while Misty-Bleu wiped a lost tear that had rolled down her cheek. "William, he's right. We have never, ever seen anything like this. I don't know what to say? We have spoken to excellent oncology specialists, and we are all in agreement, you are in the clear. You are healthy and will probably live to be a hundred." Joshua was still holding William's hand when he squeezed his shoulder. William nodded his head, but all he wanted to do, was to look into Misty-Bleu's tired eyes. When her eyes finally met William's, Misty-Bleu knew that it was a look she would never forget.

It was almost a promise of life, sudden relief, and severe warnings of what might or could have been. Misty-Bleu animatedly clapped her hands in excitement before she grabbed Julia and Dave and firmly embraced them. Tears of relief had begun to roll unashamedly down her cheeks when she heard what she had already known that William was going to live. Dave and Julia Carmichael frantically embraced Dr. Zahn and Joshua before they both flung their arms around William. Misty-Bleu stood staring at the tears of joy that were gushing from William's eyes but was suddenly desperate to leave them alone with one other.

She picked up her bag, and hurriedly made her way out of his ward. As she reached the closed doors of his hospital ward, she felt a hand tug at her arm. When she turned around, she found William standing behind her. "Misty-Bleu, I know you have things at the farm that you must attend to, but please stay. They will all be leaving soon …" She moved closer to him and took his hands into hers. She opened up the door and gently tugged at him to follow her. When they stood behind that big glass window, she gently squeezed his hands. "William, you have life. You're going to live. You must begin again. You have tomorrow. You don't just have tomorrow; you have your whole life ahead of you. Find someone special, someone who is more like you. Someone you could be proud of and have the family you always dreamed of. The family, I'm not sure I want. Get that house on the beach you fantasized about as a child. Be happy, just be happy. Have a good life, with someone who deserves to share your space with you. It's not me, William, it never really was …"

Misty-Bleu's tears were once again lying shallow in her eyes. She finally realized that she could never stand with pride or honour at his side. Her past would always be a reminder of the dysfunctional life she had once lived, and it would undoubtedly catch up with her over and over again. As she stood staring into his distressed eyes, Misty-Bleu knew into the very core of her that her childhood could never be erased. She continued to live with the shame of what had happened to her; a shame she never told William about and wasn't sure she ever could. "Misty-Bleu, don't do this, don't. Please don't do this …" "William, do you know why I came back here, to you? All I ever wanted was to tell you, that you … you saved me, William. As a child, you saved me, and as a teenager, you saved me. I wanted to thank you for that, and I wanted to ask you to fight for yours. I have life because you were in it, and now, now it's your turn. You have life, William …"

She whispered hoarsely through the tears that were once again, shimmering in her eyes. "Misty-Bleu, please, go take a shower, go do whatever you have to do with your horses, but then, just come back here. I am begging you. Please don't walk out on me now, not again. I want you here for my procedure tomorrow. My parents are flying back to Shadow Falls afterwards, and I just, I want to talk once I am discharged. Don't do this to me again, don't show up here, and then just leave Misty-Bleu?" William was overwhelmed by the fear that had suddenly crept up and invaded his entire being. "William, there is so much you don't know about the last ten years but, there is so much more you don't know about the years before that ..."

William placed his index finger on her lips before he interrupted her, "That's why I want to talk, please Misty-Bleu. You can't do this to me again. I want to know; I want to talk. Just give me a chance. Stick around for a while, and then ... then, if you still want to leave, I won't stand in your way. Just, not now? Just not today." William placed his arms around her and held her close against him, desperately afraid that he might never see her again. She rested her head on his chest and was once again reminded of how she adored the way William's arms felt around her. As she listened for his heartbeat, Misty-Bleu knew that she too, was not quite ready to walk away from him yet. "Okay William, I'll come back later. Visit with your parents and with Joshua while I go sort my things out at the farm, and then, I guess, I'll see you later then ..."

When Misty-Bleu looked into his eyes, she was suddenly crippled by a sense that she may never see him again. William watched her walk down the passage before she disappeared into the elevator. He turned to make his way back to Joshua and his parents who were ecstatic by the news that William's life was no longer threatened. "That is just the best news, son!" David grabbed William and again and held him protectively against him. Julia walked up to them and placed her arms around the two men she adored more than life itself. William smiled as he made his way back to his bed. "I am so glad Misty-Bleu was here, how did she find out?" William sat down slowly before he glanced up at Julia, "She spoke to Blakesley a couple of days earlier." "She looks good?" It was more of a question than a statement, one she hoped William would reassure her with. "Yeah ..."

When Misty-Bleu arrived at the farm, she quickly made her way out into the barn. She hurriedly opened the doors of Captain Nimo and Wilhelmina's stables, before she quickly placed a bridle over them. "I am so sorry I'm late." She whispered as she led her two horses out onto the field. When they reached the enclosure, Misty-Bleu hurriedly removed the bridles, and left them to run free. She stood staring at Wilhelmina who seemed passive and sluggish. She frowned and wondered whether she might have fallen ill. When Misty-Bleu glimpsed at her wristwatch, she quickly made her way back indoors.

As she was about to head up to her bedroom for a quick shower, her phone abruptly began to ring. She switched on the television screen against her kitchen wall and smiled when she realized that it was Shaun and Kevin. "My guys!" Misty-Bleu smiled, truly pleased to see, and hear from her two friends again. "Hello beautiful. Oh my, what happened to you?" "Oh, I'm just about to get into the shower. Long story! Are you guys still on schedule for your visit?" "Yes, that's why we're calling. Tickets are booked, and Kevin's family have been notified. We'll see you soon! I'll email you the details later on." "Oh, I just can't wait! I am so excited to see you, and I have so much to tell you guys!" "Yes, we have some news too! But more about that when we're there. Bryan asked if we could stop by the club one night?" "Yeah, sure, as long as I don't have to sing!" "You always end up singing …" She laughed out loud when she heard Shaun giggle. "You guys always trick me into singing! So, listen, guys, I must run! Call you later?" "Yeah, yeah. Just do something about those circles under your eyes! Kiss!" "Kiss!"

Misty-Bleu disconnected the call and hurriedly made her way into her bedroom. She unintentionally beamed when she realized that so far, it had been a brilliant day for her, and it had only just begun. After her quick shower, Misty-Bleu changed into a crocheted pair of shorts and matching top. She quickly dried her hair before she made her way into her study, and hurriedly read through her batch of emails. She grabbed the stack of books on her desk, and quickly signed them before she sent a hurriedly written email to her publisher. 'Hi Jill. I've signed the copies and have left them on my desk in my study. You know where I keep the key. Chat later!' Misty-Bleu replied to a few messages and emails before she jotted down outlined notes for her new book.

When she again glanced at the time on her wristwatch, she realized that she had spent almost the entire day working on her new novel. She dashed out to the fields and swiftly led Captain Nimo and Wilhelmina back into the barn. She brushed them down before letting them back into the stables, and quickly filled their barrels with water. After swiftly sweeping the stables and putting out enough fruit, Misty-Bleu ran back into the farmhouse, desperate to make her way back to the hospital, and back to William.

When Misty-Bleu walked into his hospital room, William was sitting straight up on his bed, going through what Misty-Bleu thought to be old photographs. When she caught his attention, he looked up and was ecstatic to see her again. He smiled and hurriedly beckoned for her to sit down on the bed, right beside him. "Hello beautiful, come and look at this. My mom brought these earlier." "What are they?" She almost squinted her eyes as he slowly handed her the photographs, one by one. Misty-Bleu gazed at them as he began passing them on to her. She was stunned to realize who the photographs were of and smiled wretchedly when she turned to face William. They were photographs of William and Misty-Bleu growing up together in Shadow Falls, and for the first time in her life, she was delighted that there was evidence of a life she had once lived with him. She was overjoyed that the promises they had once made to one another, were captured by the photographs taken many years before, when they were only teenagers.

"I've missed you, William. I don't know what I would have done if your results came back any different? I don't think, I think I couldn't … I just want you to have life even if I am not in it. I just want you to live." "I know you don't want to talk, Misty-Bleu, but just, just tell me you were alright, then, after you left?" "I was, William, I was. I coped. Someday soon, I'll tell you all about a universe you helped me create …"

He laid down on his back and lifted a photograph out in front of him. Misty-Bleu nestled down beside him and stared at the picture he was holding in the air. "How could we have known then how things were about to change and turn out so horribly for us?" William whispered sadly when Misty-Bleu turned and snuggled in his arms. He pulled her closer, and gently kissed her on her lips. "I've missed you so …" She placed her arms around him and buried her head under his chin. She knew at that very moment that there was nowhere else in the world she'd rather be. "We had so many dreams." He whispered softly. "I still dream them …" Misty-Bleu whispered back as she fell asleep in his arms.

Misty-Bleu woke up in the early hours of the morning

after spending the entire night asleep in William's arms. Unlike the previous morning, Misty-Bleu awoke early and gently climbed off his bed, careful not to wake William just yet. She carefully made her way into the bathroom, and hurriedly brushed her teeth before combing her long, unruly hair. She gazed at herself in the mirror, and for a moment, she could hardly believe that she had found her way back to William, even if it was just for a while.

She thought back to the last time she stared into a mirror and was reminded of the inexplicable power failure and flash of light in the elevator only the day before. She glowered when she tried to make sense of what had happened and was at once aware that her hands had turned ice-cold. Again, she felt fear and uncertainty make its way into her heart, leaving her to gasp for breath at her inexplicable emotions. She shrugged it off and quickly made her way back to William. When she walked into his room, she was pleased to find Joshua at his side. "Hi Misty-Bleu, how is he?" "Good morning, Joshua, he's great. Are you doing his surgery?" "Yep, the lucky winner!" She moved closer and gently took his hand, "Please take care of him for me ..." She smiled and before he could respond, William had woken up.

She walked silently beside William when he was wheeled into theatre less than an hour later. Misty-Bleu was tremendously grateful and utterly relieved that the procedure held no danger at all for William, or for his well-being, and that it would be a quick operation. "Wait for me, Misty-Bleu ..." William whispered groggily after being administered his pre-op medication. Misty-Bleu squeezed his hand and smiled bravely while secretly terrified that something might go wrong. "I'll wait for you forever, William Carmichael."

When William closed his eyes, and fell asleep, Misty-Bleu let go of his hand and stepped back from the gurney. Joshua squeezed her shoulder as he made his way into the surgery. Misty-Bleu was seated in his visitor's chair in his hospital room when they wheeled him back in less than thirty minutes later. She was enormously relieved, yet utterly surprised that he had woken up and was sitting straight up on his bed. "Hello beautiful ..." He was in high spirits and evidently relieved to see her waiting for him. "William, are you okay?" "I am perfect, and ready to go home!" He winked when he clutched her hand in his. She turned back to Joshua and frowned. "Can he go home?" "Yep, it was such a small incision on his thigh. No point in staying here. We managed to suction out all the cells and William is as good as new." Joshua smiled and shook his head, as he immediately signed William's discharge papers.

Alice VL

AFTERLIGHT

Alice VL

5

Misty-Bleu was happy to drive William home, and when they reached his house, his parents were anxiously waiting to greet them before they left to return to Shadow Falls. William was sad that they were leaving so soon, but at the same time, he understood that his father's fishery was left un-captained while he was way. It was a word Misty-Bleu had used often in her stories; a word she felt belonged in the dictionary. She giggled softly knowing that unmanned was a better choice, although not as explanatory as un-captained.

Julia had prepared breakfast and was happy for Misty-Bleu to join them. She slid in next to William, who had begun sipping on his coffee. "How have you been, Misty-Bleu?" David was eager to set his mind at ease, after they so carelessly meddled in her life so many years earlier. "I've been good, thank you for asking, Mr. Carmichael." She smiled at him, hoping to set his mind at ease. "How are your parents doing?" Julia lowered her fork, anxious to make peace with her role in their departure. "Mom, what is this? Bacon?" William glowered at his mother, desperate to shield Misty-Bleu from what had begun to feel like an interrogation. "Yes, just as you like it." David had to know, "Do you live around here, Misty?" He was by no means at all, ready to absolve himself for his reckless behaviour of the past. She smiled bashfully before she looked him bravely in the eye, "I do, I live about ten minutes out of town, on a farm."

She smiled before she turned to William, unsure of what to say next. "She actually owns a Christmas tree farm dad, and is a bestselling author …" He winked at her, and secretly took her hand underneath the table before he gently squeezed it. "That's right, I thought I recognized the name. You've just come back from a book signing in Bronlyn, is that right?" "Yes, that's right." "Joshua tells me she sings too. He so badly wants her to join him on stage, but apparently, Misty won't hear of it!" William squeezed her hand tighter and smiled lovingly at her. "That's because I can't sing." Misty-Bleu giggled timidly.

She blushed, and hurriedly turned away from him. "Oh my, you've certainly come a long way. We are so proud of you, Misty-Bleu." She glanced over at Julia before she lowered her head and turned her attention back to her breakfast in front of her. "So, tell me more about your Christmas trees?" David was truly interested in learning more about her love of Christmas trees. "Each year I plant a hundred or so. In October, I open to the public. They can pick out any tree they want free of charge,

provided that they return the tree by no later than February."
Misty-Bleu hurriedly gave David a run-down of her Christmas tree
farm.

"She is aiming for a million trees, dad, isn't that
something?" William was proud of Misty-Bleu. He was
immensely proud of her for following her dreams and reaching
each goal she set out to achieve. "A million trees? Wow, you must
have an enormous farm. I can just imagine the number of staff
you must have to keep the farm in tip-top shape?" "It will hold a
million trees, and no, I do the work myself. Once in a while, I
might get a plumber or carpenter out, but mostly, I can manage."
She laughed out loud before she brought the serviette to her
mouth. "You have a beautiful laugh, Misty, I've missed that."
William became serious almost at once. He was oblivious to the
fact that his parents were seated around the very same table,
watching him as he gushed over her.

Misty-Bleu quickly helped Julia wash up before they set
off to the airport. She sat in the backseat with Julia, while David
and William drove upfront. Each time Misty-Bleu glanced at the
rear-view mirror, she caught William staring at her. She would
smile bashfully when he winked at her. She stared out of the
window as they were driving through the city streets, and she
wondered why she had never run into him before. For six years,

she had lived in the same city as he did. She drove the same streets and highways as he did, and they regularly shopped at the same stores. She would often drop in at Café Del Mare, which was on the corner of William's office. She regularly attended the pub he would often attend with friends. Misty-Bleu sighed and realized that it all came together at exactly the right time.

After they stood watching the Carmichael plane take off, Misty-Bleu turned to William and placed her arms around his neck. "It was so good to have had this time with you again, William. I am so glad that you are going to be okay, and it was so wonderful to see your parents again." William frowned, "Stop, Misty-Bleu. It sounds like you're saying goodbye? You're not leaving, you are coming with me. Joshua has organized a semi reunion at the beach just down the road from my house. You still have friends that really want to see you again, plus, we're celebrating the fact that I am going to turn into a really old man someday. Blakesley will be there, and she really wants to see you." When he took her hands into his, Misty-Bleu felt a sharp pain stab at her heart. The mere thought of reuniting with their old friends scared her almost to death. She had begun to shudder profusely, and when she turned back to William, he could sense the overwhelming fear that had begun to invade her. "I … I don't know William? It's been so long …" "It's been too long, Misty-

Bleu. Don't be afraid, I'll be there, right beside you, I swear. The moment you want to go home, we can leave, okay?" She lowered her arms and bowed her head, before she let out a weary sigh, "Alright, but we go in separate cars, okay?" "That makes no sense, but okay. They really want to see you. They need to know that you're okay, and that you did okay." He took her hand as they silently made their way back to his car.

When they pulled up at the beach in separate cars, Misty-Bleu at once noticed how all their friends had gathered around a bonfire they had built on the beach, just like they did when they were teenagers. She was at once unnerved by the mere thought of seeing her old friends again, especially with the dark secret she had kept hidden inside of her for almost her entire life. When William reached her, she hesitantly and nervously turned to him, before she abruptly grabbed his hand, "You go ahead, just give me a minute or so to compose myself. I promise I won't run off; I just need a minute." William squeezed her hand, and nervously kissed her on her forehead, before he made his way towards their friends. Misty-Bleu stood in silence as she watched him join the crowd. She wondered what he would think of her if he ever were to know the truth about her. The truth she had hidden as a child, but the same truth that she could no longer hide from him or from the world. Words she had written down as she bore her soul to the world, which were now printed, and sold in thousands of stores. It would be only a matter of time before his curiosity got the better of him. Not too long from that very moment, William would hold a copy of The Afterwards in his hands and read all about her dark and troubled childhood. She cringed at the thought of him reading about the beatings and abuse, and she prayed that she would have the courage to tell him before any book could spill her devastating and crushing secrets.

When she climbed out of her car, Misty-Bleu quickly straightened her crocheted shorts and pulled them down as far as she could, suddenly bashful about the length. She brushed back her long blonde hair and was happy to realize that excitement had replaced the anxiety that made its way into her heart only moments before. She grabbed her mobile phone and her car keys, and hurriedly made her way over to the crowd. She had barely taken two steps towards them when Blakesley came running up to meet her. "Misty-Bleu!" She yelled out excitedly before she flung her arms around her. Misty-Bleu giggled when Blakesley almost lost her balance. She laughed out loud and was at once happy that William had convinced her to attend the reunion. "Blakesley? Look at you, pretty girl, wow!" Misty-Bleu stepped back as she scrutinized her old friend from head to toe.

"No girl, look at you! Wow Missy, you are beautiful! You know, we were all just saying how beautiful you must be now."

Misty-Bleu embraced Blakesley once more before she hurriedly glanced around her. She was happy to recognize the familiar faces from high school, and she was pleased to have met Joshua before their get-together that night. Misty-Bleu took Blakesley's hand and made her way over to the crowd before she lovingly embraced her friends one by one. When she reached William, she quickly wiped a lost tear that had rolled carelessly onto her cheek. She smiled up at him and placed her arms around him. "And you, William, you, I've missed the most." She whispered softly in his ear before Carmen unexpectedly joined them.

Misty-Bleu and Carmen never quite agreed on much at high school. She found Carmen overpowering, blunt and competitive, and when Carmen lost out to Misty-Bleu during class elections, she would clearly make her mean streak known. Carmen adored William, and would often and shamelessly, throw herself at him. Misty-Bleu was horrified that she made no secret of the fact that she found William utterly irresistible, and that there was not much Misty-Bleu could do to stop her from pursuing him. They were never friends, but nonetheless, Misty-Bleu was happy to see her again. "Hi ..." Carmen slid in beside William, almost as though she had become territorial when it came to him. Misty-Bleu could have sworn she had turned instantly hostile towards her, and she was suddenly relieved that they had arrived separately. "Hi, Carmen ..."

She stepped back, and quickly glanced around her. "So, I'm going to go sit over there, with the girls." Misty-Bleu was suddenly uncomfortable, and hurriedly turned around before she made her way over to Blakesley, and the rest of their girlfriends. Before William could protest, Misty-Bleu had taken her place on a blanket, next to Blakesley. "What's the matter with you, Carmen?" William was at once agitated by Carmen's rude behaviour. "She mustn't think she can just walk in and lay her filthy paws on you again after all these years." William was instantly irritated and flabbergasted all at the same time, "She can do whatever she wants. How many times do I have to tell you, Carmen, we are just friends? I am sorry if you think I led you on, but we agreed to be just friends, after, you know?" Carmen was having none of it, "And how many times do I have to tell you, William, I am not going to wait for you forever. Misty-Bleu was gone, she left, remember? I was there to pick up the pieces, and I'll be damned if she gets her claws into you again!" William's irritation turned into visible anger almost at once, "It's not your decision to make. It's mine, and nobody asked you to stick around, Carmen, I wish you wouldn't!"

William turned to Joshua, afraid that their argument might turn into a nasty scene. Misty-Bleu caught glimpses of their argument, and for a moment, she wondered what had happened between them, while she was away. The men were standing around the fire while the women were seated on a blanket on the beach, sipping champagne directly from a bottle. It felt to her as they were all talking at once, and she could hardly believe how much they all had grown, yet, how they had all stayed exactly the same.

Misty-Bleu caught unintentional glimpses of William often. She was constantly reminded of how attractive and handsome he was, and she questioned why he had remained single, or what the on and off was that he spoke of earlier. Blakesley told Misty-Bleu of her new house on the beach, while Carmen enjoyed boasting about the new hotel she had bought and had begun re-modelling. Ida was proud of her brand-new beauty salon, leaving Misty-Bleu to feel as though she could hardly measure up to their standards, or compete with their successes. When her eyes trailed over to William once again, she noticed him looking back at her, and for the first time since seeing him again, she became self-conscious almost instantly.

Alice VL

William could not take his eyes off her as she sat listening to their friends reminisce and laugh about the old times, and all they had been through as children. He watched her nod her head often, and he gazed almost hypnotically at her when she brought up her arms as she spoke and told them of her own adventures. He smiled sadly when he was once again reminded of how animated she would become when engaging in conversation. He noticed her catch a glimpse of him often, and he couldn't help but recognize the sadness that were telling a thousand stories through her eyes. Each time he winked at her; she felt the blood rush to her head. She was sure that she had turned bright red. Misty-Bleu realized once again how his presence overpoweringly captivated, and entirely consumed her.

"So, Misty, what have you been up to these days?" Blakesley was eager to learn more about her childhood friend. "Oh, well, nothing as exciting as all you guys. I have just written a few novels, and I run a Christmas tree farm with two horses on it. It's nothing as fabulous as all of your lives." She responded in an almost whisper when she was once again reminded that she could in no way at all, compare to the standards as set out by her friends. "Oh wait, you're the Misty-Bleu Buchanan?" Ida sat up straight and blurted out in excitement. "Didn't you used to do a column called Murphy and Me? A few years or so ago? For the

Coral Hill Times?" Misty-Bleu smiled and nodded her head. "I love her! I think she's great. Wow Misty-Bleu!" Misty-Bleu cringed thinking back to the column that depicted her embarrassing moments with a chap called Murphy and his law. "It's not that a big deal, it's not at all as glamorous as you think ..." Ida seemed almost star-crossed listening to Misty-Bleu, "I think you're fabulous! And I heard somewhere that you did a few gigs with Bryan Shaw and his band?" Misty-Bleu was instantly mortified, "Oh no, that was just, I mean ... I never ... no, I just write." Misty-Bleu was horrified that her girlfriends were suddenly aware of her stage acts with Bryan. "You should hook up with Joshua, he has a great voice and is quite the superstar. He regularly tours and has actually won a Grammy or two. But what he really wants is just to be a doctor. You two will make a great couple." Carmen blurted out, desperate for a reaction from Misty-Bleu. Misty-Bleu felt her heart hammer in her throat when she caught a glimpse of William who was staring intrusively at her. "I mean, that ship has sailed with William, right?" "Carmen!" Blakesley was angered by Carmen's blunt, but unexpected intrusiveness. "You guys are more off than on. I think your ship with William has sailed a long time ago." Blakesley turned to Misty-Bleu who had lowered her head. "No, we're just taking a breather ..."

Misty-Bleu felt as though someone had taken her heart

into their hands and began squeezing mercilessly at them. Her heart raced as she felt the blood drain from her face when she listened to Carmen talk about her relationship with William. In her wildest dreams, Misty-Bleu could not imagine a world where William would love another. Never did it cross her mind that he would devote and submit himself to another. It scared Misty-Bleu to realize that after all the years, she was a fool to think that he would be waiting for her. She shook her head at the brutal reality that William might have found love somewhere else, and that he might have replaced her a long time ago.

William was keenly aware of the sudden, pained expression on her face when he hurriedly made his way over to her. "Misty-Bleu, are you okay?" He knelt down beside her and placed his hand on her shoulder. She gazed up at him, desperate that he wouldn't notice the tears that were threatening to bucket from her eyes. "I'm fine, William, I just ... it's late and I must go ..." She sprang to her feet and hurriedly waved a goodbye to her girlfriends before she turned back to William. "It was so good to see all of you again. I'll see you around sometime ..." She hesitantly turned away from him, but swiftly ran from him as she made her way back to her car. Carmen shot to her feet and grabbed William by his arm, knowing that he was about to give chase after Misty-Bleu. "William ..." "Carmen, stop! What did you say to her?" Carmen let go of his arm, and lowered her head, "I just told her the truth, someone had to?"

William followed Misty-Bleu, and when he reached her car just as she was about to slide in, he turned her around to face him, suddenly aware of how red and puffy her eyes had become. "I have to go, William. I never planned to be around for this long. I wanted to find you, and I have and now, William, I have to find me. I have to find where I belong again. It's clearly not here or in the past. It's not here with our friends. It's not with you. The plan was never to just walk back into your life. It was never my intention to try and pick up where we once left off. We can't … we just can't go back to before, to the way we were." She whispered through the tears that had begun to roll relentlessly from her eyes. "My friends are flying in tonight and are staying at the farm for a week or so. I'll call you, okay?" William's heart began pounding relentlessly in his chest, "Misty-Bleu, I can't let you walk away from me like this. I can't do this again …" William pressed her against her car as he clutched her face in his hands and lowered his head just enough to kiss her. Misty-Bleu closed her eyes, and placed her arms hungrily around his neck, squeezing him firmly against her. His hands trailed down her body, and when he reached her waist, he pulled her firmly against him. Misty-Bleu's body had come alive as she savored each touch his hands made on her skin. She kissed him more turbulently, and softly moaned out for him. "William …" William lifted her up and pressed her against him before she reached down and unzipped his jeans. She maneuvered herself perfectly, and when he pressed himself against her, she held onto him with all her might. She held his head in her hands as she lustfully stared into his dark, enthralling eyes. He looked back at her as he gripped her tighter. "Take me away, William, let's go so far …" "God, Misty-Bleu …" She threw her head back and moaned as he held onto her for what felt like clinging to life. When he stopped moving, she freed herself from his grip, and lowered her head in sudden and unexpected disgrace. She quickly fixed her tangled hair, and hurriedly turned away from him, unable to look him in the eye. "Shakes, they'll be at the farm any moment now. I have to go. I have to, I can't stay."

Her voice faded into the night when she realized that she was unable to respond to what had just happened between them. "I'm not going to walk away, Misty-Bleu. I am never going to walk away from you, don't ask me to. I won't. We need each other, we need this life …" "I'm not, William. I'm not asking you to walk away. It's just, there are things you don't know, and I couldn't survive losing you again. I would rather die than watch you walk away from me because of my past." William lifted her face just enough for their eyes to meet, "Then tell me, Misty-Bleu!" She hung her head in shame, and whispered softly, "I can't …" "If you can't tell me that, tell me what just happened here?" She looked away, "I don't know, William? It just happened; I must go!"

Misty-Bleu slid into the driver's seat, and after struggling to get her keys into the ignition, she was finally able to turn the key and drive off. She kept glancing back at her rear-view mirror. She felt her heart sink when she saw him standing there, watching her leave.

Alice VL

AFTERLIGHT

Alice VL

6

Shakes arrived at the farm just after midnight on that very same night. Misty-Bleu was elated to welcome her two friends into her home, and ecstatic that they were a timely escape of the events over the past few days. After spending hours catching up and chatting into the early hours of the morning, they all made their way to bed shortly after two the morning. Misty-Bleu was up again just before sunrise to walk Captain Nimo and Wilhelmina out to the enclosure before the sun was about to rise before she hurriedly made her way back into the kitchen. She was at once startled to find Shaun waiting for her with a cup of coffee at the kitchen counter. "You are up early!" She smiled and kissed him on the cheek. "Where is Kevin?" Shaun handed her a cup of coffee, and smiled boisterously, "Getting dressed. We were thinking of going to the mountain today and do some shopping afterwards. Do you want to join us? I was hoping we could stop off at Bryan's for one of his famous gigs? I checked in when we got here, and he will be performing tonight." Misty-Bleu giggled while sipping at her coffee, "Oh, no thank you. You just want me on stage again! Besides, I have to Skype with my publisher today." "Speaking of, I loved The Afterwards. I love that you had the courage to write your story. I couldn't put it down, and nor could Kevin. Misty-Bleu, it all seems so surreal?" Shaun placed a protective arm around her just as her gate bell rang. "Expecting anyone?" She was at once bewildered and wondered if Shaun or Kevin were perhaps expecting any guests. "Nope, we're not? We just got here."

Misty-Bleu frowned and was at once staggered to hear William's voice at the other end of the intercom. "Shit!" She belted out nervously as she buzzed him in. "Are you okay?" Shaun frowned and made his way over to her. "Yes, I'm fine. I'm ... shit." Both Shaun and Misty-Bleu made their way to the front door as William's car pulled up in the driveway. "Who's this?" Shaun smiled sheepishly without saying a word. "Just a friend, and wipe that smirk off your face!" Misty-Bleu was in no mood to explain her relationship with William. "Hey ..." William waved as he made his way up the steps of her porch. He kissed her on her cheek, before he turned to Shaun, "Hi. I'm William." William extended a welcoming hand out to Shaun. "Oh, hello. I'm Shaun, Misty-Bleu's guy." Shaun smiled while scrutinizing William from top to bottom. "Oh Shaun!" Misty-Bleu laughed before she nervously made her way back into the kitchen.

"Coffee, William?" Misty-Bleu asked with her back

turned to him. "Yes, thanks." William sat down on an empty bar stool next to Shaun, who was unable to rid himself of the sheepish grin he had been sporting since William arrived. He pulled his hand up to cover the side of his face when Misty-Bleu turned around, before he rudely whispered, "Is he *that* William? *The* William?" Shaun could no longer contain his curiosity. Misty-Bleu sighed and at once, lowered her head before despondently shaking it. "What William? Which William? As in *me*, William?" William was entirely confused when he glared over at Shaun. Misty-Bleu looked up and gazed into his dark eyes, unsure of what to say next, or how to explain what Shaun had meant. Shaun leaped from his seat when he realized that William was oblivious to his part, and an entire chapter devoted to him, in Misty-Bleu's book. She shook her head once more, before she wretchedly let out a faint whisper. "This cannot be happening ..."

"*What* William is he talking about? *What* can't be happening?" William became frustrated when Misty-Bleu remained silent after Shaun swiftly left the kitchen. Before Misty-Bleu could respond, Shaun swooped back in with her book, and placed it firmly on the counter, "This one, turn to page 152, you can skip everything else." He slid the book over to William before he once again, rushed out of the kitchen. "See ya later!" He shouted out as an afterthought, and before Misty-Bleu could

Alice VL

protest, the front door shut firmly behind him with Kevin waiting for him in the car. William was puzzled and took the book before paging to page 152 instantly. "My safe place called William Carmichael." He read her words out loud before he glowered searchingly at Misty-Bleu. "Not here William, not now. Please, I'm begging you, not now. I can't stop you from reading it, but I can ask you not to read it here, in front of me. I am begging you."

Misty-Bleu desperately pleaded with him. She was in no way at all, ready or equipped for William to know all about the secrets of her childhood. She was not ready to face him with all that she had been hiding from the world, or the questions she knew would follow. She was at once overawed by humiliation for all that had once happened to her, and all that she once was. When he instinctively read the first paragraph of page 152, William swiftly excused himself, "Then, I'll leave …" Before taking the last sip, William abruptly placed his cup of coffee on the counter, and hurriedly seized her book in his hands. Misty-Bleu couldn't protest or oppose him, and in an instant, William was gone. She was utterly horrified that he had left with The Afterwards in his hands.

She was devastated that he would soon know the truth about her and her childhood. The few pages he was clutching so tightly between his hands, contained the secrets of her past that she had kept hidden from him and from the world for most of her life. They were untold stories of a life she had lived. A life that had betrayed her, and a life that had almost destroyed her. In all her years before her afterwards, Misty-Bleu was desperate to shield William from the reality of who she was, and where she came from. Yet, she was desperate for him to know how he had saved her. In an instant, he held her life in his hands, and was about to discover and learn of the scars that were unseen to the rest of the world.

The Afterwards was a painful memoir and recollection of Misty-Bleu's life, and her life with John and Susan Buchanan. A family that mercilessly betrayed her and failed to shield her from the monsters that had lurked inside their home, and the monsters that had lived inside of them. It was a story of horror and violence. A story of fear and excruciating sadness. Misty-Bleu had never wanted the world to know her story, yet when she began writing it, it was simply an attempt to make sense of her emotions and anger. An attempt to heal, and to reassure herself of the fact that she did nothing wrong. The more Misty-Bleu penned down on paper, the angrier she became at those she once loved and trusted. She relived in terror her many nights of anxiety and fear that was forced upon her. She could vividly recall how terrified she was when the doorknob of her bedroom door turned at night. She thought back to John's whistle, a sound she had grown to hate. Whenever John whistled, she knew that it was her cue to be ready for him.

She hated how the littlest things brought back memories of a story she would rather forget. Misty-Bleu felt immense pain at the sheer consideration of what she was compelled to endure as a child, and then later, as a teenager. She was angry that they hurt her, devastated that they had betrayed her, but what she could never forgive them for, was that they so carelessly took her away from William. When she had written the final chapter of her book, she was cautiously nudged that the time had come to add a voice to her story. With an assumed name, she published her words of pain and horror, but at the same time, she also told the story of the little boy who saved her. Before she would fall asleep at night, she would see his eyes in front of her. In her dreams, they would haunt her, nudge her to survive the night, for him.

They would beg her to face the monsters of her nights, so that she could show up for him in her mornings. From the darkest of Misty-Bleu's tempestuous nights, a different life awaited her in her mind, and in her dreams. When she sat with William in her dreams, she was free, even if only for a few hours. As the morning light would approach, she would become brave once more, and face her normal one more time. Misty-Bleu would laugh and smile along with the world, yet her soul struggled with the agony and cruel tortures of her nights. She would forget her home for a moment during the light of day, but each night, the monster would find her, and again, she in turn, would find William to escape to. She would close her eyes and wait for him to rescue her, to hold his hands out to her and gaze into her eyes. She would drift off into a world where William would take her, dance with her, and shield her from the torment her body was enduring at that very moment. She cherished the moments that she had invented in her mind. She valued and guarded them safely.

Her struggle was her secret, her broken heart was veiled, and her demons, she would fight silently. There were nights that William felt so far away from her, that she would pray for death to find her. She would beg God to release her from the cruelty that was tainting her soul and take her away from a world where she would no longer suffer so severely. When Misty-Bleu's afterwards began, she had by then, been away from William for almost two years. She felt entirely disconnected from him, but at night, she would hunt him, and each night, she would find him. Long after she was relentlessly banished into the afterwards, her nights still belonged only to William, her safe place.

Alice VL

AFTERLIGHT

William had made his way into his home almost an hour after he had abruptly left Misty-Bleu's farm, clutching her book firmly in his hands. He anxiously walked over to a sofa that overlooked the mountains in the leafy suburb in Cotton Road where he had moved to almost six years before. He stared at her cover, and felt intense fear and hesitation make its way into his entire body. As he stood staring at the little girl walking hauntingly through the woods, he's body began to tremble slightly. He hesitantly opened The Afterwards and began to read her story, from the very beginning. As William turned page for page, he continuously gasped for air when he realized that she had lived her childhood right in front of his eyes and under his nose, while hiding her darkest secrets from him, and from the rest of the world. Secrets she never told anyone. Secrets of a little girl's soul that was battered and bruised by a man she called her daddy. A little girl whose mother berated her whenever she cried out and spanked her afterwards for her whimpering. He read about a father that would beat her when she spoke, and he read about a mother who would tell her little girl how she despised her, and how she wished she had never been born. When William reached page thirteen of her book, he violently slammed it closed, and disrespectfully hurled it across his living room, overcome by rage and anger. He clutched his head in his hands, intensely sensitive to a restricting lump that had begun to bulge in his throat. William was horrified by all that he had read only moments before, and desperately tried to recall the moments when he should have known.

Moments he thought he should have seen the signs of. As William sat reflecting on their childhood, he hurriedly swabbed at the tears that were rolling thoughtlessly from his eyes. He hesitated for a moment longer, before he made his way to where the book had landed on the floor and picked it up before he slowly ambled back to the sofa. As he stood staring at the cover once more, he realized that it was a book that had suddenly become his very worst enemy. William carried on reading as he struggled to come to terms with the reality of what he thought could never happen to Misty-Bleu. As he read on, he read about rejection and damnation. He read about the parents that had turned their back on their only child because she had had enough of their physical and mental abuse. He read about an eighteen-year-old that was desperate to save herself from her fate. William was saddened to realize that she was too late. He read about the day she found herself in the police station and told them her story. He read about court cases and blame. Blame from her family and how enormously she blamed herself. He read how her mother and father rejected her for coming forward, and he read of her intense loneliness and overwhelming fears afterwards.

At first, he questioned why it was that she failed to reach out to him, and then he blamed himself for failing to see the signs. He wondered why it was that she did not turn to him, and when he reached page 152, he realized that she did. She always and persistently, turned to him. In her mind, he saved her and yet, she was immensely ashamed of all that had happened to her. She was horrified that she could not stop her father, and she was devastated that he gave her no choice but to turn to the authorities. She was ashamed to tell him, and the world, the truth. She was appalled by how small she felt compared to him. William was astounded by the fact that she felt worthless in proportion to him. He suddenly understood what she meant when she told him not too long ago, that she wanted to be wonderful, first. When William had read the final page, he closed the book to Misty-Bleu's story. He placed the book beside him and leaned back into his couch. A floodgate of tears opened up inside of him, as his tears ran unreservedly and unforgivably down his cheeks. He felt physically sick, and he felt as though his heart had shattered into a million pieces. He was angry, he was sad, and he was devastated that she faced, what she called the devil, on her own so many times before. He wanted to see her. He wanted her to understand that he did not know about any of monsters she was fighting, but that he wanted to fix her. He wanted to set things right for her, and he wanted to mend the pieces of her broken heart.

William grabbed his car keys and dashed out to his car. As he frantically wiped the tears that had continued to roll down his cheeks, he blindly made his way back to Little Dreams, back to her farm. Misty-Bleu had just reached Captain Nimo and Wilhelmina when she unexpectedly noticed William's car make its way back through the gates of Little Dreams, the farm she had so lovingly made her home. She was at once unnerved to see him drive up to the farmhouse but was instantly thankful that the sun was about to set, and relieved that Shakes had not returned from the mountain yet. Misty-Bleu was exhausted by the thoughts that had managed to run around in her head since William left with The Afterwards earlier. She was terrified that he would finally reject and discard her. She was horrified by what he might think of her, and she feared more than anything else in the world, that he would turn his back on her. Misty-Bleu stood staring at him but could not quite discern the expression on his face. When he switched off his car, her legs grew weak underneath her, and her heart began to stammer profusely.

He hurriedly made his way towards her at the enclosure, while she clung to Captain Nimo, desperately afraid and appalled by the untaught expression on his face. When he reached her, he stopped and stood silently as he stared blankly at her. He opened his mouth but was at once painfully aware that he was unable to utter a word. Misty-Bleu sensed his loss for words and discomfort, and opted to invite him into her farm house, "Do you want to go into the house, William?" Misty-Bleu whispered hoarsely, desperate to hide the anxiety that had begun to overwhelm her. He nodded in silence, and hurriedly turned away from her. "I am just taking Captain Nimo and Wilhelmina back to the stables. Will you go inside and wait for me?" William stopped, and turned back to face her, "Captain Nimo and Wilhelmina? You named your horses after me?" William Carmichael was astonished by the unexpected discovery that she had named her horses after his second, and third names. A cold shudder rushed down his spine at once. "What can I say? You were my entire heart, Elijah Nimo William Carmichael." She chuckled bashfully when she said his names out loud, just as she had a million times before when she was only a little girl. "I'll accompany you to the barn. Shall I take Wilhelmina by the girdle or bridle, or whatever this thing is called?" Misty-Bleu laughed out loud when she noticed the confused look on William's face. She handed him Wilhelmina's bridle, before she led Captain Nimo back to his stable. When they reached the stables, she gently brushed both her horses while William stood watching her in silence. He noticed once again how her beautiful blonde hair flowed gently down her back and could not imagine how her frame could hold all her hair. He had forgotten how tiny she was and thought back to The Afterwards once again.

"Misty-Bleu, how could they do this to you? None of that seems real. I mean, it feels as though these things only happen in horror movies. I never knew …" Misty-Bleu stopped brushing Wilhelmina's mane and bowed her head in shame. The tears had unexpectedly began to shimmer in her eyes, when she realized that he had read her entire book. "I didn't want you to know …" She whispered through the uninvited lump that had made its way back into her throat. He walked up to her and gazed wretchedly into her eyes. His heart ached for the way she looked back at him. What he saw in her eyes, was something William never wanted to see again. He was sure that he could see the crushing pieces in her glacial blue eyes. He wiped a lost tear that had rolled deplorably from her eye, and determinedly, held her face in his hands, "Misty-Bleu, you say that, that I saved you?" She immediately grabbed his hands and held them firmly in hers. "You did, William, you were my safe place, you still are. I still go there sometimes. I still go there. It is so beautiful there, and sometimes, I never want to come back here. I just want to live there with you, forever. None of this happens there. I'm not the same person there. I am different. I am worthy. I am whole. Untainted." He pressed her against him and held onto her with all his might, afraid of letting her go. "Why didn't you tell me?"

He gently pressed her head into his chest when she began to sob. William held her firmly as she wept relentlessly in his arms. When he lifted his eyes to the sky, the tears he tried so hard to hold back, began to roll unashamedly down his cheeks. Misty-Bleu gently pulled away when she felt him shudder and gazed sadly at him. "Please don't cry, William. There's nothing anyone could do. Nobody could help me. Nobody could save me from them, but me. I am okay. Look at me. I did good, William. Even though I am so ashamed of all of that, I am still okay. I did this all my way, William." William swallowed back profusely, "Don't you ever be ashamed, Misty-Bleu, don't ever be ashamed of what they did to you. Don't ever excuse what they did to you, do you understand? You said you aren't worthy of me; don't you ever say that again. I never, ever want to hear you say that again! I loved you! I love, love you! I love you, so much, Misty. I always thought that we would be together someday, and today ... today, I know we will be. I can't live without you. I don't want to. I can't leave you to live without me, I don't want to. I will do, Misty-Bleu ... I will do whatever it takes to love you, and be with you, and save you over and over again if I have to. If you need me to. I am willing to bend the laws of nature if that's what it takes."

He sighed and took in a deep breath, "There is nothing that can keep us apart. There is no world that can separate us, ever. Not even death, do you understand, Misty-Bleu? Not even death. Never even death." William whispered as he lowered his head and gently placed his lips upon hers. Through her tears, Misty-Bleu kissed him while clinging desperately to him. "Hey, Misty-Bleu!" Misty-Bleu was yanked back to reality when she heard Kevin call out to her. William stepped back, and hurriedly wiped the uninvited tears that still laid wet on his cheeks. "Hey, handsomes!" Misty-Bleu waved before she swiftly made her way to Shakes. "You guys have a good day?" Shaun frowned when he realized that Misty-Bleu's eyes were red and swollen. "What happened, Misty-Bleu?" She smiled halfheartedly, but sure that her world would be kinder to her, "Nothing, I'm okay. What would you two like for dinner?" Seeing William behind her, Shaun knew that they were intruding, "We had something already. Kevin and I are pooped, straight to bed for us!"

When Kevin saw William standing in the barn, he grabbed Shaun by the hand, and hurried inside. Turning around, Misty-Bleu realized that William was standing directly behind her. "Misty-Bleu, let's get out of here?" She took his hand after she closed the doors to the barn, "Let's ..." They strolled hand in hand to his car in silence. He opened the passenger door for her, and when she climbed in, he hurriedly made his way around to the driver's seat. "A quick dinner and then, then we need to talk, just a little bit more, okay?" Misty-Bleu nodded her head before she leaned back in her seat before William switched on the radio. Misty-Bleu smiled when she heard Joshua Stark's Grammy winning song, 'Touch me' come on the radio. "Oh listen, it's Joshua!" William smiled and turned up the radio.

Alice VL

7

When they entered Joe's Pub and Grill, Misty-Bleu was pleased that it was dark and filled to capacity. It was loud, and it left her relieved to know that William would not bring up the details of her book while they were there. They made their way over to a quiet table in the corner and had barely sat down when a waiter approached them. "Good evening, my name is Charlie, and I will be serving you for the evening. Can I get you anything to drink?" William smiled and hurriedly turned to Misty-Bleu, "Wine?" "Yes please. Red and, a big one!" She giggled as she glanced back at Charlie.

They had only just placed their order when the band began to sing their next song. Misty-Bleu hurriedly turned around and was surprised to find Bryan Shaw on stage. Charlie had only minutes before placed their drinks on the table, when William recognized Joshua from across the room. He waved when Joshua saw them but hoped that they could enjoy the evening without interruption. "William, hey bud! Misty-Bleu, nice to see you again! Did you see who's playing tonight?" Misty-Bleu nodded her head and waved at Bryan when he recognized her. "You must, must do a song with us!" "Oh no, I haven't had nearly enough to drink!" She giggled as she sipped on her glass of wine. Bryan rushed over, and grabbed Misty-Bleu by her arm, "One, just one, Misty-Bleu!" "No, please Bryan! I am so rusty!" Joshua turned to William, "Bryan and I promise, just one!" William smiled and gazed over at Misty-Bleu, "I would love to hear what the craze is all about … you know I've never heard you sing, right?" Misty-Bleu smiled, and turned back to Bryan, "Fine! Just one! My song! Oh, and Josh, you are going to duet with me! Don't think because you are a hot-shot, Grammy award winning superstar that you can't lower your standards and belt out a tune with me!" "My pleasure, ma'am!" He bowed before he took Misty-Bleu by her hand, and hurriedly led her onto the stage.

"Ladies and dudes! We have a special treat and surprise for you tonight!" Bryan held the mic in his one hand, and his guitar in the other. "Not only did Joshua Stark agree to grace us with his presence, but we have Misty-Bleu Buchanan, the author and quite the singer on stage with him. For one song only! Please welcome our very own superstars!" The entire crowd erupted in applause, while women were left shouting and chanting Joshua's name. Misty-Bleu laughed out loud when she glanced around her and realized for the very first time that Joshua was in fact, a superstar. Bryan handed Misty-Bleu a mic, and when she turned to Joshua, she was pleased that he was already holding his. "'It's Coming Back,' okay?" She hurriedly gave him the song title, before the music started to play. They both turned to face the crowd when Misty-Bleu kicked off the song, and Joshua quickly found his place in the duet. She stared at William who was watching her from their table in the corner.

William's mouth hung open as he listened to her sing. He was stunned that he had never heard her sing or seen her perform before that night. She sang beautifully, but she sang sorrowfully. His heart ached as he sat listening attentively to every word and each tune she belted out. He swallowed back past the lump that had showed up once again when he noticed the tears sparkle in her eyes. She sang as though she was alone on stage, and as though she was alone in the room.

She closed her eyes, desperate to shut off the tears that were threatening to silence her. She turned to Joshua who had stopped singing, and stood staring at her, stunned by the mesmerizing rendition of a song she had written for Bryan, only months before. When the tears began to roll down her cheeks, he lifted his mic, and picked up where she could no longer continue. She stood smiling at him, deeply indebted by the fact that he had taken over when he did. When the song was finally over, Misty-Bleu turned back to the audience and bowed gracefully. She smiled at Bryan and Joshua, before she handed her mic back to Bryan. "Thank you for having me." She whispered hoarsely when Joshua hugged her, "Wow, Misty-Bleu, you should do this. You were amazing!" She smiled sadly, "I just want to get back to William, but thank you." Misty-Bleu murmured softly before she hurriedly made her way off stage, and back to William. When she reached their table, he stood up, and seized her in his arms. "Wow, Misty-Bleu, I never knew this about you?" He held her firmly against him while stroking the loose curls that were flowing down her back. Within seconds, the audience began to chant her name loudly. "Misty-Bleu! Misty-Bleu! Misty-Bleu!" She peered over William's shoulder and quickly looked up at him. "Can we get out of here?"

"Yeah ..." He took her hand, and quickly led her back out to his car. When they reached his home in Cotton Road, he turned off the engine, and sat quietly for a moment before he turned to face Misty-Bleu, "Misty-Bleu, I can't just let this go. I need to talk. Come in just for a moment and let's just talk. Let me say the things I need to say, and then, then we never speak of any of this again." Misty-Bleu smiled sadly. She knew that she had to face William, and that she owed him an explanation.

When they walked into his house, William shut the door behind them and showed Misty-Bleu to a couch in the living room. She nervously sat down before William sat down beside her. "I ... I don't know where to start William. I am just so uncomfortable talking about this. It's just hard, you know?" William took her hand and rubbed it gently. "When we were little, I ... I just wanted to be gone from this life, you know?" She paused to take in a deep breath when she finally realized that she could no longer silence her voice and remain quiet. "You made me want to carry on, and you made my life so much better but, when I got home each day, it was like stepping into hell." William was at once confused by what Misty-Bleu was saying. "I don't ... I don't want to talk about what happened, but I do want to tell you, and I never told you this, but I want you to know that you saved me, William. It's like, it's like you don't hear me when I say that you saved me. You don't seem to understand how important you were for me to live?"

Her voice began to shudder, and her heart felt as though it was being ripped apart as the tears began to stream from her eyes. "What happened, Misty-Bleu, what happened to you when you left?" William was at once panicky, and afraid of what she might say next. "I don't want to ... I can't, William. It wasn't just after we left, it was always, but it was so much worse after we left. At least before that, I could see you each day, but when we left, there was no-one. It was just hard." Misty-Bleu was sure that

Alice VL

a floodgate of tears had caved in, and suddenly opened inside of her. William held her in his arms, knowing that Misty-Bleu was in no way at all, ready to talk about all that had taken place in her life, and all that she had lived after her afterwards.

She gently pulled away from him, and quickly wiped the tears from her cheeks, before she turned away from him, "William, each night when my doorknob turned, I would close my eyes and panic, but only until I found you again. You would wait for me, and then you would take my hand. We used to sit on the beach and just be quiet. You would dance with me under the stars, and we would laugh. And then ... then, when I opened my eyes, it was all over. My monster was gone, and all I had was the memory of you and I. I loved you in my mind, William. I lived you in my mind. I have always, always loved you in my mind. In my mind and in my dreams, you took me away from those that were destroying me. I could never have survived if you weren't under the same sky as I was."

She lowered her head and began to fidget, "I never felt the pain, I never felt him. All I could feel was your hand in mine, and your arms around me. I was never afraid because you were there in my other world. I knew that, and I knew that if I had died, it would be alright, because then, I could live there with you forever. You made me strong, and you made me so happy. You gave me something to dream about, and you, in my mind, you loved me." She paused as she struggled to find the words to tell William that she was alright.

William listened to her tell him how she would meet him in her dreams and was saddened that he could not save her in her reality. "I'm so sorry, Misty-Bleu, I wish I knew." She frowned when she looked into his eyes, "No William, no! I'm glad you didn't know! I didn't want you to know! Nobody could have saved me. I never wanted you to know, and I never wanted you or anyone to pity me. I was ashamed of all that. I was ashamed of who I was. I didn't want people to know." She placed her hand on his cheek, desperate for him to understand that she survived on her own, with him in her heart and her mind. "I'm okay. I did okay. I don't see them. I don't hear from them. I did okay. I've had such a good life since. I have the farm. I have my Christmas trees, and I have my horses. I write all these crazy stories in my head, and that makes me so happy, William. I have my books and people read them. Can you believe that they actually pay me for my madness? I am doing all I ever wanted and dreamed of. My dreams have all come true, so, I'm doing okay." Misty-Bleu was desperate for William to shed the guilt that had begun to attack his entire being. "Now, William, you must be okay. You must have life too. Be great, William, with someone wonderful, and have wonderful. That's what I want for you, life. I don't want you to settle for brokenness. I don't want spoilt goods for you. You deserve more. You are more than this. My life is wonderful, William, but I am not, and I don't know if I could ever be?" William stared at her in disbelief, flabbergasted by the fact that she had no idea how far he went to love her again. She had no clue of the price he knew he would pay someday, for loving her again. "I love you, Misty-Bleu, you are my wonderful. You've always been my something wonderful. I guess maybe that's why I wanted to give up so easily when I heard I was dying. I had nothing that meant much of anything to me. You were just gone. I never, ever heard from you again. I didn't even know if you were still alive. When I was a little boy, you were that wonderful something in my life and then, then I lost you. And when ... when I heard that I was sick, I didn't care so much. Death would have been a welcomed escape, but then you showed up. Just like that, Misty, you showed up. I couldn't ... I didn't want to leave you. I didn't want to hurt you. I needed you. I need you now. Sometimes, I feel as though I made a deal with the devil to be here with you." He took her into his arms and kissed her gently as his tears bucketed violently from his eyes. Misty-Bleu got up from the couch and pressed him backwards before she climbed onto his lap. She took his face in her hands, and feverishly kissed him as she felt her entire body come alive for him yet again. Her hands trailed down to his trousers as she desperately tried to loosen them. She moved closer until she could feel him inside of her once more. She moved slowly as she gazed into his eyes. He held her around her waist and gripped her tighter as she squeezed her legs against him. He clutched her firmly, and when it was all over, he buried his head in her chest. "I love you, Misty-Bleu. I love you." She placed her hands around his head, and rested hers on his, "You are my entire heart, William Carmichael." Misty-Bleu lifted William's face, and took his hands, "I need you to be okay, William. I can't see you like this. You are punishing yourself for something you couldn't control." When William gazed into her icy blue eyes, he knew that it was time they both forgave themselves. "I've … I have some things to tell you too, Misty … a confession …" He knew he had to tell her about his parents' role in her leaving, and then, he knew he had to tell her about Ana.

When his mobile phone rang almost immediately, he grabbed the phone from his coffee table, and sat straight up. Misty-Bleu slid off of him and sat down beside him on the couch they had made love on only moments earlier. "Hey …" Misty-Bleu sensed the immediate discomfort in his voice. "You land tomorrow? Wow…" By the panicky look on William's face, Misty-Bleu became uncomfortable at once. William was immediately

Alice VL

caught off guard by the unexpected call. He was about to tell her about Ana LaRue, a woman he had been dating for the past couple of months. He had met her through Joshua a little over a year ago, but it was only recently that they had begun seeing each other.

Ana was a dancer in Paris, and although she spent most of her time there, they saw each other regularly when she would fly to Coral Hill once a month. William enjoyed her company, but what he appreciated more was the fact that they saw so little of each other. He admired and respected her, but he knew he could never love her the way she loved him. Misty-Bleu got up from the couch and hurriedly straightened her clothes. She was keenly aware of the fact that William was on the phone with another woman, and although she could not hear the conversation, she began formulating a picture of the discussion by how he was responding to her. "Yeah, all's well. See you tomorrow. I've been discharged and it's a clear bill of health, just like I said it would be!" He hung up and tossed the phone on the couch next to him before he rushed over to Misty-Bleu who was about to walk out his door. He grabbed her by her arm, unsure of what to say to her. "William? Are you seeing someone, other than your supposed on and off relationship with Carmen?" Misty-Bleu was at once sensitive to the unexpected tears that had begun to burn in her eyes. William bowed his head, still unable to explain. "Before you, Misty-Bleu, before the hospital and before you came back, and after Carmen …" "William! You couldn't tell me this today, before … before you and I, before we … again? You couldn't tell me this the other night?" She freed herself from William's grip and stepped away from him. "I am not this person, William, I am not. I don't do this sort of thing. You should have told me before!" She raised her voice and was at once disgusted at herself and horrified by how easily she had given herself to him. "Misty-Bleu …" Again, he didn't quite know how to explain Ana to her. "Where is she? Where has she been? Where was she when you were in hospital? You never said anything!" Misty-Bleu yelled out in horror. "She is in France, and she dances there. She dances with 'The Swan's.'

William was at once defeated as he ran his hands through his hair. "You should have told me about her, William." "I know, but all I really wanted was you. I just wanted to be with you, and when I read your book, nothing made sense. Everything for me changed in the hospital and nothing was like it was before. Nothing else mattered. I didn't even think about Ana. I haven't even thought about her once. All I wanted was you." "William, take me home, please. This was such a big mistake. Just take me home." William was horrified that Misty-Bleu referred to them as a mistake. "A mistake? How can you say that? I love you, I always have, Misty-Bleu. We could never be a mistake! I won't let you call us that!" She was at once overwhelmed by anger, "I bet you tell Ana that too. I bet you never even thought of me while you were with her!" "Don't do this, don't belittle what we have. Don't disregard our history like this, Misty!" "History? That is exactly what this is, and where it should have stayed. We are in the past. You and me, William, are in the past. We were just kids! What were we thinking?" He could not lose her. William could not let her go. "What do you mean, what were we thinking? I love you! And I know, I know that you love me! You and I, we're ancient, Misty. I don't care about Ana. I was just about to tell you about her, and I have no problem ending things with her!" "No, don't do that! Don't! I am not that person! Don't leave her because of me! I will never forgive you for that!" When he tried to take her hand, she pulled away from him and hurriedly made her way to his car.

As they drove through the streets of Coral Hill, Misty-Bleu was growing increasingly frustrated by the niggling tears that were continuously rolling down her cheeks. She wiped them away as often as she could, desperate to shield her heartache from William. William gazed over at her often and was overcome with fear by the possibility that he would never see her again. He watched her swab at the warm tears on her cheeks, but could in no way at all, disregard the anger that had made its way into her heart.

Alice VL

AFTERLIGHT

Alice VL

8

When William reached Little Dreams, Misty-Bleu leaped from his car, and frantically ran into her farmhouse, desperate to get away from him. William sat motionlessly in his car, while watching her until she disappeared through her front door. He sat gazing through the windows of her lit house, as she frenetically made her way to her study. From where he was sitting, he had a perfect view of her. He watched her lean against a wall, slide down onto her knees as she clutched her head in her hands. He saw her curl up on the floor, as she pulled her legs up to under her chin. He watched her entire body shudder as she completely broke down and sobbed violently while lying in a foetal position.

Misty-Bleu was listening to the sound of the darkness that had entered her heart. The pain that had entirely engulfed her was almost too much to bear. She closed her eyes, desperate to return to her safe place, there where William belonged to only her. She wandered around aimlessly in her mind, desperate to find him. She moved quicker, and when she could not find him there, her entire body began to ache. It felt to her as though someone had taken a sword and plunged it right through her heart. She could barely breathe through her sobs, and she gasped for air when she felt as though she was beginning to suffocate.

There was a faint knock on her study door, and when Shaun walked in without waiting for a response, he rushed over to Misty-Bleu, and immediately seized her into his arms. Her eyes were red and swollen, her face drowned out by her tears, and her entire body was quivering through her painful whimpers. "What happened, pretty girl?" Misty-Bleu anxiously swabbed at the tears that continued to bucket down from her eyes before she sat up straight to face Shaun. "I … I went over to William's place and we, it happened. It just happened Shaun, and then … then she phoned him. He never told me he was in a relationship. I thought Carmen was who I would have to deal with. I thought, I just thought Carmen was it, you know?" Misty-Bleu burst out crying again, while Shaun held her firmly against him. As she sobbed in his chest, Kevin heard the commotion coming from her study, and hurriedly made his way to Misty-Bleu and Shaun, just in time to hear her tell Shaun about William. "Misty-Bleu, so what? It's not like they're married?" Kevin made a valiant attempt to cheer Misty-Bleu up. "She dances in France. Have you ever? I can't compete with that? Besides, I am the other woman? I don't want to be the other woman?" Shaun hurriedly interrupted as he nodded at Kevin. "And you write. You are on the New York bestseller's list. So what? I'm sure you're a lot prettier than she is? Don't you think that perhaps *she* is the other woman? That you are the one that belongs to William? That maybe, you came first?"

William placed both his hands on the steering wheel of his car when he suddenly lowered his head. His heart was pounding, and his mind was racing at the mere sight of watching Misty-Bleu come entirely undone. He watched as Shaun and Kevin did their best to console her, but he wondered whether Misty-Bleu was not about to give up completely. He could not bear to see her fall apart, while there was nothing he could do to change what she had heard when he had spoken to Ana. He slammed his fists onto the steering wheel in utter anger and frustration. "I did everything for her! I cannot give up; it would all be for nothing! I sold my soul for her ..." He whispered silently before he opened his door, and in frenzy, he made his way back to her front door. Kevin placed his arms around her and held protectively onto her. Misty-Bleu lay down on the rug again and sobbed violently as Kevin did his best to console her. Shaun was just about to place his arms around her when William stormed inside. Shaun and Kevin turned to look at one another before they both suddenly got up. William hurriedly made his way past them as they headed out to the kitchen.

He knelt before Misty-Bleu, and wiped the warm tears that were once again, streaming carelessly from her eyes, "Misty-Bleu ..." He whispered sadly. When she recognized his voice and abruptly sat up, she was desperate to wipe away the hair that were shielding her face from him. "William? Why are you still here?" "I can't, I can't leave you like this. I can't walk away from you like this, Misty-Bleu. Even if I wanted to, I couldn't. Even if choose to, I can't. It's too late to go back to before, Misty. I don't want to ..." He sat down beside her and took her hands. He squeezed them firmly and sat with his head bowed. "William ..." She fell onto his lap and began sobbing again. He leaned down and pressed his head against hers. "It's always just been you, Misty-Bleu. Not Carmen, and not Ana. Only you. Only ever you. Just give me a chance."

Misty-Bleu turned onto her back and gazed up at him through the tears that seemed to continually roll down her cheeks. "I don't want you like this, William. I can't have you like this. It's just not right ..." She whispered sadly, before she got up to her feet, and turned away from him. "You must leave." William hurriedly leaped to his feet, and grabbed her before she reached her study door, "No, I'm not leaving you like this." "Leave, William, leave! Go! Get out! I don't want you anymore!" She shouted out before she ran upstairs and dashed into her bedroom. She collapsed onto her bed, and lay shuddering when she heard her front door close. Only moments later, she heard his car pull away. Her love for William had turned into a love, and a life that could never be. After all she had been through, and all the mountains she had to climb to become worthy for him, in the end, she felt she would never be worthy of him at all. He had so easily moved on with his life after her. It scared her that he found it so simple to give his heart away to another. She laid wondering if he ever really thought of her in the time that she was gone, and she wondered how he could tell her over and over again that he loved her. She questioned whether what he felt for her was in fact pity, and not love. Misty-Bleu hated the idea of him pitying her, and when she turned onto her side, she closed her eyes and locked up her safe place.

It was a place she would remember fondly until the day she died. It was a home she found refuge and solace in, a place she would run to and get lost in as often as she could. It was a world that promised her a life and love with William, but it had turned into a creation that betrayed her. Her very own world had lied to her and deceived her. Misty-Bleu no longer wanted to sit on the beach or dance under the stars in their own unique little world. It was a figment of her imagination, and nothing more. It was time to shut her escape off, and face the world head on, without William. All she wanted, was to tell him that he had once saved her. She wanted him to survive, and she wanted him to live. Now that she could tick off all she came to do, it was time for Misty-Bleu to place William and her past behind her and carry on living in her very own wonderful. "Goodnight, William ..." She whispered tearfully before she drifted off to sleep in a world filled with blackness.

Alice VL

AFTERLIGHT II – HALF LIGHT

"In the half-light, she found him, and she lived him."

1

Misty-Bleu wanted to close her sore and tired eyes and drift off into a bottomless sleep. She wanted to willingly surrender to the darkness and get lost in the nothingness around her. She wanted to lay still, and feel no hurt, no sadness, no heartache, and no destruction. She was desperate for numbness to show up and make it her turn. She did, by no means at all, want to return to the world she had escaped to, when the real world would heartlessly come crashing down on her. For as long as she could remember, it was her anchorage. A sanctuary built by her soul, and introduced to her heart, but for only her, and only for William.

It was where she could leave her sorrow and torment behind, whenever she wanted to. All she had to do, was close her eyes over here, and open them again, over there. As she thought about the sanctuary she had run away to so many times before, she shuddered when she realized that it had turned into a haunting and frightening nightmare for her. She missed how magical it was when she first created it, and she longed for the days when she knew nothing of him. She hunted the days that their love was a blank canvas she could alter and tailor-make to suit the hankering of her heart. Her reality with William, would surely and mercilessly follow her into her place of refuge, and it would repellently remind her of the certainty that he was no longer only hers to love.

There was nothing left for her to dream of, and there was nothing left for her to hope for. There was no longer any way she could find him there and pretend that their real world did not exist. As she lay staring at the ceiling, she was sure that she could physically and forcibly feel her heart shatter into a million tiny fractions, as though it was altogether unacceptable that there were still too many fragments that had remained intact, and passionately preserved. She incessantly swallowed back on a throbbing, overriding swelling in her throat, as she desperately tried to shut off the tears that were threatening to drown and suffocate her.

She turned onto her side, and at once, she caught a glimpse of the seemingly crucial flickering of a little blue light on her mobile phone. She was instantly exasperated that she had failed to turn it off earlier, and when she glanced over at the screen, her heart almost missed a beat when she discovered that it was a text from William. 'Misty-Bleu please, I am begging you, don't walk away from me like this.' Overcome by the sudden, yet unexpected antagonism and resentment that had instantly made its way into her heart, she promptly replied, but immediately regretted her response. 'You lied to me!'

As William re-read her message, he was once again desperately afraid that he might have lost Misty-Bleu again, perhaps forever this time. 'I swear Misty-Bleu, I will tell Ana. Just give me a chance.' She replied at once, 'No William, no. Tell Ana whatever you like, but don't make this about me.' 'It *is* about you, Misty-Bleu.' 'You see, that right there is my problem. I don't want to be that person. I don't want to be that girl. You made me that person! You turned me into the kind of woman I hate the most!' 'What do you want me to do? I don't care what anyone thinks, I love you. You love me! I know you do, I know, Misty ...' 'I don't want to! I don't want to love you! I hate that this happened! I hate that we went so far.' 'I don't. I will never regret anything. You don't know what you're saying, after everything, no, Misty. I am not going to let it end like this!'

The messages between them went back and forth for almost an hour. William grew increasingly distressed by her replies, while Misty-Bleu came extremely close to renouncing the unrelenting prodding of her heart. Without responding to his last text, Misty-Bleu switched off her mobile phone, and tossed it next to her on her bed. She pulled her quilt up to cover her head, before she curled up into a foetal position once again.

She rocked back and forth, desperate to escape the excruciating pain that was beginning to physically torture her. She closed her bloodshot and distended eyes, and could again, almost hear the splintering of her already vulnerable and broken heart. When she tightly squeezed her eyes, she rocked herself to sleep without slipping out into what was once, her hideaway. She slipped further and further into sleep. She quietly glided into a place where there was nothing but darkness and detachment. Where hearts remain intact for a few hours, and where tears are safely hidden behind the eyes. There where she would feel no fear or sorrow. A sleep where her entire body did not erupt into a catalytic shock wave, and where she could safely shut her eyes and wrap up her heart, to both her worlds.

There was nothing in either worlds, that could console or reassure her that her heart would survive the torment it was enduring at that very moment. Her realms had both turned against her, and they had both bowed to demonic sprites that were inhumanely conquering the very core of her. One world she was unwillingly compelled to survive and function normally in, while the other was a world she had conjured up, and created when she was only a little girl, simply to find refuge and solace in. It was a design that she had altered, modified and amended as she grew older, yet it was that very distortion that had savagely turned against her in the end. It had callously ricocheted back to her, when all that she had loved and cherished so powerfully, was imprisoned between her two worlds, causing her immense demonstrative misery and substantially debilitated her with crippling pain.

Misty-Bleu no longer knew where she fit in, or to which world she belonged. They had both treated her unkindly, and they had both launched severe assaults on her heart, differently, yet the same. They were both deceitfully remorseless towards her, and they both played their roles perfectly in viciously tainting and disfiguring her soul. They sought no forgiveness from Misty-Bleu for attacking her all at the same time. They showed no penitence for propelling her into a damnation she was sure, would eventually defeat her, and finally stop her heart. She was convinced that her heart could in no way at all, endure the tremendous aching it was tolerating, and survive even only for one more day. The fears she had faced in this world, was nothing compared to the terrors she knew was waiting for her in the other, the one in her mind, the one she once felt the safest in. She could not quite decide which of the two she dreaded the most. They had turned out equally powerful and equally dispiriting. She was staunch in her belief that something had drastically changed or gone horribly off-course, and that there was an enormous fault in the stars.

When Misty-Bleu awoke in the dead of the night to the inexorable thrashing of her heart, she sat up straight, and restlessly glanced around her in the dark. Her entire body had exploded into an unyielding palpitation, while her hair was soaked in feverish perspiration. She tossed and turned, and when she was unable to fall asleep again, she climbed out of her bed, and quickly slid on her robe. She soundlessly tip-toed down the flight of stairs, careful not to wake Shaun or Kevin, and speedily made her way outside, through her back door. It felt to her as though the walls were closing in on her. She was desperate to sneak out for a much-needed breath of fresh air. When she quietly closed the back door behind her, she gazed up at the sky, and was at once, captivated by the stars that were putting on a magnificent light show for her. She breathed deeply before she let out an enormous sigh. She stared out straight ahead of her and was once again delighted by the picturesque image that had awaited her, night after night.

Alice VL

AFTERLIGHT

The image never disappointed her, and she smiled as she gazed out in front of her. Looking back at her, were her Christmas trees. Thousands of White Spruce, Cottage Pine, White Pine, Virginia Pine and Balsam Fir trees were lined up in almost a hundred rows, and they welcomed her with open arms. The rows and trees were endless, and when Misty-Bleu hurriedly ran out into the plantation, she could almost smell Christmas.

Misty-Bleu adored Christmas. She savored the smells, and she feasted her eyes on the blinking lights that showed up during the happiest and silliest season of the year. She loved listening to the laughter of children as they carefully picked out the perfect Christmas tree. She fell in love with and became enormously addicted to the air on the farm during Christmas each year. It was filled with magic. The stars seemed brighter, and the moon felt closer. Misty-Bleu was sure that her Christmas trees were the reason for all the enchantment of the season, and she could almost visualize how they all came together year after year and cast a spell in the air over her Little Dreams. Even though Misty-Bleu had spent the last six years alone on her farm during Christmas, she never felt alone while surrounded by her beautiful trees. It was almost as though Christmas began right there, right in front of her, and right in the center of her little farm.

When she found herself on the path that would lead her

Alice VL

right through the Christmas tree plantation, she felt her heart come alive again. She spread out her arms and brushed each tree as she slowly passed them by. She closed her eyes and carried on walking down a path she had cut out right in the center of her magical trees. When she had been walking for what felt like hours, she sat down underneath an enormous Fraser Fir, and rested her head against it. She smiled again when she thought of her dream to light up each tree during Christmas. It was a dream she had dreamed of as a child. A dream she had committed to chasing after when she first began planting them, and a dream she would hunt for the rest of her life. She dreamily gazed up at the stars that were lighting up the sky for what felt like only her, and took in a deep breath, "One of these days, you have to land on my trees, and light them up, one by one." She whispered sleepily to the stars before she closed her eyes.

Alice VL

"Misty! Misty-Bleu!" Misty-Bleu abruptly opened her eyes when she heard the faint and distant, yet frantic calling of her name. She sat up straight, and bewilderingly glanced around her, almost as though she had no idea where she was. When Misty-Bleu realized that the sun was about to rise, she was startled to discover that she had fallen asleep at the bottom of her Fraser Fir, right in the center of her plantation of Christmas trees. She quickly clutched her robe, and folded it snugly around her, at once acutely aware of an icy chill in the air. As she scrutinized her surroundings, she realized that a dense fogginess had entirely surrounded, and impenetrably engulfed her. She groggily wiped her weary, not-quite-awake eyes, before she heard her name being called out once more. She listened closely and was horrified to recognize William's panic-stricken voice. "Oh no, shit!"

Misty-Bleu was about to get up when William suddenly appeared in front of her. She sat as though frozen in time when he appeared through the thick mist that was resting lower in the air than usual. He slowly approached her, before he knelt beside her, and smiled gloomily at her. "It's cold out here, Misty. How long have you been out here?" She quickly glanced around her, "I, I don't know? I couldn't sleep." "Have you been out here all night?" "No, I mean, some of the night?" He lifted her by her arms and helped her onto her feet before he clutched her icy cold hands into his. "What were you doing here in the middle of the night?" "I just, I just couldn't sleep." He came to an abrupt halt, before he turned her around to face him. "Listen to me, Misty. I don't care what you think or how you feel about Ana, or even your supposed part in our breakup. I am breaking up with her because I love you. I love you. I choose you. I don't care how it looks to the world; I choose you. I want to be with you, and I don't want to waste any more time. There just will never be enough time, Misty …" He lowered his head, and gently shook it before he gazed at her again, "Whether or not you will have me, breaking up with Ana is my decision. I don't love her. I can't see myself spending the rest of my days with her. I don't have the time to waste on someone I don't love." She stared into his wretched eyes, unsure of what he was saying, but overcome by sudden fear and uncertainty. "What do you mean? What's the matter? What's going on, William?" He was at once aware of the fear written all over her face, "Nothing, I mean, I'm not sick or dying, or anything like that. It's just that, if almost dying taught me one thing, it is that we are on borrowed time. We don't know when we will someday leave this world, and I don't want to spend any of it away from you. This is why I am here, and this is why you are here." She lowered her head before taking in a deep breath, "William, I can't be with you like this. I just can't. I am not built like that. I am not made for such things." "Please, Misty, nothing is as it seems. I am begging you, don't walk away from me like this." She lowered her head again, unable to look into his eyes for even a moment longer.

"When she comes back, and when you look into her eyes, ask yourself who and what it is that you really want. You haven't seen her in a while, and you might just feel differently when she is standing in front of you." Misty-Bleu lifted his hand to her heart and stared at it for just a moment. "Then, do what you must, but not for me, William. And give it time. You must promise me that you'll take a few days, and really think things through. I mean, she is someone, William. I am only me. When Shaun and Kevin go back to Bronlyn, come back to me, or say goodbye to me. I haven't spent much time with them, and I want to clear my head. I am not thinking clearly anymore, you know? I don't want us to see each other until then. This is what I am asking of you, this is what I need you to promise me." He gently touched her cheek, "I already know what I want. I already know who I want, and it's you. It has always been you, Misty-Bleu. My feelings won't change, and my answer will always be you." He placed his arms around her, and held her firmly against him, before she returned to the farmhouse, and he back to his house on Cotton Road.

Misty-Bleu had spent the remainder of the week with the

Alice VL

pair she lovingly referred to as Shakes. They were out shopping and visiting ethnic restaurants from early morning to late evening. Kevin had made appointments with a handful of art galleries who showed an interest in his art. While he attended his many meetings, Misty-Bleu and Shaun would spend their free time in corner Café's and smoke-filled pubs. "Misty, our visit is coming to an end, and I hate to leave you. Won't you come back with us for a few weeks?" Shaun grew increasingly apprehensive regarding her state of mind, as the days passed since William had discovered the truth of Misty-Bleu's childhood. He felt immense guilt for his role in exposing her secrets to William, and he could no longer stomach her suffering as he watched the sadness entirely overwhelm and consume her. "I can't. I can't leave Captain Nimo and Wilhelmina for so long, and plus, you know I have deadline on my new book. Maybe I'll close up shop and join you for Christmas?" "Alright, but don't get floppy with Skyping us regularly, okay?" "I promise. I won't." Shaun took a sip of his coffee, before he placed it back down on the table, and took her hand, "He loves you, Missy. I know, I know, I don't know anything. I don't know William, but I do know what a man who loves a woman looks like. I know Missy, what a man that is afraid to lose someone, looks like. You have to trust me." She lowered her head before she freed her hand, unable to say a word in response to what he had just said. "Don't you think he lied about Ana because he was afraid he would lose you? You know, I Googled her, she has nothing on you." She shook her head before she eyeballed him, "Oh Shaun! I am not that person! I am not cut from that cloth. I can't be the other woman. I am not like that." "You are too hard on yourself. It's William's choice, don't take that away from him." "He should have told me. He should have given me a choice. I would never have, you know?" "Oh Misty, you have to move with the times. Don't be so stubborn, and stop being such a prude. We all have done it at one point in our lives. William loves you, not Ana." "And, I love him, Shaun. I would never have come through all the shit I have if it wasn't for him. I wouldn't have survived if William wasn't under the same skies as I was, but I wanted to get things right and this, none of this right and nothing about this feels right." She paused to take in a deep breath, "What if ... what if I am just unfinished business. What if he forgets who we once were? What if he realizes I am not who he wants? What if he breaks my heart again?"

Shaun clutched her hand, and placed his other hand over it, "You are afraid, Missy. Ana has nothing to do with this! You are afraid, terrified that he'd leave you!" As Misty-Bleu stared into Shaun's hazel eyes, she knew that what he was saying, was irrefutable. "You have to trust him with this. You have to take a chance and try. I was afraid too when I first met Kevin. I didn't want to get married, and now, look at us! We are about to start a family! Missy, you deserve this too." He got up from his seat and placed his arms securely around her. "He is not your father, Missy. And if it all goes to shit, Kevin and I will always be here for you."

The day before Shaun and Kevin were to board their plane back to Bronlyn, the trio ran into Joshua while on one of their final shopping sprees. "Misty-Bleu, hey!" Misty-Bleu stopped dead in her tracks when she recognized Joshua who was wearing a baseball cap, while hiding behind dark sunglasses. She giggled as he hurriedly made his way over to them. "Josh, fancy running into you here at the Waterfront! I almost didn't recognize you." Misty-Bleu was happy to see his familiar and friendly face again. "Yeah, I know. That was the idea. It's such a pain having to disguise myself in public. Anyways, I'm glad I ran into you. We're having a get-together on the beach tomorrow evening. I would love it if you and your friends joined us?" She hesitated for an instant, "I don't know? I mean, Shaun and Kevin are leaving tomorrow night. I'm not sure we could make it." "We can make it!" Kevin exclaimed in excitement, eager for one last night out with Misty-Bleu and her friends. "I mean, we have to be at the airport just before midnight. That leaves us with plenty of time for one last get together." Kevin was adamant that they spend one final night out on the beach. "Okay then, that's settled. Thanks for the invite, Joshua." Misty-Bleu smiled disparagingly when she realized how eager Kevin was for one last night out before they returned to their busy, fast-moving lives in Bronlyn. "It's great to see you again, Misty-Bleu, I am so looking forward to seeing you all there tomorrow evening." He hugged her before he turned and went on his way. Misty-Bleu let out an enormous sigh, before she gripped Kevin's arm, "You know William is probably going to be there, right?" "Really, I didn't, I wasn't even thinking of William." He grinned slyly before he hooked his arm into Shaun's and strolled into the next over-priced clothing store.

Alice VL

When Ana landed at Coral Hill Airport early that same evening, William was anxiously awaiting her return at the airport. He was in no way at all thrilled to see her and was at once vanquished by the very idea that he would be compelled to take her back to his house and pretend that all was as it had been for the past few months. When she caught a glimpse of him waiting for her, Ana clutched her handbag, and ran into his arms. She fervently kissed him after she flung her arms around him. William placed his arms around her waist, and instinctively turned his face away when she wanted to kiss him again. "I am so glad to see you! I've missed you!" She yelled out excitedly before she clasped him against her. "How are you? Are you okay? What do the doctors say?" He loosened her grip on him and took her hand as they scurried to leave the airport. "All's clear." "I was so worried about you. You look tired? Stressed?" "Yeah well, it's been a rough couple of days ..." He sighed before he turned away from her, unable to look her in the eye.

"Well, I am here now. I can't wait to be alone with you!" She beamed wildly as they strolled over to his car. She enthusiastically began to tell him about her stay in Paris, and that she would form part of a show in Spain later that month. She excitedly expressed how animated she was to be back in Coral Hill, and that she wanted to spend a quiet evening at home with him. William became agitated as she gushed to no end about her performances, and how she loved the stage. When his mind turned back to Misty-Bleu, he was no longer listening to a word that Ana was saying.

They drove out of the airport in silence while Ana was busy responding to texts, emails and calls on her mobile phone. William listened to her tantrums, and for the first time since he had met her, he was instantly put off by her immoral behavior. She was conceited and proud. She was rude and overbearing, but more than anything else, Ana LaRue was the spoilt daughter of well-known and well-respected movie producer, who was sought out by all large movie houses. Her mother had died when Ana was barely two years old, leaving her to be raised by a family of nannies. Stefan LaRue travelled extensively and did his utmost to make up for his absence by showering her with gifts. Ana was accustomed to getting what she wanted, and nothing was too big or too extravagant for his daughter. She was fierce and headstrong in her pursuit of worldly desires.

She was happiest when she could dominate the people around her, and she thrived when she could so effortlessly instill the fear of backlash of a scorned LaRue on all those she classified as lesser around her. She was instantly mystified by William's failure to pursue her when she had first met him. He had barely greeted her, and he quickly excused himself once they were introduced. Ana was disappointed that he did not find her as breathtaking as all her lovers once did. She was puzzled, and she was relentless in her quest for him, simply because he showed no interest in her, or any desire for her. She was wholly curious about, and entirely unprepared for his lack of enthusiasm for her, and when she reached the decision to hunt him, there was nothing in the world that could stand in her way.

Joshua had once told her about Misty-Bleu, the girl William had spent most of his life pining for. He told Ana how ill-equipped William was to commit to a new relationship after she had left Shadow Falls, and that he doubted there would ever be another to successfully claim his heart. Ana was intrigued by the girl that held such enormous power over him. She could barely imagine that one person could imprison another's heart so entirely. She would often mention Misty-Bleu's name to him, desperate to learn more about the girl who entirely unnerved her, but William would make an excuse to leave, or change the subject almost immediately.

When they reached his house on Cotton Road, William kept the car running, and turned to Ana, handing her the keys to his house, "I have to be back at the office. There are a few things to tie up, but I'll see you around seven?" William had no trouble lying to her. He had no desire to be alone with her just yet. He knew how daunting and intense she could be, when all he sought was to be alone with Misty-Bleu. "You're going back to work?" Ana was at once disappointed that he had not rescheduled his day, as he did each time she flew in. "I'm so sorry, Ana. I know you just got back. But, you must be exhausted. We'll have a quiet dinner tonight. It will give us a chance to talk." William subtly tried to prepare her for a conversation his heart felt was long overdue. He had no idea of how to tell her that Misty-Bleu had returned to him, and that his heart would not let her go. He could not imagine spending one more day betraying both his heart and his soul. He could not live as he did before Misty-Bleu showed up on the park bench, and chaotically, claimed her place in his heart once again.

As he pulled out of his driveway, Ana watched him drive off, and was at once intimidated by the fact that he did not look back at her. He drove off without as much as a goodbye wave, something had had never done before. She replayed the casual way in which he mentioned that they talk later that evening, and she could not shake the feeling that she had come home to pandemonium, and that everything between them had been altered. Her heart began to trounce into her throat when she unlocked his front door and made her way inside.

Alice VL

AFTERLIGHT

William spent the remainder of the afternoon in his office, behind a closed door. He tried his utmost to busy himself with long overdue paperwork, desperate to take his mind away from Ana and off of Misty-Bleu. As hard as he tried, he was unable to discard the look on Misty-Bleu's face when he found her at the foot of one of her Christmas trees. The sadness in her eyes was a piercing reminder of all the heartache that had relentlessly hunted her through the years. It was evidence of a shattered life, and it was proof of the destruction she had once survived. William sat staring out through his window, feeling trapped in a life he had no control over. He wanted to bundle Misty-Bleu up into a cocoon and shield her from all the heartbreak that seemed to target her. He lowered his head and knew that she would be the only woman to lay a claim to his heart. He knew everything there was to know about her. He knew each colored spot in her eyes, and he knew what it meant when she pulled up her nose. He could effortlessly recall each freckle on her nose, and he knew how she would hide in his shadow when the world targeted her and turned its cruelty on her. He could not stop thinking about the night they made love on the beach, and he replayed their lovemaking in his living room. He had never before felt his body come alive, as it did when Misty-Bleu's body touched his. He had never before hunted another's body, as his hunted hers. Every inch of her. He closed his eyes

Alice VL

and could almost smell the scent of her around him. When he glanced at his wristwatch and realized that it was almost time to leave, he looked around at the papers that were untidily stacked on his desk. It felt to him as though the world had crash-landed on his shoulders when he realized he had barely made a dent on the pile in front of him. William grabbed his car keys and his mobile phone, before he despondently made the twenty-minute drive back to Cotton Road.

When he sauntered through the enormous front doors of his almost two-hundred-year-old Cape Dutch home, he was at once disconcerted to find Ana waiting for him at the dining room table. He closed the front door behind him, and instinctively placed his car keys on a sideboard at the entrance before he made his way towards her. She had laid out the table, poured him a glass of wine, and lit the brand-new candles he had bought only days before. William disparagingly ran his fingers through his hair and grasped at once that ending their relationship would be considerably tougher than he hoped it would be. "What's this?" He tautly made his way to an empty seat across from her. "I wanted to make you something nice to eat. I've missed you." He glanced over at the gracefully laid table and realized that he had all but lost his appetite. "You shouldn't have gone to so much trouble, it's just the two of us." "It's a special occasion ..." She smiled broadly before she sipped on a glass of water in front of her. "You're not having any wine?" She smiled at him, "No, which brings me to my surprise. I couldn't wait to get here and tell you! I am pregnant!"

She enthusiastically clapped her hands and squealed in delight. William stared blankly at her. He in no way at all, expected her to tell him that she was going to have a baby. It felt to him as though the blood had instantly drained from his face. He stared at her immensely surprised, while overcome by utter disbelief. "What? You're what?" "I found out just a day before I landed, isn't it wonderful?" William stared at her, as he frantically tried to absorb all that she was saying to him. He was devastated to hear her tell him that she was going to have a baby, his child. He instantly lowered his head, and profusely swallowed back on an all-familiar lump in his throat that was instantly threatening to silence him. All he could think of was Misty-Bleu, and how he was about to lose her once again, and this time, forever. "William?" Ana was at once confused by the indignant expression on his face. "You always said that you want to be father?" He looked up at her, and smiled sadly, "Yeah, I do. This is just so unexpected." He could in no way at all, turn his back on Ana. There was nothing he could do to change the harsh and heartless twists that fate had so carelessly brought into his life. He could by no means at all, ignore the fact that Ana was pregnant, and that he was responsible for her condition. As much as he loved and adored Misty-Bleu; as tremendously as he regretted his connection with Ana, it was a situation he had placed himself in, and would have to see through right to the end. His heart ached as it broke into a thousand unseen pieces right before her eyes. He could barely imagine a life without Misty-Bleu, and he at once questioned all he thought to be true and fair. "Are you upset?" Ana grew increasingly anxious at the untaught and unchanged expression on his face. His eyes were weary and sorrowful, and his smile seemed forced. "No, no. You just caught me off-guard, that's all."

He got up and made his way over to her. He knelt beside her and took her hands into his. "It's just, I didn't see this coming. I didn't ... I just thought it would be something we planned, you know? I mean, we are apart so much with your job and mine, that's all." He squeezed her hands and smiled disappointedly at her. "We can get married. Before anyone knows if you like?" Ana was desperate to calm her sudden fears. William glowered, before he lowered his head, "Let me just process all this first." He got up and made his way back to his place at the dinner table. He had downright lost his appetite, but picked reluctantly from his plate, desperate to mask his utter horror and discontentment at the news she so calmly gave him. "What did you want to talk

Alice VL

about?" She lowered her fork and gazed up at him. "Oh nothing. I can't even remember ..." He smiled again but lowered his head almost at once. He could not tell her how desperately afraid he was of losing Misty-Bleu. She could never know how she ached for her, and how he will spend the rest of his life catching his breath when she inevitably and persistently conquers his mind. She will never know how close he came to claim back his entire heart from her, and that Misty-Bleu would be the only woman he would dream of for the rest of his life.

Alice VL

2

When they arrived at the beach shortly before sunset the following evening, Misty-Bleu took her place right in the center of Shaun and Kevin, and proudly hooked into their arms. As they approached the gathering crowd, she recognized the familiar faces of her friends. "You look gorg, Misty-Bleu!" Shaun nudged her and squeezed her arm as they made their way towards the group. She wore a simple pair of shorts with a matching summer's top. She ended off her look by letting her long blonde hair flow carelessly down her back. "Those legs!" Kevin winked, leaving Misty-Bleu mortified that she had not allowed herself more time in the sun. "You guys are the best!" She winked graciously at the two men on either side of her arms.

When they reached the familiar faces that were assembled on the beach, Misty-Bleu hastily glanced around, desperate to find Joshua. From where she was standing, she noticed him standing in front of William, a short distance from the rest of the crowd. "Misty-Bleu!" When his eyes caught hers, he rushed over to her, and hugged her, "I'm so glad you came. Where are your friends?" Misty-Bleu hastily turned around and noticed both Shaun and Kevin were entangled in conversation with Bryan Shaw. "Yeah, they're over there." Misty-Bleu chuckled bashfully. "Can I get you a drink?" Joshua casually took her hands and smiled at her. "Shirley-temple?" "Coming up!" When he turned to leave, Misty-Bleu squinted her eyes as she glanced around her, hoping to find Blakesley. She had just noticed that she was caught up in conversation with Carmen when she felt a warm hand on her shoulder.

"Misty-Bleu …" "William, shit, you scared me!" "I'm sorry, I didn't mean to frighten you. Listen, can we go somewhere and talk? Alone? I really need to talk to you. It really can't wait, and you're not taking my calls?" When Misty-Bleu was about to respond, she was at once aware of a tall brunette that had invited herself to join them. She hooked her arm into William's and smiled lovingly up at him. "Here you are! I've been looking for you?" William lowered his head and grew increasingly uncomfortable. "Hi. I'm Misty-Bleu Buchanan." Misty-Bleu extended a welcoming hand out to the long-legged, beautiful brunette who was not about to let go of William's arm any time soon. "I'm Ana LaRue, pleased to meet you. How do you know William?" "I, we, we actually grew up together. We're really old friends." Ana frowned before she turned to face William. "*That* Misty-Bleu? The girl from Shadow Falls?" William reluctantly and nervously nodded his head. He was desperate to get Misty-Bleu alone, afraid that Ana's presence might wholly demoralize her. He wanted to tell her about the baby before she heard it from Ana.

He was desperate to make her understand that he loved her, and would give up everything for her, if she asked him to. He wanted to whisper in her ear and beg her heart to wait for him. Even though he could not turn his back on his child, his soul could not let her go either. "Pleased to meet you, Misty-Bleu. I've heard so much about you from William's parents, and Joshua. Though, William doesn't say much. Are you back? I mean, do you live around here now?" Misty-Bleu hesitated for a moment, "I've been back for a while actually. I live on a farm just a few minutes out of the city." "Oh, by a while you mean?" "Six years or so, more or less." Ana shot a disgusted scowl in William's direction, who in turn, was staring at Misty-Bleu. "Here you go!" Joshua arrived with her punch just in time. "Oh, hi, Ana, when did you get back? Can I get you a Shirley Temple too?" Joshua reluctantly embraced Ana who had become unsettled and intimidated by Misty-Bleu's presence in that very instant. "Yesterday. I landed yesterday. No thank you. I can't do the alcohol thing anymore. I suppose I can share our good news with you?" She turned to face William, before she turned back to Joshua, deliberately avoiding

Alice VL

Misty-Bleu's icy stare, even though she intended her to hear every word. "Well, welcome back! Oh, do tell, we are waiting in anticipation." Joshua smiled broadly. "We're, we're going to be parents. I'm pregnant! We are a little surprised, but it really couldn't come at a better time!" William's heart began to trounce lavishly as he caught a peek of Misty-Bleu who had at once, turned worryingly pallid. She intuitively lowered her head, unable to look any of them in the eye. Ana turned to Misty-Bleu, who had distinctively gasped for air, as though she was fighting with all her might, just to take in a single breath.

She swallowed back on that ever-evasive lump that had begun warning her of its arrival before she instinctively glanced over at Ana. She was dismally sensitive to her tears that were indecently attacking her eyes. William had to control every single fragment of him when he detected the utter devastation and destruction in her eyes. All he wanted to do, was to seize her in his arms, and carry her away. He wanted to shield her from anything that could threaten to hurt her ever again. He gawked over at Ana, and for an instant, he cursed the day he had met her. "Congratulations! I am so happy for you both. Really, I am. Please excuse me, I ... I want to find Shaun and Kevin. I must run. Nice meeting you ..." She was stammered by Ana's broadcast, and she was saddened by William's silence. She hurriedly turned away without even so much as looking at William. As the tears began to blind her when she walked away from them, she had no desire for Ana or William to recognize the vulnerability that had entirely infected her. Her body had begun to attack every inch of her, and the cold began to carelessly conquer her. William turned to Ana, who was staring arrogantly at Misty-Bleu as she walked away. "Really, Ana? You blurt it out here, like this?" "I didn't know it was such a big secret? Why can't Misty know? What's the big deal?" "Not like this, Ana!" William turned away from her, and speedily followed Misty-Bleu. "Misty-Bleu!"

She covered her ears with her hands, desperate to ignore William who was not far behind her. She was desperate to escape him and began running when she could not ignore his voice. William ran after her, and when he caught up to her, he grabbed her by her shoulders, and pulled her around to face him. "Misty-Bleu. God, Misty-Bleu …" His voice trailed off when she lifted her eyes to meet his. What William saw in her eyes, was something he wished he had never seen, and he ardently prayed to never see the devastation in her eyes again. Her blue eyes were as frozen as ice, yet, surrounded by puddles that were about to escape from their corners. She could no longer mask the anguish that had altogether engulfed her, as she abundantly swallowed back on her torment. "I didn't know, Misty-Bleu, and I didn't plan for this. I still want to tell her. I still choose you. Misty-Bleu, I choose you. I don't care if she's pregnant. I will, I swear, I'll be there for her, but I choose you. Please hear me. I will give it all up. I choose you. I love you. It's you, only you."

William had become desperate as he once again, pledged himself to her, despite the fact that Ana was going to have his child in a few, short months. She bowed her head before she hurriedly swabbed at the tears that were relentlessly drizzling from her eyes. She walked closer to him, and placed her hand on his chest, "William, you must choose your child. A few weeks ago, you were sure you weren't even going to live, and now, now there is a child in your future. A life you never thought you'd have. How can you not choose your child? You must. You must choose your flesh and blood. That's what I want for you. I want that for you. I want you to have life. I don't want this, William. I don't want children. I don't want a family. I don't want to be a mom, but you, you've always wanted to be a dad, and you are going to be wonderful at it. You should do this. You deserve this." She wiped a lost tear that had unrestrainedly rolled down his cheek. He grabbed her hand, and squeezed it before he interrupted her, "Misty-Bleu, I can't. You, I choose you. Please have me? I want you more. I need you more than I'll ever need a child. I choose you." She looked into his eyes and noticed the desperation staring back at her. "But, William, I don't want you anymore, not like this. I can never be happy; you can never be happy. We can never be happy like this. You can't turn your back on your son or daughter, your blood? No, I won't let you. Let me go ..." She smiled wretchedly through her tears, before she turned away from him.

William watched her make her way over to where Shaun and Kevin were standing, while entirely crushed by the certainty of what she had just said to him. By the way she so casually told him that she no longer wanted him, almost tore his heart into a million shreds. He was devastated and angry at the universe, and at that very moment, he cursed the day Misty-Bleu once walked into his life. "Hello beautiful ..." Shaun embraced a tearful Misty-Bleu who smiled at him, desperate to cover up her sorrow. "We were just talking. You must do a song with Joshua. For us, before we leave?" Kevin took her hand and lifted it in a swinging motion. "No, not tonight, guys." "Misty-Bleu, that's no way to say goodbye to your two guys. One song, just one?" Joshua and Bryan smiled when they noticed how unashamedly Kevin was begging her. "Fine, fine! Josh?" "I am always game, Misty-Bleu, it is always an honor!" "Whatever, you are the superstar!" She chuckled as she followed Joshua to the guitars that were waiting for them at the bonfire. The crowd had instantly formed around them when they began strumming the ever-familiar cords.

"Can you do 'Tougher?' Joshua stopped and turned to Misty-Bleu. "What are you talking about? I am the queen of Tougher!" She at once began belting out the chords before Joshua joined her. She avoided William's glimpses and kept her focus solely on Kevin and Shaun. Every now and again, she gazed over at Ana who was possessively holding onto William's hand. While she sang, she made a concerted effort to pay attention to the lyrics that constantly seemed to empower her, even if only while the song lasted. She gazed over at Joshua often, who was watching her closely.

Joshua was at once, disturbed by the emotions that had made its way into his own heart. The pain and sorrow in her eyes, told him a thousand stories of agony and torment. He was entirely caught off-guard by the storms that were raging inside of him as he listened to her sing, and he shamelessly scrutinized her as she belted out the lyrics to his song. He was wholly consumed and bewitched by her powerful voice, but he could in no way at all, make sense of the sudden and urgent need to hold her close to him. When the song was over, Misty-Bleu hurriedly placed the guitar down next to Joshua, and swiftly made her way over to Shaun and Kevin, "It's just under an hour to check-in. We better go." Misty-Bleu whispered to Shaun in an attempt to escape

William and Ana's intimidating presence. "We've got time?" "No, not really, please, let's go ..." Misty-Bleu tugged at Shaun's hand who in turn, was surprised by her sudden desperation to leave. "Thanks for a great evening, guys. I just, I have to get these two property moguls slash artists to the airport." She stuttered severely as she hurriedly explained when Joshua and Bryan made their way over to her. William walked up to Kevin and Shaun, and extended his hand out to them, "It was a great pleasure to meet you both. Have a safe trip back and I hope you come back soon." "Yeah, me too. You should come out to see us when Misty-Bleu comes to visit, perhaps for Christmas?" Kevin's voice trailed off when Ana joined them. She smiled self-righteously one more time, when she glanced over at Misty-Bleu.

Misty-Bleu turned away from them, and hurriedly made her way back to her car. As she approached her car, Shaun appeared at her side, and grabbed her by her arm, "What was that back there?" "She's pregnant, Kev, Ana, she's pregnant." Misty-Bleu opened her car door and hurriedly slid in, frantic to get as far away from William as possible. When Shaun and Kevin slid into the passenger seats, they both stared at her, shocked and in a haze of utter skepticism, "What?" "Yeah, just that. I don't want to talk about them." She hurriedly swabbed at the unsolicited tears that had no plans to leave anytime soon. "Missy, come back with us?" She smiled at Kevin who was frantic to comfort her. "Guys, I can't."

When they reached the airport almost an hour later, Misty-Bleu was once again distraught by the fact that their visit had ended so soon. She hugged each tightly, and when they turned to leave, she burst out crying. As they disappeared into their terminal, she realized that she had never felt as alone, as she had at that very moment.

Alice VL

3

When Misty-Bleu returned to her farm just after one in the morning, she was at once discouraged to find William's car in her driveway. When she made her way to her front door, she found him sitting on the steps that led up to her porch. "William?" "Yeah, I know. I shouldn't be here …" He lowered his head into his hands and began to shudder slightly. Misty-Bleu was immediately saddened to notice how defeated he appeared to be. She sat down beside him and fidgeted with her car keys. She had no inclination of what to say to him. "I never thought things would be this hard for us, you know?" She smiled gloomily at him, before she glanced down at her hands. "We could not have imagined how things would turn out when we were kids." She chuckled and shook her head. "Misty, there are things I wish you knew, that I just can't tell you. I wish I could. Maybe then, things wouldn't be this hard." Misty-Bleu was confused by what William wasn't telling her, "William, there's nothing you can say that will change anything. I love you so much, but I can't let you turn your back on your baby. I will never be able to live with myself. I'd end up hating myself for that, and you'd end up resenting me for the very same thing." "Misty …" She interrupted him almost at once, "What will you do if your kid comes looking for you? What if you wake up in ten years, angry at me and angry at the world? What if in years from now, you still desperately want children, and I don't? How could you ever live with yourself knowing that you have a child somewhere in this world, that you don't know? A child you gave up in a moment of desperation?" He shook his head before he turned to face her, "I can't lose you. I don't know what else to do? I don't know how to change this?" "William, we had this. We had our childhood and then, we had this. It's enough for me. It was always enough for me. Seeing you again is enough. Be who you were before I came back, have your wonderful." "You are my wonderful. I love you, Missy …" She felt intense pity for William at that very moment. "And you will love your child and you will love Ana too. I swear it."

Misty-Bleu rose to her feet and held her hands out to William. He got up and placed his arms firmly around her. She held onto him as though she might never see him again. She breathed him in one last time, and she tried to take in everything about him for one last moment with him. She could not help but wonder why it was that she fitted so perfectly in his arms. She could not quite decide why it was that his heart felt like home to her. He reluctantly walked away from her, and slowly made his way back to his car as she watched him leave. When he reached his car, she battled enormously against an undeniable urge to run after him and ask him to leave it all behind. To forget Ana and forget their child, and to come back to her. She wanted to tell him that they could go far away. They could settle in a little town where no-one knew their names, and no-one recognized their faces. She wanted to tell him that she could write her stories from anywhere in the world, and that her trees would keep the farm warm for her.

When he climbed into his car, Misty-Bleu knew that their love was one that could never be. She watched him drive through the gates of Little Dreams, sure that she might never see him again. As she stood staring at the lights that were slowly disappearing from her view, she could barely hold back the tears any longer. She dropped to her knees as she clutched her belly. She cried out in torment, overcome with an excruciating ache that had begun to manifest physically. She wanted him back. She wanted to feel his arms around her, and she wanted him to hold her, and only her against him. As she lay pleading with the powers above the stars, she knew that William Carmichael would be the man she would miss forever. She crawled into her farmhouse, and in the darkness without switching a light on, she slowly made her way upstairs. The house seemed darker than usual while the silence and absence of Kevin and Shaun began to weaken her. When she reached her bedroom, she disintegrated on her bed, and buried her head in her pillow. She released the tears that she was so desperate to shut off only moments ago. She cried for the only man she had ever loved and lost all at the same time. She sobbed uncontrollably for the humiliation of her shattered heart.

As she had done each morning for the past six years, Misty-Bleu awoke just as the sun was about to rise. She hurriedly slipped on a pair of track pants and a sweater before she made her way out to the barn. She was happy to see that Captain Nimo and Wilhelmina were ready for her to lead them out into the fields. She first placed the bridle around Captain Nimo and led him out to the enclosure. When she made her way back to Wilhelmina, she was once again nudged by a sensation that Wilhelmina was not at all, her usual self. She hesitantly placed a bridle around Wilhelmina, and slowly walked her out to where Captain Nimo was waiting for her.

When they began trotting around the fields, Misty-Bleu sat on the fence, and stared worryingly at Wilhelmina. She appeared thinner and slower, almost sadder. She could not quite decipher what it was about her that was different and made a mental note to call her vet when she returned to the farmhouse.

Alice VL

While still staring at the two horses in front of her, Misty-Bleu heard a car pull up in her driveway. She quickly looked back, and spotted Joshua behind the wheel. She waved when she recognized him and smiled broadly as he made his way towards her. "Josh! This is a nice surprise, to what do I owe this pleasure?" She was truly happy to see Joshua again, and suddenly, she no longer felt so entirely alone. "I just, I know that it's none of my business but, I just wanted to see if you're okay?" Misty-Bleu smiled sadly and knew at once that William had sent him to check up on her.

"I'm fine ..." She lied, but was in no way at all, ready to spill her heart to Joshua Stark. He gazed out over the horses that were trotting and galloping through the fields of the enclosure and smiled when he noticed how beautiful the two horses were. "They are lovely." "Yep, they are such spirited animals." Without taking his eyes of the horses, Joshua became slightly nostalgic, "My father used to say that the truest form of soulful love is found in the eyes of a horse." She smiled as she gazed at Wilhelmina. "I am worried about Wilhelmina. I think, I don't know, but she looks as if she is ill?" "I'm not a vet, but I wouldn't mind taking a look for you?" "You would?" "Sure ..." Joshua smiled before he opened the gate and hurriedly made his way over to Wilhelmina. Misty-Bleu swiftly descended from the fence and followed him.

Joshua gently stroked Wilhelmina, and slowly moved his hand over her belly. He whispered indistinctly to her, before he began stroking her mane. Misty-Bleu frowned, unsure of what to expect. "She's not ill, Missy. She's going to have a filly. It's hard to tell how far along she is but congratulations!" Misty-Bleu beamed before she too, stroked Wilhelmina's mane. "Oh Wilhelmina, you had me worried there for a second." She sighed with reprieve that her beloved horse was not ill and became excited almost at the same time at the very prospect of having another horse on the farm. "Would you like a cup of coffee?" Misty-Bleu glanced over at Joshua, who was still stroking Wilhelmina. "Yeah, that would be great. Thanks."

They walked side by side as they both made their way into her farmhouse. When they reached the kitchen, Joshua sat on one of the empty bar stools at her kitchen counter. Misty-Bleu handed him his cup of coffee before she took a seat across from him. "So, Misty-Bleu, I came to ask you to audition for The Academy. It's an awesome opportunity, and one of the prizes is a recording contract with a record label. I just think that you have a great voice and an amazing talent that shouldn't be wasted. Now with William …" Misty-Bleu lowered her head as she sipped on her coffee. When she placed her cup on the counter, she lifted her head and frowned, "I am not a singer. I'm no performer. I've never wanted to be one. I am horribly uncomfortable on stage, and I would never want to do that for anything else other than fun. I love this farm. I love my trees and horses. I just want to write, Josh, that's all I want to do. That's what I did before William, and that's what I will do now. William and Ana don't change a thing, and you don't have to find things to distract me." Joshua sighed, before he lowered his head, "It's just, well, what if things get too much for you. It can be mighty lonely out here on the farm, and you just don't seem like yourself anymore. I'm not trying to distract you from your life. I just really think you should try it and see where it takes you. You might really find your passion in it? And you are so good, Missy ..."

His voice trailed off, when Joshua realized that he had no way of telling her how terribly worried William was about her, and how he was desperate for her to find some kind of interruption from all that had taken place in the past few days. "I am tired, Josh. I am exhausted. I won't lie, it has been a rough few days and William, I love him. I am always going to love him. My heart will never let him go, but I have to go on without him. I did once before, and I will again. I must. I have to." Joshua placed his hand on hers, and smiled sadly, "I am here too, Missy. If you need me, just call." When his hand touched hers, he was once

Alice VL

again aware of an untaught tremor in his heart. There was something about Misty-Bleu that captivated him from the moment he first met her. From deep within the very core of him, he knew that she was not like any other woman he had ever met. She was someone he was comfortable around. Someone he could speak easily to. He was devotedly in love with her voice, and he admired her flawless beauty. Before he allowed his mind to wander off too far, he reminded himself that William came before him, and the unspoken rule between friends weighed heavily on him. "Thank you, Joshua. I'll be okay …" She smiled before she placed her empty coffee mug in the basin. "Well, I'm off. I have a long day, but I hope to see you soon?" He hugged her gently before she walked him out to her front door. "Yeah, I hope so. You know how to get here?" Misty-Bleu winked shyly before she waved him goodbye.

Alice VL

4

Misty-Bleu had no sooner typed 'The End' on her latest novel, when she took her calendar, and hurriedly scribbled down the same words to mark the end of another book. She was horrified to discover that an entire month had passed since she saw William for the last time. She sat back in her chair and stared at the screen in front of her. For a moment, she could not quite figure out how she managed to survive an entire month without him. She smirked when she thought of Joshua who had regularly stopped by the farm. They would have dinner together often, while Joshua helped out whenever Misty-Bleu was repairing or painting, or simply just changed a light bulb for her. She grew increasingly excited to see him, and considered him a great comfort to be around, and a wonderful shoulder to cry on.

As the days passed by, Joshua grew progressively fond of Misty-Bleu, and immensely enjoyed her company and being around her. He would often accompany her into the city, and they would spend hours in a Café somewhere, enjoying a simple cup of coffee with one another. Joshua remained respectful of her, but more than that, he appreciated William and Misty-Bleu's past. He by no means at all, cared to jeopardize his relationship with either of them, and was happy to simply remain friends with Misty-Bleu.

Misty-Bleu had written two songs for Joshua that she had given him, hopeful that he would record them. She loved writing so much more than singing, and when he recorded them both, she was elated to hear her words flow from his mouth. He regularly nagged her to write more music for him and planned an entire record with her songs on it. Even though he persistently begged her to perform duets with him, she refused, and made it clear that she was happiest writing the songs for him. She never asked about William or Ana, and he never approached her with news about them. They enjoyed each other's company, and Misty-Bleu would nag him endlessly to join him at the recording studio, where she would get lost in a world of poetry with music. She was happier, and she no longer felt as lonely, as she did only a few weeks earlier.

William had almost spent the entire month as though trapped in a foggy cloud. His days were becoming longer and longer at work, while Ana all but moved in with him. He would come home long after she was asleep at night, and he would leave for the office before she woke up as often as he could. Even though he had grudgingly acceded to the veracity that Misty-Bleu was lost to him forever, he could not bring himself to devote all of himself to Ana. He would regularly make a strenuous effort to remain loyal to her and their relationship for their child's sake, but when he was alone in the dark, it was Misty-Bleu's eyes who came back to haunt him. He would sit staring at his mobile, and it would take enormous exertion not to text her. On one of those late nights while William was still at the office one evening, Joshua unexpectedly called him on his mobile. "Hey buddy, where are you?" Joshua was eager to catch up with William again. "Still at the office." "Come on out to Joe's, we haven't had a beer in weeks." William glanced at his wristwatch, and agreed almost immediately. "Sure, see you in twenty?" "Great, I'll keep the beer cold."

When William walked into Joe's less than twenty minutes later, he instantly noticed Joshua sitting at the bar. He swiftly made his way over to him, and after placing his car keys and mobile phone on the counter, he sat down on an empty bar stool beside him. Joshua was happy to see his friend again. He placed his hand on his shoulder and could at once detect the drained and scuffed look on William's face, "Hey Will, glad you made it. You look like shit." "Yeah, work you know?" "You should take it easy. You are getting too old to still be a workaholic." William let out a faint chuckle before he sipped on his beer. "So, how are things with Ana and the baby?" Joshua sipped on his own beer before he turned back to William. "Oh, you know? She is taking up a position at a dance academy somewhere here in Coral Hill. I must say, despite everything, I am beginning to look forward to being a dad." "Yeah, you've always wanted to be a dad." William let out an indistinct sigh, before he sipped on his beer again. "So, how are you? Don't you have a ten-day tour coming up soon?" "Yeah, I leave next month. I am tired of juggling my music and my practice. Thankfully, Missy, well, she's a great friend and writes quite a bit of my music for me." Joshua could kick himself for mentioning Misty-Bleu's name.

William grimaced before he took another sip of his beer. "How is she?" "She's great. I mean, you know?" William nodded. Joshua could hardly ignore the wounded manifestation on his face. "Are you two? I mean, is there something going on between you two?" William had no intention of asking Joshua about his relationship with Misty-Bleu but blurted it out before he could stop himself. "Oh no, we are just friends. I like her, she's great, but nothing like that …" "Because, I mean, she deserves to be happy. She deserves someone more like you." "No buddy, there's something sacred about dating your best friend's girl, or ex girl, or whatever. No, I enjoy her company and if she was anyone else, things would be different, but no. I know you still love her, Will

Alice VL

and I know, I know she loves you."

William ordered beer after beer, and by the time Joshua stopped counting, William could barely stand up straight. "This life is so fucked. I mean, honestly, it is fucked! Have you ever stopped to think how screwed up everything is?" William placed his glass back on the counter and turned to look Joshua squarely in the eye. "When I was dying, I saw a gap and I took it. I thought I could, fuck. Bro listen to me, you can live in a totally different fucking universe, but you can't alter fate. That fucking destiny bitch gets in the way, every fucking time."

Joshua frowned in total bewilderment as he tried to make sense of what William was saying. "Listen bro, I think you've had too much to drink. Let me drive you home." "I love her. Missy, you know? All the shit we've been through, and now this. Fucking Ana. Don't get me wrong, I will love that kid, but I just love Misty more. How fucked is that?" William nodded before he slugged back the rest of his beer.

Joshua drove William home, and when he made his way into his house, he sat quietly, trying to make sense of what William had said earlier. At that very moment, Joshua knew that he could never pursue Misty-Bleu. Her heart belonged to him, as much as she had claimed William's when they were only kids.

Alice VL

AFTERLIGHT

Alice VL

5

Fall had arrived far too soon for Misty-Bleu's liking. Joshua had called earlier and asked her to meet him at Café LeParis at the Waterfront later that morning. Misty-Bleu woke up feeling as though she had barely slept the night before, but hesitantly agreed to meet him for a quick cup of coffee. When she sluggishly strolled into the warm and cozy coffee shop, Misty-Bleu was relieved that she had worn a warm jersey. It was misty and cold, and the wind was unapologetically stripping the leaves off the trees. When she caught a glimpse of Josh waiting for her, she nippily made her way over to him, before he got up and hugged her warmly, "Hey, thanks for coming." "I just realized, I haven't really been to the Waterfront since Shaun and Kevin left. That must be about six weeks ago." She smiled before she sat down on an empty seat across from Joshua. "I've ordered cappuccino's, extra thick cream." Misty-Bleu smiled and nodded before she pulled her jersey over her hands. "So, listen, Missy, other than your fabulous company, there is another reason I asked you here ..." "Oh? What's the matter?" He knew he had to do something. He had to intervene before both Misty-Bleu and

William end up destroying themselves. "Nothing. Nothing's the matter. It's just, have you heard from William lately?" Misty-Bleu bowed her head and was at once relieved when their coffee arrived. She placed her hands around her coffee mug, before she looked up at Joshua. "No, he has a lot on his plate and needs distance from me." As she lowered her head to take a sip, she became nauseous at once. She turned her head and hurriedly placed the mug on the table, while Joshua noticed her turn pale almost at once. "Missy, are you okay?" "I, I'm suddenly not feeling so well?" "Can I get you a glass of water?" "No, I need to get out of here, these smells …" She grabbed her bag, and hurriedly made her way out of Café LeParis. Joshua quickly pulled out a couple of bills and placed it on their table before he caught up with Misty-Bleu. Misty-Bleu stopped and turned to face him, "I'm so sorry, Josh, I feel awful." When he noticed how pale she had turned, he was instantly concerned. "Listen, my practice is just around the corner. Let me check you out?" "No, you don't have to, honestly, I'll be fine." "Misty-Bleu, it's just around the corner, I insist."

Misty-Bleu smiled nervously, before she hooked her arm into his, and walked over to Joshua Stark's medical practice. When they entered his consulting rooms, she was relieved that there were no patients waiting for him and smiled when she

Alice VL

noticed his young assistant behind the reception counter. "Loretta, this is Miss Buchanan, a friend of mine. We'll be in my office, what time is the next patient?" Loretta quickly paged through her diary before she gawked up at Joshua. "In about an hour ..." "Great ..." When they entered his office, Joshua showed her to an empty seat across from his desk. She reluctantly sat down and placed her bag on the floor.

"I don't think I've ever seen you with your doctor cap on. It looks good on you." Joshua smiled before he shifted in his chair. "So, I'm not going to ask you to fill out any forms. Is there anything in your medical history I should know about?" Misty-Bleu was taken aback by the sudden change in his demeanor. She had never seen him in a professional capacity before, and she could not quite shake the feeling of being bullied by Joshua Stark. "Uhm, no, nothing." "Good, hop onto that bed over there, let me check you out. Don't worry, I won't make you change into one those horrible gowns. This is just a quick look-over." He grinned from ear to ear, before he got up, and pointed to a bed in the corner of his office.

Misty-Bleu got up and nervously made her way over for her examination. She laid down on the bed and became anxious almost at once. "You see, this is why your friends can't be your doctor!" He chuckled as he tried to make light of their very uncomfortable situation. When he began examining her mouth and throat, Misty-Bleu was overwhelmed by discomfort, and began to shudder slightly. Joshua caught glimpses of her often and could not help but feel as though he was drowning in the puddles of her eyes. As he lowered his hands, she cringed slightly when he examined her breasts. "What's the matter?" He at once lifted his hands and stared at her. "Nothing, just sensitive?" "Alright, your glands are slightly swollen, but I am going to do a quick urine test to rule out any infection. It is possibly that your immune system has taken a little bit of a knock. You should eat better, and more often." She got up, and quickly made her way into the room next door. After she handed Loretta her urine sample, she took her place in front of Joshua once again.

Barely ten minutes later, Joshua came back in and hastily, yet tensely, took his seat across from her. He sat back in his chair and gazed into her worried eyes. "Is everything alright?" Misty-Bleu felt the blood drain from her face by the way he was looking at her. He leaned forward and fidgeted with his pen. "Yeah no, everything is great. It's just, you and Wilhelmina are both in the same position, you're pregnant." Misty-Bleu felt as though he had slammed a bucket of ice in her face. She stared at him in disbelief as she replayed his words over and over again. She glared at him in total incredulity, desperate to find something to tell her that he was simply messing with her. The longer she looked at him, the more she realized that it was no joke, and no mistake. Praying desperately for Joshua to say something, she felt the tears tingle in her eyes. When she opened her mouth, she was once again reminded of the familiar, yet enormously restricting lump in her throat. "Misty? Are you okay?" Misty-Bleu tried not to blink, afraid that her tears would come crashing through her eyes if she did. She swallowed back continuously, but when the lump grew larger, she lowered her head, and burst into tears.

Joshua got up from behind his desk and sat in the empty chair beside her. He lifted her chin just enough so that he could look into her eyes, before he took her hands into his. "Is it William?" Misty-Bleu nodded her head before she turned away from Joshua. Joshua freed her hands and leaned back in his chair. He impulsively ran his fingers through his hair before he sat up straight and rested his elbows on his knees, "You have to tell him." "No, Joshua. No. Please. You can't tell him either. He can't know." "You can't ask me to lie to my best friend, Missy?" "I'm not. I am just asking you not to say anything. I don't want him to choose, Josh. I don't want that." "He has a right to know, and he has a right to be informed before he is placed in a position he doesn't want to be in." "Joshua don't tell him. Legally, you know you can't, but as a friend, I am begging you not to tell him." Misty-Bleu grabbed his hands and squeezed them firmly. "You know I won't, Missy, but what will you do? You can't hide it forever?" "I know, Josh. I don't know what to do. I just need time to think things through." Joshua gently rubbed her hand, "Just don't do anything stupid, okay? You have time, take it, and think about this."

She nodded her head before she hurriedly swabbed at her tears. "I am going to give you Aidan Quinn's number. He is a colleague of mine. Make an appointment to see him as soon as possible. He is extremely busy, and often has a two-month waiting list. If you can't get in to see him soon, give me a call. I'll see what I can do." "Thank you, Josh, for everything." "Also, I must warn you. He is a mutual friend of William too, so I wouldn't say anything about William to him." "Okay ..." "In the meantime, take these. They will help with the nausea and will feed your immunity until you start feeling better." He quickly took his prescription pad, and jotted down a couple of things for Misty-Bleu to pick up from the pharmacy. "Thank you, Josh. I am going to pick this up right now." "Are you going to be okay?" He got up and helped her to her feet. "Yeah, everything is just a little chaotic in my head. I mean, I never thought, I never saw this coming? I never wanted to be a mother, you know?" "It happens, go get some rest. Things will look better in the morning." Joshua embraced her before she walked out of his door. Misty-Bleu hurriedly made her way back to the Waterfront, where she had left her car parked.

As she passed Café LeParis, she heard a familiar, yet unnerving voice behind her. "Misty?" She abruptly turned around and was horrified to find William and Ana walking hand in hand. She at once thought of the child she was carrying inside of her, just as Ana was carrying William's child. She shook her head and was stunned for just a moment when she considered the malicious and heartless twists life was handing her. "Hey ..." She whispered softly before she lowered her head, desperate not to make eye contact with William. William was at once overwhelmed by fear when he caught a quick peek into Misty-Bleu's eyes. He could have sworn that she was crying, but he was taken aback at once by the overpowering sadness and discomfort that told him a thousand stories of heartbreak. He instinctively took her hand into his, before he released it only moments later.

"You okay?" He could not shake the feeling that something was wide of the mark with Misty-Bleu. "Yeah, fine. How are you guys?" "We are fine! William and I are just here for a quick breakfast before we head on over to Joshua. I am hoping for a quick referral to Dr. Aidan Quinn. I hear you can't see him without a referral. Only the best for this little Carmichael." Ana smiled proudly before she rubbed her belly, all the while, fixing a triumphant smile at Misty-Bleu. 'This cannot be happening ...' She thought silently, as she shook her head when she realized that they both would be sharing a doctor, the father of their children, and that their children would carry the same last name. "Well, good luck with that. It was nice seeing you both again, I must run."

She waved them goodbye before she turned and hurried back to her car. When Misty-Bleu slid into the driver's seat, she leaned forward and placed both her hands onto the steering wheel. She lowered her head and began to sob irrepressibly. She wanted to curse the universe, and at the same time, scourge the day she walked back into William's life. She hated that she gave her body so spontaneously to him, and now she was about to pay the price of her carelessness, for the rest of her life. She thought about what Joshua had said when he clearly asked her not to make impulsive decisions, but at that very moment, Misty-Bleu could consider no other way out. Her entire body had erupted into a quake when she heard her car door open. Looking up, she saw William standing right beside her. "No, William, no. You don't get to stand here and watch me fall apart like this! You don't get to see me cry!" She shouted out, suddenly enraged by

Alice VL

the fact that he had been watching her cry when she thought that no-one could see her. William placed his arms around her and held her firmly against him. "Oh God, Missy. I can't do this. I don't know how much longer I can go on like this?" She buried her head in his chest before another wave of violent sobbing erupted inside of her. She placed her arms around him and held on as though her life depended on it. They held onto one another for what felt like forever, and when Misty-Bleu finally felt she could breathe again, she looked up at William whose own tears had begun to roll recklessly from his eyes. She withdrew from him slightly, and when William knelt in front of her, she took his trembling hands into hers. "We'll get better at this, William. I promise." William could no longer hide his sorrow, "I don't want to get better at anything that doesn't include you. Misty, I can't. I swear to God I can't do this." "Stop, William. Just stop. This is how it is. This is how it must be. You and I, we've already shared a lifetime together. We should stop ignoring the signs and accept that this world, this lifetime, is not ours." "I don't believe that Missy. Don't ever tell me things like that. I love you. We will love each other beyond universes and through a million lifetimes! Don't say things like that!" "No, William, no. I loved what we had. I loved the idea of you. I loved you once but no, I don't love you now. I care so much about you, but I don't love you, and I just wish, I wish you would leave me alone."

Alice VL

AFTERLIGHT

She felt her heart splinter into a thousand pieces when she saw the proof of agony and pain in his eyes. William went ice cold when he heard her tell him that she no longer loved him. "I don't believe you, Misty-Bleu!" "Believe it because it is what it is! Go, William! Go back to Ana, go back to your child, and go back to your life! Stay out of mine!"

Misty-Bleu pushed him away, and hurriedly slammed her door shut. When she pulled away from him, she felt her legs grow weak. It felt as though her heart was about to explode and shatter into a hundred little shards. She hurriedly wiped at the tears that had once again begin to spill from her eyes, and when she looked back in her rear-view mirror, he was gone.

Alice VL

6

When Misty-Bleu slid to her knees, she gently placed her hands on Wilhelmina's wearied head. Her beloved, thoroughbred Murgese was lying on her side, moaning as she struggled to birth her filly. It was colder than usual when Misty-Bleu frantically reached for her mobile phone. She began to shudder slightly as she tugged at her jersey to cover up her chilly hands. Out of pure frustration, she dialed Dr. Baxter's number, the trusted veterinarian she had come to know since her move to Coral Hill. "Dr. Baxter's Ark, good day?" Misty-Bleu was relieved to hear Justine's friendly voice on the other side of the phone. She had met the young, friendly assistant when Dr. Baxter came out to Little Dreams when she first brought Wilhelmina home almost six years before. Justine had only recently graduated from high school, before she took up a position as assistant and receptionist for Dr. Baxter. Six years later, Justine had enrolled in college, and was only two years away from graduating as a veterinarian herself. "Justine, it's Misty-Bleu. Wilhelmina has been in labor for hours. Please, she's not doing so well. Please can Dr. Baxter come out?" "Oh, my gosh, Misty-

AFTERLIGHT

Bleu! Dr. Baxter is on a call-out, and busy with an emergency surgery on premises. I'll have him get to you as soon as possible. Take down Dr. Drake's number, perhaps he can get to you sooner?" Misty-Bleu hurriedly memorized the number, and swiftly ended her call to Justine. She frantically dialed the number Justine had given her only moments before and was at once devastated when her call remained unanswered.

While clutching desperately onto her phone, she rubbed her forehead with the back of her hand and continued to caress Wilhelmina, unsure of what to do next.

Alice VL

It was only a few days earlier that William had listened to Ana's confession after he confronted her about her pregnancy. "Ana, you must be what? Six or so months along? When is your appointment with Aidan for your first ultrasound?" "I'm waiting to get an appointment, you know that?" William took his mobile phone, and immediately dialed his friend, the much-sought-after gynecologist, Aidan Quinn. "Who are you calling?" "I'm calling Aidan to see if we can't get an appointment soon. This is ridiculous!" She gasped for air before she belligerently took the phone from his hand. Unable to look him in the eye, she shamefully turned away from him. "What are you doing?" "I, I've got it covered." "No, Ana ... obviously, you don't. How long has it been since Joshua sent the referral through to his office?" She turned around to face him, clearly aware of William's mounting agitation. "Next week, William, I'm sure I'll see him next week. He is extremely busy, you know that?"

William's eyes trailed down to her belly. He realized at once that he had barely looked at her in the last few months. He could not identify what should be a growing bulge and was at once appalled by the suspicion that perhaps, she had been deceiving him. "You, you're not even showing yet? We should at least go see Joshua." She bowed her head in disgrace, unable to face William, but sure that she could no longer carry on lying to and deceiving him. "I, I didn't want to tell you …" She hesitated as William slowly, yet nervously approached her. "Tell me what?" "I mean, you've been so stressed lately." He grabbed her by her arm, and squeezed it in growing frustration, "What aren't you telling me, Ana?" "William, I … I lost the baby. A few days after we went to see Joshua, I miscarried." William released her arm as he instinctively turned away from her. He brushed his hand over his mouth and became enraged almost at once. "I'm sorry. I wanted to tell you, but I couldn't. I just thought that I'd get pregnant again. It was supposed to be only a matter of time …" He turned around, and when Ana saw the untrained expression in his eyes, she felt a wave of untaught fear invade her entire body. "You miscarried and didn't tell me? And then, you thought you could just get pregnant again, and I would never know?"

He could not quite decide whether he was immensely relieved, or whether he was blinded by anger. Anger at her for withholding the truth from him as she concocted a plan to trap him, yet again. He was enraged by the circumstances that ended his relationship with Misty-Bleu. Because of their child, William was forced to let her go. He was fuming when he realized that Ana had so carelessly considered tricking him for a second time. "You tried to get pregnant again? Without telling me? Were you even pregnant?" "I didn't think? It's not such a big deal. I mean, I didn't lie to you about being pregnant!" Ana raised her voice through utter desperation when she realized without a doubt, that William was about to walk out on her, and that she would lose him forever. "Really? How will I ever know the truth?" He stormed off to his bedroom, before slamming the door behind him. Ana made her way over to a couch in the living room and burst into tears. She had barely dried her tears when there was a faint knock on their front door. Ana hesitated, before she made her way over, and was relieved to find Joshua standing there. "Hey, come in. I am so glad you're here." Joshua was at once unprepared for Ana's red and bulging eyes. "Is everything okay?" "Yeah, I'll get William." She turned and speedily made her way into their bedroom. "Joshua's here …"

When William met Joshua at the front door, Joshua could sense that he had walked in on a distressing quarrel. "I am going to the mall, see you later." Ana grabbed her purse, and without turning back, she climbed into her car and drove off. "Damn, this is awkward …" Joshua tried to make light of the situation before William showed him to the kitchen. He took out two beers, and after handing Joshua one, he sat down on an empty stool at the kitchen counter. Joshua sat across from him and sipped his beer. "So, bro, what's going on? You could cut the atmosphere with a blunt knife." William shook his head before he took another sip.

Alice VL

"She's not pregnant. She claims to have miscarried, and instead of telling me, she tried to get pregnant again. What did she think? That I wouldn't notice?" Joshua was stunned to hear what William had to say. "Oh man, that sucks. What are you going to do?" "I don't want a kid with her. I'm not sure if I even really like her. Living with her these past few months almost drove me crazy. She's conceited and egotistical. I can't do this, Josh, not with her." William swallowed back on his beer before he placed the bottle on the counter. "Yeah, I never could quite get what you saw in her. I mean, she is beautiful and successful, but she's, she's just not like us, you know?" William nodded before he turned to get another beer from the fridge.

"You should go see Misty-Bleu ..." Joshua blurted out suddenly. He had once sworn to Misty-Bleu that he would never expose her secret to William, but in no way at all, did he promise to stay out of their relationship. "Ah man, I don't know? The last time I saw her nearly ripped me apart. She is so angry at me. I just can't stomach seeing her like that." "Yeah, but, she's hurting, bro." "She told me that she no longer loves me, and she never wants to see me again." "She didn't mean it, Will. Like I said, she's hurting and when we hurt, we do the strangest things. Just go see her, what have you got to lose?" William nodded before he squeezed Joshua's shoulder. "I first have to deal with Ana, fuck."

Alice VL

AFTERLIGHT

When Ana walked into the house on Cotton Road later that evening, William had calmed down slightly, and was sad to detect the pained expression on Ana's face. He sat at the dining room table and showed her to an empty chair across from him. "You're breaking up with me, aren't you?" Ana whispered as she sat down across from him. William bowed his head and nodded lightly. "This was never going to work, Ana. It was only a matter of time. We would have had a kid shuffled between our homes in the end. You can't say you were happy? I know I wasn't ..." William paused to take in a deep breath. When he gazed into her eyes, he was at once aware of the tears that were about to roll onto her cheeks. "I know you don't love me, William, but I know you care. Isn't that something to work on? I love you. I have enough love for us both." She grabbed his hands, as she desperately pleaded with him. "Ana, you are beautiful. God, you are so beautiful. You are a great dancer. Why would you want to be with someone who can never love you like you deserve to be loved and cherished?" "Because I love you. I love you. I want you. I want to be with you. I want to try. I want you to miss me, as I miss you when I'm away. I want you to love me. I will do anything, William, anything you want, just don't, please don't leave me?" Her desperation grew as she squeezed his hands tighter. "I can't live like that, Ana. I can't betray my heart like that." "But, you can love me, William. You can learn to love me?" She suddenly rose

Alice VL

to her feet and pulled him up against her. "It doesn't work like that. I can't choose who to love? I can't switch on or reconfigure some invisible setting inside of me? My heart already knows ... my heart already knows what it wants." "I just don't get it? I mean, I know this is all about Misty-Bleu, right? I'm not stupid, William, but, why her?" William lowered his head before he freed his hands from hers. "I don't know, Ana? I would swop universes to be with her. I don't know why? I can't tell you why? There are so many ways that I love her, and I don't want to tell you. I don't want to hurt you." She immediately lowered her head, "Yeah ..." He placed his arms around her and held her securely in his arms. Ana sobbed miserably when she realized that no matter how much she begged and pleaded with him, William Carmichael would always choose Misty-Bleu.

Alice VL

William had finally plucked up the courage to drive out to Little Dreams, desperate to see Misty-Bleu and tell her of all the events that had unfolded only days before. When he drove up the driveway that led to her farmhouse, he noticed that Captain Nimo was actively trotting around in the fields, but that Wilhelmina was nowhere to be found. He glanced over at the barn, and when he saw the door standing open, he instinctively made his way over to the stables. He walked in quietly and could immediately hear Misty-Bleu's heartbreaking sobbing. He paced up to Wilhelmina's stable and stood as though frozen in time when he saw Misty-Bleu on her knees, frantically dialing a number on her mobile phone. He could not miss the apparent distress on her face, but when he noticed her protruding belly, he was horrified to discover that she was keeping a secret from him. His jaw dropped, unable to ignore what he had just seen. He felt his heart hammer in his throat, as fear began to invade his entire being. "Misty-Bleu?"

She was startled to hear William's croaky, yet flabbergasted voice behind her. She hurriedly turned to face him, and could no longer restrain the tears that were threatening to rush from her eyes, "I don't know what to do? Dr. Baxter is in surgery, and I can't get hold of Dr. Drake. Wilhelmina, she's been struggling all day. If she doesn't get help now, she will die, and her filly will die too. I don't know who else to call? She won't let me leave her … she won't let me get up and get help …" She desperately pleaded with William, as he hurriedly made his way over to her. "Have you tried calling Roger Mack?" She intrusively shook her head as William took his mobile phone from his pocket. He dialed Roger Mack's number before he paced back to the barn door. "Hey, it's me, William. Listen, you're just down the road. A friend of mine's horse is in trouble, can you help?" Roger agreed at once, "Hey Will, of course, text me the address. I'll leave now."

Roger Mack was a man William had met only a year or so before. They were both guests at Aidan Quinn's birthday bash, and the two struck up an immediate friendship. They soon discovered that the four friends, including Joshua, attended the same university years before. William hurriedly texted him the directions to her farm before he made his way back over to Misty-Bleu. "He'll be here in five minutes, Misty-Bleu, don't worry." Misty-Bleu smiled as she hurriedly swabbed at her tears, "Is there anybody you don't know?" William knelt beside her, and placed his hand on her swollen belly, "Why didn't you tell me?" Misty-Bleu lowered her head, unsure of what to say next. "I … I just, I didn't want you to have to choose." She whispered almost inaudibly, ashamed that he had found her so utterly vulnerable.

Alice VL

Before William could respond, they were both aware of the sound of a car making its way up her driveway, "That should be him, I'll go meet him." William leaped to his feet and swiftly made his way out of the barn. Misty-Bleu straightened out her jersey and cleared the hair that had loosened itself from her braid, from her eyes. "You're going to be okay, Wilhelmina, just hang in there. Help is here ..."

When William and Roger Mack entered the barn, Misty-Bleu sighed and smiled, instantly relieved. "Is this Wilhelmina?" Roger rushed over to the horse that was moaning in agony. "Yes." Roger knelt down beside Wilhelmina, and gently stroked her belly. "We'll get her filly out in no time ..." He frowned when he caught a glimpse of Misty-Bleu who had turned ashen, but whose cheeks were glowing a bright, scarlet red. "Are you feeling okay?" "Yes, I'm fine now." He instinctively pressed the back of his hand against her forehead before he got up and hurriedly made his way over to William. "Get her to a doctor. She has a fever and is burning up. I'll stay here with Wilhelmina." William frowned, before he made his way over to Misty-Bleu and placed his hand on her cheek.

"Misty-Bleu, you're burning up. I'm getting you to a doctor now. Wilhelmina will be fine. Roger will stay with her." He reached down and helped her to her feet. When he realized that

Alice VL

she could barely stand up straight, he placed a steady arm around her waist. "I had an appointment with Aidan Quinn today, but with Wilhelmina ... you know?" "Yeah, I'm taking you there right now." "No, he doesn't work like that, I waited two months to get this appointment." William hurriedly helped her to his car, before he took his mobile phone from his pocket. "You should have called me; I would have gotten you in. Or you could have just called Josh, he would have scheduled an appointment on your behalf. I'm calling him now." He shut the car door, and swiftly made his way over to the driver's seat. "Thanks, we're leaving now," was all Misty-Bleu could hear before he ended the call.

William slid into the driver's seat and placed his phone in the console between them. "He's waiting for you. Is there anybody I can get to stay here at the farm?" "No, I have an interview at four with a husband-and-wife team. I just thought that, with the baby and the Christmas tree season coming up, and the horses ..." William understood at once, "Yeah well, you should have some help here. I'll take care of it."

When they reached Aidan's office, William frenetically took Misty-Bleu by her hand, and led her indoors. She had begun to shudder slightly, while she felt her entire body burn up as though on fire. "Hi Miranda, Aidan is expecting her ..." "Yes, you can show her in." William clutched her warm hand tighter, and hurriedly led her into his consulting rooms. "Hey Aidan, thanks so much for seeing her." "Hey, Will! Yeah, Joshua actually called to hear if she showed up. This must be Misty-Bleu?" He extended a welcoming hand out to Misty-Bleu, whose shuddering hands had turned ice cold. "Hi, Misty-Bleu, so sorry you couldn't make it earlier. If I had known it was you, I would have seen you so much sooner. It's so good to finally meet you. Josh has told me so much about you." He smiled when he introduced himself but was at once disturbed when he became aware of her fever. "You're burning up, how far along are you?" "I'm … I'm not sure. I was supposed to have an ultrasound today, but I think around 22 weeks?" "We'll check that out in a moment. Are you getting cold?" "Yes, I can't seem to warm up?" She whispered as she began trembling uncontrollably. "You're burning up, Misty-Bleu. I'm going to do a quick ultrasound, and then admit you to hospital. You've probably just picked up a bug, but I don't want to take any chances." "I've had it before when one of my horses became ill or pregnant. It was diagnosed as Stallion Fever, the last time I felt like this." "Oh, you own horses? Any one of them expecting?" "Yes." Misty-Bleu's voice was shuddering. "Well, I'd like to check just to make sure. Even so, fever needs to be broken, and you need to keep hydrated. Once the fever has broken, you can go home. It's not serious at all, but you are pregnant, and any fever is never good for the unborn baby. I'm going to give you something to bring down your fever, before we begin the ultrasound, okay?" "Thank you. I never really know where to place you. I thought you were a specialist gynaecologist, but I recognize you from research I did for one of my novels a couple of months back. You are a fertility scientist too?" She blabbered out in admiration before he hurriedly pierced her skin with a needle. "I just never stop studying. My greatest achievement will be when I can successfully transplant a womb someday." "Yeah, he's kind of a genius." William interrupted and let out a faint chuckle.

On Aidan's instructions, Misty-Bleu groggily made her way to the next room to change into a robe for her ultrasound. When Aidan was sure that she was no longer in hearing distance, he turned to William. "What a beautiful woman." "Yeah ..." William smiled forlornly as he gently nodded his head. "So, Will, do you want to go out to the reception area and wait for her there?" "I'm not going anywhere, I'm staying." "What are you talking about?" William placed his hands on Aidan's shoulder, "That's my kid, Aidan ..." Aidan frowned at once while utterly confused by William's confession, before instant recognition set in, "Oh, right. Oh?" "Yeah, long story ..."

Misty-Bleu silently made her way onto the bed before she bashfully turned to William. "You don't have to be here?" "I want to. Are you feeling any better?" "Yes, thank you. Whatever he gave me, that was the good stuff, we should get some more." She smiled and winked at William, relieved that she had stopped shaking, before she hurriedly turned back to Aidan as he made his way around to the ultrasound. "So, this is going to be a little cold, but we want to make sure we can see your baby's progress, and make sure that everything is alright, okay? We want to listen for the heartbeat, and then I'd like to determine how far along you are. We also check for deformities, or anything really that might be of concern." Misty-Bleu smiled and shuddered all at the same time when Aidan applied the sonar gel. He turned the machine on, and almost instantly, Misty-Bleu could hear her baby's heartbeat. "Well, that's a good sign. Perfect. The baby's heartbeat is precisely what I would expect it to be, healthy and strong." He smiled at an obviously relieved Misty-Bleu. She turned around and looked up at William who was standing at her head. She smiled sadly when she detected utter desolation in his eyes. "Everything looks perfectly fine. You are actually 24 weeks and 5 days along. Your baby is healthy, normal, and everything is progressing as it should. Do you want to know what you're having?" Misty-Bleu smiled again, before she turned to face William one more time. William took her hand, and gently squeezed it. She was sure that he was veiling his tears behind his glistening eyes. "Can you seal it in an envelope for if, and when

Alice VL

we decide we want to know, Aidan?" "Sure ..."

Aidan winked and turned his attention back to Misty-Bleu. He gently placed his hand on her forehead and was at once relieved that her fever had broken. "Dr. Quinn, I am feeling a whole lot better. Please can I go home? I promise to call if the fever starts up again, and I will take plenty of fluids. I can't leave Wilhelmina now, and I have no-one to take care of the farm." Aidan frowned, and before he could object, William interrupted him, "I'll stay with her and watch her, I promise." "Alright then, but you are going to get these from the pharmacy, and make sure that she takes them and gets enough food and fluids in, okay?" "Yes sir." William smirked when he noticed an enormously relieved Misty-Bleu. When she slipped back into the changing rooms, William took a seat across from Aidan who had begun writing out her script. "I mean it bro; you have to keep an eye on her for the next 48 hours. She can't be alone; it could flare up at any moment again." "She won't be. I'll stay with her for a few days." "So, is this the girl you reconnected with? Before Ana?" "Yeah. That whole thing with Ana was just an enormous mistake. She had me totally fooled." "Yeah, but how do you know this is your kid?" "I just know, Aidan. We met up again about six months ago when I was in hospital. We were together like *that* from the very first week, so, I know." "Okay then, she seems like a nice

Alice VL

person and she's definitely gorgeous. Successful and a great voice, I hear. Joshua just said the other day, how he wished she would take that further." "Joshua talks a lot about her? She has her horses; she farms Christmas trees and she's a successful novelist. She definitely doesn't need to trap me, but she's not a limelight sort of person, never was."

Alice VL

When they reached her farm, Misty-Bleu sat quietly before she turned to face William, who was getting ready to climb out of his car. "You don't have to stay with me, William." "I know I don't, but I did give Aidan my word." "I have the interview in a few minutes, and I want to go see how Wilhelmina is doing." "Roger's still here, so let's go see how she is doing. I'll do the interviews for you while you get into bed, before I run out for the script, okay?" "William, seriously, you don't have to do any of this." "Stop, Misty-Bleu, just stop, okay?"

Misty-Bleu smiled before she climbed out of his car, and almost ran into the barn. She had wanted to ask William about Ana, but for only the day, she didn't really want to know. She did not want to be reminded of Ana, and how they were creating a life together. She did not want to hear about their baby, or how excited William and Ana were to meet their child. When she reached Wilhelmina's stable, she was relieved to find Roger hunched beside a perfect, new-born filly. She burst into tears before she hurriedly made her way over to her precious horse, who was standing as proud and as tall as any new mother should. "You did good, my girl. She is beautiful. I am so sorry I wasn't here. You did so good." Misty-Bleu stroked Wilhelmina before she turned to Roger Mack. "Thank you so much, Dr. Mack. Are they okay?" She swallowed back on an enormously restricting lump in her throat as she hurriedly dabbed at a tear that had rolled down her cheek, overcome by relief that Wilhelmina had survived. "They are both fine. I'm glad to see you are feeling better. Is everything okay with you?" "Yeah, just Stallion Fever, but I'm feeling like my old self again. I'm just so glad that Wilhelmina pulled through, and that you came when you did. Thank you, so much."

William swiftly made his way over to where they were standing, and offered an extended hand to Roger Mack, "Thanks bud, will you send me your bill?" "Oh no, no, please don't do that." Misty-Bleu was mortified that William had offered to pay Wilhelmina's bill, "Just mail it to me, please, Dr. Mack ..." "It's no problem, Misty-Bleu. I don't bill my friends. So, let them rest. They'll be fine and by the look of things, you need some rest too?" She shook his hand and thanked him politely for helping Wilhelmina deliver her filly. "I'm going to walk Roger to his car, when I come back, straight to bed, okay?" She nodded and smiled before she turned back to Wilhelmina. "What are we going to call ... oh, I see it's a colt?" She silently tip-toed over to the brand-new addition to her family, and gently stroked the colt that was clumsily reaching for Wilhelmina. "What about Midnight?" She whispered while admiring his pitch-black fir. William had barely returned to the stable, when Misty-Bleu filled their water pales, and closed the stable doors behind her. He clutched her hand into his and led her back into her farmhouse. When they reached her bedroom, he quickly lifted the covers, before she climbed in and laid her head on her pillow. "Midnight is beautiful. I'm so glad they are both okay. I don't know what I would have done if anything happened to Wilhelmina ..." She whispered sleepily before William gently covered her up with a quilt. "My list of questions is on the dining room table for Eduardo and his wife, Maria Lima ..." "I can hire people; I've been doing it for years. Now get some sleep. Afterwards, I am going to slip out and collect your script, okay?" "Okay ..."

Misty-Bleu whispered as she placed her hand on her belly and fell asleep almost immediately.

Alice VL

7

When she opened her eyes, Misty-Bleu noticed that her blinds were closed, and that only the light of her lamp was lighting the room just enough to see William asleep in a chair next to her bed. She sniggered softly when she saw him sit up straight, yet fast asleep. Misty-Bleu climbed out of her bed and softly tiptoed over to him. "William?" She whispered softly, not wanting to frighten him. He at once opened his eyes and was alarmed to find her standing in front of him. "What? What's the matter?" He stood up in a panic. Misty-Bleu giggled in her sleeve when she detected the sudden and unmistakable panic in his voice. "Nothing, really, nothing is wrong. I know … I know it's completely the wrong thing to ask but come lay on the bed with me. You'll be exhausted in the morning if you try and get some rest in that uncomfortable chair." She took his hand and led him back to her bed. She opened the covers for William to climb in beside her, and they both sat up, staring at one another. "Well, I am wide awake now!" He giggled when he pulled the covers over him. "Yeah, me too." "So, while we're bright-eyed and bushy-tailed, let me ask you this … why didn't you tell me, Misty-Bleu?

Alice VL

About the baby?" "It's not that I didn't want to tell you, I did, I just didn't want you to choose between any of your children." "But that should have been up to me, my choice." "Yeah, but how could I ask you to make a decision like that, William? Ana came before I did. She was here before I was. You and I, I mean, we weren't really even dating? I got pregnant so quickly. And, I never wanted children, you know that?" William touched her cheek and smiled, "You came long before she did, Misty-Bleu. You just slipped out for a while, but anyways, it would have been really awkward, I know that. It's just, you should have told me, and we could have made it work, one way or another." "Could have? What do you mean, could have? Can't we now? What happened, William? You haven't even told me why you are here? Why did you come here today?" "Yeah, I guess I owe you an explanation. I mean, Ana wouldn't go for her ultrasound, and then I eventually became suspicious about the excuses she was making day after day after day. I tried to call Aidan Quinn, but she wouldn't let me. She didn't want to go. Then she came out with the story that she had lost the baby and hoped to get pregnant in the meantime. It was all just a load of bullshit, if you ask me." "Wow. She did that? I'm so sorry, William, I don't know what to say?" "I'm not sorry, Misty-Bleu. I know it sounds terrible, and I know I sound like a monster, but I am so thankful to God that she's not pregnant." "Yeah, and yet, here I am. What a screwed-up world."

Alice VL

He took Misty-Bleu's hands and held it firmly against his chest. "Don't say that, Missy. I love you; I do. I love this child, and I want to do this with you, okay? I choose you. From my hospital bed, I chose you. You have no idea how I chose you, you just don't …" She smiled sadly before she clutched his face in her hands, "I love you. Always. I've loved you always, William. I don't think I can be here, in this world, without you." Misty-Bleu suddenly remembered the envelope that Aidan Quinn had written their child's gender on. She grabbed it and waved it out in front of William. "Do we want to know?" "I can't decide? Can we wait a while longer? I mean, the surprise of it, you know?" "You don't think the baby is enough of a surprise?" She placed the envelope back on the pedestal beside her, and gently laid her head on the pillow. "Only if you hold me while I sleep …" William laid down behind her and held her protectively against him. "Joshua is having his birthday party at Gillian's Stadium tomorrow afternoon. I was thinking, with Eduardo and Maria moving into the guest house tomorrow, and if you're feeling up to it, maybe we should go?" "Oh? You've hired the couple?" She winked before she giggled softly. "Yeah, I like them." "In that case, I'd love to go with you." He kissed her gently on her forehead before she drifted off to sleep.

Early the following morning, William secretly called

Alice VL

Joshua when Misty-Bleu made her way out to the barn to check up on Wilhelmina and release her beloved horses out into the field. He watched her from her bedroom window, as she led them out one by one. He beamed when he noticed again how her belly was growing, and for a moment, he was sure that he would never again see anything as beautiful as she again. He stared at her for a little while longer, and when she brought Midnight out, he hurriedly reached for his mobile phone. "Josh here ..." "Hey buddy, many happy returns on your special day!" "William? Hey bro. Thanks. Don't tell me you won't be making my party?" "No, of course we'll be there, Misty and I. But listen, I have a huge favor to ask?" "Sure, anything." "I want to surprise her with revealing the gender of our baby at your party. Can I give it to Maria who can make the arrangements with your caterer or party planner?" "Yeah, sure. You know about the baby?" Joshua frowned when he heard William excitedly plan their gender reveal into his birthday party. "Yeah, long story. Wait, you knew?" "I mean ..." "Josh, you knew, and you didn't tell me?" "Come on bro, you know I can't. Doctor-patient privilege. I did ask you to go and see her, remember?" "Right, text me the number of your party planner as soon as you can ..."

His voice trailed off before he hung up on his call to Joshua. Even though he was immensely disappointed that Joshua withheld the fact that Misty-Bleu was pregnant, he at once brushed it off, and conceded to the fact that it was his duty as a doctor. He rushed downstairs to find Maria, who had just made her way into the farmhouse. He hurriedly handed her the envelope and texted her Joshua's party planner details he received shortly after he ended his call to him. After quickly going over her to-do-list, William was satisfied that all was going exactly according to plan.

Alice VL

When they reached the stadium later that same afternoon, Misty-Bleu was at once intimidated by the large crowds of guests that were attending Joshua Stark's birthday party. She held onto William's hand, and at once straightened her summer dress, keenly aware of how tight-fitting it had become. When she caught a peek of Joshua approaching them, she quickly wiped her loose flowing curls from her eyes. "Wow, look at you Misty-Bleu!" He steadily embraced her, and gently stroked her belly. "You are such a sight." "Happy birthday, Joshua." She swiftly kissed him on his cheek. "Happy birthday, buddy ..." William shook his hand, and handed him a neatly wrapped gift. "Thank you, please, come join the party. I'm glad to see you are doing so much better. Aidan said you were struck down by Stallion Fever?" He placed his arm around Misty-Bleu before he led her to her empty seat at a table. "Thank you. Yeah, but it only lasted a day or so."

William and Misty-Bleu had barely taken their seats when she heard someone frantically calling out for her, "Misty-Bleu! Misty-Bleu! Oh, my gosh!" She turned around to find Bryan anxiously running towards her. She smiled broadly when she recognized his familiar face, while trying to think how long it was since she had seen him before that night, before she impatiently bolted from her seat, and hastily ran to meet him. "Bryan! You seem to pop up everywhere I do!" She flung her arms around him and lovingly embraced him. "Pretty girl, look at you! I mean, when did this happen? What are you doing here?" He stepped back as he cautiously scrutinized her. "Hi ..." William had appeared beside her and smiled cautiously at Bryan. "This is William. William, this is Bryan, an old band mate of mine." "*The* William? Yeah, that's right, I remember him from, you know? But I do remember him from the beach, if my memory serves me?" Bryan frowned when he shook William's hand. Misty-Bleu lowered her head, utterly mortified when she realized that he was referring to her book, The Afterwards. "I hear that a lot, and yes, we did actually meet on the beach a few months ago." William winked and placed his arm around Misty-Bleu. "So, Misty-Bleu, we have lots of catching up to do by the look of things." She giggled timidly before she placed her arm around William. "Yep, you should come over soon, there are so many things going on at the farm, and its almost Christmas." "That would be great! So anyway, I better get my butt back to the stage. Hope to catch you before you leave?" Misty-Bleu nodded and smiled, before Bryan broke out into a weak excuse of a trot, as he returned to the stage. "Ladies and gentlemen! Welcome to Joshua Stark's 30'ish birthday! Thank you for having us! We hope you'll enjoy the party!" Bryan shouted into the mic before he turned to Misty-Bleu, "Misty-Bleu, come on, one last one for the

Alice VL

band! It was a special request from the birthday boy!" Misty-Bleu glared at Bryan before she glanced over at William, "Go on ..."

He clapped his hands before Misty-Bleu rose to her feet and made her way over to the stage. She had barely reached Bryan when he handed her a mic. "Hi everyone. Thank you for having me. I must admit, I am so under-dressed and over-bellied for this." She teased nervously before turning back to Bryan. "We are going to do a little number from Joshua's album, 'The Ultimate Fantasy'. The track is 'Stronger than we are.' I hope Josh forgives us for this. Happy birthday, Josh. You have been such an amazing friend, and I am so honored to know you. You have taught me to be stronger than I ever thought I was and for that, I thank and salute you. Are you ready?" Misty-Bleu shouted into the mic before all the guests broke out in applause. When she looked out in front of her, both Joshua and William had made their way to the stage. Misty-Bleu smiled at William and whispered into the mic, "This is for you, Carmichael, it's always been for you."

The crowd was mesmerized by her voice as Bryan and Misty-Bleu began singing a duet which was a little bit of pop, mixed in with a little bit of rock. Misty-Bleu sang as though she had been performing on stage for all of her life, and when she glanced down at William, he smiled sadly at her, but beamed with pride. "Wow, William, this voice. I mean, wow! I just never get enough of her singing …" Joshua was instantly drawn to Misty-Bleu's performance, but he could not admit how entirely bowled over and bewitched he was by her beauty. "Yeah, she just blows me away when she performs. It's as though her soul comes out through her songs."

When the song was over which seemed far too swiftly for the party guests, Misty-Bleu laughed out loud as Bryan excitedly embraced her. William and Joshua applauded her flawless performance, while the rest of the guests cheered excitedly in approval of her faultless recital of the famous Joshua Stark's number one best seller. "More! More! More!" The audience began to chant as Misty-Bleu was about to leave the stage. She hurriedly glanced over at William who smiled and nodded in pride. She lifted her hand and indicated with her index finger to the guests, "Only one more!" Bryan handed her the mic once again, and with no time to waste, she sang a song she had written for William shortly after she was forced to say goodbye to him, back in Shadow Falls. Her eyes straggled over to him, and she could in no way at all, take them off of him until the song was over.

While she looked at him, she was suddenly overcome with fear, and could not quite place her finger on what had terrified her so intensely and so suddenly. As she gawked nervously at him, she was sure that it looked as though he was fading away from her, almost as though he would be gone if she blinked. Growing increasingly anxious and unable to shake the feelings that had begun terrifying her, she shut her eyes, before she hurriedly opened them. She was at once relieved to see him standing there in all his glory, as he was only moments before. As she sang her song, she still couldn't shake the feeling that something was wrong with that very moment. She suddenly felt so far-removed from him, as though he would be gone from her soon.

William smiled when he noticed her hurriedly dab at the tears that had begun to glisten in her eyes. He could hardly ignore the pained expression on her face, and he wondered what was going through her mind as she stared at him. Again, he was captivated by her eyes, and the thousands upon thousands of stories they would tell him. While he stood wholly engulfed in her performance, the entire crowd broke out in applause one more time as Misty-Bleu swiftly made her way over to William, who had gently lifted her off the stage. "Are you okay?" He was at once staggered to find the tears rolling pitilessly from her eyes. When she stood lifelessly in front of him, he was once again overwhelmed by fear, and it felt as though someone had taken his lungs into their hands and were squeezing the life out of them. "Misty-Bleu?" "I'm fine, everything is just fine. I just, I missed you. I keep thinking something's going to happen and destroy all of this? Like, something isn't right in this moment? I keep thinking that I'm going to wake up, and nothing will be this way? Like this is all going to end soon, and there's nothing I can do to stop it. Something doesn't feel right, William? I am scared to death that, that this isn't real. I know I'm being silly, but I just can't shake this feeling?" William lifted her chin and kissed her, desperate to calm her down. "I love you, Misty-Bleu, there is nothing that's not right, right now. Nothing is going to end, don't think like that." "William, you must listen to me. Something is wrong. When … when I was singing, it looked like you were disappearing, like you were becoming invisible?" "Misty-Bleu, I have no idea what you are talking about?" "I know. I know it sounds crazy, and perhaps, it was just my imagination, but I can't forget what I saw. It is scaring me! I can't lose you, William! I can't! I won't ever survive losing you!" He placed his arms around her and kissed her passionately. "You won't lose me, ever. I am not going anywhere, okay? It's probably just the lingering effects of Stallion Fever."

"Okay then! Misty-Bleu, William has a surprise for you." Misty-Bleu turned around, and turned back to face William, before she looked back at Bryan who was still holding the mic in his hand. William took her hands and squeezed them gently. Joshua nodded at Bryan, and in a perplexing commotion, pink smoke was released from all four corners of the stage. Joshua placed his hand on William's shoulder and signaled for him and Misty-Bleu to look up. When Misty-Bleu lifted her eyes, they immediately caught a banner that read, "It's a girl!" She burst out crying before she turned back to William. He took her in his arms and swirled her around and around. When he finally placed her back on her feet, he held her face in his hands. "We're having a little girl …" Misty-Bleu erupted into laughter as she feverishly wiped the tears from her cheeks. She hugged him tightly, before she looked up at the smoke again. William stood behind her and watched as Bryan released pink balloons into the sky. "I am going to get us a soda to celebrate!" William whispered in her ear as she stared at the balloons that were floating around in the sky.

It had become darker suddenly, and the wind began blowing viciously through her hair. "Hurry up!" "Sure, be right back." He kissed her on her cheek before he made his way out to the bar behind the stage. Misty-Bleu lifted her eyes one more time, but this time, her eyes didn't hunt the balloons. She folded her arms around her waist, as she stared at the changes in the sky. Her heart was pounding when she was once again nudged, that something was terribly wrong in that moment.

When William placed his order for a glass of water and an ice-cold beer, he felt a hand rest on his shoulder. Abruptly turning around, he stared questioningly at the strange face behind him. It was an older man with glowing, silvery hair. He glared at William through his piercing blue eyes, yet he seemed friendly and harmless to William. "It's getting darker. By nightfall the portal will be closed." William frowned when he heard the old man whisper. "What are you talking about?" William felt shivers run through his entire body when he heard what the silver-haired stranger was telling him. "You know what I'm talking about. You slipped through, and you brought her with you. If you don't send her back, she'll be stuck here forever. And so will you." William lowered his head as his heart began to thrash at the speed of a freight train. "You have to let her go, now, today." "I can't. I don't want to send her back. I don't want to leave her. I need more time with her. Our daughter ..." "There is no more time. For each soul that passes, there is only one opening, and only one closing of the portal. We don't get to decide how long it is opened for. Only He does." He pointed up at the sky. "This is yours. Misty-Bleu will have hers someday, but this is your last chance to send her back. If you don't, your soul and hers will be trapped between this world and the next. A world between life and death, forever. You will never be able to move on." "She won't survive. I don't want to move on." "You should never have given her a glimpse into a life she could have had with you. She doesn't know that it is simply a peek into a world that could have been. She thinks it is all real." "I know. God, I know." "If you love her, you must send her back to live as she should and die as she should. Your souls will be lost for all eternity. Can you live with that? Are you prepared to take responsibility for her soul? Are you prepared to lose her forever when The Man upstairs has had enough? It's not up to you to trick the stars."

William shook his head and turned to catch a glimpse of Misty-Bleu. He saw her talking to Joshua as she gently stroked her belly. He looked back at the silver-haired old man that stood in front of him only moments before, but he was gone. William hurriedly glanced around him but could not find him anywhere. He looked up at the sky and noticed how the sun was disappearing fast. Glancing at his wristwatch, he knew that time was running out for them. He anxiously made his way over to Misty-Bleu when pure panic began to set in. He took her by her arm, and quickly led her away from the crowd. Misty-Bleu grew apprehensive as she tried to decipher the untaught fear on William's face. It was a look she had never seen before, and it scared her almost to death. "William?" "Misty-Bleu? God, I don't know how to tell you this. I am so, so sorry ..." "What William? What? You're scaring me!" It felt as though she could barely breathe when she heard the crushing shudder in his voice. "You have to go back ..." "Go back? Go back where?" "Misty-Bleu, listen to me. This isn't real. None of this is real. Nothing is as it seems." Misty-Bleu's heart began hammering so profusely, she could hardly breathe. "I, I don't understand? What are you saying?" "You've slipped through a portal with me, Misty-Bleu. I pulled you through. I couldn't stand to see you in so much pain, so I pulled you through. A long time ago, I pulled you through ..." She gasped for air, unsure of what William was telling her, "William? What are you saying! What portal?"

She glanced around her and was at once confused by the fact that they were unexpectedly alone and stranded at the stadium. The stage was empty. There were no party tables or balloons. There was nobody else in sight. There was no-one else, but them. "I ... I didn't make it, Misty-Bleu. When I got sick, I didn't make it. You need to remember; you must try and remember those last months before ... before I left ..." She clutched at his shirt, and began tugging at him, "You were fine, William! You were fine! I was there! You were fine! I was there when your results came in! I was there!" "No, Misty-Bleu, listen to me! I wasn't fine! You just didn't want to face it and blocked it all out when I slipped out. They … they admitted you to a psychiatric hospital in the days after, and you just kind of checked out of your life. Of your world." She let go of him and tried to make sense of what hi was saying, "William! What are you talking about! You are making no sense!" "I couldn't see you like that, so when the portal was still open, the one I slipped into, I watched you for a while and then … then, I just couldn't see you like that. Your soul died, but your body was still alive. I had already died, but it felt as though I was dying over and over again when I saw you like that. I grabbed you and pulled you into this world. One I created for us, for you and me to live in. Just like you used to. I remembered how you told me how beautiful it was, and how we lived there. So, I took you back to the elevator in the hospital, do you remember? When the power went out? I went back to that moment, and I pulled you through and changed all of this. The morning of my results. I took you back there, and we began again. We changed the outcome. We picked up from there, from that moment, in the elevator." Misty-Bleu began pounding at his chest with all her might, "William? No! No!" She fell to her knees and held onto her belly with all the strength she could muster up. He knelt down in front of her and placed his hands over hers. "I thought that; I just thought we could do this forever, but we can't. I didn't know, Misty-Bleu. There are rules and, you must go. You have to go back." "No, no, William no!" "The portal will be closing soon, and if you don't go back, your soul will be stuck here forever. You will loiter as a prisoner in a world that I can't be a part of, even though I so desperately want to. I have to leave just as you have to." "Don't, don't say these things! What about our daughter? What about our life? The farm? The Christmas trees! Is nothing real?" "They are all real, Misty-Bleu, and they are all waiting for you. Wilhelmina will have her colt, and you will have your daughter someday. It's just me, I'm not real. Our life isn't real, you and me, we're not real. Our daughter isn't real, but you will have her someday, with someone else. You must go back, without me. You must go back to your world." Misty-Bleu collapsed in his arms when she felt the entire world spinning around her, before darkness entirely invaded her, and pulled her into a deep, dark, and bottomless pit. "Oh God no, William! No!"

Alice VL

AFTERLIGHT

8

"Misty-Bleu, Missy, can you hear me?" Misty-Bleu opened her eyes, and groggily glanced around her. The white walls blinded her and began closing in on her when she realized that she was trapped in a room with four white walls waiting to swallow her up. She frantically searched the room for William, and when she realized that he was nowhere to be found, she cried out in excruciating agony for him. "William! William! William! Come back! Don't leave me!" Her tears began to bucket mercilessly from her eyes, and when she gazed down at her flat belly, her entire body began to convulse hysterically. "My daughter! Where is she? Where am I?" She swabbed violently at the tears that were drowning out her face. She glanced over at Joshua who had called her name only moments before and glared beseechingly into his eyes. "Joshua?" "Misty-Bleu, do you remember me?" He smiled sadly when he noticed the recognition in her eyes. "You, are you even real? I mean, did we meet, like, really meet?" "Yeah, when William was in hospital. Do you think we never met?" "Where am I?" "You're in The Garden House Care Center, you've been here for a while ..." "My farm?

Little Dreams?" "The farm is fine. William hired a couple to take care of your horses and your trees before he, well, before he left. I have been checking in for you. I hope you don't mind? When I found out that you don't have family, well, I just didn't want to see the place fall into disarray. It's beautiful there ..." Misty-Bleu was desperate to pinpoint what was real, and what she had lived in another life with William. "How long have I been here for?" "Quite a few months ..." "William died? I don't remember, Josh, I can't remember any of that ..." She hurriedly dabbed at the warm tears that were laying on her cheeks. "You sort of checked out after William died." Misty-Bleu burst into tears when she heard Joshua say it out loud. "I don't want to be here without him ..." He took her in his arms as she buried her head in his chest. "You have to try, Misty-Bleu, this is the longest you've been awake. This is the first time you recognize me ..." "I have to be where he is ..." "He's gone, but you're still here. Please Misty-Bleu, please let me help you. I promised William I would try." "You can't help me, Joshua." Joshua gently wiped her tears, "Please let me try?" "I can't live without him ..."

As she laid her head down on the pillow, she began having flashbacks of a life she could by no means at all, remember living. She was reminded of the day that she had walked into the elevator on the morning he was to receive his test results. She thought she had returned to his hospital room, and that she was there with him, when the results came back. That was how she had lived it. That was what her memory told her. That was how she remembered it. But, as she lay reflecting on that very moment, Misty-Bleu realized that nothing of what had happened or what she had remembered, was at all real. William had helped her create an alternative universe for her to live in. He adapted the outcome of his results, and he altered their ending for her, for just a while longer. "We lived, Josh, we had a life. That's what I remember. That's what was and is real to me. We were about to have a little girl. We lived. We had a whole other life. You and I sang together a few times on stage with Bryan. You did the gender reveal for our daughter! Can't you remember any of that? Did none of that happen? I don't know what is real anymore!" She yelled out as she gazed pleadingly at him. She could flawlessly recall the life they had led after William was discharged from the Coral Hill Oncology Hospital. "Was this all in my mind? Am I going crazy?" Joshua took her hands, and gently held onto them, "Misty-Bleu, it's normal to create an alternate reality when you lose someone. That's how some people cope with the pain and reality of losing someone they love, but you have to start healing. You can't keep going back there, it's not real. It is only in your head." "Don't! I didn't create anything! It was real! It happened! You know nothing, Joshua! We lived, even though it

Alice VL

was in a supposed portal through a moment in time, as William called it, we had a life! You were there! Don't tell me you weren't! How could you be there and not know? How can you live a life here and there? It doesn't make sense!" "Misty-Bleu, that's because you can't. There is no such thing as a portal, or a moment that freezes in time. It does not exist. I was with you at the hospital with William when he passed away. We were all there at his side. Don't you remember anything about the days that followed?" "No, no! No, Joshua, no! I don't remember that! I don't remember any of that!" She yelled out while interrupting him, not wanting to hear what Joshua had to say any longer.

She turned her back to Joshua and stared blankly at the white wall in front of her. She was at once unwillingly transported back to the day William told her he was dying. As though she was watching a movie play out in front of her, she remembered it as vividly as she remembered all she thought was real, and all she thought she had lived with William. He had pleaded with her to return to the hospital that same day, the day she thought she ran from the elevator, and back to him. Instead, she remained in the elevator and drove out to her farm for the shower she so desperately wanted to take. When she returned to the hospital later in the day, she was overcome and deathly afraid by the defeated look on William's face. He was visibly crippled by sadness, anxiety and immense fear had engulfed his entire body. She was horrified to determine the extreme exhaustion on his face, and she instantly knew that the results were not what they had both hoped for. Fear had begun to conquer and repellently consume her, as her heart began to trounce aggressively. She took his hands into hers and tried to find something in his eyes to tell her that everything would be just as she had said it would be. "What is it, William?" She glanced around her, and at once, she wondered where his parents were, and if his friend, Joshua, whom she met that same morning, was still around. "Misty-Bleu, come sit here next to me …" She could hardly ignore the trembling and frostiness of his hands. "What is it, William?" "They've, they've given me my results and, they've informed me of my prognosis …" William began explaining as calmly as he could what his diagnosis was, and how they wanted to approach his treatment, despite his grim prognosis. As he tried to explain word for word what he was told only minutes before, Misty-Bleu was sure that, at that very moment, her heart was about to stop beating. She felt her stomach turn and began to panic. Her heart could not bear to hear the finality in his voice, and her soul was overcome with a pain so excruciating, she was sure her body could not survive such an enormous amount of torture. "William?" "I have cancer, Misty-Bleu. It has spread throughout my body. They were right, it is in my thigh …"

Alice VL

He continued to explain as steadily as he could but was unable to hide the tears that were appearing at the surface of his eyes. Misty-Bleu got up from where she was sitting and turned to face the wall. At that very moment, she realized that she was not prepared for what he had told her, and she knew at that very moment, that it was something she never wanted to hear again. The word cancer was a word that was never used in her entire life. A word that had never made its presence known in her family. She never once considered the fact that it could happen to somebody she knew, let alone the only man she had loved, and for her entire life. "It can't be, it must be a mistake. You don't look sick, William?" She whispered tearfully before she lowered her head and gave in to her emotions as she began to forcefully sob. William got up from his hospital bed and stood behind her before he placed his arms around her. Misty-Bleu turned around to face him and rested her head on his chest. She could no longer hold back the flood of tears that were building up from inside her soul. "No, William, no. Please tell me, please tell me that ... that you'll be okay?"

She listened to the beating of his heart, and could barely imagine that it would stop someday, not too far from that very moment. She listened to the rhythm of what was keeping him alive, and how perfectly normal it sounded to her. When she looked up at him, she realized that he was crying too. They stood in silence as they clung to one another. They were both lost for words and held onto each other as though he might be gone by nightfall. "I ... I'm going to start treatment as soon as possible, Misty-Bleu. I am not giving up. I'll do all that I can and that is asked of me, but the doctors have prepared me for the worst, and I need you to prepare for the worst too. It doesn't mean I am giving up." William was desperate to prepare Misty-Bleu for the fate that inevitably awaited him. "No, William! No! We are not going to let this happen! We can't! Do you understand me? You have to fight this for us! For me! I just, I just found you again! I found you, William! I can't ... I can't go back to before, without you. There is so much you don't know about me, so many things I want to say to you." Misty-Bleu became frantic and lowered her head in his chest again. She said a silent prayer for mercy, and if mercy was no longer available, she prayed to change places with him. William was everything she never was, and Misty-Bleu felt that it would be only fair for him to be spared, than for her to walk the earth without him. She could not even begin to imagine her life without him. It was not an option for her, and she refused to accept that it would come to that. Misty-Bleu knew that her life was nothing without him, and that she would simply exist, and lead an existence without meaning, if he ever had to leave her.

Alice VL

She was angry that she had stayed away from him for so long and becoming wonderful for him no longer seemed as significant. It was at that very moment that Misty-Bleu understood how William was her pillar of strength. Her only support of an existence, and that she survived her childhood, simply because he had lived in hers. The idea that William would become deathly ill someday and possibly die, was something she had never once considered. It was something she was too afraid to even imagine. She rejected the reality that William could be taken away from her. It was only the night before that she saw him for the very first time since she had left Shadow Falls. She could not help but whisper into her soul how cruel life was treating her, and how it had continuously chewed her up, and heartlessly spat her out. He appeared healthy, and only moments before, he was excited about his future. They still had their entire lives ahead of them, and in less than twenty-four hours, Misty-Bleu felt that it had all come to an abrupt, and cold-blooded end.

When she mentioned how she might perhaps audition for a competition at The Academy only the night before, he was keen and excited to accompany her to the audition, even though he had no idea she could sing, until Joshua Stark recognized her from her on-stage performance in Bronlyn. "How can one-day change so many things?"

Alice VL

AFTERLIGHT

Misty-Bleu whimpered as the intense sadness that had entirely overwhelmed her, penetrated deep into her soul, allowing for a brand-new batch of tears to flow from her eyes.

Alice VL

AFTERLIGHT

Alice VL

9

"Misty-Bleu, you must remember! You need to remember so that you can heal, so that you can leave this place!" She once again heard the frustration in Joshua's voice as he called out to her, and when she gazed up at him, she felt his hand firmly clasped in hers. "Come on, Misty-Bleu. You must think back and remember!" "I can't do this. I don't want to. It hurts. I want to go back to our life. I want our little girl. I want to go back to where he is." She turned away from him, and allowed her mind to slip out, back to William. Back to the life she wanted to remember, the only life that she could bare to face. She wanted to go back to the portal where she was sure, he would still be waiting for her, and mend her shattered heart.

William was wholly reluctant to begin treatment and remained stubborn and head strong only days before his first round of radiation was to begin. Misty-Bleu had hurried home for a fresh change of clothes, and when she returned later the afternoon, Dave, Julia, and Joshua were in his room. When Misty-Bleu walked in, she could almost see the tension that was hanging in the air. She quickly placed her bag on the visitor's chair, before she walked up to him. "Hey, what's going on?" She gazed nervously into his eyes. Julia walked up to her, and placed her hand on her shoulder, "He's refusing treatment. The same treatment that could save his life!" Julia yelled out in frustration. "What? Why? You said you'd do what it takes?" She stared incredulously at William, who had lowered his head. "I want kids someday ..." His voice trailed off, and before he could carry on, Misty-Bleu interrupted him, stunned by his carelessness. "You'll be dead!" "I can't live out the rest of my life, not being able to have children!" "You won't, you'll be dead!" Misty-Bleu raised her voice as fear began to engulf her. "I need to be able to have kids!" William raised his voice only slightly, as Misty-Bleu stood staring at him in disbelief. "You need to be alive to have kids!" She shouted at the top of her voice, desperate to make him understand that without the treatment, there would never be children. "Stop saying that!" He grew increasingly frustrated by what Misty-Bleu was saying to him. "No!" "Get out!" He yelled again when he realized that she was overcome with anger for him. "Leave! I never asked you to come here!" "I won't! And you can't make me!" He walked up to her. "Try me!" Misty-Bleu realized at once that there was no way she could convince him of anything at that very moment. "Fine!" "Fine, and don't come back!" William was exasperated by her sudden anger. "I won't!" She yelled without turning around. "Ever!" He yelled again before he turned his back on her. "Fine!" She responded before she grabbed her bag, and hurriedly left his room.

William sat on his bed and shook his head. He ran his fingers through his hair, before he looked at Joshua who stood motionlessly and in silence, alongside Dave and Julia Carmichael. "Leave me alone, please." They all huddled together and walked out of his hospital room. William laid down on his bed and stared at the ceiling in frustration while hearing Misty-Bleu's words echo in his mind.

When Joshua came by later that night, he once again brought up the options for his treatment. William reluctantly agreed, after Joshua once again, emphasized the fact that he needed life to father children. The following evening, after all the forms were signed to commence treatment, he suddenly turned to Julia who had been discussing his treatment regime with a nurse. "She won't take my calls; her mobile is off." The nurse peeked through her glasses at William. "Are you talking about the lady with the blonde hair who's been here on and off?" "Yeah?" "She's in the nurses' lounge. She's been camping out there since yesterday." William frowned before he hurriedly made his way down the passage.

When he opened the double doors to the nurses' lounge,

he saw her curled up on a couch, fast asleep. Slowly making his way over to her, he knelt beside her before he gently wiped the hair that were covering her face. Her eyes flickered, and when they opened, he smiled sadly. "Hey ..." She sat up straight, before her heart began to hammer wildly. "Hey, what's the matter?" "Nothing. Have you been here the entire time?" "No? Only a crazy person would do that." "Well, then you should meet my girlfriend. A total psycho, but she's mine and I love her." He gazed lovingly at her, as she stared at him with a thousand questions in her eyes. "I am so sorry about yesterday ..." "Me too, William." "So, listen, I begin treatment tomorrow morning. It's just, those babies in your eyes, I need it to be me." She placed her arms around him and held him against her. She kissed him gently, before she took his hands, "I don't, I never wanted kids anyways. I need you."

Alice VL

AFTERLIGHT

It was only seven months after his first treatment began, that William was rushed to hospital during the night. Misty-Bleu spent all her free time with William at his house in Cotton Road, and even spent her nights writing her novel when he was asleep. She would rush back to her farm each morning to catch up with her publisher and reply to emails and messages. As the sun was about to rise, she would lead Captain Nimo and Wilhelmina out onto the fields, before she would speedily make her way back into her farmhouse. After a quick shower and a cup of coffee, Misty-Bleu would rush back to William. She would spend the entire day with him at his house, and when he was scheduled for treatments, she would drive him, and stay with him for the duration of his stay at the Coral Hill Oncology Hospital. She spent her nights with him, afraid that he may become ill during the night. The side-effects were horrendous to witness, but Misty-Bleu was sure that it would ultimately cure him. William grew increasingly silent, but the sadness in his eyes was what almost killed her. They hardly spoke about their dreams anymore, and when Misty-Bleu tried to make new plans with him, he would become angry at her.

The night that she rushed him to hospital, she abruptly woke up during the night when she heard him having trouble breathing. Although he kept reassuring Misty-Bleu that it would pass, she knew that it could quite possibly be the beginning of the end for both of them. While calling for an ambulance, she prayed to her God that He would spare the life of the man she loved more than anything and take her instead. When the ambulance failed to arrive within minutes, Misty-Bleu piled him into her car, and rushed at the speed of lightning until she reached the emergency room. It had been a long and hard road for them since he began treatment. William became extremely weak and was ill for most of the time. Misty-Bleu was devastated to watch him surrender to his illness, but she was comforted by her insistence that he would recover fully. For her, there was no alternative. She refused to accept that his cancer treatment would be in vain, and that the debilitating side-effects would be for nothing. She reminded him each day that it would all be over soon, if he never gave in, and submitted to his illness. When William was having a good day, they would once again dream about their future together. They would laugh about the past, and they would talk about all the twists and turns life had in store for them. He told her about Ana LaRue, a dancer he had dated on and off, and who was dancing to her heart's content in Paris. He told her how beautiful and intimidating she was, but he reminded Misty-Bleu that she was the one his soul loved.

Misty-Bleu slowly revealed all the secrets of her

childhood, but she could never go so far as to give him a copy of The Afterwards. His good days made Misty-Bleu happy. Those were the days that she optimistically believed that everything would be okay in the end. Then there were days that William nurtured desperation and attempted to prepare her for the worst. Those were the days she would fly into a fit of rage, before she would break down, and climb into bed with him. She would lay down beside him, just to hear him breathe. Each time he would mention the possibility of his death, Misty-Bleu would place her hands against her ears, and rush off out of his bedroom, while her tears flowed unreservedly from her eyes. As much as it entirely crushed her soul, it nearly killed William to leave her. It almost stopped his heart each time, while he pretended to be stronger than he really was. He knew that Misty-Bleu was fragile, and he could in no way at all, tolerate seeing her so entirely misplaced and defenseless. He spent most of his days worrying about her, or what would become of her when he was no longer close to her. He focused solely on her emotional state of mind, as he tried to spare her heart any avoidable hurt and agony. William knew that no matter what he said to her, or how desperately he tried to comfort her, there was nothing he could say to cleanse his body of the disease and make it all better again. He could not go back into time and alter the malicious and callous twists that had awaited them. There was nothing he could do to alter their future. He was powerless and utterly incapable of rescuing her from the torment and suffering he knew, was waiting for her. There was no way in the world, he could prepare her for life after he were to leave, and for the first time in his entire life, William Carmichael was convinced that he had miserably failed Misty-Bleu, in the worst way possible.

For most of their days, they paraded in front of one another with courageous and valiant faces, but late at night, Misty-Bleu would sit in the dark, and desperately cry for him. There were nights that she bargained with God, and selfishly begged him to rather take the life of a homeless person, but to spare William for her. She tried to make Him understand that without William, she would die too. She wanted God to know that she could not function without him, and that He may as well pick her up when He comes for William.

Misty-Bleu, Joshua and his parents were called to his bedside the very night she rushed him to the emergency room. It wholly shattered her heart to finally acknowledge how much damage the cancer had done to the boy she loved with her entire heart. Seeing him fighting for his life, tore into Misty-Bleu's emotionally crammed body, and there were times that she wished the disease would get her too. Misty-Bleu stood outside of his hospital ward, while Dave and Julia Carmichael were at their son's bedside. She could not hear what they were saying, but by the expressions on their faces, she knew that William was perishing. "William is asking for you, Misty-Bleu …" She turned around to find Julia standing in front of her, as her tears rolled inexorably from her eyes. Misty-Bleu hesitantly made her way over to him. Taking his hand into hers, and at that very moment, she knew that tomorrow would never come for him. Misty-Bleu was instantly blinded by her tears, and for the first time in her life, she welcomed that ever-familiar, and restricting lump in her throat that she knew, would silence her. "Misty-Bleu, I never wanted you to see me like this. This was never the way I thought it would be. You know I love you, right?" William swallowed with enormous exertion, as he tried to say goodbye to her. "No William! It can't be! We just spoke about our dreams! I came back to you! Don't let it be for nothing!" Misty-Bleu cried out to him, as she begged him to hold on for her. "Misty-Bleu, please, let me go …"

William was exhausted. He was suffering. The pain had increased immeasurably during his last few days. He was desperate to hold on, but he was tired, and at the same time, desperate to let go. Misty-Bleu stared at him, stunned, and convinced that he was giving up too easily. She was angry at him for asking something of her, he knew she could never do.

Alice VL

"William! How can you leave me? How am I supposed to carry on without you?" Misty-Bleu screamed at him through her streams of tears. "I don't want to leave you, Misty-Bleu. I just can't be here anymore, but I promise you, I will always be in your life. I will find you in the next, I swear it. Just, Joshua ... let him help you. Let him take care of you, Misty-Bleu, for me. He knows what to do, let him. I swear, Missy, I will find you in the next ..."

When Misty-Bleu stared into his dark eyes, she noticed for the first time how the life had begun withdrawing from him. She could see that William was exhausted. She lowered her head onto his chest, as he held her with all the strength that was left inside of him. Misty-Bleu sobbed irrepressibly as she begged him to fight just one more time. One last fight. As she begged and pleaded with him to hold her tighter, his breathing became labored and shallow. "William! No, please God, no!" She pleaded with William and then, she pleaded with her God. Julia placed her arms around Misty-Bleu, as they both stood sobbing sadistically when they realized that William had left them. She climbed onto the bed with him and clung to him while praying that he was still there. She desperately pleaded with God to breathe life back into him. When Joshua rushed in, followed by a handful of nurses, she grabbed his hands, and implored him to try and resuscitate him.

Joshua shook his head while looking down at her and

turned off the machine that had only seconds earlier, signaled that William's heart was no longer beating. Julia and Joshua pulled her away from William, before she left the hospital screaming hysterically, and fighting them through her hysterics. Misty-Bleu broke loose from Joshua and the Carmichaels and fled straight to her car. When she slid in, she lowered her head, and rested it on the steering wheel. Joshua ran after her, and when she noticed him approach her, she started the engine and drove off before he could stop her.

While driving back home to Little Dreams, the rain came crashing down in front of her, as thunder and lightning lit up the sky. She could barely see the road in front of her and knew how fitting the weather was. She wondered if the raindrops, and the enormous bolts of lightning knew that William Carmichael had just left her world. She couldn't help but wonder if they were in fact, lighting up his way as he left the earth. What she did know was, that it would be the darkest day in her entire life, no matter how bright the lightning was, or how low the stars would lay above her. It would be the one day that would be remembered for finally destroying her heart, and ultimately shattering her soul for once and for all. It would become the day that Misty-Bleu was sure, she could never survive. She silently prayed to God to have mercy on her heart and end her life on earth too. She begged Him to reach down and take her to William. "I have to be where he is ..." She shouted out through the tears that were gushing ruthlessly from her eyes. Misty-Bleu wanted to turn around and go back to William. She wanted to hold him against her and breathe new life into him. It never once crossed her mind that he could die. She never once believed or considered the fact that his life could be over, without any prior warning. For the first time in her life, Misty-Bleu felt completely alone and abandoned. She felt punished for all that had happened to her, and she blamed herself for angering God.

She glanced around her and noticed how people were beginning their days just as the sun was about to rise. She was angry that they were going about their lives, as though nothing was different, when her entire existence was falling apart around her. How could they act so normal when nothing mattered to her anymore, and when she could hardly breathe? She held her breath, desperate to stop breathing, but when her body took over and breathed for her, she slammed her fists into the steering wheel, and cried out in desperation. She wanted the world to feel what she was feeling. She wanted the strangers on the road around her, to take the smiles off their faces, and understand the pain she was in. She wanted the world to stop and become silent for William. They had no right to start their days and carry on, as though he was never here.

Joshua at once sprang into his car and followed Misty-Bleu home. He could in no way at all, get the look of utter devastation and despair on her face, out of his mind. He felt a jolt from the pit of his stomach when he replayed her sorrowful wail over and over in his mind. He was desperate to reach her, afraid of what she might do if she were alone.

It was only days before that William called Joshua over after Misty-Bleu had left to pick up his script from a local pharmacy. When Joshua walked into William's house on Cotton Road, he found him sitting quietly on the porch. "Hey buddy, how are you feeling?" Joshua hurriedly made his way to an empty seat next to William. "Ah, you know?" "So, what's up?" William turned to Joshua and looked him gravely in the eye. "I'm not going to get out alive, you know that?" Joshua lowered his head, before he nodded sadly. "I'm okay with that, Josh, I'm at peace with all of this. It's just, Misty, she believes that I'm going to get better. I've tried talking to her, I've tried preparing her for what you and I both know is going to happen, but she just won't hear it." Joshua shook his head before he looked over at William again, "Joshua, you've got to do something for me when I'm gone. You must help her. I've spoken to my parents, but you Josh, you must help her. Promise me …" "I don't know how to help her,

William?" William placed his hand on Joshua's shoulder, "Give her time, and then, get her into The Academy. Let her grieve through her music. I've seen her on stage, and I've seen how her fears are never really so very far off, but there's something that happens to her on stage. Something beautiful, do that. Let her do that." Joshua smiled, and nodded miserably, "I'll do what I can, I promise."

When Misty-Bleu arrived at Little Dreams, she sat in her car for what felt like forever. Finally, after opening her door, she found Joshua standing beside her. Misty-Bleu crumpled into his arms and sobbed vehemently into his chest. He held her in silence, and when he began to quiver slightly, she knew that he too, was bitterly falling apart at the loss of his best friend. "It will get better, Misty-Bleu, you have to believe that. He is free from suffering; he is free from pain. It just, it's better ..." He whispered softly as he dried the tears from her eyes. "It's better?" Misty-Bleu stepped back, and glared at him, before she interrupted him. "Better? Better!" She swallowed back profusely, as she continued to yell hysterically at him. "You say it's better? How can it be better? How can William's death be better? Better than *what*, Joshua? Better than having life? Better than *what*?" Joshua stared at her in silence, unsure of how to respond to her. For the first time in his life, Joshua Stark was silenced. "Just leave me alone!" She urgently made her way to her bedroom before she slammed the door behind her. Instinctively, she dialed William's voicemail just to hear his voice. "William here! Leave a message, and I'll get back to you!" Her heart began to batter when she heard his comforting and acquainted voice. The voice she fell in love with as a little girl, and the only voice responsible for the broadest smile on her face. He sounded exactly like the boy she left behind in Shadow Falls.

He sounded like the man she found again on a park bench of the Coral Hill Oncology Hospital, but he did not sound like a man riddled with cancer, that would be gone from her in a few months. She dialed his number over and over again, and each time his soothing voice told her to leave a message for him to call her back. For a single moment, Misty-Bleu considered leaving him a message, begging him to come back to her. She was desperate for him to call her back and tell her that they were permitted phone calls from Heaven.

Misty-Bleu reached for her photo album from underneath her bed and paged nostalgically through the photographs of William and of her. She relived each moment in each photograph, and although it by no means whatsoever, eased her pain, she could once again feel him with her. "William, come back to me. I'm not going to make it …" She whispered as she looked up and fought the tears that were desperately trying to escape from the corner of her eyes.

Not knowing what else to do, Joshua put on the coffee, and sat at the kitchen counter, before he buried his head in his hands. Discouraged by his own heartache and overwhelming sadness, he had no idea how William expected him to help Misty-Bleu. He was at once enraged at his friend for asking him to do the impossible. From the very core of his gut, he knew that nobody could save Misty-Bleu, but William. There was nothing he could do to help her find life again. All that she had ever valued and loved, had left with William when he closed his eyes for one final time. All her hopes and all her dreams were caught up in his soul and left the world with him. She was caged and imprisoned in her grief, and there was nothing he could do to release her from the chains that were wearing her down.

It was much later when Joshua finally had the courage to check in on her. He was relieved to find that Misty-Bleu had fallen asleep with her photo album on her chest, as she lay clutching her mobile phone. He covered her with a quilt, and gently kissed her on her forehead. Joshua suddenly realized that there would be extremely hard days ahead of her, and he prayed for some relief for her. Joshua slept on the couch that night, and almost each night afterwards.

Alice VL

Misty-Bleu remained in bed, and kept her curtains tightly drawn. He would check in on her each morning, carrying a cup of coffee for her, but Misty-Bleu would turn her back on him the moment he walked in. A little while later, Joshua would come back in to clear away her coffee mug, only to find it untouched. He would bring her something to eat during the day, but he would take it back to the kitchen when she refused to eat. He could hear her sob her days and nights away, as she lay curled up under the covers in her dark bedroom. Some mornings, Joshua would walk in and through utter frustration, pull her curtains wide open, but the moment he walked out of her bedroom, she would get up and close them again.

Joshua began taking Captain Nimo and Wilhelmina out to the enclosure each morning before the sun was about to rise, and at night, he would walk them back to the barn where he brushed them down just as Misty-Bleu would do. He would scan through her emails and respond to any messages that he deemed important. He had secretly taken her mobile phone, and kept the battery charged as he checked for messages and took her phone calls. Joshua did not leave Little Dreams even for a moment, and on the second day, he asked Julia to pack up, and bring fresh sets of clothes for him.

The evening before William's memorial service, Joshua

hesitantly knocked on her bedroom door before he walked in. Misty-Bleu laid curled up in the center of her bed, mumbling incoherently to herself. Joshua stood unresponsively as he stared at her and tried to make sense of what she was saying. He could not help but notice how she was fading away into the darkness, and he could no longer bear to see her slowly giving up. "Misty, it's William's memorial service tomorrow, you must get up. You must get out of bed." He sat down on the bed beside her, where she laid with her back towards him. He gently touched her shoulder, before she slowly turned to face him. Joshua was horrified to detect the dark circles around her bloodshot, and distended eyes. Her beautiful blue eyes had turned a dark, misty gray, and her skin tone had turned ashen. Her long, blond tresses were wildly trying to find a place on her head, and when she peeked through her hair at him, he knew that Misty-Bleu had finally given up, and entirely surrendered to the blackness that had overwhelmed her. "I have to be where he is ..." She whispered softly, before she turned away from him. "I have to be where he is. I've been talking to my angel, and, he said that it's okay ..." Joshua turned her around to face him, suddenly overcome by a crippling fear. His heart was pounding fiercely. He was convinced that Misty-Bleu could hear the hammering from inside his chest. "Misty-Bleu? What did you do? What did you do!" He shouted out at the top of his voice, while lifting the quilt that was covering her. He was horrified to discover that she was lying in a pool of blood, and when he grabbed her hands, he understood where it had come from. She had slit her wrists with the blades of a razor she had taken apart. She smiled at him, before her head fell backwards, and her mouth began turning blue. "Misty-Blue! Missy! Stay with me! Oh God, Missy!" Joshua shouted out in angst as he pressed the quilt down on her wrists, desperate to stop the bleeding. He grabbed his mobile phone, before he frantically dialed the emergency number of his hospital, and hurriedly summoned an ambulance to her address. When he tossed the mobile on the bed, he held her in his arms, and pleaded with her to stay. "Oh God, Misty, please stay with me!" He begged her over and over again.

"I've got to be where he is …" She mumbled as she closed her eyes to this world and opened them in a world where William was waiting for her. In the portal, there where she had to be. She remembered nothing of the months leading up to his death, and was at once, taken back to the elevator of the Coral Hill Oncology Department.

Alice VL

AFTERLIGHT

Alice VL

10

Misty-Bleu turned around, and laid staring at Joshua as she relived the night William died. For months, she watched him lose his battle, while she firmly believed that he would survive, and for months, she was trapped between the four walls Joshua had her locked in. Yet, and at the very same time, for months, she had lived with William in a portal. "Why did you save me?" Misty-Bleu whispered in anger to Joshua, as he sat staring at the tears that were shimmering in her eyes, once again. "You remember? Oh God, Missy, you remember?" Joshua handed her a glass of water, and hurriedly wiped away the warm tears that had begun to roll onto her cheeks. Misty-Bleu became enraged at once and sat up straight only to smack the glass from of his hands. As it fell to the ground and shattered into a hundred pieces, she grabbed a broken shard and mindlessly, lifted it to her throat.

Joshua struggled with her as he tried to seize the broken shard of glass from her hands, and as they wrestled, he slipped, and fell back onto the cold floor of her room. He felt an unknown warmth trickle from his chest, as he frantically gasped for air. He could not speak, and when all he could hear were desperate gargling sounds coming from his mouth, he knew that Misty-Bleu had stabbed him in the struggle. He laid staring ahead of him, suddenly acutely conscious of how bright the light above him was. His eyes grew heavier as he fought to keep them open. Misty-Bleu hovered anxiously over him as her body began to tremble uncontrollably. She dropped the bloodstained shard of glass, and frantically knelt over him. She stared at the wound in his chest, and realized at once, that she had wounded him. "Joshua! Joshua!" She shook him violently, and frenetically shouted out for help. When her bedroom door opened, she was at once relieved to see what looked like a doctor and a couple of nurses, rush in. Misty-Bleu was at once restrained, as she stood staring at Joshua lying unconsciously on the floor. "Help him! Please, I didn't mean to hurt him!" She hysterically pleaded with them to save Joshua's life.

As the voices became distant, Joshua closed his eyes and drifted off into a deep, unnatural sleep. He felt no pain, yet his eyes were too hefty to keep open. Before he fell asleep, he heard Misty-Bleu plead with him to open his eyes, but he was suddenly overcome with exhaustion. When he opened his eyes again, he glanced around him in mystification. There was nothing, but what seemed like sky that had entirely surrounded him. He glanced down at his chest and saw no indication that he was stabbed only moments before. In utter bewilderment, he looked up, and was astonished to find William standing over him. "William?" Joshua rose to his feet and grabbed William's hand with both of his. "Am I dead? Did I die?" "No. You lost quite a bit of blood and slipped into unconsciousness, but you'll be okay. They're working on you now …" William smiled wretchedly as he squeezed Joshua's shoulder. "Where are we?" "We're in between somewhere. Like a portal, a half light. I know it sounds crazy and, I'm not quite sure how this works really …" "A portal? Is this what Misty-Bleu was talking about?" "Yeah, I should never have pulled her through. What happened to you today, was all my fault. I alone did this." "So, wait. She wasn't making it all up?" Joshua was overcome with shock, and at once devastated that he hadn't believed Misty-Bleu. "I wanted for us to stay here, you know? It's just, it doesn't work like that. The portal opens, but it closes again. Joshua, you have to go back, and you must take care of her. Forgive her for hurting you, she didn't mean to, it was an accident. You have to bring her back to the living. You must help her live again. I should never have brought her here. I should never have let her live here, with me." "She's never going to survive this, you know? For months, she just left. She clocked out. She believes in this world, this portal. She wants to come back here …" "She left because I gave her somewhere to go. She will live if you help her. You must help her, bro. Now you can

Alice VL

understand what happened to her and where she was. You know about the portal. You know what I've done. Don't tell her it wasn't real, don't tell her it never happened. Give her something real to live for again. Give her something to look forward to, one day." "She can't, William, she can't live without you. Twice, she tried to take her own life. Nothing I can do will help. I've tried for months. I can't get through to her. She keeps slipping out, it's like she checks out the moment she remembers. She's going to find a way out permanently. I can't help her, William. I can't keep my promise to you."

"You must stop her. She has life. She must live. If she finds a way out, she'll be stuck in a whole lot of nothingness forever. She will be trapped in a world between mine and hers. She can't take her own life. You must tell her that. You must convince her of that." "No, William. She doesn't care. She already thinks that there, here, is the only place she'll ever find you. Just stop! You brought her here into this world that you call a portal. You gave her a glimpse into a life you both could have had. She talks about a daughter? You lived here with her, and you created a whole new memory for her. One she is clinging to and slipping out to. She is there in that world without you, with one foot in this world with you. I can't change this. I can't change what she's lived, even if it wasn't real to the rest of the world. It was real to *her*. You made it real for her. It was a kind of a real, William. Just like this is, here, you and me! You have to go back, William. You must go back and fix this." "I can't go back?" "Yes, you can. I'll stay, and you go back. Take my place, bro. Go back as me." "I can't ask you to do that?" "You're not asking me to do anything, Will. Go back. She's not going to make it if you don't, and I just can't see her like that. You weren't there that night when she … you didn't hear her say how she was talking to her angel. I can't, I love her, William. I do, but she, she is never going to make it without you." "She won't know it's me, Joshua?" "No, maybe not, but you will know, and you will know how to help her. I don't. I can't help her. Nothing has worked. You know her better than anyone else does, you will know how to help her." "What about your life, Josh? Your amazing life? Your music? You are a superstar?" "Ah, I think I'm going to like it here much more. Besides, imagine the music you two can make together? You will be me, William, but it will be you. You will inherit all I do, but just don't mess with my name." Joshua winked playfully as he tried to find humor in their untrained situation. "I don't know, Joshua? Isn't that like bending the rules way too much?" "And you haven't? You've already taken it too far, William. Go fix things. You were given a raw deal, and so was she. Go fix her. Go set this right."

Alice VL

William lowered his head as he firmly clutched Joshua's hand in his. "The Academy, William, that's what will save her, you were right. It must. Do your homework on this, okay buddy? They've invited me to host and judge the competition, while performing with the finalists. All the contestants will be staying in a house over a period of time. I'm not sure for how long? The contestants will be eliminated one by one. No outside world interference, nothing. Just you, the counselors, and the contenders. I took the liberty of entering her, and she made it through to the finals. Start there, William. All the information is on my desk at my practice. Start there." William leaned forward and placed his arms around Joshua. He hugged his friend, before he dolefully retreated from him. "I'm going to miss you, buddy. You know that when the portal closes, you can't change your mind, you can't go back?"

William was anxious to take Joshua's place, but he was terrified that Joshua might regret changing places and changing lives. "I was done with that life anyways, bro! I know you love Misty-Bleu; I know you do, but I also know that I cannot help her. You should never have died. She loves you. She needs you. Not me, she doesn't need me." "I don't know what to say? I sure am going to miss you. Thank you for taking care of Misty-Bleu, thank you, my friend."

Alice VL

AFTERLIGHT

William embraced Joshua again, before everything around them turned black.

Alice VL

AFTERLIGHT

Alice VL

11

William groggily opened his eyes, and anxiously glanced around him. The white walls around him unnerved him at once, and the bleeping of machines around him seemed almost too familiar. He sat up straight as his heart frantically began to race. He was at once reminded of a time that the bleeping of a machine was all that was keeping him alive. He felt a sharp pain originate from his chest, and when he looked down, he noticed that a bandage had been placed on the stab wound to Joshua's chest. He smiled broadly, as he sighed an indebted sigh for his friend, Joshua Stark. "It worked; I can't believe it worked!" William blurted out as he glanced around him. He could barely fathom the idea that he had returned to a world, he never wanted to leave in the first place. He had returned to Misty-Bleu, even though she would recognize him as his best friend, Joshua Stark. William was ecstatic at the mere notion of having been given a second chance with her. He at once thought about the daughter they would have someday, and he smiled gloomily when he thought of Joshua, who would never live to meet her. "You're awake! Welcome back, Dr. Stark ..."

Alice VL

He swiftly lifted his head and turned to find a young nurse adjusting the fluids in his drip. "Where am I?" "Do you remember anything?" "Not really, I mean, I'm a little hazy on the details." "Ms. Buchanan stabbed you with a shard of glass. The police are here and will want to interview her soon." "No please, it was an accident. We struggled and she dropped the glass as I grabbed for it. It was all just an accident, a horrible misunderstanding. Please, keep the police out of this. She is very fragile at the moment, and a patient of mine." He reached for the nurse's hand as his heart rate suddenly increased to a dangerous level. "Alright, you must keep calm. I'll go see them now, just please calm down." She had just propped William's pillows underneath his head, desperate to make him comfortable, when she made her way to the nurses' station. As she approached her colleagues, she noticed two policemen waiting to interview her.

William watched them through the enormous glass window of his hospital room and was instantly relieved when they looked over at him, before they turned to leave. He peeked over to a mirror directly across from him and was not quite prepared for the image that stared back at him. He was no longer William Carmichael. He was no longer the man Misty-Bleu once fell in love with, and he would never again be the man she would recognize as her one great love. His heart remained intact, and

Alice VL

his soul still belonged to him, but all there was about him that she once recognized and loved, was gone forever. To return to her, William knew that he had to change all that was unique and familiar about him and transform into Dr. Joshua Stark. If he were to love her one more time, he would be compelled to love her as his closest friend, Joshua Stark. He would have to find a way to make her fall in love with him, all over again. He felt a sudden twinge rush through his heart when he realized how daunting it would be, to convince her to give her heart to another man.

William was suddenly intensely afraid of his ability to step into another man's shoes, while his memories of his life as William Carmichael, would continue to haunt him for the remainder of his life. He was terrified that Misty-Bleu would shun him, and he was scared to death of the fact that she may never survive losing William, him. He was saddened by the reality that he could never see his father or mother, through the eyes of their son again. He had no idea how to step into the untutored life of Joshua Stark, and he had no clue as to how he would veil his secret from the world, and for the rest of his life. He thought back to the moments they spent in the portal. He reflected on the life they had created, and he relived their ups and downs. His mind drifted back to the magical time while they awaited the arrival of their daughter. In their portal, the in between he had pulled her into, there was an immense reason to live, an enchantment the universe conjured up only for them.

They were both given a second chance for a new start and a new beginning. As though it had happened in their world, William knew that the memories of what they had lived after life was stolen from him, would have to remain a secret, even though Misty-Bleu would live the remainder of her life with her memories of the portal, and he with exactly the same. They would wander through life, remembering the same things, the same events and precisely the same emotions. They would miss the exact same moments, yet he could never tell her that it was him, and that he missed those moments too. He could never let her know how he lived with her during their time in the portal, and he could never allow her to catch a glimpse into his memories of their alternate universe. All that had happened in their in between could never be shared in memories with Misty-Bleu.

He had no inkling as to how to win Misty-Bleu over, for Joshua. He had never had to persuade her to love him before. They were instinctively drawn to each other and came together almost unnoticed. Intuitively, they were thrown and hurled towards one another, and they welcomed it with open arms. They loved each other from the very beginning, and it was something William knew, Misty-Bleu cherished and would never betray. When he thought back to The Afterwards, he became enraged once again, as he considered all that she had been through, and all he had failed to protect her from. He was angered by the abuse and anguish she had suffered, and he was horrified by the torture and misery she was enduring at that very moment. The torment of his very own death.

As William lay thinking of Misty-Bleu, he swore to never leave her side again, and that he would sacrifice his life to save her and give her hope for a life with him again, even if it had to be as Joshua. He would remind her heart of the love hers had for him, and he would never stop proving to her soul that he had come back to her, even though he could never tell her the truth. He knew that eventually, her soul would recognize his, and that she would love him, once again.

William again reflected on all the occurrences that had taken place in the portal. For a moment, he could barely distinguish between what was real in this world, and what was real in the portal. He did not quite know where to draw the line, and how he would pretend that they never lived in an alternate reality. He could never let her know that Joshua had sacrificed his life in this world, simply so that he could return to her, and love her in her world, one more time.

Alice VL

Alice VL

AFTERLIGHT III – NEW LIGHT

1

"Perhaps tonight it will be his eyes I see, his touch I feel and his warm breath on me. Perhaps, after tonight, I will no longer search for his soul in someone else's body. Perhaps tonight, my search will be over."

William sat in silence in the visitor's chair next to Misty-Bleu's bed, in the white-walled room she had chosen to shut the world out from. He sat gawping at her as she slept, and thought back to a moment in time, back in the portal, when he had once before, kept a watchful eye on her. It was the same day he had discovered that she was carrying their child. The day her beloved Wilhelmina birthed her colt after tremendous strain and great difficulty. He thought back to the vision that awaited him when he walked into her barn and found her resting on her knees, on bales of straw that covered the floor, as she feverishly stroked Wilhelmina's long mane. Her plait had come undone, as she incessantly wiped away the dampness on her forehead. His eyes shadowed down to her belly, and what he saw, left him speechless and for a moment, he was unable to move even a single step forward. For an instant, he stood limply as he considered the secret her belly had revealed to him. He longed for their existence in their in between, and he ached to have Misty-Bleu buried safely in his arms, one more time. He was desperate that she fights one last battle to salvage the wreckage of her broken heart, yet he was confounded by the reality that his death had heartlessly and ultimately, destroyed her. He unwittingly shook his head in utter revulsion and despair, as he reflected on her torment at the hands of her parents. She had persistently remained strong-minded and driven to free herself from their cruelty. She fought courageously to remain resilient and incorruptible through the horrors of all she had endured under them. He was enormously honored by her unfaltering bravery, and he was proud of how they remained powerless, and unable to break her. It saddened him immensely to accept the fact that the only thing it ever took for her to surrender to an existence of wretchedness and darkness, was his final breath in this world.

"Come back to me, Misty-Bleu ..." He whispered sadly as he soothingly caressed her damp cheek. He could no longer stand to see her tears escape from the corner of her eyes and roll relentlessly onto her cheeks. He dried her tears as often as he could, but he was unable to abolish her grief as she lay there sleeping. Every so often, she would shudder slightly, and call out his name before she would turn around and erupt into a violent outburst of inconsolable anguish. William leaned back in his chair and closed his eyes, before he said silent prayers to a God, he hoped would forgive him for breaking her heart, and then again, for seizing her, and fleeing into the portal with her. He could never expunge her memory of the life they had lived in, in their in between.

It scared him almost back into the clutches of death, to consider the penalties of his impulsiveness. It was an escape she did not ask for, or had a choice or a say in. She would spend the next few years of her life recalling every aspect, and each moment of her time in the portal, as though it had taken place in the real world. She would devote her coming years to yearning for the daughter she almost had, in a life she so desperately hankered after. They were memories that would linger inside of her until the day it would be her turn to leave this world. He was desperate to release her from her memories of an event where she thought he would survive an illness she was never prepared for. For the remainder of her life, their survival in the portal would come back to haunt and taunt her, over and over again.

Alice VL

Alice VL

Misty-Bleu was immensely relieved to find Joshua asleep in an empty chair next to her bed. She smiled forlornly but was profoundly indebted to him for the hurt and aggression she had inflicted upon him. She was thankful and deeply appreciative of the fact that he seemed to have fully recovered from his wound. She was devastated by the reality that she had almost taken his life in a moment of pure anger and sheer desperation. It would be a moment that she would live contritely, for the rest of her life. As she lay watching him, she could not help but feel a powerful sense of unanticipated ease that had exuded from Joshua. She glowered slightly when she reflected back to a time in their portal, that William once lay asleep in a chair beside her bed in her farmhouse at Little Dreams. A time when she was eagerly awaiting their child, in a moment she had so much to hope for and look forward to. She thought back to how dreadfully Wilhelmina had struggled to birth her calf, and how William had stepped in, and saved the day for her, and for her beloved purebred Murgese. That was the exact day he had found her again. The very day he had discovered that she was carrying his child. Misty-Bleu grinned unintentionally when she thought back to how William's mere presence would brighten up her darkest and loneliest days. He unequivocally mastered the uncanny ability to connect with her soul, and to love her in a way, no other man ever could, or would ever hunt to after him. She closed her

Alice VL

eyes, frantic to conjure up the image of his eyes in her mind.

"Josh ..." Misty-Bleu's voice faltered somewhat, as she almost indistinctly whispered his name. She reached out and touched his hand and was instantly unprepared for the sudden rush of exhilaration that had begun to overwhelm her entire body. She immediately pulled back her hand and lifted her head before she sat upright on her bed. She glowered liberally at him as she stared directly at his sleeping face. She grew increasingly anxious as she tried to make sense of the abrupt, yet unanticipated emotions that had begun to arrogantly flicker inside of her. She was in no way at all, prepared for the emotions that were beginning to taunt her. She could not identify with or relate to the sensations that were beginning to frighten and unnerve her.

William groggily opened his eyes when he felt her hand touch his, and at once beamed with joy, when he noticed her upright on her bed. At the same time, he frowned tensely when he realized that she had fixed a secure, yet interrogative glare at him. He at once sprang from his chair, and summarily made his way over to her bed before he sat down beside her. He nervously took her hand in his and gently squeezed it, while he tidied away her hair that had wildly cluttered her face. She gasped for air when he touched her, again overawed by sensations she had hardly been acquainted with or could even begin to understand. "Hey, beautiful …" He whispered gently before he kissed her on her forehead, relieved that she had finally woken up. "I'm so sorry, Joshua, I'm so sorry. Are you okay?" She spontaneously flung her arms around his neck as she wept inconsolably in his arms. The mere thought that she had come so close to ending his life, was almost too much for her to stomach. "Hey, please don't cry. I am fine. It was just a scratch." He held her possessively against him and was at once deeply grateful to Joshua for having given him the ability to return to her, and feel her against him, for one more lifetime.

Misty-Bleu held onto him, once again exposed to the untaught feelings that had intensely overawed and silenced her. For the first time since William had left her, she felt disturbingly, yet wonderfully safe again. She felt an irresistible responsiveness in his arms and for a moment, she felt as though her heart was wholly acquainted with his. The scent of his skin had left her feeling delightfully unscathed and warmly sheltered. Her heart gently sputtered in vibrancy as she rested her head on his shoulder. For the first time in what felt like forever, there was not a single tear that had threatened to gush from her eyes. She soaked up the feelings of weightlessness she had unsuspectingly welcomed into her soul. William retreated slightly before he lifted her chin scarcely enough for their eyes to meet, "Misty-Bleu, listen to me. You have to let me help you, okay? You owe me this one chance to help you. You owe me a chance to try and help you recover, and if I can't, you can walk away. I won't stand in your way. I will let you walk away, and I will leave you to do what you need to do, whatever that is. But please, just let me try and help you get through this. You can't question me, and you cannot back out or change your mind. You must give me a fair chance." She smiled miserably as she listened to him pleading with her. She could hardly grasp why it was that he had never given up on her, or why he had stuck around for her. She revered in his perseverance, and she trusted his willingness to help her through her crushing pain, and destructive loss. She knew that she was obliged to give Joshua an opportunity to help her, even if it was to simply pacify her own conscience and integrity.

She realized then that it was up to her to play her part and meet him midway. Even though she knew into the innermost core of her that she would never recover from losing William, she was obligated to them both, to get up and place one foot in front of the other, even if it was only one day at a time. She had almost cost Joshua his life and yet, he was holding her protectively in his arms, begging her to let him help her. She knew at that very moment, that he should in all fairness, despise and rebuke her for the damage she had inflicted upon him. She was keenly aware of the fact that she needed help, and that she could no longer cling to the hope that William would meet her in the portal, even only one more time. Joshua was right, she owed him a chance and she owed herself a chance.

"Okay …" She whispered hoarsely as she folded her arms around her waist. "Okay, Josh. What do you want me to do? I just … I just can't stay here anymore. I need to get out of here. These walls are suffocating me …" "You don't have to stay here, Misty-Bleu. The Academy has invited you to participate in their annual superstar competition. It's not as depressing and solitary as it is here. You can sing and dance, and you'll make friends with people that are more like you, okay? There are twelve of you, and I'll be there every step of the way with you. It'll be like living at college again. We are going to stick around there for a while. I want you to promise me you will give it a shot, and that you won't hurt yourself. You have to try and work with me, okay? They can't know we know each other, alright? For me, for William. The farm is fine. Your trees and horses are fine. Everything will still be there when you're ready to face the world and go home again. But, if you don't agree to this, you will be forced to stay here, and there is nothing I can do about it, do you understand?" "Is there anybody at the farm, the couple you mentioned earlier?" She was at once overcome with worry for the beautiful horses that she adored and prized so immensely. "Yes, I'll go into detail a little later, but there are people taking care of the farm for you. You must not worry."

"Let me guess? Eduardo and Maria?" She whispered almost inaudibly as she lowered her head. William pretended not to hear, and was again, reminded of the incidents in the portal. For an instant, Misty-Bleu was sure that she could feel William close to her again. The way Joshua had gently spoken to her, reminded her of how William would talk to only her. She closed her eyes as she tried to breathe in the memory of how it made her feel at that very moment, afraid that not too long from that very moment, Misty-Bleu might forget all she had once known and remembered about him. They were moments she was frantic to cling to, and desperate to hold onto. She wanted to lock away all that she was not ready to let go of yet, and bury it in a chamber of her heart where she could go anytime she wanted, and invoke them whenever she needed to. She kept her head bowed and replayed all that Joshua had just told her. She shook her head before she lifted her eyes and stared into Joshua's. She smiled sadly when she realized that it was the first time she had looked so intensely into his eyes. It instantly reminded her of her Fraser Fir Christmas trees on the farm, and she anxiously surveyed them when she spotted what seemed like a million yellow spots.

"Okay, Josh, if that's what you ask of me, I will try. I can't promise you anything. I can't promise it will work, but I do promise you here, today, that I will try and that I will do my very best. But, at the end of the competition, you have to stop. You must promise to stop trying to fix me?" "That's all I am asking, Missy, nothing more." William reached into his pocket and pulled out a sealed envelope with her name on it, "I have a letter for you from William. He left it for you. I just wasn't sure when to give it to you? I'll leave you alone to read it. Just call if you need me." Her heart began to beat fiercely when she took the letter from Joshua. Her hands were quivering as she held it possessively in her hands. William lovingly stroked her cheek before he turned to leave. "Josh, wait. Why? I just want to know why?" She huskily called out to him before he turned around to face her again. "I mean, why all this? Why are you doing this? You don't really know me? You certainly don't owe me a damn thing. You've, we've only really met a few times. And yet, you've been here for me since that night. Since that night, you haven't left my side, why?" Her tears had slowly begun to glisten in her eyes. William walked back to her and placed his hands on her shoulders. He gently wiped the thawing tears from her cheeks, before he achingly kissed her on her forehead, "Because, William loved you

Alice VL

more than life itself. Because William made me swear, and because ... because Misty-Bleu, William needs you to survive this. Because, you are worth fighting for, and because Missy, this is what we do for those we love."

William had penned the letter to her only moments before. From that very same hospital chair next to her bed, he wrote her, desperate to pass it off as one he had written before he had died. He hoped that it would give her an insight into his emotions before he passed away, and he prayed that it would guide her, and show her the way from that moment forward. He was anxious to find a way to reach her through his own, authentic voice. He wanted to comfort her, but more than anything, he needed her to survive. He was frantic to let her know, that he, William, needed her to survive.

'To my darling Misty-Bleu,

I know that if you are reading this letter, I am no longer here with you. I am so sorry that I had to leave you, I so wish I could stay. I would just about do anything to stay with you. I pray for you to carry on, and if you make it through to the finals, you have to go through with it, for me. Don't be mad, you need to do this! Yeah, yeah! Josh helped me conspire against you! I know that singing was never in the stars for you, but I want you to try it. Even if only to find your place in the world again. Please don't be mad that we sent one of Bryan's recordings of you in. Misty-Bleu, I know you are feeling anger and hurt at the moment, I felt it too not too long ago. You will get over this, and you will get through these days, but first, you must know a few things. I am there with you, always. When you think you feel me, it's because you do, and I am there. When you feel something normal or familiar, it's because I am right there with you, trying to show you. When you think you see me in someone else, perhaps I am or perhaps, I am just close by. I know things are going to get so rough for you, but you must promise me to try and find me in all that I've left behind for you. Let Joshua help you, for me. Give him a chance, Missy, he wants to help you. Find me there with him and let him help you. Listen to him. Feel him and hear him. Look closely and know ... know how much I want you to let Joshua help you. He is a great man, you know. We've had some beautiful moments together, and you have so much love inside of you, it will kill me all over again to see you waste it just because you think I'm gone. I'm not. I've simply slipped out for a while. I know ... I know you will go through a period of magical thinking, Misty-Bleu, apparently, that happens and is a thing. But when it's over, please, please let Joshua help you. I'll be waiting for you anytime you need me, but you must live again and if you think you can't, you must at least try. I love you, Misty-Bleu. William

Alice VL

AFTERLIGHT

P.S. I am so much closer than you think.'

Misty-Bleu folded his letter and placed it back into the envelope. She pressed it against her heart before she got up and walked over to a window. She gazed out and peeked at the world below her. She smiled when she gazed up into the sky and knew that William was looking down on her. "Wait for me …" Misty-Bleu whispered, and for the first time since William's death, she did not feel as though her heart was about to stop beating.

Alice VL

2

The days following her awakening left Misty-Bleu in an aimless and wandering haze. She was convinced that her emotions were placed on a roller coaster, but that it had been rocketing her to darker downs, than to perkier ups. She would laugh out loud one moment, and merely a moment later, she would fall to her knees, and cry out in excruciating agony. She was tremendously susceptible to violent outbursts that would threaten to erupt within her more often than she would care to admit to. She was wrathful and indignant. She was enraged by the endless wheel of emotions that would overwhelm her when she least expected it. She detested her life; she hated that William was gone and would never return to her. She experienced emotions that left her devastated and crushed, all at the same time. When she became silent, Misty-Bleu was no longer sure who she was angry with, or what it was that had triggered her unanticipated impressions.

She would flare up for no reason at all. Misty-Bleu would surrender entirely and completely fall apart, and into a bottomless pit of nothingness, the one she had lived in not too long ago. She would berate herself for her debility, and she would become infuriated with all around her. She made a conscious decision to ignore all Shaun and Kevin's calls to her, and she snubbed both David and Julia Carmichael's messages to her. She had instructed the staff at the clinic to withhold all communication from the outside world from her. She made it clear that she would not at all, take calls or see visitors, other than Joshua Stark.

William would make an enormous effort to pacify Shaun each time he called for Misty-Bleu, but after a while, he no longer knew what to say or how to excuse her behavior. He could not compel her to make contact with the outside world, but he prayed that she would reach out to them soon. There was nothing he could do, to calm the uproars inside of her, or quieten the chaos that would absolutely overpower her when she least expected it. He would watch her fall apart, and then he would watch her get up again. As he guarded her from a distance, he watched her desperation to cling to life by grasping at invisible straws. William was afraid that she might ultimately surrender to her anguish, and slip out just as quickly, as he had slipped back in.

The night after she had read William's letter, she was shaken and stunned to uncover how incensed she was with him.

Alice VL

She was angry that he had left her. She was outraged by his death and then, she became resentful towards the portal he had snatched her into, even if it only occurred in her mind and through her hallucinations. She was aggravated by the fact that he had allowed her a glimpse into a life they should have had. She longed for the daughter she thought she would have, and she yearned terribly for the life he had promised her in their in between. She was livid that he had damned her back into a life she would be duty-bound to live in, without him. When her anger was finally replaced by downright despair, Misty-Bleu was humbled by her opinions and bitterness towards him. She knew from the bottom of her heart, that William did not willingly choose to leave her. If the portal had been real, and not merely a deluded figment of her imagination, he must have grieved too. For the first time since coming back from the portal, she understood how challenging it must have been for him to let her go and send her back to a life he was obliterated from. She sympathized with the unspeakable pain he had hidden from her, while he knew from the very beginning, that he was inevitably going to die, and leave her behind. William loved her, and he had chosen her for him, over and over again. She blatantly criticized and harshly scolded herself for not once considering all that William had gone through.

Alice VL

AFTERLIGHT

As the time came closer for her to leave the clinic, Misty-Bleu was determined to try and escape that deep, dark and damning pit she was regularly flung into, just as she promised Joshua. She was committed to making a valiant effort to deal with and move past her grief. She bravely swore to discard the memories of her period of magical thinking when he lived with her in the portal. She wanted to apologize to Dave and Julia Carmichael for ignoring their messages, and for placing great distances between them. When Misty-Bleu folded William's letter after she had re-read it for the umpteenth time, she hurriedly made her way to Joshua, and begged him to allow her a phone call to William's parents. William agreed at once and stood silently as he listened to Misty-Bleu express herself without excusing her behavior. She profusely apologized for her questionable conduct, and how selfish she had been shortly after he had died. She whispered almost indistinctly how desperately she regretted not considering their own sorrow, or the fact that they were grieving him just as she was, perhaps more. She told them how she was sure that she might get better, and that she was engaging in a brave, and courageous battle to conquer the demons his death left her with. When her call was almost over, she finally told them how greatly she valued their support of her, and she thanked them for checking up on her when she checked out of this world. Before she said goodbye, she told them how

Alice VL

grateful she was to them for bringing William to her.

William stood quietly as he listened to her beg his parents' forgiveness. His heart dropped right down to his feet when the raw emotion on her face overwhelmed her tiny body and left her in a catalytic shudder. His heart regularly missed a beat when he heard the utter and severe desolation in her voice. More than once, he was forced to engage in rigorous exertions to remain an outsider right in the center of her conversation with the parents he could never embrace again, even only once. He came dangerously close to falling apart and confessing his secret to Misty-Bleu more than once. He was frantic to pull himself together without her noticing his failure to conceal his emotions when he bravely fought against his reactions. He battled enormously to regain his composure with each crushing whimper she would let out.

When she handed him his mobile phone, she cautiously placed her arms around him, and clasped him securely against her. She held him for a moment longer than she should have, but she could not discard the relief his arms brought to her. "Joshua, please forgive me for what I did to you. I am so, so sorry. You are all I have now. I truly didn't mean to hurt you. Please just don't, don't leave me?" She whispered tearfully as she stood facing him. William was desperate to recover from the wave of emotions that had come plummeting down on him only moments before. She was determined to look him squarely in the eye, without falling apart in front of him. She was adamant to make herself stronger, and she was unwavering in proving to who she thought was Joshua, that she was engaging in an audacious warfare to free herself from all the pain and anguish that had crippled her for months. "I was so selfish, and yet, you stick with me? That is something only William has ever done for me. He would be so enormously proud of you, you know? William was so lucky to have you as a friend, and I am too, Josh." William took her hands and brought them to his lips before he gently kissed them. Misty-Bleu stared at him while utterly perplexed by his mannerisms, and wholly insecure about what to make of the unpredictable that were beginning to invade and dominate her all at the same time. "Misty-Bleu, of course, I forgive you. I know you didn't mean to hurt me; I know that. Stop punishing yourself, stop doing this to yourself. It's over. It's behind us. Just forgive yourself too." She smiled gloomily, before she leaned into him as closely as she could. She rested her head on his chest and was at once comforted by the sound of his rapidly beating heart. She sneered softly, and tightly closed her eyes. She could breathe again.

For the first time in what felt like an eternity, Misty-Bleu could breathe without having to fight for every little breath of fresh air. She silently prayed to God and begged Him to give William a message from her. She wanted God to tell him that she was no longer angry at him, and that she missed him awfully. She wanted God to take him aside and explain her emotions to him. She hoped that God would comfort him each time she would fall apart, and re-assure him of her promise that she was going to do whatever it took, to make him proud of the combat she had engaged herself in. She placed her arms around Joshua, and held firmly onto him, as she inhaled the wonderful and addictive scent of his skin. When he placed his arms around her, she was sure that she could feel a slight tremor in his body. He lifted his head and closed his eyes, as he desperately tried to memorize how magnificent she felt in his arms. Misty-Bleu wanted to stay like that forever. After William, Joshua's arms were the safest place for her to be.

William stood as though frozen in time when he held her pungently against him. He stroked her long, blonde hair as she rested her head against his chest. His heart began to race when he recognized the intimacy of Misty-Bleu in his arms. He savored the moment and knew at once, that moments like those were fleeting. He had always found solace in her arms, and he silently wished that they could remain that way forever. He breathed her in and held his breath for what felt like an eternity before he released the accumulated air in his lungs just before they were about to explode. His heart came alive, and his soul was ensnared with hers. There was no escaping his love and desire for Misty-Bleu. As he held her in his arms, he knew into his soul that there was no way at all, he could ever have left the portal, without her.

Misty-Bleu continued to wrestle with her emotions with each day that followed. She had no idea of how to carry on without William. She felt as though she was simply crawling through her days, wandering around mindlessly and in a complete daze. She didn't want to let him go. She didn't know how to purge the months she had spent with him in their in between. As determined as she was to convince herself of the harsh reality that it was simply a fragmented portion of her imagination, her heart refused to accept that it was never real. She had no inkling of how to take the first step forward and carry on as though William's existence with her in the portal, had never happened. It had come to be the most intense fraction of her survival. It was what kept her rational, and it was all she had left to cling to. A glimpse into a life they could and should have had, but memories she knew, no one person in the world could take away from her. It was real to her. It was real to William. It was a world nobody would believe ever existed, but it was a haven she would treasure intimately, and defend with her entire being.

Alice VL

She spent the following weeks before her admission into The Academy scripting songs about William to sing to only him. Songs that would allow her to be angry with him, and songs that gave her unspoken permission to yearn for him. They would be words her soul would shout out through her lips and remind him of how penetratingly she adored him. Songs Misty-Bleu was sure would bring him back to her, even if only in her heart and in her mind. She valued the moments she would consent to her songs to bring him back to her, and at times, she was sure that she could feel him wrapping himself around her. She sang about losing him, she sang about loving him, and she sang about how desperately she wished he had stayed with her. She told him how foolish she was to have wasted the years trying to become wonderful for him, when he was all she needed to be extraordinary. All she had ever needed from him; was the millions of ways he had loved her. She told him how repentant she was that she could not save him, and she pleaded for him to linger for just a while longer and wait for her in the portal. She finally knew where he was, and where she could find him. Without intending to, she begged him to seize her up and back into their life in the portal, if only for one final moment. Only, Misty-Bleu knew that one more moment would never be enough for her. She wanted him in her forever. She wanted to reclaim their life in the portal away from her world, even if it was never real. She wanted to remain there with them, even if it meant that they would linger in nothingness for all eternity. She wanted their hearts to melt into their souls only one more time, and she desperately ached to feel her daughter inside of her, just one last time.

William would watch her closely, as she wandered around purposelessly, and as she waited for her journey to The Academy to begin. He had often caught glimpses of her when she placed a convincing and protective hand on her belly. It would overwhelm and crush him each time his eyes would fall upon her, yearning for the child he had introduced her to in the portal. She would close her eyes and let out conquering tears for the daughter that was almost hers. He remained as close to her as he could, and rarely went into Joshua's surgical practice anymore. He had contacted a colleague over at Coral Hill Oncology Center and handed over his practice for the duration of their stay at The Academy. William was surprisingly elated by the fact that he had become a superstar almost overnight, even if it was Joshua Stark's name that claimed his stardom. He sang often, while blissfully flabbergasted by how brilliant his voice sounded. He fell in love with the stage, and although he knew that it was never truly his voice, he took it in his stride, and belted out tunes every chance he had. It was an enormous adjustment for William to step into the life of his closest friend, whom he had missed dearly. He was careful to avoid careless mistakes, and he was cautiously aware of all the finest details of Joshua's life. He was abruptly obliged to learn and adapt to Joshua's ordinary habits and behavior, and he was careful to maintain contact with some of his closest friends. William familiarized himself with every nook and cranny of his friend's life, and by the time The Academy opened for the contest, William was convinced that he could persuade the world that he was the famous, Grammy award-winning Joshua Stark.

On Misty-Bleu's final morning at the clinic, William had arranged for a phone call between her and Shaun, who had grown increasingly anxious to speak to her. He was relieved when he detected the enthusiasm and animation in her voice, when he was finally able to speak to her. "Shauny! I am so glad you called!" She was honestly pleased to hear his voice on the other end of the phone. "My beautiful! It is so good to hear your voice! How are you?" "I'm okay, I'm leaving this morning. Joshua is driving me to the bus stop at the airport. We'll be travelling by bus to The Academy." "I am so glad you're doing this Bleu-girl! You are going to win this thing!" She sighed when she contemplated spending the next few months in a house full of strangers. "I don't care, Shaun. Not about any of that. I just promised Josh, and I mean, I owe him that. I just don't want to let him down …"

"Yeah well, you nearly slaughtered him with a shard of glass!" Shaun let out a nervous giggle before Misty-Bleu burst out laughing. "That's not funny, Shauny! It was an accident!" "I know, beautiful. So, I'll call you when you're in the house, okay?" "Okay, my guy. I love you guys, who knows? Maybe this Christmas I get to spend it with my guys?" "We would love that! Get well, Misty-Bleu, we miss you so much. We love you."

She hung up the phone and smiled sketchily when her eyes caught a glimpse of William's. "Ready?" "Yes, I am. As ready as I'll ever be." She winked at him, before he picked up her bags, and led her out to his car. He promptly opened the passenger door for her before he anxiously made his way over to the driver's side. When he climbed in, he turned to Misty-Bleu, and took her hands into his, "This is going to be just what the doctor ordered, me, what I ordered, seeing I am the doctor here ..." He whispered and stuttered all at the same time before he flashed a broad smile at her. Once again, Misty-Bleu was restlessly unsettled by Joshua's unmistakable sense of intimacy. It had instantly reminded her of how often William would grab onto her hands and hold them tightly in his, each time he climbed into the car with her. She found herself slipping back into one of the many moments with him in the portal, and for an instant, she couldn't quite tell what was real, and what wasn't. She hesitated for a second, before she freed her hands from his. She smiled tenderly at him, before she turned, and gazed out through the window. Misty-Bleu leaned back into the seat, and eagerly allowed her mind to drift back to William. She was once again transported back to the portal, and she impulsively replayed their in between in her mind. She dreadfully longed for their world, and she desperately missed William. She longed to feel joy again, and she was fraught for a moment of reprieve from the excruciating heartache that had relentlessly hunted and enslaved her. "Are you okay, Misty-Bleu?" She smiled sadly when she turned to face him. "Yeah, just, ...just remembering."

William knew she was thinking of her time in the portal, and he smiled when he reminisced over the life he had created for them, not too long ago. "You know, they say that a memory is not that of an actual event. It's simply a memory of the last memory you had of the event. They say that you shouldn't trust that too much, it becomes distorted and compromised each time you return to it." Misty-Bleu smiled again and knew that there would be nothing in her entire universe, that could distort any memories of the life she had lived with William, even though it was in another dimension of time, and solely in her mind. "Yeah, I guess, but they are mine, and you never said anything about me having to rebuff them." He nodded his head, as they drove in silence to the airport. He could not argue with the point she had just made, but William was not quite sure he wanted to. He was secretly elated by the fact that they both were living with the same memories, even though he would never be able to share any of them with her. They were there for him too, to slip back to whenever he wanted to. He smiled when he peeked at her often, and realized that she was smiling more frequently, and that the sparkle in her eyes, were not because of tears.

When they reached the bus terminal at the airport, William quickly unloaded her bags from his car, and handed them to her. When she took them from him, he nervously embraced her. "So, I won't be there until Monday. Get yourself settled in. If you need me, call me, okay?" He handed her a mobile phone, before he closed the passenger door behind her. "I got you a new mobile. I've punched in my number, so text me or call me. I mean, if you just want to talk, or if you need anything, okay?" She smiled and tossed the mobile phone into her sling bag, before she turned around and leisurely made her way to a group of young men and women seated on a bench behind the bus stop. She glanced around her, and quickly found an empty seat amongst them. She leaned back and waited patiently for their journey to begin.

When William pulled the car off to the side of the road a

Alice VL

few meters away from her, he climbed out and made his way around the back of the car before he leaned against it. He watched her shuffle in between the rest of the contestants and smiled when he realized that she had not attempted to hide herself from them. He was excited to begin this journey with her. It would be his only chance to win her back. He was frantic that Joshua conspires with the moon and the stars, to alter her heart, and nudge her back into his, even as Joshua. He was sure that he could pull it off, but at the same time, he knew that it would cost him everything, if he failed. He owed it to his friend, who willingly offered up his life, to find his place in Misty-Bleu's heart again. It was up to him to save her from her heartache and anguish and bring her back into a world she had learned to despise.

"The bus is late …" Misty-Bleu whispered softly and irritably to herself while she anxiously glanced at her wristwatch. They were a small, intimate, and young group of musicians that were impatiently seated at the bus terminal outside the Coral Hill International Airport. They were intolerantly waiting for their bus to arrive, to take them on what was meant to be the journey of a lifetime for most of them, except for Misty-Bleu. She did not share their animation or enthusiasm for the weeks that lay ahead of her. It was a journey the rest of the finalists were thrilled to begin, one they had waited for, for many months.

Alice VL

AFTERLIGHT

For months, they had all competed against their country's best and most talented musicians, the most supreme their nation could offer. They had auditioned almost a year before and were carefully screened and selected from thousands of hopeful entries. It was a wait which seemed to drag on forever for these finalists, as they tirelessly counted down the days for their voyage into stardom to finally begin.

Excluding Misty-Bleu, there were eleven other contestants who were to participate in the much sought-after vocal talent competition at The Academy of Music in Claremont, a city almost 300 miles from Coral Hill. A contest that took place only once a year, with only a dozen finalists that would compete against one another, in front of audiences that would fill the world-famous Superbowl. Over and above Trevor and Darren, the remaining ten contestants were all female contenders. They were selected from across the country to participate in a competition that would crown only one a winner, that brought with it a record deal from MFL Records and a year's residence in Nolan's Creek. It was a country, almost right across the world and on the other side of two oceans. It was an opportunity to rub shoulders with the best and sing their way to stardom amongst the most superior of them all. It would shoot the winner to celebrity status where they would record their very first album and release a single the night the winner is announced. It would be a further six months before the ultimate champion was to be crowned and publicized, and eliminations would take place every other week, following their first month in The Academy.

Misty-Bleu received the news from Joshua that she was selected as a finalist with mixed emotions, in a time that she was desperate to withdraw entirely from the world, and from the competition. She wanted to be alone with her thoughts, and secretly, she was desperate to slip back into the portal with William. She longed for him, and she ached for the life she had left behind, in a world Joshua had told her, she had conjured up in her feeble mind. She was exhausted by the torture her soul was enduring, and she was beleaguered by her inexorable tears. Her heart could barely survive its intense heartbreak, and her body reminded her of the pain it was forced to endure because of her frail heart. She had no desire at all, to live in a house with total strangers for the duration of the competition. She wanted her little farm, her horses, and her trees where she would no longer have to pretend that she could survive the crushing reality of William's death. It was only after she had stabbed him almost to death, that she agreed to participate in a valiant attempt to redeem herself for what she had done in a fit of rage.

After she had read William's final letter in which he

revealed his last wish for her, did she pour her entire soul into surrendering to his desires. Being selected as a finalist for a singing contest was something she had never dreamed of or set out to reach. Misty-Bleu could not ignore her lack of enthusiasm to win, and she couldn't care less that she was carefully chosen as a finalist for the coveted and world-class title. She readily admitted to herself that it was not what she had ever wanted for her life, or what had mattered much to her. She was never comfortable in the limelight, and she regularly cowered away, and hid from the spotlight. She had only ever wanted to write her stories, where she lived many existences with the characters that would incessantly haunt her. She fell hopelessly in love with each of them, and she would sit back and listen carefully when they took over from her and told their stories all by themselves. Once she had ended their fairy tales, she longed for them, and would often wonder how they were, and whether their tales were in fact, finally over. It was extremely hard for her to let go of their influences in her life, and when she was forced to submit them for publication, she felt as though she had lost an enormous chunk of herself in the process.

Their lives all remained unfinished to her, and she was desperately afraid to say goodbye to them. While they were still in her mind and while the stories remained only between her and her characters, they remained intimately connected to her. They were the family she never had, and they were what kept her sane on the days she felt so entirely alone and far-removed from the rest of the world. When her novels were ultimately, yet reluctantly published, she would never open or read any one of them again. She felt bizarrely detached from the intimacy they had once so faithfully shared. She had found in writing, what she never could in people. She was Misty-Bleu Buchanan, author and Christmas tree farm owner, and there was nothing else she needed, or no-one else she wanted to be. Misty-Bleu had always dreamed of owning a Christmas tree farm, and all she wanted after she bought Little Dreams, were the two horses that would keep her company, and help her survive in a world, she felt utterly isolated in. The only reason she felt so compelled to go through with the contest, was simply because she owed Joshua the chance to heal. To herself, Misty-Bleu willingly confessed that she too, was anxious to recover from the debilitating pain that would engulf her, and bring her to her knees, when she least expected it.

She was guilt-ridden for hurting the one person that refused to give up on or neglect her. He was the only person that refused to lock her away in a clinic for the mentally ill and forget her when she checked out of this world. She was tormented by the fact that she could just as easily have taken his life through her reckless actions, and she was haunted by the certainty that he refused to abandon her, even though she did not deserve his kindness or compassion.

While she sat in the crowded bus stop surrounded by enthusiastic and eager contestants, she tried to consider what it was, that she had left to live for. She could barely convince herself to imitate enthusiasm, even if only for Joshua. She did not want to intentionally disappoint him after all she had inflicted upon him, but she simply could find no reason to carry on without William anymore. She sat in silence between the chatty group of contenders and listened to their electrifying squeals as they waited impatiently for their bus to arrive.

Alice VL

3

When Misty-Bleu reluctantly walked into The Academy, she was met and welcomed by the Chief Administrator and Project Organizer, Mr. Donahue. Misty-Bleu thought him to be in his late fifties but found him pleasant and eerily comforting. He spoke in a soft and gentle tone when he warmly received and welcomed her into the home she would be sharing with him, and the rest of the finalists. He turned around to find the rest of the finalists standing behind him. He clasped his hands together, before he addressed the eager group. "Good evening, ladies and fellows. I am Mr. Donahue, and I will be your go-to guy for the duration of your stay. As you are all aware, we have regular counselors and tutors who you will all meet on Monday morning. We have meetings each Monday morning promptly at eight, so be sure to be dressed, and in the lounge by then. If any of you are late, you will not be permitted to use any of our facilities until you've made an appointment with myself for remedial action. Do any of you have any questions?"

He glanced around at each one of them, as they nodded their heads in agreement. Mr. Donahue swiftly explained the rules of the house, as well as the schedules for their rehearsal sessions and mealtimes. It was decided that each Monday morning, each student will be given an hour to rehearse and perform in the recording studio, while another is to spend time writing lyrics, or practicing instruments in the library or music studio for the remainder of that week. Mr. Donahue showed each of the finalists to their bedrooms and made a concerted effort to get to know each one individually. He was informed of each student's past and given a brief history on each one of them. When it was Misty-Bleu's turn, Mr. Donahue was eager to show support for her, "Misty-Bleu, we are going to become great friends, you and I. I've been told by the board of The Academy that you have a great voice. We believe in music, and we believe in the therapy of music over here. Heal with music as opposed to being stuck in an institution, which is nothing to be ashamed of." He placed a comforting and protective hand on her shoulders and hoped that she would learn to trust him and confide in him in during her stay in The Academy. Misty-Bleu knew that he was referring to her stay in the clinic, and thanked him for his kind words, before she turned away from him, and closed her bedroom door behind her.

She sat on her bed, plagued by humiliation. It unnerved her that he knew of her time spent in the mental institution.

Alice VL

Misty-Bleu never sought sympathy or pity, even as a child. She desperately needed tolerance and indulgence, and as far as she was concerned, there was no one person in the entire universe, that was quite prepared for, or equipped to understand how she felt. They could not begin to sympathize with her loss, and they could in no way at all, begin to understand how her world around her had fragmented into a million tiny shards. All she needed to survive the life she was left behind in, was William.

She instinctively took her mobile phone from her sling bag, and quickly texted Joshua. "Hi, I'm here." She had barely placed her phone down on the bed, when the bleeping turned its blue flashing light on. William was just about to drift off to sleep when the text alarm on his phone startled him. He grabbed his mobile phone, and curiously read her message, before he smiled sadly, but replied at once. 'Glad you're safe. How is it?' 'It's okay, much better than the clinic.' 'What are the other finalists like?' 'I don't know? Loud, giddy, I don't know? But Mr. Donahue is nice.' 'Yep, he is a really good guy. So, I'll see you on Monday. Text or call whenever you want.' 'I miss you, Josh. I wish you were here already.' William re-read her texts to him, and was at once, desperate to join her in that big, busy, and chaotic house. He smiled without responding, and hurriedly placed his phone back on his nightstand.

Alice VL

AFTERLIGHT

When Joshua failed to respond to her last message, she pulled out a photograph of William from her suitcase and had no sooner looked at the image staring back at her, when a lost tear rolled unsympathetically down her cheek. She gazed at him for as long as she could before she whispered how desperately she longed and ached for him. "I want to be where you are …" She whispered again and traced his entire face on that photograph. The corners of the photograph were beginning to fray, and the ageing ink was beginning to fade. There was evidence that the photograph was once torn in resentment or fury, or perhaps while overwhelmed by the shatters of her broken heart. When she turned it over, she noticed again how she had desperately glued and taped the photograph of him back together. She looked at each wrinkle and fold on that photograph and was ashamed to admit they were there because she had once crumpled it, and impulsively banished it into a waste bin. She frowned when she noticed the stains that she had left from the teardrops that once fell onto it. She slowly and carefully traced his face with her fingers, as he looked back at her. She gazed achingly into the eyes, that looked back at her a thousand times before. In his eyes, she could find a million stories, and each time she joined him in that photograph, she saw something different. Sometimes, there were stories of pain, suffering and sadness. And at other times, there were tales of uncertainty, confusion,

Alice VL

fear, frustration, and desperation.

But mostly, his eyes let her know of the love there was once for her, and only for her. When her eyes trailed down to his mouth, she hungrily touched them, before she smiled wretchedly. It was as though she could feel them at her fingertips. She could barely stop her bottom lip from quivering, when she remembered again, how his lips felt against hers. She remembered the way they kissed her, and she could once more, hear their messages to her heart. Her eyes began to scrutinize every inch of his face, and when they detected that all-too-familiar dimple around his mouth just below his cheek, she beamed involuntarily when she remembered how he once laughed from the very hub of his stomach. She remembered how it would begin with a smile and a frown all at the same time. And, as though a countdown to an explosion had begun, he would erupt into a laughter that could silence the entire world, as they searched for the happiest and most beautiful sound in the biosphere.

She paused when her eyes rested on his hair. She gazed with sadness at his dark, not quite black hair that was wildly blowing in the wind, and she remembered how he used to run his fingers through them when they argued. She remembered how he once used to sit with his elbows rested on his knees while deep in thought and twirled a lock of his own hair with his index finger. For a few moments, that photograph of him reminded her of love. An honest, crazy, and mad kind of love she thought, she would know forever. That photograph was what reminded her of where and when she was introduced to a kind of love, she never thought she would find. It was a love that trapped her beneath his eyes and kept her from seeing others around her. It was a photograph of a man she knows she will miss, for the remainder of her life. A photograph of a place and a time where fairy tales were real, and butterflies lived inside of her.

Misty-Bleu stared for just a moment longer, before she placed the photograph in a drawer of her nightstand. She hurriedly unpacked her bags, before she took her notebook, and began writing a letter to him. She wrote him to tell him that she had finally agreed to participate in the competition at The Academy, and what the house looked like. She told him about the other contestants, and that she doubted whether she had much in common with them. She gave him a short rundown of Mr. Donahue, and she told him that she felt safe around him. Misty-Bleu then told him that she loved him, and that she thought of him each minute of each day. She said that she would leave her entire life behind in a heartbeat if she could be where he was. She ended off her letter by telling him that nothing much mattered anymore, and that he was her entire heart.

The weekend passed by especially sluggishly for Misty-Bleu's liking. Saturday and Sunday were a scheduled period for all the contenders and counselors to get to know one another and become acquainted with all there was to learn about the finalists. Misty-Bleu was sad that Joshua would only arrive on Monday, but she secretly hoped that he would show up before then.

William had grown increasingly nervous at the prospect of stepping into The Academy as Dr. Joshua Stark, the well-known surgeon and Grammy-award winning superstar who had travelled the world extensively and performed on almost every stage in the world. When Misty-Bleu entered The Academy, William took the opportunity to check in at Little Dreams. He saw to it that Eduardo and Maria were well-equipped to run the farm without a glitch in her absence, and he informed them that he would be away for a few months. He left his number with Eduardo, as well as Misty-Bleu's new vet, Dr. Roger Mack. He sent an email to her publisher, informing her of Misty-Bleu's acceptance into The Academy, and he requested that she forward all her emails to him for the next few months.

AFTERLIGHT

Alice VL

4

The finalists had spent the weekend lazing around in the lounge, around the pool, or acquainting themselves with the studios. The young women were overly excited about meeting the handsome Joshua Stark, who was scheduled to become a permanent fixture at The Academy for the next six months. They gushed shamelessly about the undeniable attraction and sensuality he radiated so effortlessly, and they became lightheaded whenever his name was mentioned. Misty-Bleu smiled when she listened to their gushing and the infatuation that surrounded him and was sorry that they had never experienced with a man, what she had. She secretly tried to place herself in their shoes, as she desperately attempted to see Joshua through their eyes, but she gave up soon enough when she realized that she had never looked at him, in the same way they all did. She never fell prey to his lure, and she never once felt swept off her feet by him.

While having a cigarette outside on a hammock, a habit she had picked up at the clinic, Misty-Bleu heard the women giggle as teenagers did, and as they wagered on who it would be that ultimately walked away with the much sough-after title and record deal. She had no desire at all to join in and wager any bet, and she was even less interested in discussing Joshua Stark and his desirability. For a moment, she considered telling them that she had stabbed him with a glass shard only weeks before, as she grew desperate for them to leave her in peace. She remained friendly and respectful towards them at all times, but she preferred to be alone. They all had realized this about Misty-Bleu soon enough and kept her at a safe distance after Sylvia had tried to include her in their conversation. "Hey, Misty-Bleu!" Sylvia, the youngest of the finalists shouted out to her, "How gorgeous is this, Joshua Stark?" Misty-Bleu shrugged her shoulders and realized again how she had never noticed or looked at him in the way she had looked at William. "Is he?" She whispered to herself before she tossed her cigarette away.

Although Misty-Bleu was adamant to keep to herself at mealtimes, all the finalists around her were eagerly informing one another of how excited they were to be there, and they could not miss a chance to speculate as to who would win the competition. All Misty-Bleu could do was spend her days thinking of William, and the life she was left trapped in without him. She ached for him mostly during the night. It had reminded her of a time when she would climb into bed with him and lay snugly in his arms. She missed feeling his arms reach out for her, and she desperately longed for the shelter of his body. She replayed the intimacy of their first night on the beach, and it suddenly dawned on her that it was just one more liaison they had shared in the portal. It was not real. What was real, was that she could no longer turn to him, or bury her sorrows in his chest. She could no longer rest her head on his shoulders and calm the storms that were persistently brewing inside of her. She could no longer flutter like an angel without fear around him, almost as though she was breathing in sacred air. All she was left with, were the nightmares that were never too far off. Visions that relentlessly pursued her and haunted her until morning came. She would close her eyes, desperately afraid of the combats and demons of the night, and when she awoke in the morning, she would be exhausted by her bitter battle to cling to a life, she was desperate to leave. It was William whom she would never stop dreaming of, and it was William whom her soul sought out in everyone else around her.

When Monday morning arrived, after what felt like a month of Sundays, Misty-Bleu was momentarily disoriented when her alarm clock awoke her that morning. She hurriedly glanced around her, and again, she longed for the serenity and familiarity of Little Dreams. She longed for Captain Nimo and

Wilhelmina, but more than anything else, she longed for the trees that she could get lost in when the world around her became too loud. She longed for her normal, and she missed the days she could type 'The End' on a novel which always left her feeling accomplished. Those were the feelings that she was sure, were guaranteeing her of her extraordinary that was out there, waiting just for her. She was desperate to reclaim her life as it was before she had found William in Coral Hill Oncology Center, but she knew that the more she tried to let go of her past and her life before him, the more she would yearn and ache for him.

After taking a quick shower and combing back her long, unruly hair, Misty-Bleu quickly slipped into a pair of jeans, and a loose-fitting sweater. She cautiously, yet excitedly made her way to the kitchen that overlooked the communal living room area, where Mr. Donahue had only moments before, begun to address the contestants. She hurriedly looked around her and was at once disappointed that Joshua had not yet arrived. Misty-Bleu glanced down at her wristwatch and sighed with relief when she realized that she was perfectly on time.

"Good morning, Misty-Bleu. Did you sleep well?" Mr. Donahue instantly noticed the drawn and tired look on her face when he caught a glimpse of her in the kitchen. "Yes, thank you." She was at once unnerved when the rest of the finalists turned their attention to her. She quickly turned around and grabbed a tub of yoghurt from the fridge. "Are you alright there? Can you hear me?" "Yes." She replied almost inaudibly, before she took a spoon, and began eating her yoghurt. "Right! I trust you all are comfortable in your bedrooms, and that you're all settled in? Do you all understand the house rules?" They all nodded in agreement before he began introducing the mentors, one at a time. "First off, we have the very talented, and much sought-after Mr. Raul Shanaed, who will assist you all with music compilations, and who will evaluate the songs you sing. Then, Ms. Jenny Parker who will assist with writing and poetry, and finally Ms. Barbara Terry, who will be responsible for choreography and performance routines in general. She is a qualified counsellor, and well-respected in the psychiatric industry, so any of you who need to talk, go see her."

After introducing the students to all the mentors, Mr. Donahue paused to take in a deep breath. "And lastly, you are probably all dying to meet Dr. Stark, who will be extremely hands-on, and will oversee each one of your performances in The Academy for the next six months?" Mr. Donahue smiled when he noticed the excitement build among the contestants. "Before I introduce him, I'd like to first give you all a little bit of background on him. Not only is he a brilliant and respected doctor in Coral

Hill, but he too, has won several Grammy awards in the past, and has just released an album that went straight to number one in nine countries. He is the famous, but reluctant superstar, Joshua Stark who leave women wild at concerts!" Mr. Donahue burst out laughing when the finalists began cheering before they erupted into an animated applause. "He wanted to be personally involved with each of you during your stay here this year. Not only does he have his own record label, but he will personally spend time with each one-off you and select one student to attend a concert he has lined up at the Superbowl in less than two weeks from now!" The students shot to their feet as they screeched in excitement and grew impatient to meet him. Misty-Bleu giggled softly while eating her yoghurt, and realized for the first time, what a hot-shot Joshua Stark was in the industry. She shook her head when she realized how competitive they would become, as they would desperately fight and compete for the honor of performing alongside him. She smirked when she recalled that sharing a stage with Joshua Stark was something she was well-acquainted with, even if it was merely in her life in the portal. Performing alongside him with a packed Superbowl, was the last thing on her mind. "It is with great pleasure that I introduce ... Dr. Joshua Stark!"

Mr. Donahue clapped his hands, before Joshua entered

Alice VL

the room. He grinned from ear to ear, as he hurriedly made his way over to Mr. Donahue. Misty-Bleu could barely deny that there was certainly a uniqueness about him, and his presence was enough to brighten up any room. She chuckled sympathetically when she watched the women jump up and down while overcome with excitement, before they vigorously began to encircle him. Trevor and Darren, the only two men in the house, quickly rose to their feet, and joined in the crowd of what could easily have been mistaken for over-excited teenagers. As Misty-Bleu gawked and grinned at the spectacle right in front of her, she scowled unwittingly when she caught a glimpse of Joshua. She could at once notice the exasperation on his face when she detected how entirely out of place, and uncomfortable he seemed. It was peculiar that he would react so unusually to a gathering crowd, when she assumed that he had women falling over their feet to meet him. She stared for a moment longer and could swear he appeared to be as someone who had never commanded such attention than at that very moment.

Shortly after the finalists all frantically introduced themselves to Joshua, Mr. Donahue instructed them to calmly take their places again. William winked at Misty-Bleu when he finally spotted her in the kitchen. She was flabbergasted by the reaction of the finalists who turned out to be his greatest fans, but she seemed wholly unaffected by his presence or the commotion and chaos that had surround him only minutes before. She glanced over at him and smiled before she placed her empty tub in the waste bin.

He found it invigorating that Misty-Bleu was so unlike the pretentious women he had met before, and that she was not at all affected by Joshua's stardom or celebrity. To the world, he was Joshua Stark, the superstar, but all he really was, was the man she had lost, and who was caught up in his best friend's body. Joshua was more than a superstar. He was a beautiful man, and women all around the world found him irresistibly attractive and appealing. Joshua was tall and slender. His dark brown hair had a wild streak, and his green eyes seemed to break down into a million yellow spots. He was regularly featured in the tabloids dating famous women who would unashamedly throw themselves before him, and flirt brazenly with him.

Misty-Bleu was not at all captivated or prejudiced by his popularity, and she was not quite sure if it was because she never knew much about him when she had first met him. To her, he was William's best friend, and the man she had almost killed. She would never know how he was able to keep her, and what she had done to him, out of the news, but she was incredibly thankful that the world did not know her connection to Joshua. He had become her friend in the months after William had died, and she owed him so much more than she was willing to admit. She knew that if she had never met or known William, she would find him arrogant and rude, and she would by no means at all, pursue a friendship with him. She thought him to be suave and slick around the ladies, and she thought he was too ridiculously aware of his charm and good looks.

As Misty-Bleu stared out ahead of her, Mr. Donahue signaled for her to take her place among the rest of the students in the living room. When she found an empty seat between Justine and Margie, Misty-Bleu sat down quietly, as she desperately tried to blend in amongst them. "Misty-Bleu?" She looked up at once when she heard Joshua address her. William was again intrigued by her and could not contain his admiration for her long blonde hair and sad, arctic blue eyes. A sadness he alone was responsible for. Misty-Bleu was blissfully unaware of her beauty, as she had been all her life, but when William looked at her, it was as though he was seeing her for the very first time. William would habitually remind her of her flawless beauty, yet Misty-Bleu never quite believed him, and shrugged it off when she became shy immediately after. "Yes?" She whispered bashfully, before she lowered her head and crossed her legs. She was uncomfortable by the sudden silence where a pin could drop, and the entire group would hear it. She nervously folded her hands as she began to shudder slightly. "Welcome ..."

He smiled when he noticed how unexpectedly self-conscious, she had become. "Right people. Let me explain quickly how this will work. Joshua has a show starting next Friday at the Superbowl. He will be listening from behind closed doors to each of you, and by the end of the day, he will reach a decision as to who will be performing with him. This person will then spend the weekend and the following week with Joshua to rehearse for the show and will perform alongside him. The lucky performer will leave with Joshua on Thursday next week and return the following Monday. I must stress that this will in no way at all, interfere with the competition or place prejudice on any one of you. Is that understood? It is a wonderful opportunity, but it has no weight in the competition." They all nodded, as they excitedly clapped their hands again. After he dealt out session schedules to each student, Misty-Bleu was relieved that she was booked into the very last slot of the day in the studio. She was in no way at all, attracted to performing alongside Joshua. All she wanted was to get through the next six months, if she were to last that long, as effortlessly as possible.

After their quick morning meeting, each finalist headed out in their own direction. Misty-Bleu retreated back into her bedroom and took out her song book. She had been working on a song she had written for William, and was anxious to finish it, by working on the music for her lyrics. She had just began singing it softly, when she found herself slipping back into a misty fog, as her tears began to bucket from her eyes. "I wish you were here with me." She became quiet, before she whispered inconsolably into the unseen, invisible abyss that was waiting to swallow her in.

"Misty-Bleu! It's your turn in the studio!" Trevor knocked urgently before he called out frantically from the other side of her bedroom door. She hastily glanced at her wristwatch and could barely fathom how the entire day was almost over, and that she had spent most if working on her song. She was caught up exclusively in the world her song had promised her, and she completely lost all track of time. Misty-Bleu grabbed her notebook and raced to the studio. She was at once mortified that she was late, and highly apologetic to find Mr. Shanaed patiently waiting for her. "Something wrong, Misty-Bleu?" He frowned slightly when he saw her dash in, in a frenzy. "No, nothing's wrong. I'm just, I'm sorry I'm late, Sir. I wasn't aware that it was so late. I wasn't paying attention to the time." "That's alright, it's only five minutes anyway." He stepped aside and showed her into the studio. "So, Misty-Bleu, we've asked each student to sing their own song, one they may have written. Are you comfortable with that? Do you have anything you have written or are working on?"

Misty-Bleu was not in the least bit prepared for performing or rehearsing one of her own songs, and she could hardly sing a song she had previously written for Joshua, given it happened in the portal. She felt completely out of sorts, as though she was hurled from her comfort zone, as she frantically considered each song she had ever written. "I … I, don't know, Mr. Shanaed. I've only just finished something that I've been working on all day. Maybe I could try it?" She stared at him with uncertainty and anxiety in her eyes. He nodded, and gently squeezed her shoulder. William was watching her through a two-way mirror from the next room and was again reminded by how intensely intrigued he was by her, the woman he travelled between dimensions and through universes for. When Mr. Shanaed returned to the adjoining room, William was sure that he could categorize the sudden sullen expression on her face. He was convinced that Mr. Shanaed could see right through him, and who he was, and what Misty-Bleu meant to him. "What do you know about her?" He blurted out, obliged to question Mr. Donahue about Misty-Bleu, as he did with each student before her. It was of utmost importance that he veiled the truth of his connection to Misty-Bleu and keep up the farce of his identity. "Well, only about her. She's a very private person, and difficult to get through to. I know she is a successful author, and that she owns a farm in Coral Hill. Apparently, a Christmas tree farm. But other than that, we know only what we've been told by the clinic she has only recently been discharged from. If my memory serves me, she was hospitalized following a break-down after her boyfriend died and had a hard time recovering from her loss. I don't really know much more. She is extremely talented, which is why we've invited her here." Mr. Donahue replied hesitantly, as he scrutinized her from the other side of the mirror. "What is the song called, Misty-Bleu?" "When you were here with me." She hurriedly glanced down at the sheet of music in her hands before she handed it to Mr. Shanaed. "It's just a rough scribble, I'm not quite finished with it." "Okay, are you ready?"

He took the sheet of music and handed it to the band who were ready to accompany her on the guitar and the piano. Although Misty-Bleu was nervous when she began to sing, she somehow managed to get caught up in her song as she drifted away from the studio, and back into the portal with William. She was so utterly enthralled by the lyrics and the life she had shared with him over there, that she failed to notice that her tears had begun to roll brazenly from her eyes.

Alice VL

While he listened to her sing her song for him, William could not deny the agony Misty-Bleu was feeling, and he could in no way at all, deny the sorrow that had made its way into the very core of him. Mr. Donahue remained eerily silent. They were both mesmerized and captivated by her voice, and equally enchanting, yet heartbreaking performance. They sat up straight in their seats and watched the tears gush from her eyes, as her voice began to shudder hoarsely. William swallowed back a few times, desperate to keep up the pretense, but he could barely stand to see her come undone right in front of him, and only because of him. She was falling apart mere meters from him, and there was nothing he could do to rescue her from the anguish and overwhelming destruction that was entirely consuming and submerging her. He swallowed back again on a powerful lump in his throat as he desperately tried to hide the tears that were brimming in his own eyes. As he watched her echo her sorrow and longing for him, all William could think of, was to burst through the studio doors and seize her into his arms. He wanted to hold her against him and put all her broken pieces back together for her. He wanted to tell her that it was him, William, the man she was pining for, the man she was dying for. He wanted to beg her to see him, to look past Joshua, and see him. He wanted to ask her if she could feel him from the very pit of her stomach, there where there are no lies on their bodies. He

Alice VL

wanted to ask her if her soul recognized his.

William wanted to hold her against him and tell her that the portal was real, and that their life was out there waiting for them. He wanted to tell her how dreadfully he loved her, and that not even death could separate them. He wanted her to know that he could never let her go, not even when he took his last breath here, and his very first over there. But, as William sat with one foot as Joshua and the other as the love of her life, he knew that he could not willingly crush, or confuse her anymore. William could not risk losing his second chance with her if he told her the truth. With a thrashing and wincing heart, he turned to Mr. Donahue, desperate to keep up the charade and appear touched, yet unhampered by her heart-stopping performance. "What exactly happened to her?" William already knew the answer, but he knew too that if he had failed to show curiosity behind her performance, it would immediately raise suspicion. He made eye contact with Mr. Donahue, as he stared enquiringly at him.

When he realized how deeply her song had affected him, it took Mr. Donahue a moment to gather himself before he could respond to William. He was hesitant, and felt his own heart miss a beat when he quickly considered all she had gone through in her very short life. "It's such a sad story, Joshua. She lost her boyfriend to cancer only a short while ago. It seems they were very much in love, childhood sweethearts or something like that. Her parents treated her really badly. There appears to have been severe abuse from them both, and well, there are people that are worried that she might never be able to function normally in this world again." Mr. Donahue tried his best to answer as accurately as possible, but still, he could not turn away from her performance, or her song. William was once again distraught when Mr. Donahue gave him a rundown of her life, one that he had already known intimately, and lived with her. He hated himself for putting her through the devastation his death had brought her, and again, he despised her parents for discarding her place in the world.

When Misty-Bleu's song was finally over, she was horrified to discover that she had fallen to her knees and allowed her tears to flow spontaneously from her eyes. She swiftly leaped to her feet, overcome with mortification by the emotions that had carelessly overwhelmed her, and taken over her performance. She glanced over at Mr. Shanaed, who was making his way over to her. "That was beautiful, Misty-Bleu. Did you write that song yourself?" She nodded sadly, before he placed his arms around her and hugged her tightly. Misty-Bleu gently pulled away from him and lowered her head. "Well done, Misty-Bleu, it was beautifully written and beautifully sang. Your performance was second to no other here today." He smiled before he made his way back to the piano. When Mr. Donahue entered the studio, he headed straight over to Misty-Bleu. "Do you think you could do another one?"

William was desperate to hear her sing another song and urged Mr. Donahue to request one more from her. He was not quite ready to let her leave the studio and realized that her music had affected him as though he was a junkie, addicted to his drug of choice, and desperate for his next fix. "Another one of my own?" "Yes, if you could?" Mr. Shanaed approached them, and was instantly concerned by his unusual request, "I think that's enough for one day, don't you?" "That's okay ..." Misty-Bleu smiled before she handed Mr. Shanaed another sheet of music. He irritably took it from her and made his way back to the piano as Mr. Donahue left the studio and returned to William behind the large two-way mirror. "Misty-Bleu, are you sure you're up for this? You don't have to do this?" "It's called 'The Photograph,' Mr. Shanaed."

When the music began to play, Misty-Bleu belted out another of her songs she had written to William, but this time, she appeared to control her feelings, and was far more prepared for her emotions, than she was with her previous song. William was again fascinated as he listened to her sing, and although she did not fall apart this time, he was once again aware of the sorrow in her eyes. The earth-shattering tremble in her voice, was unmistakable and cataclysmic. He felt so deeply sorry for her, and wanted to somehow, ease her pain, and bring her back a little of the joy she had once known.

When she ended her song without as much as missing a tune, Mr. Donahue thanked her and complimented her on a well-written and well-sung song. She smiled shyly, before she said a hurried goodbye, and quickly made her way out to the pool. William stood staring at her, and when he could no longer see her, he turned to Mr. Donahue, "Are we done for the day?"

"Yip. That was the last one." "Alright then. I think that Misty-Bleu's voice is strong enough, and best suited for my concert at the Superbowl. I think that she far outweighs the rest of the finalists, and I think she will be a good fit. What do you think?" "I fully agree. I'm just not sure she is emotionally ready to perform in front of thousands of people?" Mr. Shanaed had walked in only moments before, and turned to William to voice his own concerns, "She is good. She is the best The Academy has ever seen, and she will be a superstar someday, but she needs time, and she needs to heal. I don't think this is a good idea. I don't think we should let her leave here; she needs time."

William frowned when he heard them both object. He

understood their concerns, but he could not pass off a chance to be alone with her, and to be close as she navigated her way through her heartbreak. "I'll keep a close eye on her. We'll spend so much time rehearsing, she will eventually learn to focus on her performance more, than her pain. I swear, if I feel that she can't cope, or if I feel she won't be a good fit, I'll pull the plug on her performances straight away. In the meantime, I am going out for some fresh air." He placed his hand on Mr. Donahue's shoulder, before he left through the studio door.

William was keen to check up on Misty-Bleu after her performance and subsequent breakdown in the studio. When reaching the pool, he found Misty-Bleu seated alone on a garden swing that overlooked the pool. He saw her drag on a cigarette and thought back to a time she wouldn't be caught dead with one in her hands. He smiled when he remembered how she would berate him for smoking, and how she was relentless in getting him to quit. He anxiously made his way over to her, and when Misty-Bleu noticed him approach her, she was alarmed and wholly surprised. He sat down beside her, before he lit a cigarette in silence. "Joshua! When did you start smoking?" He grinned when he noticed the repugnance on her face. "Around the time you did." "You should quit, your voice?" "Yeah? And what about yours?" She turned away from him, at once repulsed by the filthy habit she had picked up during her stay at the clinic. "Tell you what, Missy? I'll quit the day you do, okay?" She grinned faintly, before she took another drag.

William thought back to the night that Misty-Bleu walked back into his life. She had sat down beside him as though there was nothing in the world that could keep her away from him. She was determined to walk back into his life, and trample through the puddles of his heart, one more time. Just as he was doing, at that very moment. "Cold, isn't it?" Misty-Bleu nodded as she gazed up into the sky. "Yes, but I don't mind the cold." She looked over to him and sneered. "I'm glad you're here, Josh. I've missed having you around. I like seeing you every day." Misty-Bleu pulled her sleeves over her hands, but still could not seem to warm them up. "Are you okay?" "I … I'm fine, it's just hard living here, when all I want is to go home to Little Dreams. I'm not such a fan of house rules and schedules, and I hate pretending that I don't know you. I miss my life, and I just miss William." "I know, Misty-Bleu, I miss him too. I lost my best friend. I miss Jo, William so much more than I thought I could. I know what you're going through, and I know it's tough." He nearly slipped up, when he tried to tell her how profoundly he missed his friend, Joshua. Misty-Bleu became agitated before she turned to face him. By the untaught expression on her face, William knew that she was once again overcome by anger, and that her wounds were causing chaos and raging storms from deep within her. By the look in her distressed eyes, he knew that a ball of fire was rummaging inside of her, and she had no idea how to let it out and, calm the raging tempest inside of her.

She did not want to talk to him about William, but at the same time, she wanted Joshua to understand that he could never feel the way she felt, at that very moment. "You don't know what I'm going through, Josh. You think bringing me here is going to fix me! You think that all this makes you the hero! Why are you doing this? For publicity? Or do you think that William would pat you on the back for this one day? He is gone, Joshua! Gone! I don't want your pity, I don't want you to pity me, please, I'm begging you, don't you ever pity me ..." Misty-Bleu was overcome with emotions of uncertainty, anger and fear all at once. "Don't think because you are Joshua whoever Stark, and William's best friend that you know how I and other normal people feel or function! You don't know! Your world doesn't let you know! Why are you doing this? Why are you going so far? I never wanted to sing! You don't even really know me! And this so-called therapy through music that you have forced me into? A competition I never wanted to be a part of; what is this? I promised you I'll try, but I didn't sign up for this! I owe you; I know that! I almost killed you, and for that I am sorry, but this, how am I going to get through this? I just don't know? I don't know how?" She became silent, before a fresh batch of tears threatened to bring her to her knees, "I wish you would believe me about the things … the life we had once. I wish I could talk to you about it! Maybe then, maybe then you'll see, and understand …" She tossed her cigarette, and hurriedly swabbed at the remorseless tears that were carelessly reminding her of how close they were to flooding her eyes and slip down onto her cheeks. She immediately shot to her feet and turned away from Joshua, frantic to make her way back into the house.

"Misty-Bleu, wait! I didn't mean to presume anything! You have a great voice, and William was always so proud of your singing. He used to watch you sing with so much pride. I just thought that maybe … I just want you to get better, and I just wanted to talk. This is what William wanted for you, and even if you can't see it now, things will get better, I swear it." William grabbed her arm before she could run back into the house. She at once freed herself from him and hesitated before she sat down beside him again. "How do you know what William wanted? Where did William ever watch me sing? Where? How could you have known he was proud of my voice when he never once saw me perform?" "I … I know he; I know that Bryan, he just said so,

Missy. I don't know?" William was desperate to disguise the fact that he had slipped back into their moments in the portal. "Bryan? Right. I should have known you and Bryan were behind leaking the recordings to William. Joshua, I know what you're doing, but I also know where you're from, and where you come from. William always said that your fame and celebrity, your looks and all of that, could make people do anything you wanted them to do. I don't want to talk about it, okay? I am here, and I am trying, but don't try and tell me that it will get easier, and don't try and tell me what William would have wanted."

"William loved you, Misty-Bleu, that I do know. There is nothing in this world or the next that I am surer of, and this, you quitting like this, is not what he wanted or would ever want. I know you're in pain. I know you are struggling to cope. I want to listen. I am here for you, but you need to talk to me. Not for this competition, not for other contestants, I am here for you, only for you." When William placed his hands on hers, he realized how cold she was. He took off his jacket and placed it around her shoulders. He was desperate to get through to her. He was eager to remove the blindness that his death had caused her. William could barely control his emotions when he heard the brokenness in her voice, as she reprimanded him and accused him of ulterior motives. He moved her hair just enough to catch a glimpse of the wretchedness in her eyes. When he placed his jacket around her, Misty-Bleu was uncomfortable at first, but could not discard a feeling of contentment when she felt him so close to her. The warmth of his body was spilling over into hers, and it made way for an enormous sense of awareness and refuge.

She was instantly confused by her emotions, and tried to identify what it was about Joshua, that had made her feel safe again. She was engaged in an inner and bitter warfare with the untaught emotions that were brewing inside of her. She loved William, but she was beginning to sense emotions around Joshua that she had never felt before. They could in no way at all, compare to the intensity of her love for William, but there was a flicker inside of her, each time she heard his voice, or felt his touch.

"So, Misty-Bleu, what you wrote in your book about William, why did you never tell him about all the shit that was happening to you when you were little?" He was desperate to break the awkward silence between them. "How do you know about that book? William would never, he would never tell anyone. Did William even know about that book? William never knew. I never told him. Oh God, Joshua, I don't know what's real anymore? I don't know any more what happened and what didn't. I mean, I am going crazy trying to distinguish between this world and that one, the one you think made me crazy …" "Oh, I'm … I'm sorry. No, Misty-Bleu. William did know. He must have bought it. I saw the book at his place once, and I asked him, and he told me just a little bit. I honestly don't know anything else, except that your parents were unreasonably strict with you, but that he never really knew anything about your childhood circumstances." "William had my book?" Her eyes trailed over to his, but William could scarcely look her in the eye. He nodded before he lowered his head, desperately afraid that he might reveal his true identity to her.

She took in a deep breath before she turned away from him. "I don't think you're crazy, Missy. I never did. I just think that; I think your mind just created an alternate reality for you. I think that perhaps, that's how you coped with losing him. I don't think it makes you crazy." William was frantic to validate their life together in the portal. He wanted Misty-Bleu to hold onto what they had, the life that was promised to them. He wanted her to acknowledge their wonderful, and he prayed that somehow, she might reach for that life again, with Joshua, the man he had come back as.

William was yet again reminded by how effortless it was for Misty-Bleu to command his attention. He lit another cigarette and handed it to her. She reluctantly took it from him and noticed him light another one for himself. "The songs in there, were they all written for William?" "Yes …" William lowered his head and shook it in anguish. "When he died, I wanted to die. I lived a whole other life, Josh. I know you don't believe me, and I know that sometimes you think I'm imagining it all. I know you think that I made it all up, and I know how ridiculous and utterly far-fetched it all sounds, but we had a whole other life. He was never sick. We had so many problems at first with Ana, and then I mean, you were there as well, and so were Kevin and Shaun, Blakesley and Bryan. Everyone was there. There was bad there too. It was so real to me. We were going to have a little girl; you did the gender reveal at your birthday party. I felt her inside of me, and sometimes, I still feel her. I know it sounds bizarre, but she is missing from me, you know? She was so real, Josh. My body aches for her. And Aidan Quinn? You referred me to him … wow, Josh, when I say it out loud, it all really does sound crazy, totally crazy!"

When she listened to herself tell Joshua of their life together in the portal, she burst out laughing as her tears bucketed wholeheartedly and without apology or permission, from her eyes. She knew that the very idea that she was trapped in another universe with William, seemed utterly ludicrous to any sane person. "You don't sound crazy, Missy, none of this does, it's just, the world, you know? The world doesn't understand this sort of thing. The world can't believe that this happens … they just can't think like that." William placed his arms around her when he realized that she was laughing and crying, all at the same time. "Yeah, it kind of does sound crazy …"

She leaned against him, just as she had done a million times before when a floodgate holding a thousand tears were getting ready to escape through her eyes. He held her close, deeply saddened by the torment Misty-Bleu was suffering. She leaned deeper into him and closed her eyes. She sensed William into her soul, as though he was sitting on the very spot Joshua was sitting on. She felt familiar. For an instant, her heart was no longer shattering, and for a moment, her soul was silenced. "I miss him so much. I wish I found him sooner. I was I never left. I wish so many things, Josh." Misty-Bleu whispered hoarsely through the tears that were drowning out her face. William stroked her hair, but could not at all, utter a word through the confining lump in his throat. He was defeated and wholly conquered by her vulnerability, and he was close to falling apart, when he realized for the first time, how immensely he had failed her.

"I don't think you are crazy, Misty-Bleu. I think love is so extremely powerful, and can do anything, and he loved you. I mean, he never stopped speaking of you. I believe it was real to you, and you know what else, Missy? Who makes these rules anyways? Who's to say there isn't a portal that we can slip into once in a while? What if it was all real in another kind of universe? What if the rest of us, the rest of the world is crazy for not believing in loving beyond dimensions and time as fiercely as you do? A love so powerful it could continue through the sands of time?" William had grown progressively anxious for Misty-Bleu to forgive herself for believing so wholeheartedly in the portal. He wanted her to consider a possibility of a dimensional kind of love, one he knew truly existed. He wanted her to believe that their love was magic, and that the fairy tale and the butterflies were always real.

When Misty-Bleu finally stopped crying, she retreated from Joshua, relieved by what he had just said. It felt to her as though a mountain had been lifted off her shoulders, even though she knew he probably did not himself, believe what he had just said to her. She smiled as she dabbed at the warm tears on her cheeks. "I'm sorry, Joshua. Now I got you talking crazy too. I better go inside now. You are beginning to sound completely irrational to me now." Misty-Bleu let out a faint giggle when she got up and smiled at him.

William stared at her and again, he thought that she was

without a doubt, the most beautiful girl he had ever seen. He knew at that very moment that he would never see anything like her again. He was intensely attracted to her and her vulnerability, and he desperately wished that he could carry even a small amount of her pain. In all his twenty-nine years, he had never experienced heartbreak and never imagined that it could be as painful, as seeing it manifest in Misty-Bleu's tiny frame, and through every part of her body. It was as though he was seeing, feeling, and living it through her eyes, the girl he had loved for all of his life. William's own pain was questioned when he considered the fact that he had never lost her. Not even for a moment. He had snatched her from this world the moment he had left and carried on living with her in another. When the portal was about to close, he slipped back through to be with her again. He had not missed a single moment with her. He had no idea of how excruciating it was for her to lose him. As he sat there, considering a possibility of losing Misty-Bleu, fear and horror immediately immersed him, and entirely consumed his every thought.

William sat out on the swing at the pool for a while longer. He could not abandon the utter anguish that was threatening to destroy her. He had to make it better for her, although he had no idea of where to begin. He was sure that the harder he tried to fix his biggest mistake when he abducted her into the portal, the worse he made things for her. He tossed his third cigarette and was at once angry and disappointed by how his body had once failed him. The body of William Carmichael that had become ill and withered away. He could make no sense of why he became ill, and he wondered why he was flung into a living hell with the dreaded disease he could not conquer. William got up from the swing, and reluctantly made his way back inside. When he entered the living room, he found Misty-Bleu fast asleep on the couch, in front of the muted television. He tiptoed closer to her and was again caught entirely off-guard when he noticed her tears laying damply on her cheeks.

William hurriedly made his way upstairs and picked up a quilt from his bed before he made his way back down to her. When he reached her, he gently covered her, and could not resist wiping the tears from her face. He sat on a chair across from her and stared distraughtly at her as she lay sleeping. He could in no way at all, discard the vivid memory of her performance in the studio earlier, and felt a dejected tug at his heart each time he would look at her. He hated that she appeared so broken. He could not bear to see her so utterly distressed and in such anguish. He hated the fact he alone, was responsible for all the shattered pieces of her heart. He wanted so desperately to wake her, and tell her that it was him, William, the man she was trying to recover from. He wanted her to look into his eyes, and past Joshua's, and find him there. He wanted to ask her to find him in the things she once knew so well. As he closed his eyes, William knew that his own crushed heart and bruised spirit could not feel that much pain and survive for much longer.

Misty-Bleu awoke during the night to find Joshua asleep on a chair across from her. Once again, she gasped for air when it reminded her of the night, she woke up to find William asleep in a chair, across from her. She smiled sadly, before she got up and instinctively covered him with the quilt she found over her before she quietly made her way up to her bedroom. Misty-Bleu was totally unaware of how traumatized he was by her pain, or that he had spent hours watching her sleep.

Alice VL

AFTERLIGHT

Alice VL

5

Misty-Bleu was abruptly awakened by Sylvia, who was anxious to inform her that Mr. Donahue had summoned all the finalists to the living room. She told Misty-Bleu that Joshua had chosen a finalist from their group to appear on the show and perform alongside him, and that he was about to make the announcement himself.

Misty-Bleu reluctantly dragged herself out of bed, and when she glanced at the reflection in her bathroom mirror, she sighed when she realized how distended her eyes were. "Shit." She whispered angrily when she realized that there was nothing she could do to get the swelling down, or make the redness in her eyes disappear. She was mad at herself for crying through most of the night, and she berated herself for laying out her heart to Joshua, when she could barely whisper her heart's anguish to anyone else. It was something she had never done before, not even to herself. Misty-Bleu knew that she was close to breaking down, and frantic to shout out to the world how terribly broken she was, and how desperately sore it was. She wanted to plead and beg those around her, to look into her heart and take away the pain that she could no longer stand. It had become excruciating for her to carry around the aching and absolute anguish in silence, while she desperately tried to mask her shattered heart from the rest of the world. Ever since William had died, Misty-Bleu lingered in her grief, and was feverish to avoid facing the demons her emotions evoked, her outrage and tremendous fear. There were times when all she wanted to do, was to break down and let it all out, even more so when Joshua was around her, but as she would open her mouth, her silence would deafen her. She wanted to plead with Joshua to help her, and make the pain go away. She wanted to beg him to bring William back to her, but she knew that even he would never be able to mend her shattered heart.

Misty-Bleu admired Joshua Stark and the way he would sail through her emotions with her. She felt unanticipated shelter with him, and she knew that he would never turn his back on her. He had sworn to her to help her, and it made her feel safe. It lessened her pain, and it renounced her fear, even if only for a moment. But, at the same time, Misty-Bleu knew that there was no cure for her soul, and that nobody could fix the wrong and injustice, she was sure had been done to her and to William. All there was about her life, was unfinished. All there was about the portal, remained as a stench in the air, and incomplete. There was nothing in her life, that was neatly closed off or tidily put away. There were loose ends all around her, and she had no idea how to move forward in her unfinished life. Although life had carried on, and even though William's family had begun to cope with their loss, Misty-Bleu's life ended the day he died. They could hardly consider a reality where Misty-Bleu had died along with him, even though she was still alive to the world around her. She sighed at the image looking back at her in the mirror, before she hastily made her way downstairs.

As she made her way into the living room, Misty-Bleu noticed that all the finalists had gathered around and were anxiously awaiting Joshua's announcement. She quickly sat down on the living room floor, and hoped to go unnoticed, and become invisible to the rest of them "Good morning, guys!" Mr. Donahue greeted them, as he began the meeting. All the students greeted him enthusiastically and in anticipation of his announcement, while Misty-Bleu simply smiled when he glanced over at her. "So, as you all know, Joshua was evaluating your performances yesterday, and has rather quickly chosen a student that will be performing with him next weekend. I want to make it clear to each one of you that he was impressed with all of you, but unfortunately, he could only choose one." Mr. Donahue was careful to keep them motivated, and he hoped that the students would not walk away from that meeting, feeling as though they were not good enough. He turned to William who had stepped forward. "Okay!" William rubbed his hands together, before he began addressing the finalists. "It was such a difficult decision to make, and I must assure you all that you are all very talented, and that each of you deserve a spot on any stage! Misty-Bleu? I was very impressed with your performance yesterday, and your voice and songs are equally strong. I think that your voice is best suited with mine, and I hope that you will join me at the Superbowl next weekend. I think it will be a great success, and it will be a huge honor! All you have to do is say yes?"

Misty-Bleu was flabbergasted to hear him call out her name. He could not know how often they shared a stage in the portal, and she wondered if he had ever heard her sing before her performance in the studio the day before. She could not quite believe that he had chosen her for his concert at the Superbowl. "Me?" "Yes, you!" William smiled when he saw the disbelief in her eyes. The remainder of the finalists had begun embracing her, as they shouted out in joy and excitement, yet, all that Misty-Bleu wanted to do, was creep into a hole and disappear. "Guys! Guys, let's calm down for a minute." Mr. Donahue desperately tried to regain control of the meeting, when he noticed how claustrophobic Misty-Bleu became. "Misty-Bleu? Are you ready for this? There is a lot of hard work ahead of you." Mr. Donahue smiled tenderly at her, and even though he was not entirely convinced that she was ready for such an enormous audience, he was secretly pleased with Joshua's choice. He was convinced that giving her something to look forward to, might just be what she needed. "I guess ..." Misty-Bleu was not quite sure why he had chosen her, but was sure that Joshua was once again, trying to fix her. "Okay then! You will spend the rest of this week and the whole of next week rehearsing with Joshua, where after you will leave for the Superbowl. Okay? I promise you; this won't influence your evaluation when it is time for eliminations." Mr. Donahue swiftly explained all that Misty-Bleu could expect over the next few days. "Joshua? You and Misty-Bleu can use Studio 3 for the rehearsals, and if there is anything you need, please let me or Ms. Parker know, alright? We'll carry on as usual with the remainder of the finalists." Mr. Donahue uttered softly, before he turned back to Misty-Bleu. "Misty-Bleu, you can go with Joshua. We promise not to disturb or interrupt you both until after the show. There will be no schedule for you until then, so you are free to rehearse with Joshua whenever you want." He smiled at her, before she got up and followed Joshua to Studio 3.

When they entered the studio, William made his way over to a cushion on the floor and signaled for Misty-Bleu to join him. "You okay?" He smiled when she sat down beside him. "Joshua, I mean, you never really heard me sing until yesterday. I just ... I don't think I'm the right person to perform with?" "You are the only person I am comfortable with, Misty-Bleu. There is nobody else I'd rather share a stage with. I've always known you could sing. I've seen Bryan's recordings. Now, we have much hard work ahead of us, but I was thinking that for the show, we open with your single, 'When you were here with me,' then perform a duet? Maybe 'The Photograph?' I can do a few songs after that, and we can end the concert off with another duet, 'Stronger than we are,' which I love, by the way! What do you think?" Joshua became excited as he quickly ran through the songs he had planned for their performance at the Superbowl. "Stronger than we are? You've heard it? You want to do a duet with 'Stronger than we are?'" Once again, Misty-Bleu was entirely overwhelmed by all that Joshua knew about her. Again, she was caught between her life here, and the life she had lived in the portal. "I mean, I must have heard it somewhere. I am pretty sure it was the song Bryan recorded. Anyways, what do you think?"

William was again dangerously close to slipping up as he desperately tried to separate himself from this world and the one in the portal. "Yeah, I mean, if you think so? It's your show." He stood up and held his hands out to her. "It's *our* show, and I do.

Alice VL

Come on, let's start!" He took her hand and led our out to the center of the studio. "Let's start with your songs first. Tomorrow, I'll rehearse mine and then, we can start on the duets together ..." He made his way over to the piano, before he began playing the music for her first song. After her initial hesitation, Misty-Bleu sang the song she had written for William, almost exactly as she did the previous day. Once again, she was crushed as she came undone right in front of his eyes. He was devastated when he watched her fall apart and was once again reminded of the pain that was not about to renounce her any time soon. He could not bear to see her in so much distress and misery, but at the same time, he could not disclose the feelings of desperation that were welling up inside of him. He had never felt as much torture, as he did at that very moment. It made him sick to the stomach when he realized that, for the first time in his life, just looking at Misty-Bleu could kill him, all over again. He stopped playing the piano, and walked over to her, on her knees, and crying out in pain.

"William ..." He heard her whisper his name over and over again. He placed his arms around her and held her tightly against him. He wanted to comfort her and tell her that she would be alright, but he could not find the words to tell her that she would forget all her anguish soon, without revealing himself to her. He knew that no matter what he said to her, he had crushed her heart, and when he died, he took what was left of her, with him. As he held her trembling body against him, he was stunned to realize that he had turned into her worst enemy. He wanted to reach out to her and ask her to trust him to make it better, but he was no longer sure it was a promise he could make, without telling her the truth. William tried to make sense of his own emotions as he held her in his arms. They were sensations he had never felt before, and never wanted to feel again. "Misty-Bleu …" He lifted her chin, as he wiped the tears from her eyes. She stared into his eyes, and for a moment, she could swear that it was William's eyes staring back at her. She glowered as she searched for something in his eyes to tell her he had come back to her. As she hunted him for just a moment longer, she knew that her desperation was blinding her, and that it was Joshua staring back at her. "I'm sorry, Joshua. I told you I'm not the right person for this. I can't do that song without falling apart." Her voice trailed off as she rested her head against his chest one more time. "Misty-Bleu, you can do this. Just give yourself time, you are too hard on yourself." He took her face into his hands, entirely caught up in the devastation of her pain, and the life they were promised in the portal.

He tasted the salt of her tears when he leaned forward and gently kissed her. His heart erupted into one big shudder when he felt her lips against his again. He needed her more than the air he needed to breathe. He wanted to commandeer her into his arms, and forever hold her against him. He wanted to promise her that he would do all he could, to make the world a better place for her. He distraughtly sought the power to bring him back to her; the William her heart had recognized, but no matter how fiercely he would fight to win her heart, he would never have the power to make Misty-Bleu as happy, as he once could.

Mr. Donahue softly knocked on the studio door before William called for him to come inside. "Listen, sorry to interrupt …" His voice trailed off when he noticed Misty-Bleu's devastating tears. "Are you okay, Misty-Bleu?" "I'm fine, sir …" She turned away from him and hurriedly walked over to the window, as she frantically dabbed at the tears on her cheeks. "Joshua, there's a phone call for Misty-Bleu. Do you mind if she takes it quickly?" When Misty-Bleu heard him tell Joshua about a phone call for her, she anxiously made her way back to where they were standing. "Who is it?" She frowned as she tried to figure out who would be calling her at The Academy. "It's a Shaun fellow?" Misty-Bleu clapped her hands, and hurriedly left the studio when William nodded his head in agreement. She ran downstairs, and swiftly picked up the phone when she reached Mr. Donahue's office. She was at once excited to her Shaun's familiar voice.

Alice VL

AFTERLIGHT

"Hello, gorg, how are you?" "I am so glad to hear your voice, Shaun. I'm okay, how are you?" "Fine! Congratulations on being chosen for the show at the Superbowl, Joshua called us earlier! This is really a big deal!" "Thank you, handsome, but I don't know if I can do it?" Misty-Bleu whispered into the phone and prayed that no-one would hear her hesitation. "Give yourself more credit, Missy. You'll be fine, and your guys will be in the audience. Joshua has arranged tickets for Kevin and I! We miss you so much." "I miss my guys, how is Kevin?" "Dreamy as always! Anyway beautiful, see you then. We love you!" "I love you, too!" Misty-Bleu squealed into the phone before she hung up. When she turned around, she was startled to find Joshua unexpectedly behind her. "You're smiling!" He exclaimed out loud, when he noticed the broad smile on her face. "Yeah, thank you for arranging this call, Joshua. It means so much to me. Would you mind if we took a short break?" "Sure! I'll join you. By the way, when are we going to quit smoking?" Misty-Bleu giggled and could not quite answer him. He placed his arm around her and led her out into the garden. When William sat down on the swing, Misty-Bleu sat down beside him. "Missy, if you rather want to do another song, I am fine with it." Misty-Bleu sat quietly for a moment, before she turned to face Joshua, "No, I just need to rehearse it and sing it a lot more so that I can get used to it, that's all."

Alice VL

AFTERLIGHT

William peeked over at her often as he sat in silence. He was still overawed by the raw emotions on her face only a short while ago. He thought he could see how visibly and slowly she was dying, and she was making no attempt, to fight or hide it. It was as though Misty-Bleu was lingering, simply waiting to die. When he glanced over at her again, he wished with every fraction of him, that he could once again become the man who had stolen her heart. He secretly wondered, and severely questioned what it was about him that made Misty-Bleu love him so much.

After their short break, William and Misty-Bleu made their way back into the studio. William asked her to sit on the cushion on the studio floor, while he spent the remainder of the day rehearsing his solo performances. He dialed the kitchen and asked the staff to bring their lunch up to the studio where they could eat in private. William did not want the rest of the finalists plundering her with questions about their rehearsals, or their impending performance at the Superbowl. Misty-Bleu sat quietly as she listened to him sing. She smiled often and was surprised that she had never really noticed how brilliant he was behind a mic. At times, she could barely imagine how he pulled off his life as a conservative doctor in Coral Hill by day, and a hot-studded singing superstar by night. She looked closer at him perform behind the mic, and for the first time, Misty-Bleu conceded to the fact that he was an attractive man.

His jeans fitted him like a glove, as though they were made for only him. His teal blue-green shirt was the exact color of his eyes, and his dark eyelashes matched his hair color perfectly. Misty-Bleu scrutinized his facial features, and when her eyes found his lips, she wondered what it would be like to kiss him like she once kissed William. She was mesmerized by his voice, and entirely bewitched by his performance. For a moment, Misty-Bleu wondered why she had never really added his songs to her playlist, and when her eyes trailed back to his mouth, she touched her lips, and again questioned how his would feel against hers. When his song ended, she was at once horrified by her thoughts. She lowered her head, and berated herself for thinking of another man, in the way she once thought of William. For a moment, she had left behind her memories of him. She was entirely whisked away and utterly enthralled by Joshua's performance, that for a few moments, William's eyes were not on her mind.

When their lunch was brought to Studio 3, Misty-Bleu was pleased to realize that she had forgotten about William for a short while, and she was stunned by the sudden change in her mood. William joined her on a cushion and opened a can of soda for her. She smiled at him when he handed her the can. "Josh, I just realized, I've never heard you like that. I mean, I've never ... I've heard some of your songs, but this, wow! This was, I don't know what the right word is, hypnotic?" She blurted it out before she burst out laughing. William was speechless when he noticed her unexpected change in temperament but was relieved that she had paraded her beautiful smile for him, once again. He was completely in awe of her beauty and wanted to remember her as she looked at that very moment. William knew that days like those would not come around too often. He watched her smile and was sure she could light up an entire city. He suddenly wished he could tell her to do it more often. "Misty-Bleu, do you have any idea how beautiful you are?" Misty-Bleu did not expect him to say that she was beautiful, and was not quite sure how to reply, or whether she should reply at all. "No, listen! I'm not trying to make you feel uncomfortable, but when you laugh ... when you laugh, it's the most beautiful thing I have ever seen, or ever will see again. It's always been the most beautiful thing in my life." "William, he used to say that my smile is what got him through to the end. You sounded just like him right now, you know that? Always been?" "I mean, you know? I believe that, honestly, I do. William was a very lucky guy, Misty-Bleu, and I'm sorry ... I'm sorry that it all turned out like this." "I was the lucky one, Joshua, and I am sorry too. I would do anything, anything God asks of me, if He would just send him back ..."

Alice VL

She lowered her can of soda, before she looked him sternly in the eye. "I just keep thinking … if he had started treatment sooner, if I maybe didn't ask him to wait? If he had just started chemo or radiation, and not listened to me? If I never waited; if I just kept quiet?" The tears were beginning to shimmer in her eyes when she considered all she could have done to change the outcome. "Misty-Bleu, what are you talking about? William started treatment immediately? The day after he was diagnosed, he had his first radiation treatment. Do you blame yourself for this?" William realized in shock how overcome with guilt she was. She nodded and bowed her head before he placed his arms around her and held her closely against him. "I asked him to wait for his results … what if, what if he just had that one treatment earlier?" "You can't blame yourself for William's death? You have to believe that. If you don't, how will you ever be able to move on with your life? There was never going to be a way for William to survive, Missy. You must know that?" "I don't want to move on, Joshua. I don't want to live anymore. What kind of life is this, if the only thing that has ever mattered has been taken away from me? How cruel is that Josh?" She raised her voice through utter frustration and could not quite understand why Joshua could not accept the fact that she could never move on.

Alice VL

William sensed that Misty-Bleu was slowly releasing some of her anger and bitterness and sat in silence as he allowed her to express the rage that had been blinding her for months. Misty-Bleu got up from the cushion and moved over to the window. "You don't know what it's like, Joshua. You have a whole world of women throwing themselves at your feet. You can choose anyone you want, and they'll have you. They wait for you, you know? They wait for a sign or a hint, and when you give it to any one of them, they are yours. You don't know what it's like to want somebody, to need someone and to love them, but you can't ever have them. Do you know what you do then? You love them in your mind, just so that you can breathe again. You live in a world where they are, because if you don't, you'll die. All I had was William. All I ever had, was William ..." She turned back to him, as she hurriedly swabbed at the tears that were showing up as if on cue. William felt an immense and hollow pain tug at his own heart, when he heard the desperation in her voice, and noted how her tears were spilling from her eyes. He got up and moved over to where she was standing. "Misty-Bleu, I can't have anybody I want? I don't want any of them. As for you, I wish I could say that I loved the way you did. I wish I could love ... you ..." He frantically brushed her tears away and bent down just enough to kiss her.

Alice VL

He wanted his lips to linger on hers, as he drank in everything about her again. Misty-Bleu instinctively closed her eyes when she felt Joshua's lips on hers. She unwittingly savored his touch and was instantly aware of an unexpected thump in her heart. William kissed her more enthusiastically, as he wrapped his arms around her, and pressed her firmly against him. "Joshua?" Misty-Bleu pulled away from him, and stared into his green, puddled eyes. "Oh God, I'm so sorry, Misty-Bleu, I ... I don't know what just came over me? It just, it reminded me for a moment how you looked that night on the beach, our first night. I mean, Missy, the farm ... when ..." He at once turned away from her, utterly confused by what he was feeling, and horrified that he was about to expose himself. He lied as he quickly recovered from his almost grave mistake. What he wanted to tell her, was about the night on the beach, in the portal, when he swept her up, and made love to her under the stars.

Misty-Bleu felt a strange twinge of excitement well up inside of her, yet she was angry when she consented to the kiss she had wanted from him. When her mind turned her thoughts back to William, Misty-Bleu felt guilt make its way into her heart again. She was convinced that she was about to betray William with his best friend. It suddenly hit her right between the eyes that he had initially, mentioned the beach. She knew he was referring to the night William pressed her up against her car, and made love to her. "The beach? You said the beach, Joshua? Why did you say the beach? When? What happened there? What are you talking about?" "Let's just call it a day …" "Joshua! You said the beach! I may be crazy, but I am not stupid, and I am not deaf either!" She yelled out to him, before he abruptly left the studio. He realized straight away that Misty-Bleu was beginning to puzzle the fractions of her life back together. They both knew about that first night on the beach, but that it had taken place in the portal. He had no answers for her, and he had no desire at all, to complicate their situation for her any further. She had been through enough, and he could not allow her to endure any more pain than she had to.

William slammed his bedroom door behind him, before he laid on his bed, staring at the ceiling. He was acutely aware of the sensations that were finding their way into Misty-Bleu's body, sensations that were introducing her to Joshua. He secretly wondered if they were in fact, for Joshua, or if they were for him. Was it her soul that so loved his, that was simply recognizing his? "I have to be more careful! How long can I keep this up?" He whispered softly, afraid that he might expose all that he was so desperate to shield her from. He kept seeing her face in front of him, and he remembered the way she laughed from her belly earlier. Each time his mind would wander to her, he was overcome with fear as his heart trounced wildly.

William realized that he was falling in love with her all over again, but he did not quite understand the hurt that he was feeling at the very same time. It reminded him of the utter torture he was flung into when she so abruptly left Shadow Falls. He suspected that Misty-Bleu was beginning to look at Joshua, just as she once looked at him. He sat up, and let his legs hang from the side of his bed, when he felt his tears brimming in his eyes. He could barely breathe when he considered a reality where she would love another man, and no longer love him. He wondered how it was possible to love her so greatly, even after they were separated for years. He could not at all understand how he crossed time just to be with her again, and he could not explain how his heart needed hers to survive in any universe. She was the girl he had loved and waited for his entire life. The woman he would begin to write about in his songs. She was the girl who had once permitted him to love her freely, yet now, he would have to fight his way back into heart. She was blinded by her love for him. She could no longer see clearly, and she could not see that William had found a way to return to her once again.

For as long as she grieves for him, she would never know who was standing right in front of her. He was at once terrified

Alice VL

that she might never love him, and that she might never fall in love with Joshua. He was horrified by the fact that the real him would cripple and debilitate her for years to come. Perhaps even, until death comes for her too. He was envious of the man he once was, and even though he knew they were one and the same person, he suddenly found himself wanting to be William all over again, just for her. The real William. The authentic William. The William she was ready to lay down her life for. He wanted to earn back his title of the man that had once saved her from her nightmares of her childhood. He instinctively revisited their life together in the portal, which left his heart missing a beat. Misty-Bleu loved him unconditionally, and he so craved that love from her again, even if it had to be as Joshua.

Misty-Bleu remained behind in the studio, and rehearsed her song to William over and over, desperate to overcome her emotional breakdowns each time she sang it. With each try, she felt stronger and smiled easier, instead of falling apart. She spent the remainder of the day rehearsing and found it a welcome escape from the torment she was living through. In between continuously rehearsing the same song, her mind drifted back to Joshua, the only other man she had ever shared a kiss with. A kiss that took place only hours ago, but one she could hardly stop thinking of. Without intending to, Misty-Bleu grinned from ear to ear each time she allowed her mind to drift back to his touch. She closed her eyes, and secretly revived their kiss. It made way for a sparkle inside of her, and it replaced the emptiness within the very core of her, with slight flutters. Misty-Bleu did not see Joshua again during rehearsals and headed out to the pool after supper for fresh air, desperate to isolate herself from the other contestants. When she approached the garden swing, she noticed Joshua sitting there quietly, as he rested his elbows on his knees, just as William would habitually do when he was still alive. "Josh?" She whispered gruffly as she sat down beside him. "Hey, Missy, are you feeling better?" "Yes, I'm fine. I just wanted to say that I am sorry about this afternoon." "You don't have to be sorry, Missy. I get it, really I do." She interlocked her hands, and sat in silence for a few seconds before she turned back to him. "So, tell me more about your life. William always used to say how glamorous it was?"

William began telling her about his record company, his tours, his music, and all the advantages and disadvantages of being a star. He told her that he was never really ready to give up his practice, and that he was wholly torn between the two. He mentioned how he would often go up to his hotel room and find strange women waiting for him. Misty-Bleu giggled when she heard him relay stories of horror and disgust at the women throwing themselves at him, but at the same time, William was happy to see her smile again. It was never hard to relay stories about Joshua's life. William could vividly recall all the details Joshua had regularly shared with him. Misty-Bleu told him how she adored music, but that she hated the spotlight all at the same time. "I love music, Joshua. I love the emotions and how the lyrics come from our souls, but I doubt that I could cope with the pressure. I never wanted the stage or the stardom." "It's tough in the beginning, but you get used to it. After a while, it becomes a job, and if you're not careful, it sucks you in. I never wanted this, really. I just wanted to enjoy music and become a brilliant doctor. I never planned this life, any part of it actually." He paused when he reflected on his own life, and how destiny had horribly intervened, and brought chaos along with it. "I never, ever thought that my life would be like this. If someone told me a year ago, I'd be here today, with you, like this, I would have laughed. I never thought that we'd end up strangers, I mean, you know? Not that I really knew you. It's just, we are different people in this house and things aren't always as they seem." He stammered nervously as he stumbled over his words. Misty-Bleu thought she detected anguish and bitterness in his eyes, and she was sure that Joshua was hiding a dark secret, and excruciating heartache from her.

Alice VL

They laughed together when they told each other stories of their childhood, and when Misty-Bleu spoke about William, she remembered everything there was to remember about him. Even though she was initially beleaguered by sadness, she told him only the good stories about them. William was glad to hear her talk about him, without falling apart and bursting into tears. She had burst out laughing more than once, and she smiled instead of cried, when she recalled her memories with William. Misty-Bleu glanced at her wristwatch and realized that it was after midnight. She got up from the swing and turned back to face him. "I've got to go to bed, Joshua, it's late. I'm sorry I was such a pain earlier, tomorrow will be better, you'll see …" She bent down in front of him, and quickly kissed him on his cheek. She retreated slightly when she was once again, reminded of the kiss they shared earlier. She knelt in front of him and placed her hands on his knees. William leaned forward and smiled when he detected the uncertainty in her eyes. He leered slightly, before she leaned in until her lips met his. She closed her eyes and was once again familiar with the sensations that were rushing through her. She slowly retreated and gazed into the eyes that were beginning to haunt and taunt her all at the same time. "I want you to kiss me like before …"

She was at once desperately afraid that he might reject

Alice VL

her. He stared at her in stunned silence, before he placed his arms around her, and pulled her closer to him. Misty-Bleu surrendered willingly to him when he kissed her more fervently than he did only moments earlier. William held onto her, as he kissed her just as he did almost a hundred times before. As if in a foggy haze, she climbed onto his lap, and took his face into her hands. "I don't want you to say anything. I don't want you to speak. I don't want to talk ..." It was a moment she was familiar with. It was an emotion she knew so well. He felt like home to her, and she was desperate to reclaim one moment that could take her away from all that was fighting to destroy her. She lifted herself onto him, and when she could feel the warmth of him inside of her, she huskily cried out for him. She could not take her eyes off him, and when he gripped her firmly around her waist, his eyes were fixed on hers. She had entirely surrendered to him, and the moment that offered her a reprieve from all that she had suffered for what felt like an entire lifetime. She allowed herself to get lost in him for that one moment, and she freely submitted to him and the endless pleasures that his body offered her. When it was over, Misty-Bleu lowered her head and pressed her lips against his one more time. She kissed him gently, before she lifted herself off him. She stood staring at him through the hair that was wildly masking her face, and without uttering a single word to him, she turned away from him, and made her way back indoors.

William watched her walk away from him, as though she was never there. She had brought along inner chaos with her body, almost as though she snuck into him undetected. She had opened the door to a tempestuous storm that had begun raging inside of him. The look in her eyes bore no traces of uncertainty, and he was convinced that her touch was burnt onto his skin. For a moment, he was sure that he had imagined it all, but when he leaned back, he could still smell her on him. He closed his eyes and relived her hunger for him. He shuddered when he recalled the way he felt inside of her. It was all he needed, to once again, lose himself in the murky puddles of her heart, one he had left in a mess. William made his way back to his bedroom as though in a rambling haze. When he passed Misty-Bleu's bedroom, he stood quietly, and wondered if she was asleep. He knocked softly, and when there was no reply, he opened her door and quietly snuck in. She was asleep, with the covers pulled up so high, he could barely see her hair. He was at once overwhelmed by a powerful urge to hold her and protect her, even from herself. He sat down on the bed beside her and stared at her as she lay sleeping. "You're beautiful, Misty-Bleu, I love you. I am so in love with you. I am so sorry I broke your heart ..." He gently caressed the top of her head, and when she murmured softly, his heart hammered into his chest. "I love you too, William …"

William stood up, and leaned against her bedroom wall, as he tried to make sense of all that had happened only moments earlier. There was so much more about her grief that he did not understand. He wanted to know what it would take to make her whole again. He wanted to find a way to erase her heartache and all that had threatened to defeat her. He never wanted to see her cry for him again. He wanted to shield her and protect her from the cruelty that had mercilessly imprisoned her in her sorrow. He wanted to sweep her up, and hide her from the world, where she would never suffer through any torment again. He wanted to love her, and he wanted his daughter to find a way into their lives, one more time. William let out a disparaging sigh, before he glanced over at her once again. "Misty-Bleu, I am going to fix this for you." He whispered gently, before he walked out of her bedroom, and into his.

Misty-Bleu dreamed about Joshua that night, and even though she had surrendered herself entirely to him, she could not release the grip William held over her. She begged him to let her go, and she pleaded with him to allow her to feel something other than pain again. She fought to loosen herself from his grasp, while Joshua turned his back on her, and walked away into the night. She woke up in sweats often during the night and was overcome with guilt for her betrayal of William. She curled up under the covers of her bed, and lay sobbing until the sun finally came up. After pouring herself and Joshua a cup of coffee, Misty-Bleu anxiously made her way back to the studio, where Joshua was waiting for her. "Hi there!" He smiled when he saw her walk in with coffee. "I brought the coffee …" She whispered, and when she handed him a cup, she could not discard the images of their encounter of the previous night, from her mind. Misty-Bleu smiled tensely when she realized that she was unable to look him in the eye. "Listen Missy, I know this is awkward, but do you want to talk about what happened?" She lowered her head, and took a quick sip of her coffee, "No, can we just pretend it didn't happen, please?" He lifted her head, and when their eyes met, he smiled when he recognized how blood-red her face had turned. "If that's what you want? We never have to talk about it, alright?" She nodded, at once relieved that she did not have to answer for her unpredicted behavior.

William turned away from her, instantly unnerved that she discarded their encounter as though it had never happened. "Where do you want to start today?" When he moved over to the center of the studio, Misty-Bleu was at once sensitive to the fact that his mood had instantly changed. "Are you mad at me, Joshua?" Misty-Bleu could not shake the feeling that he had become hostile towards her. "I'm not mad at you, Misty-Bleu, I just have a lot on my mind and I ... I just didn't sleep too well." "Was it me? Was it because of ... you know?" "No, not at all. It has nothing to do with that." William lied, but knew that he could never let her know how it had everything to do with her. "Okay. I'd like to start with 'When you were here with me'. Is that okay?" She took the microphone and waited for his response. "Sure ..."

He walked on over to the piano and began playing the song he had learned to fear the most. When Misty-Bleu sang the final lyrics of her song, William was relieved that, although she had sung it with the emotions, she had sung it before, the tears that plagued her during her performance, was nowhere to be seen. He was immensely relieved and applauded her for a wonderful performance. Misty-Bleu smiled at him, proud of herself for manipulating her anger and hurt. "Misty-Bleu, that was fantastic!" He seized her into his arms and turned her around and around. She laughed out loud for the first time in what felt like an eternity, and while the joy replaced her heartache, she again, did not feel as though her heart was being ripped out from inside of her. He placed her down, before he unexpectedly turned away from her. "Joshua, what's wrong?" She was stunned when she recognized the pained expression on his face. "Misty, you are far too beautiful to carry so much pain around with you.

Alice VL

AFTERLIGHT

When I see, and hear you laugh, I can't imagine seeing you cry. I want to tell you to stop and consider that perhaps that things are not always as they seem. Sometimes, you have to believe in something bigger. You did once, remember? The portal you claimed to be stuck in? You believed it so much, that you had me convinced for a while, that half-light ..." He walked up to her and embraced her. Misty-Bleu was at once surprised by what he was saying, but at the same time, she wanted him to hold her even closer. "Joshua? I don't know if any of that was real. I *did* live a whole other life, in a whole other world, and even if it was real in my mind, I know it couldn't really have been. I'm beginning to see that. I'm beginning to question everything, and last night, you and I, it was you, not William, and I hate myself for it. I hate that it happened, but I'm not sorry. I am not sorry, Josh." "It was real, can't you feel me?" She frowned and gazed questioningly at him. "It shouldn't have happened ..." She became anxious at once when he wasn't making any sense at all to her. "Don't talk, Missy, just be quiet and feel me." He whispered, and through sheer desperation, he grabbed her hands. She pressed up against him, before she placed her lips on his. She closed her eyes and realized that she could hardly get enough of the way his lips felt against hers. She compared the sensation to a drug she would relentlessly seek and pay any price it would demand. She was slipping into a life of addiction, only it would be to a man who

Alice VL

had slipped in when she wasn't looking. He longingly kissed her back, and when he took her face into his hands, she was sure that she felt a million butterflies find a home in her stomach.

He retreated slightly, and stared into her frosty blue eyes, "Misty-Bleu, I have no idea what is going on here, and I don't know what I'm saying, but I … I am in love with you. I am falling in love with you …" "No, Joshua! No! This isn't about love! Last night was not about love! You don't know what love is!" She pushed him away, before she made her way over to the window. "Misty?" He followed her to where she stood staring at the world outside and grabbed a hold of her arm. She turned around and glared angrily at him. "I love William, I always will! I will not betray him or his memory! I can't. I will never love you, Josh! Never! Not like that! I want William!" "No, Misty-Bleu! You have to move on with your life! You speak about picking up the pieces, of getting up and fighting the cruelty of the world in your book. You speak of rising above all the hurt and of becoming wonderful! You say all these things in The Afterwards. You tell the world how you wanted to survive and how desperate you were to live, and yet, here you are!"

William's heart could not allow Misty-Bleu to surrender to her inner demons, even one more time. Misty-Bleu felt her entire world come crashing down around her when she realized

Alice VL

that Joshua had read her book, and that he knew exactly what had happened to her, through her own words. She began to quiver as her tears began to bucket mercilessly from her eyes, "You had no right to read The Afterwards!" She angrily pointed a finger at him. "Then you shouldn't have put it out there for the world to read!" "No, Joshua! No! *You* had no right!" "Well, I did! And, put that in your pipe and smoke it! It can never be unread!" He was fuming as he stood staring at the anger that was radiating through her eyes. "Joshua, my life and my past, is none of your business! What happened to me is no concern of yours! How did you even know? You keep saying William read my book, but you never said that you did!" She yelled out at the top of her lungs, when she again recalled that the only time William had ever laid his eyes on her book, was in the portal. That was, until Joshua had casually told her that he had seen the book in William's house. "I ... no, I don't know, Misty-Bleu! Maybe I just scanned through the book somewhere! Fuck, Misty-Bleu! I don't know what to say to you right now! I am telling you that I am falling in love with you, and all you can think about is that damn book! And yeah, your life is my business, it has always been!" "Always been? You are delusional!" She yelled out, before she pushed him away once again. "You are a superstar! Then, you go home, and you are a surgeon and who knows what else? Me, I am a writer, who just wants to live on my farm and love William! I don't want this life! I am not a part of this life like you are! I hate it!"

She felt as though something inside her had snapped, as she shouted out in anger and desperation, without even as much as taking a breath. "I don't care! It doesn't matter to me, Misty-Bleu, it's not what matters! None of this is! This isn't me! This isn't my life! I didn't choose this or how things turned out! I wish … I wish you could see that. I wish you could see me. You are important to me, you matter, Misty-Bleu! And if … if you could just for a second, just for a moment, stop drowning in yourself like this, then maybe you'll see, maybe you'll know that this place is not about celebrity or stardom, and that who I am is nothing and no-one!" Misty-Bleu moved closer to him and took his hands, "It is important, Joshua. We are poles apart, too different, and William … I will never say goodbye to him, Josh. I will never let him go, so don't ask me to …" "Stop Missy! Stop. Can you honestly say you don't feel anything? Can you truly, from the innermost gist of you stand there and tell me that there is nothing about me, nothing at all? Last night, you came back to me, aren't you getting the messages, don't you feel anything for me?" Misty-Bleu was stunned to detect how the tears had begun to gleam in his eyes. "Came back to you? Josh, sometimes you say things I just don't understand, and I don't know how to respond! I don't know what you mean? I do feel something. I do.

Alice VL

It scares me, and it unnerves me! Sometimes, you say things William used to say or you do things William used to do, and sometimes, I think I can feel him, like last night. But Josh, you are not William! I can't carry on looking for him in everyone else. I can't find something in you that brings him back to me and convince myself it's him. I am trying to breathe again. I am trying to feel something that doesn't hurt so much, but what I can't do is … I cannot do this to William! I am not ready! I cannot risk my heart again Joshua, and I can never risk it with someone like you, and especially not with his best friend, don't you get it?"

Joshua stood staring at her. He knew that he was only moments away from blurting out the truth. He was desperate to make her understand that she was with William, and that it was William she found in Joshua, but he knew he could never reveal himself to her. He was desperately afraid that the truth would take him away from her forever. "Misty-Bleu, William doesn't want this for you, this pain and all this anger. Please, please let me help you, please Missy." Misty-Bleu's anger was not quite ready to subside. She moved closer to him, and began thrashing into his chest with her fists, and with all her might. "Stop saying that! Stop trying to fix me! Stop telling me what William wants!" She paused to take in a deep breath. "You don't know what we had, Joshua! You have no idea of what we went through once!

You don't know how I need him to breathe. I need him to glue me back together!" She stepped back from him, and brought her hands to her face, before she broke out into a violent shudder. William placed his arms around her and held her possessively against him. She closed her eyes, before she whispered into his chest. "I am sorry about last night. I am sorry. I just want to get through these few weeks, Joshua, and then go back to my life. I won't quit, I promised you I wouldn't, but I want you to know that you don't have to save me, and I am trying, I am trying …" She stepped back from him, before she feverishly wiped the tears from her cheeks. "I know, I know you have a good heart. I know you are loyal to William. Don't, please don't beat yourself up about last night. I so badly wanted to escape all this for a bit. I am sorry." William was distraught when he realized how close she was to surrendering to her heartache again. He knew that nothing he could say to her would draw her away from William, from him. The old him. The him that no longer existed in her world, and the him that would never subsist in her universe again. He knew that he had to let go, no matter how much it would cost him, and how he would have to live in a world that once belonged to his best friend, without Misty-Bleu Buchanan. For a moment, he wondered if he was not being punished for altering fate, and cheating time. "I can't turn my back on you, Misty-Bleu, but I can promise to try to let you go."

Alice VL

AFTERLIGHT

He turned away from her and made his way over to the piano. William was crushed and felt cursed beneath the weight of her eyes. He was crippled by her sorrow, and sure that he could no longer stand to feel the enormous weight of her pain on him.

Alice VL

William and Misty-Bleu spent the next two weeks rehearsing for the show, while they kept a safe distance from each other. Misty-Bleu could not tolerate one more confrontation with him, while William could no longer find the strength to fight for a love he was once ready to sell his soul for. When they rehearsed their duets, William made a concerted effort to invite Ms. Terry to their rehearsals, so as to avoid getting as intimately close to Misty-Bleu, as they did each time they performed together. Misty-Bleu sensed the distance he was desperate to achieve from her with sadness, and at night, she often questioned whether she had been too quick to reject Joshua, especially since he had never left her side.

Without intending to, and without noticing, Misty-Bleu had slowly begun dealing with the fact that William would never return to her. He could never reach her again, and he could never love her under the same blue skies as he once did. Not a moment went by that she did not think of him, but she no longer fell apart, and she no longer wished with all that she was, to join him. Misty-Bleu found herself staring at Joshua when she thought he wasn't looking. She would be transported back to the night at the pool, and her entire body would jolt by the mere memory of him so intimately close to her. She played out the look in his eyes over and over again in her mind, and she secretly hunted her body's craving of him. Her body ached to feel his against hers again, but it was how she felt in his arms, that brought a little bit of William back to her. Misty-Bleu had finally accepted that the portal was simply a desperate figment of her imagination. It was a world she had created and ran away to when she could no longer tolerate the utter devastation and anguish that had invaded her entire being. She longed for the magic she had found in the portal, and she recalled each detail as though it was real.

She often reflected back on her time there with William, and she beamed when she relived the moments that saved her. Each time her mind wandered to the daughter she was carrying, her heart ached enormously, and she couldn't help but feel a deep emptiness inside of her; there where her daughter should be. Her body hankered after the child she was about to have, and when Misty-Bleu closed her eyes, she could almost feel her inside of her again. She missed William, and she missed the daughter she never met. Misty-Bleu hunted the fullness of her heart, but she ultimately surrendered to the fact that none of it was ever real.

William would slowly stroll past her bedroom at night and could barely walk past without checking in on her when she was asleep. He never had to compete with any man for her heart, and yet, the only man who was standing in his way, was he, himself. She pined for and sought William Carmichael. She ached for the man who was standing right in front of her, yet, she had no suspicion that it was him. The woman he had loved his entire life, had lost her heart to a man William no longer knew, and no longer understood. His mind told him that she ached for another man, while his body told him, it was he her heart recognized. He was torn between what he thought he knew, and all that he did not quite understand. He laid awake at night, unable to rid himself of the curse of her touch, and the eyes that continued to haunt him. He prayed to God, that she would wake up one morning soon, and finally lay William to rest. He wanted to wait for her. He was desperate to stay close and wait for the day that she walked out into the light, and confess to him that she had survived William Carmichael. With his entire heart, he wanted to wait, but he was no longer sure he could survive the anguish that had set its sights on him and targeted him just as it had Misty-Bleu.

Alice VL

At The Academy, the contestants were allocated Friday afternoons to receive phone calls from their families. Misty-Bleu was excited to spend an hour on the phone with Shaun and Kevin, and she looked forward to her phone calls from David and Julia. She was thrilled to realize how speaking to William's parents instantly distracted her from Joshua. She no longer joined Joshua at the pool for their rehearsal breaks, but she would sneak out on her own when The Academy was quiet, and each finalist had retired for the night. She was careful to keep an eye on Joshua, and the moment his bedroom door closed behind him, she would tiptoe out to the pool.

As Misty-Bleu began identifying the inherent feelings that were beginning to overwhelm her, she reluctantly admitted to the fact that she was falling in love with Joshua. She scolded herself for the emotions that were beginning to ignite passion inside of her, and she was utterly ashamed of her betrayal of William. She often questioned the authenticity of her emotions and craving for Joshua. She could not help but wonder whether her vulnerability and loneliness were blinding and numbing her. She was desperately afraid of loving so freely again. She was terrified to give in to him, just to lose him in the end. When William slipped out, it was a pain Misty-Bleu felt, and forced her to live with excruciating anguish and sorrow. An ache she was sure she could never survive, even only one more time. It was a soreness she knew she could never feel again, and she wished she had never loved to begin with. There were times when Misty-Bleu's thoughts drifted away from William, and straight to Joshua, and it would take her breath away. She was absolutely confused by the sensations that were causing a tingling throughout her entire body. Her stomach would turn, and a tickle would linger deep inside of her, while he was on her mind. She had no idea that a smile would form around her mouth, each time Joshua Stark's eyes would infiltrate, and consume her every thought. Each morning at breakfast, Misty-Bleu's heart would unintentionally leap when Joshua took a seat at the other end of the table. The finalists would flock around him, and pepper him with questions about his life. She smiled often when she noticed how they would compete for his attention.

William thoroughly enjoyed the attention and could finally appreciate Joshua's addiction to the limelight. He beamed as he conversed with each contestant, but it was Misty-Bleu's attention he so desperately craved.

Alice VL

AFTERLIGHT

Alice VL

6

The limousine arrived early the following Thursday morning to drive Joshua and Misty-Bleu to the Grand Belle Hotel at the Superbowl. They hurriedly said goodbye to the rest of the finalists and mentors and could not shake the discomfort and distance that had grown between them. They both sat in silence during the short drive to the Superbowl, but Misty-Bleu caught glimpses of him often.

William and Misty-Bleu were shown to their separate hotel rooms shortly after their arrival. She quickly excused herself and locked herself in her hotel room where she unpacked her luggage before the rehearsals for the show began. William matter-of-factly informed her that they would be rehearsing together early the following morning for the first show later that evening. She spent the remainder of the day in her room, desperate to distract herself from Joshua, but she could not veer away from him, while knowing that he was in the room right next to hers. She was again overwhelmed and confused by the emotions she had grown extremely sensitive to. It was as though her heart was tireless in sending her messages, and she could no longer ignore any of them. Misty-Bleu was staggered that there was a space left in her heart for Joshua, yet it was only William she thought she needed there. There were never any guarantees with Joshua, none that could persuade her of his devotion for her, as William's love had once effortlessly convinced her. They came from too different worlds, and more than anything, she feared the fragility of her heart. The pain of losing William was something she could never go through again, not even for a moment. Misty-Bleu felt into the very core of her that her heart would stop beating not too far from that moment. It was too much for one heart and one soul to bear, and she wondered at times, whether her heart would eventually turn blunt.

She laid unresponsively on her enormous hotel bed, as she reflected back on the wonderful and carefree days she had shared with William. There were so many hopes and dreams she held tucked away in her heart. All she had every prayed for, was to live them out with William before he became ill. Misty-Bleu wiped away a tear and turned onto her side. She could still see his eyes as she lay thinking of all he had suffered in the days after his diagnoses. She fell asleep growing increasingly resentful of the cruel twists that had lurked in plain sight, only days after he began the treatment that caused him to spiral into a deep, dark world of pain and suffering.

Alice VL

AFTERLIGHT

It was after eight that evening, when Misty-Bleu finally woke up. She felt surprisingly rested and calm, and immediately thought of Joshua in the bedroom next door. She got up, and quickly slipped on a jersey, before she hurriedly made her way to the room, only a few steps away from her. When she stood at his door, she noticed a light reflecting underneath it. She hesitated for a moment, but almost robotically, she knocked twice. William heard the gentle knock on his door and assumed it might be the sandwich he had ordered only moments ago. When he opened the door, he was surprised to find Misty-Bleu standing there. "Misty?" His voice began to shudder, before he forced a smile. It was only when he realized that she had probably just woken up, that he smirked truthfully. "Hey Josh, can I come in?" William stepped aside, as he made way for her to gain access into his hotel room. He showed her to a chair when his mobile phone began to ring. "Hello?" Misty-Bleu stared at him, dressed in a pair of jeans and a T-shirt. She noticed again how good-looking he was, and she wondered again, how it was that she never noticed any of this before. It took her breath away as she scrutinized every inch of him. She was keenly aware of her sensitivity to him, as her body began to relive their one night out at the pool. "No, I won't be doing autographs this evening, perhaps tomorrow." He ended the call and placed his mobile phone on his hotel bed. "Autographs, huh?" "Yeah, apparently, you can never get away

Alice VL

from it. The moment the fans find out where you are, they don't leave you alone. Anyway, is something the matter?" "Apparently huh? No, nothing's the matter. I just wanted to see you. We have been kinda avoiding each other, and I feel like it's all my fault. I don't want us to be like that with each other." She stood up, and nervously made her way over to him. "I know I've been difficult, Josh. I know what I've done to you, and I know how hard you've tried, and still try. Nobody has really stuck with me like you have, so, I am sorry. Please forgive me?" William gazed incredulously at her, while Misty-Bleu slipped deeper into the abyss, where his eyes were supposed to be. "It's ... it's alright, Misty-Bleu. Really, there's nothing to forgive." He turned away from her, and hurriedly made his way over to his hotel room door, before he abruptly opened the door for her. "I'll see you tomorrow morning at eight then?" He stepped aside so that she could pass, even though all he wanted was to keep her there. He fought the urge to seize her in his arms and hold her against him for the entire night. He wanted to whisper in her ear that he could give her the same love William had once given her. He wanted to protect her heart and give her the world. He wanted to comfort her and wipe the tears from her misty blue eyes. He wanted to sweep her up, and never let her go again. But, as he stood at the door waiting for her to leave, William knew that Misty-Bleu was not ready for him, and he doubted whether she ever would be. He was intimidated by her sadness, and at the same time, by the feelings that had consumed him each time he was around her.

Misty-Bleu was at once mortified that she showed up on his doorstep, and immediately felt unwanted and entirely out of place. She had gone to his room to make-believe that there was nobody else in the world, but the two of them. She wanted to just once more, escape the anguish that had dominated her life so severely, even if only for a short while. Yet, as she made her way through the door, she realized in utter despair, that Joshua's patience with her, had run out. "I deserved that ..." She thought sadly before walking out of his room, feeling lonelier and emptier than ever before.

Misty-Bleu had just climbed out of the shower, when she heard a frantic knock on her hotel room door. She hurriedly pulled a robe around her wet body, before she walked over to the door. She opened it slightly and was startled to find William standing there. "Joshua?" She was entirely unprepared to find him standing in front of her, especially since he was anxious for her to leave his room, only an hour ago. William stood in silence, as he framed the picture of her in front of him. Her long hair was still dripping with water, and when he lowered his eyes, he realized she had not yet dried herself. "Misty-Bleu ..." He marched into her room and shut the door behind them with force. He moved closer to her and pressed his lips against hers. His arms clutched her body against his, as he pressed her against the bedroom wall. Misty-Bleu did not fight him, instead, she fiercely kissed him back. She placed her arms around him, and squeezed herself against him, as though she was still too far from him. He retreated slightly, before he slowly opened her robe, and left it to fall to the floor. He stood still, as though frozen in time just to look at her and absorb all there was about her one more time. When he took her in his arms once again, he kissed her wildly. He held his open lips against hers, as he gazed into her ocean blue eyes, "God, you are so beautiful, I've missed you. This, I need this. I want that night on the beach …" He picked her up, without his lips leaving hers, and carried her to the oversized bed in the center of the room. Misty-Bleu stared into his eyes and was again slightly unnerved and confused by what he had just said, but she was powerless to fight him. She was defenseless to resist her hunger and craving for him.

For one night, she wanted to surrender fully to Joshua Stark. She wanted him, Joshua Stark. She wanted to feel him inside of her, and as her body responded to his, she clutched his face in her hands, and intensely kissed him as though this would be their one last kiss. "Joshua, make love to me. I want you. Do you hear me? *You*. I want *you*. I want to feel something again,

take me away from here. It's you, I want. It's you I want to feel
…" She whispered hoarsely as she held onto him. William wanted
nothing more than to carry her away into a world where she
could be only his. He wanted her to surrender to him, just as she
had done a thousand times before. He wanted to feel her body
crave his, and he wanted to feel her hands hunt him for her
pleasure. He wanted to feel her legs squeeze against him, while
her fingers carved into his skin. He wanted to feel her gentle
shudders as he found his way inside of her. He wanted to see her
throw her head back as she moaned out with pleasure. He
wanted to once more, feel the ripple run through her entire
body, as it found its way into his. It was an entire world away
from the passion they had shared before, but he wholeheartedly
embraced a kind of hunger and craving he had never known with
Misty-Bleu until that very moment. "Misty-Bleu, I love you. I love
you. I've always loved you. Even when I lost you, I loved you …"
He stammered almost incoherently as he thrust himself inside of
her. She held on to him, afraid that if she let go, she would never
feel the way she felt at that very moment.

As their bodies came together, and as their rhythms
synchronized in pure decadence, it was Joshua's arms she lost
herself in. It was Joshua's body that replaced her pain with
endless gratification. It was Joshua she hunted, and she wanted

their moment to never end. She closed her eyes as she heard him whisper into her ear, just as William had whispered to her so many nights before. She heard him tell her that he loved her, just as William had told her when her body captured and imprisoned his. He clung to her, just as William would hold her close to him. He pressed her firmly against him, and when she was sure that she felt William again, she moaned out softly. For a split-second, and for a brief moment in this world, she felt William again. Deep into her soul, and from the innermost core of her entire being, she felt and breathed William Carmichael. She had lost herself in his eyes, as she felt him become one with her again. She clung to him, and without intending to, without hearing herself moan out, she softly whispered his name, "William ..." When William heard her cry out for him, he held her tighter. He had come back to her, and her soul had finally recognized his. Her heart could not deny that it had sensed him, and for one moment where they were caught up in enchantment, their souls had found their way home.

Rolling over to his side, William noticed that Misty-Bleu had burst into tears. He knew that she was overwhelmed by what had just taken place between them, and he was sure that she understood all that he already knew but was not yet equipped for. "Missy?" He turned to her and pulled her against him. "Is it William?" "No, Joshua, no. I mean, I don't want to lie to you. I felt something with you, something that I thought I knew only with William. There's never been anyone, but William for me, and I just knew him into my soul, I knew him. And now you, it was like, it was like William, like you were him, and I am so sorry for telling you this! I am so sorry for saying that, but I am, I am falling in love with you. I am slipping so far away from William, and falling in love with you ..." She turned over to face him, while keeping his arms firmly around her. "I'm not crying because I'm sorry this happened again. I am happy. I've never felt this way since William left, and I never thought that I could ever feel this way again, but I do, and I hope to God, he doesn't hate me for it. My heart knew you; my body knows you, and it scares me." William squeezed her tighter against him and knew into the very core of him that she had felt him again. She had recognized him. It was the proof he needed that her soul had come home to his. Misty-Bleu was safe again. "Misty-Bleu, come with me. Come with me when I go on tour." "Go away from here? And Little Dreams, with you? Joshua, what are you asking me?" She sat up straight as she covered herself with the covers on her bed. "I have to leave for a world tour after the shows here at the Superbowl. I came here tonight to tell you that I've informed Mr. Donahue about it and, I can't stay until the competition at The Academy is over. I am under contract to do a world tour, Misty-Bleu and, I mean, I didn't know all the details until it was finalized. I thought there would

Alice VL

be more time. I didn't think it would be now?" "What? You're leaving The Academy?" She raised her voice, suddenly plagued by fear as the desperation began to overpower her. "My agent called me this morning. I have four months to complete the tour. I have to do this, Misty-Bleu, I must. But, when it's over, when all my contractual obligations are met, I am going to walk away from all of this. I don't want this anymore ..."

Misty-Bleu rested her head on her pillow. She could not simply leave the academy and walk away from her promise to the world, or to William. She could not leave her home and join a man she hardly knew. She was slowly weening herself off William, and she could not hand her life over to someone she was not yet ready for. William sat up right and gazed down at Misty-Bleu. "Misty-Bleu, don't think. Jus come with me. Let's run away and go so far. Let's get away from here ..." Misty-Bleu shot to her feet, and angrily threw her robe around her. "What did you just say?" Misty-Bleu was suddenly caught off-guard by William's choice of words. "What do you mean?" "You said to go so far?" "Yeah, I mean, let's just go far away." Again, William came dangerously close to revealing his true identity to her. "I can't, Joshua, I just can't." She paused while considering all he was asking of her. "We have different lives, and yes, I do have feelings for you. I do, but I don't know if it's enough to give up my life here? I don't know if I want the life, you will be living for the next four months? What if you can't walk away from all this? I don't want that life, and I can't let go of mine just yet …" "What life, Misty-Bleu? What fucking life do you have? How many times haven't you told me that you have no life? How long do you still want to cling to William, and the life you had with him? Or almost had with him?" William was enraged by how cruelly their situation had come back to haunt him. "My farm, my trees and my horses, that's my life! My books, my stories! That's my life! It may not be nearly as glamorous as yours, but it's mine and it's all I have, and I love it!" She yelled at him through the tears that were once again bucketing from her eyes. "Leave if you must! Go far away, but don't … just don't leave my heart in a mess. William has already done that! So just go!" "Misty-Bleu, I wouldn't take you away from the farm if I didn't think I could bring you back here for a weekend now and again, I swear to you. I know you'll never give up Little Dreams, and I don't want you to. I know you've dreamed of this life since you were a little girl, but I am asking you for four months, just four months?" Misty-Bleu was at once frustrated by his callous remarks, "Joshua Stark! You know nothing about my dreams as a little girl. I can't! I don't want to! You are Joshua Stark, the Grammy award winning superstar! I am nobody, and you'll forget me as soon as you're on stage again. You will forget me the moment someone blonder, and more beautiful stands in front of you! There will always be someone better, someone else you will love. You don't love me, Josh, you pity me! You are keeping your promise to William, and I ... I don't want that!" She gasped for air, before he interrupted her. "I *do* love you, Misty-Bleu! Why is it so hard for you to believe that I, Joshua Stark, love you? I don't know how else to tell you? I don't know what else to say to you? Things are not as they seem and I ... I need you to look past all that you think you know about me!"

He grabbed her by her shoulders, before he lifted her eyes just enough to meet his. Misty-Bleu frowned when she stared into them through her tears. For an instant, she wanted to go with him. She wanted to leave all her pain behind, and start a new life with him, but as she stood looking into his eyes, there was something about William looking back at her. There was something there, that told her he was close. She glowered again, and realized that perhaps, her surrender to Joshua was coming back to haunt her. She bowed her head when she realized that she had deceived William, and their life together. She was blinded by the reality that she had just betrayed William with his very best friend. She could not look past what she was seeing, and she could not understand who it was looking back at her. She recognized Joshua, but she found William in his eyes. It scared her almost to death that William felt so close to her, when it was

Alice VL

Joshua standing right in front of her. "No, Joshua, I can't! I don't know what you want me to see!"

William turned away from her and slipped on his jeans and T-shirt. He swiftly made his way to her door, and before he opened it, he turned back to her one more time. "Misty-Bleu, what do you want to do for the rest of your life? Do you want to feel sorry for yourself because William died? Do you want to live the rest of your life in self-pity? You can't change what happened, and you can't bring him back. Look at me, I'm here now. Take a closer look, Misty-Bleu, you might be surprised by what you can actually see if you really open your eyes!" He shouted at her, before he walked out the door. "I'm leaving after the last show on Sunday, Misty-Bleu, do whatever you like!" He slammed the door behind him in anger and frustration. Misty-Bleu sat on the edge of her bed when she realized that Joshua had hit the nail on the head. She was sure that she would never be enough for him and could never adapt to a life he was so well-acquainted with. Misty-Bleu convinced herself that what he needed was a glamorous dame, someone more like him.

She took out her notebook from her nightstand and wrote a letter to William. She told William that she loved him and needed him more than ever. She begged him to come back to her and help mend her broken heart. She told him about the mistake she had made with Joshua, and she begged him to forgive her. Misty-Bleu carried on writing and told William that the life he left her behind in, was no life at all without him. She wrote of the weight of his eyes, and how they haunted her through Joshua's. She wrote of the curse of his body, and how his skin was burnt on hers. She told him how his love was all she breathed for a time, but how it now hurts and blinds her with rage. She turned the page and wrote how she could barely look in the mirror anymore, and how she struggled to see anyone else in her life. She whispered through her pen that they were far too young for the kind of hurt she was feeling, and how her head and heart was in a mess. She lifted her pen and closed her eyes. It was Joshua's eyes that found her in the darkness. It was Joshua's touch she relived, and it was Joshua's voice that sent a shudder down her spine. She opened her eyes and carried on writing. She told him how numb she was beginning to feel, and how it was Joshua's eyes that was plunging her into a curse she picked up while he was gone. She wrote about her desperation to rid her of the heaviness of her heart, that was threatening to kill her slowly. She told him how she must live with the tempests raging inside of her, and she begged him to tame the ghosts of the portal that were beginning to cripple her.

She closed her notebook and slid it into the drawer of her

nightstand once again, before she climbed into the bed Joshua Stark had just shared with her. Between the empty sheets of the oversized bed in her hotel room, she could smell him, and she fell asleep with his eyes burnt into hers.

Alice VL

AFTERLIGHT

Alice VL

7

They spent the following day rehearsing for their first show together that night. They remained vigilant of one another, and careful to avoid each other as much as they possibly could. Despite feeling extremely anxious about sharing a stage with Joshua in front of thousands of spectators, Misty-Bleu was sure that the show would be a success, even if only because of Joshua's presence and performance. She regularly peeked over at him during rehearsals and was sad that he was about to leave on tour. She was devastated by the fact that he was so angry when he hardly looked at her throughout the day.

Misty-Bleu met Tracey in her hotel room, who was sent to style her hair and apply her make-up for her. She slipped on an outfit that was chosen for her, before Tracey hurriedly began styling her hair. When Misty-Bleu glanced at her alarm clock on the nightstand, she realized that she had barely fifteen minutes left before the show was to start. She wondered if Joshua felt as nervous as she did, and she was no longer sure she could pull it off. William ran into Misty-Bleu backstage, where he formally went through their routine with her, desperate to ensure that all had been planned out to the tee. Jerry McMann, a well-known public figure, and master of ceremonies, was hired to host the show, and introduced Joshua to the audience when it was time for the concert to begin.

William took a few deep breaths, before he ran onto the stage as the audience applauded and chimed his name in excitement. Misty-Bleu stood backstage and watched him greet his fans confidently, smiling broadly when the screams and yells of the audience deafened her. When William turned to her, Misty-Bleu smiled at him, and felt excitement well up inside of her. As he stood looking at her, he was once again unprepared for her beauty, and how she looked at that very moment. "Ladies and gentlemen, please welcome one of the finalists of The Academy, the beautiful ... Misty-Bleu Buchanan!" He held his hand out to her, before she slowly made her way onto the stage, and clutched his hand in hers. William was aware of the iciness in her hands and realized how nervous she had become. "Don't be nervous ..." He whispered as he gently reassured her before he tightly squeezed her hand.

"Misty-Bleu will kick off our show by singing a song she wrote while in The Academy, dedicated to love of her life. Please give her a round of applause!" He handed her the mic, and immediately walked away from her. Misty-Bleu was instantly angry for the way he had introduced her song to the audience, and when William turned back to her, he knew that she was furious with him. She closed her eyes and began singing the song she had written for William. Her heart was viciously thumping inside of her chest, and her voice shuddered with each note she reached. The audience was at once enthralled by her voice and began shrieking in approval. Misty-Bleu was surprised by how enticing the reaction from the crowd was, and for the first time on stage, she felt as though she could live there forever. She had come alive, as her voice found its place in the air that night. She smiled often when she realized what it was about a stage that so utterly enchanted singers from all over the world. She looked up at the starlit ceiling of the Superbowl, and she wondered if William could see her.

When her song had finally come to an end, she bowed to her audience as they broke out in applause and shouted for more. Misty-Bleu laughed out loud at their reaction and smiled when she saw Joshua walk over to her. He excitedly embraced her, and in turn, she held him firmly against her. "See? You were great!" He whispered in her ear and squeezed her tightly. "Guys! How about a duet with this beautiful lady?" Misty-Bleu burst out laughing again when the audience went wild with their applause and chanting. They had only just begun singing 'Stronger than we are,' when the crowd became silent. William and Misty-Bleu were entirely caught up in the lyrics while consumed by the air that they could barely breathe, as they captivated their audience through their noticeable passion for each other. They held onto one another, and they pleaded with their bodies, while their eyes were trapped by their stares. William did not care who noticed how he had surrendered to her on that stage, or how he was brought to his knees by the emotions that were entirely seizing his every breath. He could no longer hear or see those around him. The world had been silenced, and the audience had disappeared. It was only the two of them ensnared in a world, they could no longer understand.

When their song was over, the audience was entirely bowled over by their performance, and erupted into standing ovations and deafening chanting. William leaned forward and kissed her. He was deaf to the audience, and blind to the world, as he swept her up and kissed her in front of thousands of strangers who were watching their every move. Misty-Bleu pulled away from him, and turned back to the audience, before she gracefully bowed to them. She looked over at Joshua, desperate to remember the moment, and drink in all there was about him, before she walked off that stage. When she reached backstage, she turned back to watch him perform out the rest of the concert. She listened closely to each song he sang afterwards. She watched him in bewilderment, and she knew that she had fallen in love with a man who had saved her from her excruciating heartbreak. A man who had not only healed her soul, but who had saved her life when she was ready to quit so many times before.

When they ended the show with one final duet, the crowd went wild as they both bowed and waved. When they strolled off the stage, William had his arm around her waist, and as soon as they were backstage, he let go of her, and turned his attention to the producers and organizers of the show. Misty-Bleu was once again aware of how worthless he could make her feel. She swiftly returned to her hotel room, before she collapsed onto her bed. She was super-charged, but at the same time, she was defeated and exhausted. She lay thinking about the concert, and she secretly confessed how she loved the stage and the energy that radiated from the audience. She could barely contain her excitement for their performance the following night, and she felt a quiver run down her spine when she replayed in her mind, how Joshua looked at her during their performance. He had carried her away into a world where only the two of them subsisted in. He sang to her, and she sang to him as though their hearts and souls had taken over from their minds.

Alice VL

Misty-Bleu drifted off to sleep, as she laid face down on her bed, with Joshua's eyes on her mind. She woke up the following morning still dressed in her outfit, and with an unwashed face. She climbed into the hot tub and laid silently while reflecting on their performance the night before. She thought about the day ahead where they would rehearse for most of the morning, perhaps even into the afternoon. When she climbed out of the tub, she quickly slipped on a pair of jeans and a sweater before she hurriedly made her way to the Superbowl.

"What was that all about last night?" Gaby, the drummer walked beside her as they made their way onto the stage. "What do you mean?" "I saw the way Joshua looked at you, is something going on between the two of you?" "No, nothing like that. No ..." Misty-Bleu hurriedly made her way to the mic, and promptly began rehearsing without even as much as glancing in his direction.

The shows on Saturday and Sunday nights were a great success, much the same as Friday night. Although William was frantic to avoid Misty-Bleu, her heart leaped each time she met up with him on and off stage. Misty-Bleu was beginning to feel the pressure of his departure on Monday morning, and she began dreading the remainder of her stay in The Academy, without him. She suspected that it was Joshua who filled her days, and it was he that comforted her thoughts at night. It was the knowing that he was behind a door, only a few steps down the corridor. For just a moment, she considered ending all the uncertainties that were beginning to brew inside of her and join him for his world tour. It no longer seemed as important to stay and linger in a life that no longer mattered as much to her. Little Dreams would survive without her for a few months. It had been running just fine for much longer than that. She never really had any intention of competing in the competition and winning a record deal was never what she wanted. As she sat toying with the idea to leave it all behind, she was once again nudged by her overwhelming fear, to stay.

Shortly after their final show on Sunday night, Misty-Bleu slipped out from a celebratory bash that was held in their honor and headed straight back to her hotel room. She was exhausted from the late nights, and she began feeling caged in by the crowds that would tirelessly gather around her. She had barely changed into a T-vest and a pair of shorts when she heard a persistent knock on her door. When Misty-Bleu opened her door to find Joshua standing in front of her, her first instinct was to fling her arms around him, instead, she stepped aside and made way for him to enter. "Joshua? Come in …" "I've brought you this …" He handed her a newspaper as he made his way inside. She swiftly closed the door behind him, and realized it was the 'Sunday Gazette'. Misty-Bleu stood motionlessly as her jaw dropped in disbelief when she read the front-page headline, 'Local singer and finalist mesmerizes audience'. Her eyes at once caught a photograph of her and Joshua on stage, before she stared back at him in disbelief. "You are a star, Misty-Bleu, I've always told you that …" Misty-Bleu was still unable to move and could barely utter a word. "Come with me, Misty-Bleu. I can make all your dreams come true. I will love you and take care of you. I will never leave you again." He made his way over to where she was standing, as he pleaded with her to leave with him. Her heart relentlessly nudged her, and from the innermost core of her, it shouted out to her to take his hand, and leave the crippling pain and debilitating sadness behind her, in a life William had left her in. But Misty-Bleu's mind was stronger and could not agree with the nudges from her heart, or the fear that had relentlessly plagued her. "Joshua …" She took his hands and looked up into his doleful eyes. "I can't, that has never been my dream, Josh, but there is just something that compels me to you, and I don't know what it is? It scares me. I don't understand it, and I don't know what it is?"

William turned away from her, and before opening her bedroom door, he stood with his head bowed for what felt like

Alice VL

forever. Misty-Bleu walked up to him, and gently touched his face. "Give me time. I just need a minute for this, Joshua. Let me just work through this. When I entered The Academy, I was so sure that there could never be anyone else for me. When I woke up to you in the clinic and had to accept that I had totally lost the plot, I was so sure that my grief was playing tricks on my mind, but now I ... I don't understand what I'm feeling, Joshua. I don't know how to explain it to you? How don't I scare you, Josh?" He looked into her eyes, and smiled sadly, "You don't scare me, Misty-Bleu, you can never scare me. I'm leaving tomorrow morning, and I probably won't come back here. If you choose to stay behind, I won't be coming back. I've made mistakes, I know that. So many mistakes, and I can't even begin to tell you how badly I screwed up, so maybe ... maybe if you can't choose me in this life, then I should rather not come back. Maybe, you should rather have died with William, because your heart has. And you know, Misty-Bleu, I have a feeling that even if he was standing in front of you right now, you would be so blinded by your sorrow, that you wouldn't even know it." She was stunned that he had so calmly spilled words of such cruelty to her. "How can you be so cruel, Joshua?" Misty-Bleu knew at once that he was leaving her life, and even though she so badly wanted to leave it all behind, the courage to leave William behind, failed her.

Alice VL

When he walked out of her hotel room, she collapsed onto her bed, and sobbed. She curled up, and turned out her light as she lay weeping, only this time, for Joshua. She could not ignore the way his arms felt around her, and she could not discard the memory of his eyes on her. As Misty-Bleu cried in the darkness, she knew that a man like Joshua would never walk into her life again, and what she felt with him, was over and would be forgotten by morning. Joshua had remained at her side since the moment William had taken his very last breath. He had never even for a moment, left her alone in her farmhouse. He followed her to the clinic, and then he followed her to The Academy. He was always only a few steps behind her, to break her fall. He remained a few steps ahead of her, to protect her from what may have been lurking in wait. He remained firmly beside her, to take her hand and hold her upright, where she could rest her head and lean on him whenever she wanted to. She could not get him off her mind, and thought back to their night at the pool, and then again to that very hotel room. Her body ached for him. Her heart cried out for him. The closeness she felt with him, had brought William back to her, yet it was Joshua she craved and hunted. It was Joshua whose eyes weighed down heavily on her. It was Joshua's touch, that had become her new home.

She fell asleep and breathed without effort for the very

first time, when she realized that she was no longer imprisoned by William, and her devotion to him. She longed for him, and she ached for him, but she suspected that he had placed Joshua on her path for a reason bigger than she could ever have imagined. For a brief moment, she wondered whether he hadn't conspired with God to send her Joshua, as a way of saying sorry that he had to leave her. "Joshua is right, I should rather have died too." She whispered through her tears, as she drifted off to sleep.

Misty-Bleu awoke early Monday morning, just as the sun was about to rise. She had barely packed her suitcases, when she received a call that a driver was ready to drive her back to The Academy. When she replaced the receiver, she realized that Joshua would be gone from her life in just a few short moments. She knew instantly that she had made an awful mistake. Desperate to find him before he was about to walk out of her life for good, there was so much she wanted to say to him, and there was even more she wanted to confess to him. She ran over to the room next door, and pounded on his door, afraid that her heart might jump right out of her chest. When there was no reply, she hammered violently, as fear begun to wholly consume her. "They left hours ago ma'am." A cleaner that was passing by had noticed Misty-Bleu urgently banging on the door. Misty-Bleu stared at her in skepticism, before the cleaning lady carried on walking.

She was devastated. She wanted to leave with him and join him on his tour. She was finally prepared to give up her life and her past, to be with him. She knew into her soul that William would understand, and she was afraid that if she did not take the first step, she would never feel the way she felt with Joshua again. Although guilt crept into her mind over and over again, she no longer wanted to feel as shattered as she had since William had died. Joshua brought joy back to her, and she hoped from the very bottom of her heart that William would allow her to love again. She no longer wanted to be dead, while she had so much life to live. A life that she wanted to live. "He didn't say goodbye?" It felt to her as though the world had crash-landed on her shoulders, when she slowly made her way back to her hotel room.

She picked up her bags, and hurriedly made her way downstairs to the waiting car that was to drive her back to The Academy. She had barely noticed her tears shimmering in her eyes when the clerk at the front desk called out to her. "Miss Buchanan, Dr. Stark left this for you ..." She handed Misty-Bleu a note before she swabbed at the tears that were once again, threatening to escape from all the corners of her eyes.

When the driver pulled away, she opened the envelope, and slowly read the carefully folded note. She was at once

Alice VL

unnerved and horrified that Joshua's handwriting bore such a striking resemblance to William's, and she was stunned by the way he worded his letter, almost as though William had written it. Her heart immediately began to hammer profusely when she read his letter to her.

'Misty-Bleu, I'm sorry for what I said to you last night, and I'm sorry I didn't say goodbye, but I thought it better this way. I want you to know that you'll be a superstar yourself soon, and it can be a very lonely place to be. You will always be on my mind and even though you fight me so, I fell in love with you. But, William is gone, Missy. Don't throw your life away for somebody who can never come back to you. You deserve to have love. I realize that that is probably not me, but I know that William wouldn't have wanted this for you.

Love, Joshua"

Misty-Bleu wiped the tears from her eyes before she reread his letter over and over again. She was overcome with repentance for letting Joshua go. She was too late. She folded the letter and held it against her. She knew that Joshua was right. William was gone, and no matter how intensely her heart ached for him, he would never return to her. She could never slip away into the portal again, he was gone from there too. As she sat staring out of the window, she was no longer sure she wanted to go to the half-light anymore, even if he was waiting there for her. It was Joshua who her heart hunted, and it was Joshua who had consumed her every thought as they drove back to The Academy.

Alice VL

8

When they reached The Academy, she was pleasantly surprised to find all eleven contestants, and all the mentors waiting for her. As she stepped out of the car, she was bombarded with animated questions from all the finalists. Mr. Donahue at once detected her sudden distress, and hurriedly addressed the finalists. "Guys, Misty-Bleu must be exhausted. Let's give her time to rest and at least just settle down, okay? I am sure she'd be thrilled to answer all your questions later on." He placed his arm around her and escorted her back into the house. "Thank you, sir." Misty-Bleu smiled at him with deep gratitude. She was utterly relieved that he had spared her the interrogations. She did not want to discuss her time at the Superbowl, and she had no desire to answer questions about Joshua Stark. When she reached her bedroom, Ms. Parker quickly followed her in. "You were wonderful, Misty-Bleu, we all watched each show on the big screen, and we are all extremely proud of you!" Ms. Parker clapped her hands in excitement, before she excitedly embraced her. "Thank you. It was definitely an experience to remember." Ms. Parker was taken aback by

Misty-Bleu's expression, "You seem sad, Misty?" Ms. Parker could not mistake the sadness and weariness in her teary eyes. "No, I'm fine. Just tired …" "You know, Misty-Bleu, even though you can't see it now, it does get better. You need people around you to lift you up. Don't shut them out." Misty-Bleu burst into tears and sobbed in her hands. Ms. Parker placed her arms around her and hugged her tightly. "I've lost my heart again, Ms. Parker, but I can't … I just can't let William go. I see him in everything Joshua does. I feel him everywhere around me; he just won't let me love again …" Ms. Parker gently stroked her hair, "It takes time after you lose someone. It's normal to feel his presence, Missy. It's normal to feel guilty about loving again, but you have to give yourself time to heal, and you have to forgive yourself. You are not betraying William. You must find peace in all that happened, and you are allowed to love again. William wouldn't want you to live out the rest of your life alone." "It still hurts so bad, and when I think about him sometimes, I just want to die …" Misty-Bleu broke down, and slowly let out all the hurt and anger she had carried around with her for so long. "Now, I think about Joshua all the time, but I don't want to betray William either. What do I do? Joshua is gone now, and even if he was here, William will always be what stands between us for the rest of my life, because I love him too …" Ms. Parker took in a deep breath, "I can't tell you what to do, Misty-Bleu, but I can tell you

Alice VL

that the universe sometimes asks us to love more than one. Equally, yet differently. Listen to the messages from your heart and know that William will understand. You must believe that William will understand." Ms. Parker wiped the tears that had begun gushing from her eyes, before she walked out of her bedroom. Before closing the door behind her, Ms. Parker turned back to Misty-Bleu, "You have found with two men, what most people don't find in their lifetimes, Misty-Bleu. That's okay, hold on to that. Grab onto it, and never let it go."

Alice VL

William kicked off his world tour in the UK and was scheduled to appear in eight different cities in almost as many days. He had been rehearsing tirelessly to pull off his shows with success. He was frantic to step into Joshua's life and his career. He contacted Mr. Donahue often but could barely bring himself to call Misty-Bleu. He constantly thought about her and could no longer figure out how to bring her back to him.

On the Friday before the second last elimination on the second last Sunday, Misty-Bleu had settled into a routine at The Academy while the excitement began to build around the final round. She unintentionally developed a strong, yet odd friendship with Sylvia and Ms. Parker, and she looked forward to spending time in the garden or at the dinner table with them each day. She spent many evenings caught up in conversations with Ms. Parker, and was pleasantly surprised to discover that somehow, she was able to see herself in a different light, as though through another's eyes. She was pleasantly surprised to learn that all it took to feel better for a while, was to open her heart to someone who wanted to listen. She missed Joshua daily, and she smiled more often when she realized that she was thinking about William less. Her heart no longer felt as though it was being ripped out from inside of her when she thought about him. She no longer longed for her time in the portal with him, but she desperately missed and ached for Joshua who was thousands of miles away. She would often begin to type out a text to him, but her courage to send it, failed her each time. When she did think about William, she remembered what he was like before he became debilitated by his treatments, and she smiled when she realized how lucky she was to have been loved by him. She no longer felt as guilty about Joshua as she once did, and she prayed that he would return after his tour.

They were only four contestants remaining in the house, and for the first time since she agreed to participate, Misty-Bleu was thankful that she had earned a place in the top four. Sylvia was extremely nervous throughout each elimination rounds but managed to make it through each time. With the help of Ms. Parker, Misty-Bleu was able to express herself more freely, and she opened up to her often. She had spoken openly about her feelings of abhorrence towards her mother and father, and she would tell her how unfairly they had treated her as a child. She told Ms. Parker how she once thought that she deserved their anger and abuse, but that she had come to realize it was never her fault. She told her about William, and how she once planned on becoming wonderful to deserve him, and how she had wasted so much valuable time in the process. She had finally accepted that she was always worthy, and that her soul was never formed from her DNA. Her longing for Joshua had increased by the day. She missed the comfort and shelter he offered her when he was at The Academy. Sylvia would habitually turn up the radio when he came on, but Misty-Bleu pretended not to hear, and tried not to dwell on the two weeks she had spent with him. She realized in time that what she felt for Joshua was not mere and simple distraction from her heartache for William, but that she had fallen in love with the man who once loved William too. She often thought of what Ms. Parker had told her shortly after she returned from the Superbowl, and she smiled when she realized that she did love William and Joshua equally, yet differently.

The universe had asked her to love them both, and she did. She dreadfully missed William, and she held to great value the years she spent with him in her heart, but she longed for Joshua, and devotedly loved him in her mind. She acceded to the reality that she was so blinded by losing William, that she could not see Joshua as he slowly, almost undetected, found his way into her heart. It was a reality she sorely regretted, but she learned to pick up all the broken pieces of her and begin looking forward to her life without either of them. She could hardly wait to return to Little Dreams and begin her new novel. One she would write about her time at The Academy. A story she would tell of her life with William and how she thought she would never again, breathe easily. She wanted to tell the world about Joshua, and how he brought William back to her, but how in the end, he released her from the chains that were imprisoning her. She wanted the world to know that sometimes, the universe asks you to love two equally, yet, differently, and that it's okay.

Fridays were phone call days, and Misty-Bleu was ecstatic when she realized that since it was only her, Sylvia, Trevor, and Darren left behind, their calls could quite possibly be longer. She missed Kevin and Shaun, and she wondered how David and Julia were coping. She could not quite guess who would call her, but she would not mind either. "Misty-Bleu! Your turn!" Mr. Donahue called her from downstairs for her much-anticipated phone call. She ran down those stairs, almost missing a few steps in the process, but eager to have contact with the outside world. "Hello?" She shouted breathlessly into the phone. "Missy ..." It was not Shaun or Kevin, and it was not Dave or Julia Carmichael. "Joshua?" Her heart began to hammer in her throat when she heard his tranquil voice. Her hands began to tremble, while her stomach flipped and reminded her of the million butterflies that were living inside her still. "How are you?" He was almost whispering, afraid that she might not take his call. "Where are you?" "I'm heading out to Scotland in the morning. I had to beg Shaun to give me his spot on the phone. It was not easy at all, but I hope you don't mind? How are you?" She smiled suddenly when the sound of his voice immediately comforted her. "I'm fine, just terribly nervous. Can you believe that? For someone who never wanted any of this, I am terrified!" She let out a faint giggle after her confession. She was excited to hear from him, and she tried to imagine him standing in front of her. "You are a star, Misty-Bleu, you know you are. I've been thinking so much about you, and I feel like I let you down. Like I abandoned you?" Misty-Bleu remained silent, unsure of what to say to him. "I miss you. I just wanted you to know that in case you ... in case you perhaps missed me too?" William was desperate to hear her say that she missed him too. "Joshua, why are you telling me this? You're over there, and I'm over here ..." "I'll come back if you want me to? But, you have to say it, Missy. You have to tell me what you want. I don't know how to be with you? I don't know what you want? You have to say it ..." William was desperate while Misty-Bleu grew anxious and flustered. "I must go, Josh. You do what you have to do, that's all I want. Goodbye." She replaced the receiver before he could respond. She stood staring at the phone for what felt like forever, and immediately berated herself for not asking him to come back to her.

William stood staring at the phone as he considered calling her back. He felt a twinge of pain rush through his heart,

Alice VL

almost like a sharp knife that was being plunged into him by her cold and uncaring words. He was desperate to hear her tell him that she missed him too, and that she wanted him to return to her. He wanted to hear her say how she loved him, and that she was finally ready to confess to her aching for him. He could never be Joshua or live his life in Joshua's shadow. He wanted to leave all the fame behind. He wanted to go after her and tell her that he could not live without her, and that the life he was thrust into, was never a life he had chosen. He ached for her, and he came back for her. William knew that he would give up Joshua's life of stardom in a heartbeat, and that he would follow Misty-Bleu to the end of this world, and back into another.

Misty-Bleu was agitated when she walked away from the phone. She was angry at herself for denying her the love she finally knew she deserved. Her heart was crying out to her to call Joshua back, and tell him that she loved him, but her mind hauntingly reminded her that William might still not approve. She knew that she could let William go, but she was not sure that Joshua was ready to give up his life as a superstar for her. For the first time in her life, Misty-Bleu was angry at William. She was angry at him for leaving her, angry that he had given her a life with him in an alternate universe, and angry at him for not allowing her to love Joshua, and let Joshua love her. "Misty-

Bleu!" As she began climbing the stairs back to her bedroom, she heard Mr. Donahue call out to her again. She hurriedly turned back and made her way into his office where she found him seated behind his desk. "Come in! Please have a seat!" He smiled while peering over his glasses and showed her to an empty seat across from him. "Misty-Bleu, I have something very special to show you. I think you'll be very pleased ..." He handed her a compact disc. He grinned from ear to ear while scrutinizing her face in anticipation of her reaction. She hesitantly took it from him and was stunned when she realized that it was a compilation of their songs and duets that Joshua had sent her. She swiftly turned it around and was speechless when she saw that it was his latest release, featuring her, Misty-Bleu Buchanan. She gazed up at Mr. Donahue who was smiling at her. "When?" She paused when she realized that she was totally gobsmacked and lost for words. "It's titled 'Joshua & Misty-Bleu.' It is his latest release, you didn't know?" Mr. Donahue pointed to the title and beamed when he noticed the smile grow broader on Misty-Bleu's face. "No, I didn't. I don't know what to say? I didn't expect this?" "Congratulations, Misty-Bleu, it's an enormous achievement and a huge accomplishment. You did good." He got up from his seat, as Misty-Bleu got up from hers, while unable to take her eyes off the disc. "Can I keep it?" "It came for you, Misty, it's your copy." She smiled and hugged him excitedly before she ran up the stairs

Alice VL

and dashed into her bedroom. She immediately sat on the edge of her bed, and opened up the cover of the disc. On the inner sleeve of the cover, he had written a short message to her which unnerved her once more, especially when she noticed again how similar his handwriting was to William's. "You're a superstar!" She smiled and re-read the hurriedly scribbled words over and over again. She never wanted to be a superstar, but at that very moment, she was thrilled that for the first time in her life, she was considered one.

Misty-Bleu laid tossing and turning in bed that night, unable to sleep as her mind kept wandering back to Joshua and their recording. When she finally surrendered to the bout of insomnia that was not going to be releasing her anytime soon, she got up and carefully placed the disc into her player. She sat on the carpet and placed the earphones around her head. She closed her eyes, and when the music began to play, she smiled when she thought back to the show. Her heart ached for him. Her body craved his, and her eyes desperately wanted to look into his again. The thought of his lips on hers sent shivers up her spine, and the yearning for his arms around her made her quiver. By the time the music had stopped playing, Misty-Bleu was wide awake.

She grabbed her mobile phone, and softly tiptoed out to the pool and over to the swing. She had just scrolled down to

Joshua's name on her phone, when she noticed a shadow in front of her. Misty-Bleu was at once afraid and realized that the rest of the finalists and mentors were fast asleep in The Academy. She hesitated nervously, but when she looked closer, she was at once horrified by what she saw. "William?" She leaped to her feet but realized instantly that her legs had grown weak beneath her. "William?" She whispered tearfully before she collapsed on the lawn. She gazed incredulously at him, afraid to turn away from him, but terrified that her heart and mind might be cruelly deceiving her. He walked up to her, and when he stood only a foot away from her, Misty-Bleu knew without a doubt in her heart, that it was William. "Misty-Bleu, you have to listen to me. It's not William, I am not William. I am not William, Misty-Bleu, are you listening to me?" He knelt down in front of her before he took her face in his hands. "Don't be afraid. Please don't be afraid. You must listen to what I'm about to tell you. You must hear me, and you must hear all that I am about to say ..." He gazed into her frightened, yet stunned eyes, before he smiled at her. Misty-Bleu's heart began thumping viciously. The tears that had so cruelly plagued her over the past few months, returned in abundance. This time, she did not try and hide them, and she made no effort to excuse them. He was back. William had returned to her. The face she had loved the most in the world, had appeared before her. The eyes she longed for, was looking back at her. There was nothing in the world she would trade for that moment with him. There was nothing she wouldn't sacrifice, for that very instant with him, and the way he looked at that very moment. There were no traces of the dreaded cancer that had weakened him in the last weeks of his life, and there was no pain or heartache that had once crippled and debilitated him. He was William. The man she had loved and prayed for so intensely, for as long as she could remember. "I can feel you; I know you are close ..." She whispered croakily as the tears rolled unreservedly and relentlessly from her eyes. "Misty-Bleu, you must listen to what I am saying. You feel William because he is still there, with you. The person standing in front of you now, is not William, it's me, Joshua. I am Joshua, not William, even though I appear to be. It's a long story, but I am here to tell you that you have to look closer at who you think is Joshua. Look at him, Misty-Bleu. Look at his ways and look at his habits. Open your heart to hear him and recognize him. Look at him. Your tears and pain are blinding you. When you stabbed me, I found him in the portal, a kind of a half-light. You were right, Missy, the portal, you were right, it was real. It was all real. Don't you ever forget that, and don't ever let someone tell you it's not. I am so sorry I didn't believe you, but that's where I met William again. We sort of made a deal and William came back to you through me. He's been watching you die slowly Misty-Bleu, but he can't tell you who he is. He can never tell you, so I need you to see it, or else it would all have been for nothing." He took her hand, and gently squeezed it. "What are you saying? I don't know what you are saying? You're not William?" "I am Joshua, and he, Joshua, is William. Misty-Bleu, open your eyes and open your heart! William is real, and he is there! You are pushing him away because you think I am him and he is me." Misty-Bleu quickly swabbed at the tears on her cheeks, "Joshua? But the singing, the doctor that he is?" "He became me to be with you again, Missy, to save you and to love you one more time. It's amazing what your mind can take from another. I let him take my place because you belong to William, and he loves you so madly. You are not being fair to your or William's heart, it doesn't deserve this, Misty-Bleu …" Joshua placed his arms around her and held her firmly against him. Misty-Bleu was stunned and could not quite fathom all that he was telling her. "Feel me, I'm not William." She hesitated, before she freed herself from him. "What you had, you can have again, Misty-Bleu. You have a new lifetime together, make it count. Twice in your lifetime, you've been loved by William. He found a way to come back. He found you in the opening and the closing of the portal, Misty-Bleu. What happened was nobody's fault. You couldn't have saved him then, none of us could." She glowered at once, "I … I killed you?" "No, Misty, you didn't kill me. If you did, William wouldn't have been able to come back.

Alice VL

He just took my place so that he could come back to you. But the thing is, Misty-Bleu, he can't tell you. That seems to be the deal over here, we're not too sure about all the details ..." He winked while Misty-Bleu stared at him, unable to take her eyes off him. She closed her eyes as she tried to take in all he was saying. She wanted to burn the way he looked into her mind, the image of the man standing in front of her. She wanted to breathe him, and soak in all there was about him, but when she opened her eyes, he was gone.

Misty-Bleu frantically glanced around her, but all she was left with, was the darkness of the night. She walked back to her bedroom as though in an aimless haze. For a moment, she was not quite convinced that he had appeared before her, and she instantly wondered if she had perhaps, dreamed it all. She smiled when she could still smell him on her and feel him against her. For the first time since William had died, she felt excitement well up inside her, and she was sure her heart was about to explode.

When she climbed into bed, she placed the earphones around her head once more, and she turned up the music. She listened to them sing, but this time, she could hear William sing to her. As she lay listening to the sounds of their two voices come together, she knew at once that she had to win the competition. She wanted to win, to earn a place in his world. She wanted to share the stage with him, and she wanted to travel the world with him, if that is what it took to take her heart home again. It was the only way she knew how to be with William as he navigated his way through his life as Joshua. She was desperate to reclaim him, and she was willing to sacrifice whatever she had to. Through the opening and the closing of the portal, she became his superstar. Misty-Bleu knew that it was her turn to meet him halfway. It was time for her to prove her worth. She had to take the first step and save herself from her own fears and anger. Joshua and William had both sacrificed so much in keeping her heart from dying. They had kept it sacred for her, and now it was time for her to play her part. She loved William, and finally understood why she had fallen in love with Joshua. Her soul had recognized his, and her heart heard the messages from his. Her heart had reclaimed him, even when her eyes could not see.

Alice VL

9

She took her time to find, and carefully select the song she would perform for her final round. She had spent the next few days writing the song that spoke of their time in the portal, and how his love for her brought him back into her world. She wrote of how her grief and anger had blinded her to the truth, and she prayed that his heart would hear her message to him. When first walking into The Academy, Misty-Bleu had no interest or desire to compete against the other finalists, but for the first time since that day, she was extremely unnerved and anxious when their second-final round of the competition arrived that Sunday night.

Trevor was first to perform, followed by Darren. When it was Sylvia's turn, Misty-Bleu was sure that her nerves would fail her, but she pulled off an almost perfect performance. When Misty-Bleu finally walked onto the stage, she smiled gracefully at the audience and the judges, before she picked up the mic and sang 'Stronger than we are.' She sang as though it was only William in the audience, and she sang as though both their lives depended on her performance. She had barely lowered the mic as she sang the last verse of her song when the audience erupted into applause. She bowed graciously, before she hurried backstage. Mr. Donahue had swiftly made his way onto the stage, and quickly thanked the audience and proclaimed how the finalists were extremely talented, and how daunting it was to eliminate any one of them. He called them all back on stage, and quickly read out the results of the votes that were cast during each performance.

Misty-Bleu was at once saddened that Trevor was the finalist to be eliminated. They all hugged him and were sad to see him leave The Academy. Misty-Bleu was immensely relieved that she had one final chance for the much-sought-after title of Superstar. She glanced over at Mr. Donahue who stood staring at her. She smiled and nodded her head, and she knew by the look on his face that he was almost as relieved as she was, to make it through to the final round. After the final elimination round, they were only three finalists left in The Academy. The pressure had begun to mount amongst them, and they began distancing themselves from one another as they spent the remainder of their time practicing and rehearsing. Misty-Bleu rehearsed every chance she had and grew increasingly determined to perform as though she had been on stage for years. There was a studio for each of the remaining contestants, and they locked themselves in rehearsals from early morning until late at night. Even though they were given free reign to rehearse as much and often as they wanted to, they were not allowed phone calls on their last Friday before their final performances. As excited as Misty-Bleu was to win the contest, she could barely wait to return to Little Dreams, her horses, and her beloved Christmas trees. She missed her home, and she longed for the peace and tranquility of her farm. She wanted to sleep in her own bed and write one more novel before the year was over. She wanted to parade around with only a T-shirt on whenever she wanted to, and she wanted to ride the fields with Captain Nimo and Wilhelmina. She wanted to sit on her porch that overlooked her Christmas trees until the sun was about to set, and then she wanted to escape into her plantation, and dance under the stars that decorated her trees. Misty-Bleu was homesick for the home she found shelter in. She desperately missed Shaun and Kevin, and she desperately wanted William's footsteps to come up her porch. Misty-Bleu wanted to go home to the only man that was ever home to her.

Sunday evening arrived far too suddenly, and much too unexpectedly for Misty-Bleu. She was convinced that she had not spent her last week in the house performing or rehearsing as she should have. When Misty-Bleu awoke that morning, she hurriedly set out to find Ms. Parker, and in a panicky voice, she begged her for one more week to prepare. Ms. Parker burst out laughing and assured Misty-Bleu that she hardly needed any rehearsal time to win. "Misty-Bleu, you are a star whether you win this competition or not. You will go far, and as far as I'm concerned, you are our Superstar." "Do you mean that, Ms. Parker?" "Every word, Missy. Now just go do your best, but more importantly, you have fun while you're doing it. I am holding all my thumbs and all my toes just for you." Misty-Bleu smiled sadly, "I am going to miss you, Ms. Parker, and I don't think I've ever thanked you, but thank you. I am sure going to miss you." "I will miss you too, but I hope to read about you." She lovingly embraced Misty-Bleu, before she headed back to her bedroom.

The final round was to be held at the Superbowl, while being broadcast on live television. Misty-Bleu, Sylvia and Darren had packed their bags the night before and loaded them into the car as they were about to leave for the Superbowl. When they said their goodbyes to the staff at The Academy, Misty-Bleu was surprisingly sad to be leaving the home that had finally brought the light back into her life. They were all permitted a quick phone call to their families before they were to leave, and when Misty-Bleu called William's number, his phone had been switched off. She was sad that she could not speak to him before her big night, but she assumed that it was due to the time difference between them. They reached the Superbowl merely an hour before the final round was to begin. After they had changed into their outfits and were groomed to the tee, they were all led backstage where they waited for Mr. Donahue to introduce them to the world. Misty-Bleu peeked through the heavy, red velvet curtains, and when she noticed how filled to capacity the Superbowl was, her heart began to trounce in her throat. The last time she was there to perform in front of such an enormous audience, William was with her, and she was not quite sure if she could pull it all off without him.

Mr. Donahue strolled onto the stage, as though he had been hosting audiences and competitions for his entire life. He smiled and quickly removed his glasses, before he addressed the exhilarated audience. "I have had the ride of my life with this year's finalists, and I can promise you that all twelve of them are extremely talented. But tonight, we are left with the top three, the best of the best, in my opinion. All three are superstars and they all three deserve the title. I am afraid that the judges here can't solely choose a winner tonight, so I have invited a well-known, extremely successful and Grammy award-winning superstar to help us decide. I will, however, not divulge his identity right now, but I will introduce him to you, the audience, and to the finalists after the last one has performed. We certainly don't want to add any extra pressure on them just yet. Please be aware that all three the contestants are expected to address the audience before they perform, so please, be kind and show your support. Thank you all for coming out tonight. We hope you enjoy the evening!" He bowed and waved at the hundreds below him, before he hurriedly walked off stage.

First to perform was Darren. He gracefully thanked The Academy and Mr. Donahue for the opportunity he knew, only came around once in any lifetime. He stammered slightly when he gave a short speech to the audience of how The Academy had changed his life, and how he would carry the experience with him, wherever he would go. Misty-Bleu smiled when she heard the stuttering in his voice. He was a brilliant singer, and she was convinced that he would walk away from that evening, the winner of the prestigious record deal they were all competing for. When he finally performed his song, Misty-Bleu listened to him carefully. He sang beautifully and on tune, and she could not find one single blunder in his performance. When his performance was over, the audience applauded excitedly, and so did Misty-Bleu and Sylvia who embraced him when he joined them. "You were fantastic!" Misty-Bleu gushed as Sylvia nervously made her way onto the stage to perform next. "Thank you, Missy, but we all know you are the real winner." Darren smiled before he embraced her one more time.

Sylvia was unexpectedly confident when she gave a beautiful speech as she thanked The Academy and their mentors. She thanked the other eleven contestants for their role in the competition, and she thanked her parents for their devotion to her music and hopefully, subsequent career. Misty-Bleu knew without a doubt, that she was desperate to be crowned the newest superstar, and that she would be rigid competition for her. When Sylvia performed her song, Misty-Bleu detected a slight quiver in her voice and prayed that her nerves were not about to fail her. She quickly glanced over at Darren, before she frowned. "I hope they don't hold that against her." She whispered before she turned back to Sylvia as she performed for the audience and the judges. She knew that Sylvia was extremely nervous and tried far too hard to perform flawlessly. Thankfully, the audience were just as taken by Sylvia as Misty-Bleu was, and when they applauded her, Misty-Bleu was at once relieved. Sylvia had a beautiful voice. Misty-Bleu often imagined that, if an angel was to sing, she would sound just like Sylvia. "You were great!" Misty-Bleu firmly embraced Sylvia when she finally joined them backstage again. "Sylvia, I couldn't believe that came from you. It was so beautiful." Misty-Bleu was in awe of Sylvia's performance. "Thank you, Misty-Bleu! It's your turn, good luck!" Sylvia shouted out as Misty-Bleu made her way onto the stage.

When Misty-Bleu reached the mic, she at once noticed Shaun and Kevin in the audience. She smiled when she detected the excitement on their faces, and immediately waved at them, grinning from ear to ear. She was overjoyed that they had made the trip from Bronlyn to support her and was at once saddened that they were all family she had to encourage her. The audience intimidated her slightly, and when she once again looked around her, she realized she was to have the stage all by herself. "My name is Misty-Bleu Buchanan and I ... I had an opportunity to perform here at the Superbowl before. I sang a song I dedicated to someone that I loved and *thought* I had lost. Back then, I was sure that the world was black and white only, and that there are no half-lights. It was either first or new lights. I knew nothing of portals, or that they open or close, and that someone you love can slip back in, or pull you in with them. I know it sounds crazy, but the song I have chosen tonight, is called The Portal. It is about that half-light that I choose to believe in, even if only in my heart. I thought I would live in an unfinished life forever. I thought I'd never heal, but The Academy brought me back. Joshua Stark guided not only me, but all the other finalists throughout our journey, and I owe much to them. This song is about life, and that it doesn't have to end when a love does, that nothing is as it

Alice VL

seems. It is always possible to love again, all over again even if it is different, and even if it is the same. It's about someone who believed enough in me, to come back for me. Someone who thought I was a superstar. Before I sing 'The Portal,' I would like to thank all our mentors at The Academy, especially Mr. Donahue and Ms. Parker for holding me up and keeping me going when I wanted to quit. And then, I so badly want to thank William's very good friend for sacrificing himself and giving William a way back." She smiled sadly, before she brought the mic to her mouth as the music began to play. From behind the stage, Sylvia and Darren applauded excitedly, and knew at once that Misty-Bleu was in fact, their winner and newest superstar.

The audience remained quiet while Mr. Donahue and Ms. Parker wiped tears of joy from their eyes. Shaun and Kevin watched her sing as though they could hear her soul vibrate before them, and when Shaun took Kevin's hand, there was no denying that Misty-Bleu was the superstar. When her song was over, and the music faded into the background, Misty-Bleu hurriedly wiped the tears from her own eyes. They were by no means at all, tears of heartache or sadness, but rather tears of exultation.

The audience rose to their feet as they loudly applauded her performance, and when Misty-Bleu looked past them, she

Alice VL

saw Joshua appear in the distance, as William one more time. He smiled at her when Misty-Bleu fixed a sorrowful gaze upon him. She knew then that she did not have to win the competition, to find William again. "Misty-Bleu, you can stay here, let's just get Sylvia and Darren out here too." Mr. Donahue signaled for them to join Misty-Bleu on stage. "Ladies and gentleman, please welcome back ... Joshua Stark!" Misty-Bleu frenetically turned around when she saw William walk up onto the stage. He smiled at them and turned to wave at the audience. She was stunned, when she understood for the first time, that it was William who had been hiding in Joshua's body. The way he walked, and the way he would smile bashfully at strangers around him. The way his eyes would flicker when his met hers. The way his smile would form right in the midst of a frown, ready to erupt into a convulsive laughter. It was never about the way he appeared to be, it was in all the little things, that she found him again. It was in his soul that she found the proof that William had found a way to come back to her. It was right in front of her the entire time, yet, her brokenness blinded her to the truth about him and their half-light in the portal. Her stomach began fluttering as it woke up the butterflies that lived inside of her. Her heart began to hammer ferociously, and her hands began to tremble viciously. She beamed from ear to ear, and when she looked closer at him, it was as though she was seeing William again for the very first time.

"Hi everyone!" William shouted into the mic as he waved out over the audience. They erupted into wild squeals, and when Misty-Bleu gazed out over the audience, she burst out laughing. "Thank you for having me. I must admit, the talent here tonight must be amongst the best I've seen in the world. This is going to be pretty damn hard!" He again shouted into the mic as he celebrated and applauded the finalists. "Anyway, the winner has been unanimously agreed upon by myself, Mr. Donahue and Ms. Parker from The Academy. But, before I announce the winner, I have a song to sing!" He stood smiling, as he waited for the audience to quieten down. "Before I sing my number though, I'd like to ask Misty-Bleu ..." He paused, before he turned to her. Misty-Bleu was instantly mortified when the entire audience became quiet. She could feel their eyes on her. "I'd like to ask Misty-Bleu Buchanan respectfully, to withdraw from this contest." He turned back to the audience, when the entire Superbowl went silent, leaving Misty-Bleu stunned. "You see, the thing is, I fell in love with her from the moment I laid eyes on her, and I must just say, my soul must have known her from way before. She knows me, and everything there is to know about me. She is a superstar already, and she does in no way at all, need to win this competition to prove it. She is a beautiful and brilliant singer, but she doesn't belong here. She belongs on her farm with her horses and amongst her Christmas trees, with me, if she'll have me? Now that you all know how biased I am, don't you think it's only fair that she withdraws?" He yelled out to the audience before he became silent. "Yes!" They all shouted out together, before he turned to Misty-Bleu, and brought the mic back to his mouth. "Misty-Bleu, I love you. All the crooked parts of me love you. I've loved you from the moment I met you. Every second I was away from you, and for every moment I was able to spend with you, I loved you. I don't want this life as a superstar. This isn't who I am, and you know me well enough to know all this about me. This isn't you either. You are a writer, a brilliant one. You are a Christmas tree farmer, and you adore your horses, you don't belong here on this stage."

He lowered the mic and placed his hand over it so that only she could hear, as he made his way over to her. "I'm not really supposed to tell you this. I have no idea what the consequences are, but ..." Misty-Bleu moved closer to him, and quickly placed her index finger on his lips, "I already know, William, I know ..." She whispered, desperately afraid that someone might hear her. William stared at her in disbelief when she called him by his name. He frowned quizzically at her, unsure of what to say next. "Josh, he told me ..." William took in a deep breath and placed his arms firmly around her, before he whispered in her ear. "When I got back to my so-called life as Dr. Joshua Stark the famous singer, nothing mattered anymore. I kept seeing you everywhere I go. I woke up at night hearing you call out to me. There were times when I could hardly breathe, and I just wanted to hold you in my arms again. I'll never be William again, the guy you knew and loved. I'll never look like him, but I love you. I am compelled to live as Joshua Stark for the rest of this life, but I don't want all this. Let's go home to your farm and begin again. I want that little girl you and I so very nearly had. I want the life we so very nearly had once." Misty-Bleu gasped for air when William once more, validated their life in the portal. It was real. It was a glimpse into a promise from William.

He gently kissed her before he began singing his song. Misty-Bleu retreated and made her way back to Darren and Sylvia. She beamed as her heart violently thrashed in her chest, and she swiftly swabbed at the tears that had rolled onto her cheeks. He was home again. He had travelled the earth and beyond, to return to her. He found her in life, and he found her in death again. She thought about Joshua and was at once sad that he would no longer be in this world, with her and with William. She lowered her head and smiled, as she swore to herself to never disregard the enormous sacrifice he had made

Alice VL

for her heart. When William finally ended his song, Misty-Bleu walked over to him, and took the microphone from him, while constantly fighting against that restricting lump in her throat. "Joshua ..." She winked as she swallowed back one more time. "I do want to begin again if you'll have me, and if you'll have my simple life. I want our daughter. I want Wilhelmina's filly, and I want those beautiful trees. I want my books and I want you, more than anything else in this world, I want you." She paused as she took in a deep breath, "I don't know how to carry on without you, I could never learn how to?" He placed his arms around her and pressed her firmly against him. "The portal, I knew it was real, our half-light was real." She whispered as she ran her fingers through his hair. "I'm so sorry for pulling you through, Misty-Bleu. I couldn't let go of you. I thought that it was just because ... because, I couldn't see you in so much pain, and I couldn't, but, I couldn't let you go either. I just wasn't ready to let you go." Misty-Bleu's voice began shaking, "All that happened in the portal? What was real? I mean, did any of that happen? Was that a glimpse into what will be or what can be?" "It was all real, Misty-Bleu. Life picked up and carried on as it would have if I hadn't died; if I didn't become ill. Some of it just hasn't happened yet, and some will be slightly altered with me back here, as Joshua. But Missy, I lived the portal with you, and I remember everything." He kissed her while the entire audience remained silent. William turned to them when he realized that their show must go on. "I'd like to ask Misty-Bleu to announce the winner and our brand-new superstar!"

He handed her the mic, before he placed an envelope in her hand. Misty-Bleu nervously opened it and giggled at the noticeable shuddering of her hands. She turned to face both Darren and Sylvia and was overcome with excitement when she called out Sylvia's name. Sylvia almost collapsed when she heard her name being called out. William embraced her, and handed her a trophy, before he turned back to the audience, "Please allow our newest superstar to end off this magical evening with one of her songs?"

William and Misty-Bleu left the stagehand in hand, so that Sylvia could perform the very first song of the rest of her career. When they reached backstage, Mr. Donahue was eagerly awaiting Misty-Bleu. "I saw him too, that night. William, I saw him." Mr. Donahue embraced Misty-Bleu as he whispered into her ear. She gazed up at him, before she hurriedly dabbed at the tears on her cheek.

When Mr. Donahue turned away from her, William held her in his arms, and gently kissed her. "I love you, Misty-Bleu …" "I love you, William, Josh. It's going to take some getting used to!" She held him closely against him, and when she looked past the crowd that had gathered backstage, she saw Joshua standing there, staring at her and at William. She smiled when she noticed the look of contentment and peace on his face. She waved secretly, and whispered gratefully, "Thank you for the portal, for the first light, half light, and for the new light."

Alice VL

FROM MISTY-BLEU'S JOURNAL

The Half-Light

Every once in a while, I am wonderfully sure that a portal opens between the life I find myself trapped in, and his, the next. I hear a song on the radio play more frequently than usual, and I smell his cologne in the strangest of places, at the oddest of times. I abruptly awaken in the middle of the night, positive that I can feel his hand clutch mine, as he delicately whispers my name.

I *know* it's him, I *know* his voice, and I *remember* his touch. I will never forget the way his hand feels in mine. I *remember* how his hand used to feel on my face, while staring into my eyes. I search for him in a crowd when I feel him brush past me, and I close my eyes to linger in the breath-taking familiarity of what was once *him*. I unintentionally check my watch at *exactly* the same time each day, and when I start recognizing a pattern, I begin to understand that he is *close*.

Alice VL

AFTERLIGHT

I am often flung into an unresponsive haze as I cling to him once more, and I *remember* it all. During those moments, I pine for him, and I am reasonably certain that he misses me *too*. My sorrow is still *only* love; *unspent* love that has nowhere to go anymore, so when my world creates a portal for him to come back through to me, my love and longing for him finally *escapes* from the corner of my eyes. I begin to whisper when I really want to shout. I wholeheartedly welcome and embrace the opening when I should surely walk away from it. I become quiet when I stop my shuddering voice from speaking, and I *just* feel. For a while, I *can't* move forward, and I linger in the opening of the portal with him, *just one more time*. It is always *just one more time*. They are the days that *matter*. They are the days that keep my heart from dying. They are the days that allow me to breathe for *just* a little while longer.

In the opening of the portal, I no longer need *people*. All I want is *him,* and the beauty of his love for *me*. I hunt his strength *because* I no longer feel much of anything else, other than intense hankering and excruciating anguish. I pass my days waiting for the portal to open once more, so we can dance and splash around in the puddles of one another's hearts again. Without the portal, the world I am stuck in, is *simply* a life I need

Alice VL

to get away from. I can't hear much of anything, and there is barely space for me to breathe while I *drown* in the silence.

I ramble around purposelessly through this life, waiting and begging for a miracle to release all the caged love in my heart, so that I can see the beauty in *my* world, and not crave the *healing* in the next. I *want* my second chance. I want someone in *my* world to touch me again. I *want* to forget, *but only* until that portal opens again.

I will never say goodbye to him. I will never let him go. But, if you stumble across me, just love me when the portal closes again, and I am forced to come back to this world.

With love,

Misty-Bleu Buchanan

THE END

Alicevlo.com

Alice VL

Author of Lola's Secret, Pearls In Ashes, Molly, It's Me, Samantha, The Bookstore Series including The Passage of Time and A Crinkle In Time, The Weeping Prince, The I Do (Not) Series.

Alice VL